CROWNBREAKER

CROWNBREAKER

SEBASTIEN DE CASTELL

HOT
KEY
BOOKS

First published in Great Britain in 2019 by
HOT KEY BOOKS
80–81 Wimpole St, London W1G 9RE
www.hotkeybooks.com

A CIP catalogue record for this book is available from the British Library.

HARDBACK ISBN: 978-1-4714-0549-5
TRADE PAPERBACK ISBN: 978-1-4714-0822-9
also available as an ebook

1

Typeset by Palimpsest Book Production Ltd, Falkirk, Stirlingshire

Printed and bound by Clays Ltd, Elcograf S.p.A.

Hot Key Books is an imprint of Bonnier Books UK
www.bonnierbooks.co.uk

To the real Ferius Parfax.
Your worst teysan still thinks of your lessons every day.

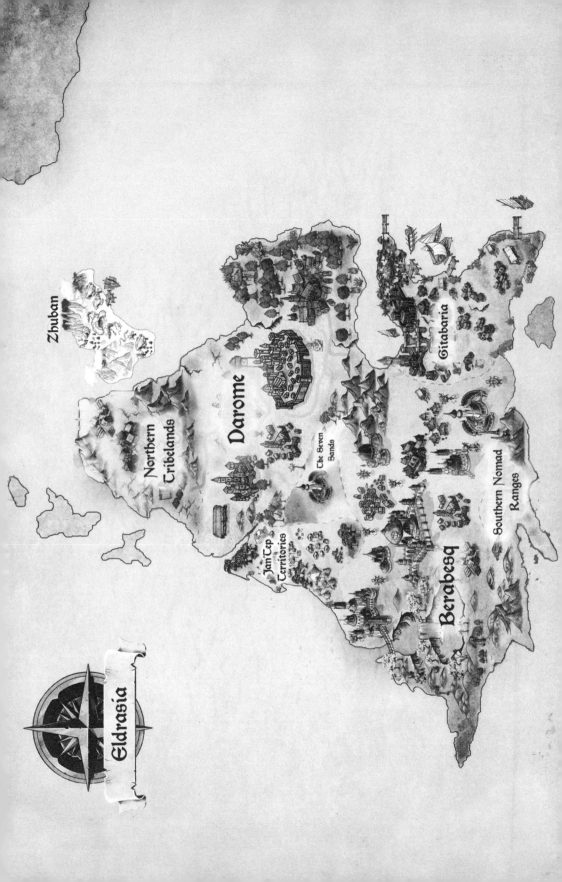

Prologue

The Card Trick

The old man dealt me an ace. Again. I picked it up only to let it fall face up next to the other ace and two jacks in front of me. One edge of the card landed on top a crumb of mouldy, dried-up bread stuck to the table. It lay there, tilted towards me as if pointing out the obvious.

'Two jacks, each with an ace,' I said. 'That's a pair of spear bearers.'

The old man leaned forward, long brown greasy hair and beard framing a crooked smile. He waved his arms in the air to show he'd just been swept up in unforeseeable circumstances.

'Lost again, haven't I?'

He glanced around the room as if he were performing for an audience. The place was empty except for one drunk snoring in the corner and a bartender doing a piss-poor job of mopping the floor.

The old man turned back to me and let one hand fall into his lap while the other motioned for the bartender to pour more ale into mugs that weren't any cleaner than the floorboards.

'You don't seem to be too good with cards,' I observed.

My irritatingly cheerful companion smiled back at me. He had perfect teeth. Filthy hair, shabby robes, thin as a rake. His sandals reminded me of those strip shows where the dancers spin bits of cloth around their bodies as they flounce all over the stage; you couldn't call them naked, but they'd catch a chill if they went outside. But those teeth? Straight. Clean. Perfect. One look at his hands revealed fingers free from calluses and nails that were neatly trimmed.

'Can't help but wonder what makes a lord magus wander into a saloon and start bleeding money at cards,' I said, tapping the pile of coins on my side of the table. I'd started the night with just one.

The old man shrugged. 'Perhaps I'm above such petty concerns as money.'

'Maybe,' I said, taking a swig of my beer, instantly regretting it. 'Then again, maybe you don't mind watching me slide coins from your side of the table to mine all night because you don't plan on seeing me walk out with them.'

The mage gathered up the cards and started shuffling again. 'They told me you were clever.'

'Be sure to thank them for the compliment.'

He dealt another hand of Country Holdup. Four cards each. Only face cards counted.

I picked up my hand, saw that all four cards were twos. The old man had just dealt me an eight-legged horse. Guess he wasn't planning on letting me win this time.

'So that's how it's going to be?' I asked.

'That's how it's going to be.' Just like that, the smile was gone. So was the pretence. 'You're going to die tonight, Kellen of the House of Ke.'

'Reckon you've got me confused with someone else, friend.'

I dropped the two of chariots on the discard pile in the centre of the table. The old man dealt me a new card, which turned out to be another two of chariots. Nice trick.

'You *reckon*, do you?' He chuckled. 'You think that preposterous frontier drawl hides who you are?'

Now that was just mean. I'd practised my drawl all morning to get it just right.

'No running away this time, Kellen,' the mage went on. 'You are who you are and I am who I am. Sure, you've got yourself a little magic. A few tricks. But you're no lord magus.'

'Never claimed to be.'

The old man snorted. 'No, of course not. What is it these Daroman barbarians call you? "The queen's spellslinger"?'

'I believe Her Majesty prefers the title "royal tutor of cards", actually.'

I dropped the deuce of trebuchets on the pile.

'"Her Majesty",' the old man repeated in a mocking whine. He spat on the table, which made it neither dirtier nor cleaner. 'That little bitch has pissed off the wrong people, Kellen. But she's too well protected – politics and diplomacy, you understand. So I've been sent to teach her a lesson by making an example of you.' He snorted then, apparently taken unawares by his own cleverness. 'Do you suppose that makes *me* her "royal tutor of manners" now?'

'Can't see how I'm going to serve as much of an example, friend, seeing as how, like I told you, I'm not this Kellen fellow you say you're looking for.'

He dealt me another card, this one bearing the number two and depicting a pair of skulls. This was particularly impressive when you consider that there is no suit of skulls in a Daroman deck.

3

'Don't suppose you'd consider teaching me that trick?' I asked.

'What would be the point?' His fingers twitched and the card went up in flames. 'Would've thought someone with your reputation for outlawry would stay better hidden, but my silk spells led me right to this place. Honestly, boy, I'm so disappointed I'm tempted to kill you now and be done with it.'

I put up my hands and offered him my most winning smile. 'Hey now, no need to be hasty. I just came in here for a drink and to play some cards. Now why don't you describe this Kellen fellow to me? Maybe I've seen him around.'

The mage snickered. 'Your height, your build.' He tossed a jack of trebuchets face up on the table. 'Your smarmy mouth, your dung-coloured hair.' He flipped the card over once and now it was the jack of blades.

'That description matches any number of folks around these parts,' I said. 'Besides, I don't think you're in any position to be disparaging other people's hair, friend.'

'And of course –' the mage flipped the jack once more in the air. This time when it landed it was the same card, but now with an elaborate black design circling the jack's eye – 'the man I'm looking for has the same disgusting shadowblack around his left eye that you bear, Kellen of the House of Ke.'

I leaned back in my chair and gave him a round of applause. 'See? Now that's some fine magic. You sure I can't persuade you to teach me these wonderful card tricks of yours?'

'You're all out of tricks now, Kellen.' He wagged a finger at me. 'Oh, you've eluded a few minor adepts, built yourself a modest reputation with what little magic you have. No doubt

4

you've impressed a few of these backwater hicks. Maybe even captivated the imagination of a twelve-year-old girl who calls herself a queen. But you've got nothing to match up against a true lord magus, Kellen. So now you die.'

I offered up a sigh of frustration. 'Like I keep telling you, friend, you've mistaken me for someone else.'

'You're going to tell me there's more than one man in these territories with black markings around his left eye?'

I shrugged. 'Could just be make-up, you know. Like a new fashion. An . . . affectation?'

'An *affectation*? As if anyone in their right mind would willingly go around with the shadowblack staining their soul?' He clapped his hands together. 'I take it back, boy. You're almost too much fun to murder. Unfortunately you've killed one too many Jan'Tep mages . . .'

He gathered up the cards, drew a small pile of them and fanned them out on the table. Eleven cards. All kings. 'If the rumours are to be believed.'

'Maybe even more?' I asked, flipping an additional card from the deck. It would have been nice if it had magically turned out to be another king, but it was the six of arrows.

'Anything's possible, I suppose.'

'This Kellen fellow sounds awfully dangerous. Aren't you the least bit anxious you might get hurt chasing him all over the Daroman territories?'

'No.'

I leaned my elbows on the table and peered into his eyes. 'You're *that* sure of yourself? You're really *that* powerful?'

'I am. But unlike the fools you've met before, I'm also cautious. That's why I made certain preparations in advance of our encounter, just to be sure.'

5

I tapped my pile of coins. 'You mean like losing a lot of money at cards?'

He chuckled at that. 'In a manner of speaking. The cards were just to keep you in your chair, which, as you're about to discover, I enchanted yesterday with magic older and fouler than you can imagine.'

I looked down at my chair. 'This rickety old thing? I hate to tell you, friend, but if it's supposed to be killing me right now, it's not working very well.'

'Kill you? Don't be silly. I want to keep that pleasure for myself. No, the chair has a sympathetic binding spell on it, Kellen. When a mage sits down upon it, the enchantment gradually seizes hold of the magic inside him. By now, even that tiny drip of power in the breath band on your forearm is enough to hold you in a grip stronger than oak or iron.' He gestured for me to get up. 'Go ahead. Try to move. The more you struggle, the stronger the spell will bind you to the chair, until eventually you'll suffocate from the pressure.'

I considered that for a moment. 'That really does sound ingenious. Can't imagine a way out of such a fiendish trap. Almost makes me wonder why nobody ever thought to try it on this Kellen person before.'

The old man giggled. 'Oh, not many can cast this spell, I assure you.'

'I'm curious, then, why the dozen or so people who sat in this chair before me today didn't seem troubled by it at all.'

Irritation crossed the old man's features. 'As I've told you, the binding only works on Jan'Tep mages. I would've thought you'd appreciate the compliment, Kellen. At least now people will have to recognise that you weren't entirely devoid of magical ability.'

'Right, right,' I said. 'Diabolical *and* considerate. And yet . . .'
I drummed my fingers on the table.

'And yet what?'

I tilted by head back to stare idly up at the ceiling. 'Well, it seems risky to me, putting so much effort into something as banal as a chair, relying on the victim to sit down on the right one.'

'No risk at all. You've been seen here every night for the past week, sitting in that same chair each time. So I made sure to be in *my* chair before you got here, and the bartender ensured no one else sat there until you arrived. Besides, I picked a night when most of these barbarians are out celebrating their little queen's birthday festival.'

'Sure, that makes sense. Still though . . .'

'What?'

'Well, this Kellen is supposed to be some kind of devilishly clever outlaw, isn't he? A genius at the art of evading his enemies?'

'Genius? No. Cunning, perhaps. He keeps a few tricks up his sleeve, certainly.'

I nodded in agreement. 'Right. Cunning. Tricky. So I guess what I'm asking is, wouldn't it be just like a cunning, tricky fellow to figure out what you were up to and then come in the night before to swap the chairs? I mean, he does seem to have an uncanny knack for survival. What if he'd just happened to sneak in here after closing time last night, put your chair here, and his chair, well, right where you're sitting now. Wouldn't that technically mean *you* were in the binding spell?'

The mage's eyes narrowed. He tried lifting his arm, only for his mouth to gape open when it didn't move. He tore at the sleeve of his robe as if it was glued to the arm of the chair. He began shifting furiously, trying to get out of his seat, but to no avail. His gyrations grew more and more frenetic until finally he stared across the table at me, lips moving silently, helplessly, as though his chest were being crushed by an ever-increasing lead weight. His eyes fluttered closed.

The room fell silent.

Then the old man started laughing.

He rose effortlessly from the chair and patted his belly. 'My, oh my. The look on your face! I swear, boy, *that* was priceless! Like watching a hangman at the gallows discovering the noose around his own neck!'

'Well now,' I said drily, 'that was quite a performance.'

The old man bowed at the waist. 'Thank you, thank you.' He sat back down and started giggling again. 'I did warn you, Kellen, that I'm just a bit smarter than those other mages you've duelled in the past.'

'Just a bit,' I acknowledged.

'I knew there was a chance you might learn of my plans, so I took precautions. I made sure the chairs were checked first thing in the morning. So after you snuck in last night and switched them . . .'

'Your accomplice switched them back before I arrived.' I looked over at the bartender who had a grimy smile on his face. 'Nice way to treat a regular customer,' I said.

The mage slapped his hands down on the table between us. 'Now then, I'm afraid that while this has certainly been entertaining, it's past time I collected the other half of my bounty, which means we have to conclude our business together.'

The bartender came over and placed a dusty bottle of wine and a corkscrew on the table.

'Don't you think you should at least offer me a glass of whatever you're celebrating with before you kill me?'

'This?' he said, holding up the bottle. 'Oh no. This I'm saving for later.' He put the bottle back down on the table, pulled a white cloth from the pocket of his robe and set about cleaning the corkscrew. 'This,' he said, holding it up for me, 'is what I'm going to twist into that black eye of yours. Then I'm going to rip the life right out of you.'

I swallowed. 'Sounds a bit barbaric for a distinguished gentleman like yourself, if you don't mind my saying.'

'A requirement of my Daroman employers,' he explained. 'Desecrating the corpses of their enemies is something of a tradition with them. Sends a more meaningful message to their little queen.'

I nodded sympathetically. 'Freelance work can be so messy.'

'I don't mind.' He turned the now gleaming corkscrew in the air. 'A lord magus rarely gets his hands dirty, but twisting this into your eye? Inflicting such horrific pain while you sit there, screaming in agony yet unable to move a muscle?' He shivered. 'Let's just say it's an idea that intrigues me. I suspect you'll suffocate from struggling against the binding spell before you die of your wounds.'

I bit my lip. 'Don't suppose I can talk you out of this? Maybe make a deal?'

The mage shook his head. He smiled one last time, showing me those perfect teeth of his before standing up, the corkscrew gripped tightly in his right hand.

'Well, dang it,' I said. 'If this is the day I meet my ancestors, reckon I'll do it standing on my own two feet.'

'I told you, there's—'

Whatever the old man was going to say next died when he saw me rise from the chair.

'That's not . . .'

I picked up the bottle of wine and noted the vintage scrawled in grease pen. Probably the most expensive bottle in the place. Must've been a good fee.

'This isn't right,' the mage said, looking very much like a confused old man discovering he's become lost very far from home.

'Maybe the spell didn't work?' I suggested.

'Impossible. My spells never fail me. *Never*.'

'Well now, that is a conundrum.' I held up a finger. 'Perhaps this Kellen fellow is vastly more powerful than you've been led to believe.'

The old man started mumbling. 'But . . . But everyone knows Kellen of the House of Ke is the weakest of mages. He only ever sparked his breath band. His magic is as weak as a child's!'

I nodded thoughtfully. 'Yes, even I've heard that. So if your spells never fail, and this Kellen fellow isn't powerful enough to break them, then, well, that only leaves one explanation, doesn't it?'

I picked up the white cloth from the table and began wiping the black make-up from my left eye.

'Ancestors! You tricked me! You're not—'

I smiled innocently. 'Now be fair, friend. I did try to warn you that I wasn't this Kellen of the House of Ke you're looking for. I mentioned it several times, if you'll recall.'

The mage reclaimed his composure and his finger started twitching into what the Jan'Tep call somatic forms. 'Whoever

10

you are, the fact that the chair didn't bind you means you've no magic to protect yourself with. So now you'll tell me where Kellen is hiding or I'll have you begging me for a quick death!'

'I'll tell you for free,' I said, tossing the dirty rag over the mage's shoulder. 'He's right behind you.'

The mage whirled around. The bartender lay unconscious on the floor. The drunk who'd been snoring in the corner was now standing behind the old man, wiping at his own left eye with the rag.

'A trick!' the mage shouted. 'A filthy trick!'

Kellen Argos – at least, that's the name he'd given when he'd hired me – smiled sympathetically at the old man. That disturbing black pattern circling his eye that we'd spent hours painting around my own was now glistening in the dim lantern light. 'It's as you said, my lord magus: I have precious little magic to work with. Tricks are all I've got.'

Completing my end of our contract, I smashed the wine bottle down on the back of the mage's head as hard as I could. Glass shattered into a hundred pieces, wine spilling all over the old man's greasy hair. He crumpled like sackcloth.

Kellen Argos knelt down next to him, listening for a heartbeat before searching the mage's robes and pulling out a bag of coins. He fished out a few of them, which he stuffed into his own pocket before handing the rest to me.

I looked inside the bag. There was a small fortune in there; enough to buy me a minor title and a nice little mansion on the outskirts of the capital if I wanted. Enough to make me suspicious. 'What's the catch?'

Kellen grabbed one of the unconscious mage's arms. 'Give me a hand with him.'

Between us, we hefted him up and sat him back down in what had been my chair.

'That seems a little cruel,' I said.

Kellen patted the old man on the head. 'No worse than what he'd had in store for me. Besides, by now his employers will be on their way here to celebrate. Maybe they'll take pity on him and hire another mage to release him from the binding spell.'

'Why not just kill him? Aren't you worried he'll tell people how you pulled this off?'

'I'm counting on it.' He walked over to the bench where he'd been pretending to sleep and retrieved his coat and black frontier hat, the band above the brim inscribed with silver sigils. 'Next time the queen's enemies want to hire themselves a lord magus to do their dirty work, they'll have to pay a lot more for the privilege.'

He headed for the saloon's swinging half-doors.

'One more question,' I asked before he could leave. 'You work for the queen, right? I mean, you're an official of the Daroman court?'

'That's what they keep telling me.'

'So why aren't there a dozen royal marshals or palace guards here backing you up?'

He set the hat on his head. It was a little too big for him. Although we really did resemble one another – enough to fool strangers anyway – he was a couple of years younger than me and looked a lot more . . . tired.

'They also tell me I don't play well with others.'

'What about next time?' I persisted. 'You won't be able to use this same trick twice.'

He swung the doors open, letting in the fading sounds of

last night's celebrations from the street outside. He turned back to me and a wicked grin escaped the corner of his mouth like a scavenger sneaking out the back window after stealing your supper. 'Guess next time I'll just have to come up with a new trick.'

Emni Urbana

City of Glories

City of Glories

There are two sides to every city. The top shimmers and shines, magnificent towers reaching high into the air, drawing the gaze of travellers for miles and miles with promises of civilisation and companionship. As to the other side? Well, as with any good trick, sometimes it's best not to look too closely at what lies underneath.

1

The Arrest

Nothing stinks like a capital city in summer. Streets already crowded with lords and labourers begin to burst as endless caravans of merchants, diplomats and those impoverished by bad harvests or foreign raiders roll through the gates in search of profit or protection. Upon a gleaming white arch at the city's entrance an inscription bearing the Daroman capital's motto beckons visitors with a promise: 'Emni Urbana Omna Vitaris'.

From The Imperial City Flows Prosperity.

Also, sewage.

That's the thing about great cities: they can solve hunger with more food, security with more soldiers, and almost everything else with more money. But there's only so much shit you can swirl around before the flagstones begin to reek.

'This place stinks,' Reichis chittered above me.

The soft flutter of fur-covered gliding flaps heralded a light thump against my shoulder as the squirrel cat made his landing. My two-foot-tall, thieving, murderous business partner sniffed at my face. 'Funny, you don't smell dead.'

'I'm fine,' I said, not eager to resume the lengthy argument begun in the early hours before dawn when I went off alone to face the mage who'd been sent to kill me. All I wanted now was a bath, some quiet and maybe a few restful hours without any attempts on my life.

Reichis sniffed at me a second time. 'You smell worse than dead actually. Is that whisky?' He poked his muzzle in my hair and sounded more than a little intrigued.

A year of living in the capital city of Darome had afforded Reichis the opportunity to expand his list of unhealthy addictions, which currently consisted of butter biscuits, over-priced amber *pazione* liqueur, several vintages of Gitabrian wines – the expensive ones, naturally – and, of course, human flesh.

'Did you remember to bring me the mage's eyeballs?' he inquired.

'He wasn't dead.'

'That's not what I asked.'

This is where having a squirrel cat perched on your shoulder perilously close to your soft, tasty human ears gets dangerous. See, squirrel cats, with their tubby feline bodies, big bushy tails, coats that change colour depending on their mood and furry flaps that stretch between their front and back limbs enabling them to glide from the treetops (or 'fly as well as any gods-damned falcon' as Reichis would insist), can – if you stare at them, squinty-eyed, from a distance and preferably through a drunken haze – look almost cute. They're not. Puppy dogs are cute. Bunny rabbits are cute. Poisonous Berabesq sand rattlers are cute to *somebody*. Squirrel cats, though? Not cute. Evil.

'Reichis . . .' I began.

His breath is surprisingly warm when it's less than an inch from your earlobe. 'Go on, say it.'

20

Ancestors, I thought, noting in the periphery of my vision that Reichis's shadowblack markings were swirling. Just over a year ago he'd wound up with the same twisting black lines around his left eye as I have around mine. Unlike me, though, the possibility of one day becoming a rampaging demon terrorising the entire continent didn't trouble him in the least. The prospect frankly delighted him.

Rescue from possibly fatal squirrel cat gnawing came in the form of a half-dozen pairs of heavy boots clomping up behind me, followed soon thereafter by the tell-tale click of a crossbow's safety catch being released. 'Kellen Argos, by order of Lieutenant Libri of the queen's marshals service, you are under arrest.'

I sighed. 'This again?'

The first tentative rasp of the crossbow's trigger grinding against its iron housing. 'Get those hands up high, spellslinger.'

I hadn't even noticed that my fingers had drifted to the powder holsters at my sides. Reflex, I guess, though by now you'd figure I'd've gotten used to being arrested on an almost weekly basis.

I raised my arms and slowly turned to find the marshals wearing their customary broad hats and long grey coats, armed with the usual assortment of short-hafted maces and crossbows – all trained on me. 'Would you like me to read the warrant?' Sergeant Faustus Cobb asked. Short, scrawny, narrow-shouldered and years past his prime, you'd think he'd appear comical next to his younger and more vigorous subordinates. But my experience with the Queen's Marshals had taught me that age does nothing to diminish how dangerous they are – only how ornery they become when you resist.

Me? I was eighteen, wearier than my years ought to allow. My shirt was still soaked from the booze I'd used to disguise myself as a drunk back at the saloon, and I was feeling more than a little crabby myself. 'What's the charge this time?'

Cobb made a show of reading out the warrant. 'Conspiracy to commit assault upon the person of a foreign emissary enjoying the protections afforded diplomatic representatives...'

Yep, that's right: the old man who'd come to kill me, being a Jan'Tep lord magus, held ambassadorial status in Darome.

Cobb went on. 'Grievous physical abuse...'

Not nearly grievous enough.

'Theft...'

Knew I shouldn't have kept any of the coins.

'Acting against the vital interests of the Daroman Crown and the people it serves...'

That one they throw into almost every warrant. Spit on the sidewalk and you've technically 'acted against the interests' of the crown.

Cobb paused. 'And there's something here about "unlawfully being an irritating, half-witted spellslinging card sharp who doesn't do what he's told", but I'm not sure that's an actual crime.'

And yet, I was pretty sure it was the *only* crime Torian was concerned about. 'Funny how she had that warrant already drawn up before anyone found the mage,' I pointed out.

Cobb grinned. 'Guess the lieutenant's got you pegged pretty good by now, Kellen.'

I was really starting to dislike Lieutenant Torian Libri. While there were no end of people in the Daroman capital intent on making my life hell, few displayed her raw determination and consistently lousy sense of humour. 'You do realise that under imperial law my rank as queen's tutor prevents you from prosecuting me for any crime without four-fifths of the court first revoking my status, don't you?'

One of the younger deputies gave an amiable chuckle. I'd let him beat me at cards last week in the vain hope I might win over some of the marshals to my side. 'Don't say nothin' about you bein' arrested though.'

'Let's go, spellslinger,' Cobb ordered, motioning for me to walk ahead of him.

Reichis gave a low growl. 'You gonna take this crap, Kellen? *Again?* Let's murder these skinbags. You owe me three eyeballs and this here's an opportunity for you to pay up.'

'Three? How many eyeballs do you think that mage had?' I asked.

One of the marshals stared at me quizzically. She must've been new – the others were accustomed to hearing me talk to Reichis.

'Who can tell with humans?' the squirrel cat grumbled. 'Your faces are all so ugly that every time I start counting, I lose track on account of needing to puke. Besides, two eyeballs was what you owed me an hour ago. The third is interest.'

Perfect. In addition to being a thief, a blackmailer and a murderer, Reichis now wanted to add loan shark to his list of criminal enterprises.

'Let's pick up the pace,' Cobb said. 'You know how the lieutenant gets when you keep her waiting.'

Several of the deputies laughed at that – not that any of them would dare cross her. Reluctantly, I trudged along the wide flagstone street en route to my thirteenth jailing since becoming the queen's tutor of cards.

'Hey, what's that?' Reichis asked, his nose nodding in the

direction of something small and flat floating on the breeze towards us, low to the ground. A playing card settled at my feet.

'Keep walking,' Cobb ordered.

I stayed where I was, staring down at the elaborate artwork on the card depicting a magnificent city on the top half. The bottom was a sort of mirror image, distorted as if reflected by a dark, shifting pool of black water.

'You drop that?' he asked, finally noticing the card.

'Sergeant Cobb,' I began. 'Before this goes any further, I need to clarify a couple of things.'

'Yeah? Like what?'

'First, I had nothing to do with this card suddenly turning up.'

'So what? It's a playing card. Not like you're the only gambler in the capital.'

As if to contest his banal explanation, a second card drifted down to land next to the first one. Then another and another, each one rotated a little more than the previous, gradually encircling me.

'What are you playing at, spellslinger?' Cobb asked, stepping back. I heard the safety catches on several crossbows unlock.

I was now standing in a ring of elaborately painted cards, their rich metallic hues of copper, silver and gold so vibrant they made the street look drab and lifeless by comparison. I turned to the half-dozen well-armed men and women charged with escorting me to jail. 'Marshals, allow me to offer my sincere apologies.'

'For what?' asked one as she raised her crossbow to train it on me.

The cards on the ground shimmered ever brighter, blinding

me to everything but the coruscating play of colours that drained the light from the world around me.

'For the inconvenience of my rescue,' I replied.

I doubt anyone heard me. The city around me faded to a flat, colourless expanse; the buildings, the streets, even the marshals themselves looked as if they'd been carved out of thin sheets of pale ivory. Reichis slumped on my shoulder and began snoring. A figure walked towards me, a lone source of dazzling colour wrapped in the twisting golds of sand magic, the pale blues of breath enchantments and the glistening purple of a silk spell.

A grandiose entrance of this type is usually accompanied by the disappointed sigh of my sister Shalla – *Sha'maat* now, I supposed – soon followed by an extensive commentary regarding my dishevelled condition and the annoyances my recent behaviour has caused our noble and much-admired family. Occasionally, though, it's my father who appears to inform me of the latest crime I've committed against our people. That latter possibility was why my hands were now deep inside the powder holsters at my sides.

Ever since I'd left my people, almost three years ago, I'd known the day would come when my father's grand destiny could no longer tolerate my miserable existence. I'd been asked on many occasions by friends and foes alike if I had a trick – some devious ruse – saved up that could outsmart the mighty Ke'heops before he could kill me.

I did. I just wasn't sure if it would work.

'Kellen.'

The voice didn't belong to my sister or my father. In fact, I hadn't heard it in such a long time that at first I didn't recognise her. Gradually, the bands of magical force began to settle, their brilliance diminishing enough that I could finally identify the apparition before me, and found myself standing there, the twin red and black powders I'd normally be using to cast a fiery explosion slipping through my fingers, with absolutely no idea what was going to happen next.

'Mother?'

The figure gestured at the cards surrounding me. 'Pick a card, Kellen,' she said. 'Any card.'

What is it with people and card tricks lately?

2

The Deck

As a child, I'd firmly believed Bene'maat was the finest mother any Jan'Tep boy could hope for. She'd been an island of patience and calm in the otherwise stormy sea of my father's unyielding ambitions and my sister's pugnacious temper tantrums. My mother's prowess as a mage was widely respected in our clan, yet her fascination with astronomy and healing revealed an inquisitive nature not solely consumed with the pursuit of magic, as Ke'heops and Shalla were. And me, for that matter.

If a parent's second duty is to love their children equally, then Bene'maat had done so admirably in a society that valued Shalla's raw talent for magic a thousand times more than my aptitude for clever tricks. And if a mother's first duty is to protect her children, well, then Bene'maat had done that pretty well too – right up until the day she'd drugged me and then helped my father strap me down to a table so he could inscribe counter-sigils on the metallic tattooed bands around my forearms, forever denying me access to the magic that defined our people as I screamed over and over again for her to stop.

Now the woman I hadn't seen for nearly three years was standing before me, placidly repeating, 'Pick a card, Kellen. Any card.'

I considered telling my beloved mother to bugger off, but my family is nothing if not persistent, so I gently settled the slumbering Reichis down on the ground and considered the thirteen cards forming a spell circle around me. I reached for the first one, which depicted architecture in the style of the Daroman capital in which we stood and was titled 'City of Glories'.

'Not that one,' she said.

'Why not?'

I heard the answer inside my mind a fraction of a second before her lips moved. 'That is the keystone. Picking it up would break the spell and end our meeting.'

I'd always been a belligerent child. Life as an outcast had done nothing to cure me of that fault. I reached for the City of Glories again.

'Please,' the voice in my mind said just before the apparition did. 'Forgive the awkward fashion in which our conversation must take place, but I've been unable to properly recreate your sister's wondrous spell for long-distance communication. I've had to rely on a much older enchantment your grandmother invented before you were born.'

For the third time she repeated the same instruction, exactly as she had before: 'Pick a card, Kellen. Any card.'

She's not really here, not even in spirit, I realised. Bene'maat must have used silk, sand and breath magic to record her thoughts and convey them to me within the cards as a series of individual messages, like a bundle of letters tied together with string, the spell encoded with specific responses based on my actions.

The remaining twelve cards fell into four suits unfamiliar to me – which is saying something considering how many decks I've encountered. In an Argosi deck, each suit corresponds to a particular civilisation on our continent. In more common sets of playing cards created for entertainment, the suits tend to represent symbols meaningful to the culture that created them. The standard Daroman deck, for example, embodies its people's obsession with military emblems: chariots, arrows, trebuchets and blades. However, the four suits of this new deck before me were unlike any I'd seen before: scrolls, quills, lutes and masks.

Had my mother devised these suits herself? And if so, what did each one mean?

I selected the seven of lutes, reasoning that no one had ever been blasted out of existence by a lute.

The figure of Bene'maat smiled and an instrument appeared in her hands. She began to play a melody that pulled at my heart so unexpectedly I gasped out loud.

'You always loved this song as a child,' she murmured. 'You used to make me play it for hours and hours whenever you were scared or sad.'

I dropped the card as if it were a spider crawling on my hand.

The figure of my mother nodded, somewhat sorrowfully, as if she'd known I would respond this way.

'Pick a card, Kellen,' she repeated. 'Any card.'

I found one that depicted a man carefully arranging quills on a scale. The caption read 'Enumerator of Quills'.

My mother's apparition was now seated at a desk composing a letter. 'My dearest Kellen. It's close to three years since last I touched your face. I had never thought such a thing possible. I always assumed you would come ba—'

'What is this?' I demanded. 'Nostalgia? Have you forgotten

29

what you did to me, Mother?' I pulled back my sleeves to show the foul counter-sigils desecrating the tattooed bands on my forearms. 'You destroyed any hope I had of becoming a mage like you and Father and Shalla.'

I hadn't expected a reply, but I felt an itch in the back of my mind and a moment later she spoke again. 'I know you're angry with us, Kellen. You have every right.'

I was beginning to understand how the magic worked. I wasn't communicating directly with my mother, but these messages were more than just words scrawled on a page. The spell was made from a more complete collection of her thoughts, capturing a single moment in time during which my mother had bound up all her contemplations on a particular topic and infused them into the card.

A spectral tear slid down my mother's cheek. 'It broke my heart, what we did. We believed we were protecting you, protecting the world from what you might become. We had no idea how wrong our actions were.'

You should've known, I thought bitterly. *A mother is supposed to protect her child, not ruin him.*

I didn't say any of it out loud though. I knew it wasn't really Bene'maat standing there in front of me, yet still I couldn't bear to say such hurtful things to my mother.

'I thank you for your gracious missive,' I said finally. 'Are we done now? I have an important appointment in a jail cell. So unless you have some miracle cure for—'

Bene'maat's arm extended, pointing now to a different card.

I replaced the one I was holding and picked up the nine of quills. The expression on my mother's face changed to a look of determination, and arranged all around her were sketches and diagrams and pages upon pages of esoteric formulae. 'Every day since you left, I've tried to find a way to undo the counter-banding. I've searched every book of lore in our sanctums, consulted with spellmasters across the territories. I read every scrap of parchment your father brought back from the Ebony Abbey, hoping to find among their knowledge of the shadowblack's etheric planes the means to repair your connection to the high magics. At times I thought I might be close . . .'

She stopped, squeezing her fists in frustration. The image of her fluttered and faded.

The spell must require perfect focus to imprint the message on the card, I thought. *Every time she lost her concentration, she'd had to stop and start a new one.*

'What do you mean, "close"?' I asked. 'Are you saying there might be a cure?'

A different card began to glow brighter than the others. The peddler of masks. I picked it up.

'So much of what I've been told has turned out to be lies, Kellen. False promises. Supposed secret methods for inscribing new sigils that resulted in nothing more than temporary illusions.'

'Then it's hopeless?'

I suppose I shouldn't have been surprised. Of all the things I lost when I left my people, the one I knew I could never get back was my magic. I'd learned to live with that fact. With my one breath band, my blast powders, my castradazi coins, and all the other tricks I'd learned along the way, I sometimes even prided myself that I could outsmart my enemies without spells. But I still woke up in the middle of the night sometimes with every inch of my skin glistening with sweat, my fingers twitching through the dozens of somatic forms I'd practised thousands of times for spells I would never cast, so desperate for the taste of magic that no food or drink could satisfy me.

Like all my people, I was an addict. My addiction was inscribed in tattooed metallic inks around my forearms. I could never sate that desire. I doubted it would ever leave me.

The apparition of my mother gestured behind me, and I turned to see the thief of masks rising above the other cards, beckoning me to take it. When I did, her voice became a whisper.

'There might be a way.'

I spun back around to see her, still standing where she'd been before. There was an uncertainty in her gaze though, as if she were afraid someone might burst into wherever she'd been when she'd created these messages for me.

'What do you mean?' I asked.

She looked as if she were struggling to get out the words without losing the concentration required to continue imprinting her thoughts onto the card. 'Our people have been . . . wrong about magic, Kellen. So very wrong, and at costs we're only now discovering. The fundamental forces are vastly more complex than we assumed and can be fashioned in ways we never imagined. There are traditions as old as our own, spread out across the cultures of this continent. Much of the knowledge has been lost even to their own peoples, but I've found traces of it within old songs and stories.'

No wonder she was having so much trouble holding the spell. To hear a Jan'Tep mage admit our people weren't the only ones who could perform high magic was a kind of sacrilege that even I found troubling.

'There is a place far from here where I believe I might acquire the means to rectify the crime your father and I committed against you, to give you back the chance to become a true mage of the Jan'Tep.' The look of determination I'd seen in her so often as a child appeared in her features. 'I swear to you, my son, there is no price I will not pay to buy back your future.'

I swallowed. My breathing was quick, my heart beating faster than it should. The prospect of what my mother was suggesting . . . But I'd travelled the long roads of this continent, seen and heard just about every kind of con game there was, performed half of them myself. Not everything is fake in this world, but nothing of value comes free.

I reached for the card depicting two figures exchanging goods as they stood beneath an open scroll. My people don't use scrolls for spells or messages. We use them for contracts.

'Come home,' my mother said, her voice more a plea than an opening bid. 'Come back to us. Your father is mage sovereign now. He has lifted the spell warrant against you.'

'Too bad he didn't mention that to the lord magus who just tried to kill me.'

The apparition of my mother gave no reply. She couldn't, of course. She would've had no knowledge of this latest attempt on my life. Besides, it was a fair bet this guy had been hired by Daroman conspirators rather than my own people.

'Come back to me,' Bene'maat repeated. 'Even if I fail to return your magic to you, still I can give you a home.'

Home. Such a strange word. I wasn't sure I knew what it meant any more.

'I've been scrying you when I could, though you're very

difficult to track,' Bene'maat said. 'Not spying on you, I promise, but I needed to see you sometimes, through a mother's eyes and not through the recounting of your sister and others.' In the haze behind her, pictures formed and faded, images of events in my life since I'd left my homeland. Scenes of violence, of pursuit, of me sitting alone after a fight looking far more miserable than even I remembered. 'The brave face you put on for those around you, this trickster's guise you've taken on, it's not you, Kellen. You weren't meant for this life. You aren't happy.'

Happy? I'd spent the past three years facing every mage, mercenary or monster this continent had to offer. I'd survived them all. Saved a few decent people along the way. Wasn't that enough? Was I supposed to be happy now too?

My mother's fingers were outstretched, reaching towards me, a desperate hope in her eyes. 'Come home, son.'

The card in my hand felt heavy. Clammy against my skin. I sank to the ground and before another could glow or rise or otherwise demand my attention, I shuffled them all together, fully breaking the circle and ending the spell. The cards became dull and flat once again, and the world around me came back to life.

Goodbye, Mother.

'Move real slow now, spellslinger,' Cobb said.

I heard the marshals shuffling behind me, fingers on the triggers of their crossbows. They seemed neither concerned nor even aware of the cards that had floated here and that I now held in my hand. I suspected barely a second had passed for them and this whole event had taken place solely in my mind.

'Hey,' Reichis growled from where he was curled up on the ground. 'Why'd you dump me down here?'

'Sorry,' I said to both him and the marshals, stuffing my mother's strange herald cards into my pocket. I picked up the squirrel cat and settled him back on my shoulder. 'Let's get a move on. Time for Torian Libri to lock us up again.'

The marshals chuckled at that, and we all resumed our march to the palace.

'You know where you went wrong with the lieutenant?' Reichis asked.

'Don't start,' I warned.

There are only three solutions his species have to offer regarding the resolution of conflicts between humans: kill them, rob them blind, or – and this is the one where Reichis derives the most pleasure from devising elaborate and intensely nauseating suggestions – bed them.

'Shoulda mated with her the day you met her,' the squirrel cat said earnestly.

'Mating works better when the other person doesn't despise you,' I countered.

A couple of the marshals following behind me broke out laughing. Reichis took their mirth as encouragement – not that he needed any. 'Nah, that Torian female desires you, see?' He tapped a paw against his fuzzy muzzle. 'Smelled it on her the day the queen introduced you two. I swear on all twenty-six squirrel cat gods, Kellen, the marshal's in heat for you.'

It was, most assuredly, not true. Also, it's highly doubtful that there are twenty-six squirrel cat gods. Times like these though? It's best not to contradict the little monster.

'Now, here's what you oughta do . . .' Reichis tried – and failed staggeringly – to stifle his chittering laughter.

35

'First, you're gonna take off your trousers. Females love that. Next, you turn around and wiggle your bottom at her. Then all you have to do is drop to your knees and start making this sound . . .'

I'm not going to describe the noise he made. Suffice it to say that it was exactly as disgusting as you might imagine. He kept making it all the way to the palace.

3

The Lieutenant

The Imperial Palace of Darome had been my home this past year, a significantly more luxurious place to lay one's hat than the string of seedy roadside taverns, flea-infested campsites and cramped jail cells that constituted an outlaw's customary abodes. That didn't make it any more comfortable though.

The outlandish opulence of palaces, with their gilded halls, stunning portraits and majestic statues, make them wonderful places to visit. But unless you were born in one? Living in a palace makes you feel small. Shabby. An intruder whose presence tarnishes the otherwise pristine perfection of their surroundings.

It was enough to make a man reconsider whether he belonged there at all.

'Now who let a lousy, no-good outlaw loose in a fine, upstanding establishment like this?' Lieutenant Torian Libri asked.

Don't pick a fight, I reminded myself. *Let her drag you off to a cell and by morning the queen will have ordered your release. After that . . .* I sniffed at my armpit, *a very long bath is in order.*

Torian was leaning nonchalantly – some might say disrespectfully – against a statue of Hephantus IV, the famously ill-tempered Daroman monarch who founded the royal marshals service more than a century ago. In life, Hephantus had broken with tradition by foregoing ostentatious royal vestments in favour of a rather plain grey leather coat better suited to concealing the knives and garrottes he relished employing on would-be assassins. To this day that same dull grey garment remains the customary uniform of nearly every marshal in Darome, save for Torian Libri, who'd dyed her own long leather coat a deep crimson.

Hides the bloodstains better, she claims.

'Miss me, spellslinger?' she asked with a wink.

At this point I should mention that, as merciless enforcers of the law went, Torian Libri was the most beautiful woman I'd ever met.

How beautiful?

'So *purdy* . . .' Reichis murmured.

The squirrel cat was perched on my shoulder, one paw resting on top of my head as he gazed wide-eyed at the lieutenant. Now, I know what you're thinking: why would a squirrel cat – especially one who claims to find human faces so ugly that every time he tries to count their eyeballs he ends up vomiting before he gets to two – be mesmerised by this particular skinbag?

'Purdiest eyes I ever saw,' he chittered wistfully.

Imagine the brightest indigo you've ever seen – brighter than the azurite ores in the blue desert region of the Seven Sands. Deeper and richer than the waters off the coast of Gitabria that the locals call the Sapphire Sea. So captivating that more than one amateur poet among the palace courtiers had been known to rhapsodise about the ecstasy of drowning in those eyes.

Me? I generally avoid drowning.

Best as I'd been able to uncover, Torian was only a couple of years older than me. A string of successful manhunts against some of the deadliest outlaws in the Daroman empire had enabled her to rise up the ranks far faster than her fellow marshals – a fact which irritated them no end.

I'd met one of her captives once. The guy swore to me – right before he was dragged off to be hanged – that he'd witnessed Torian take down six highly trained killers all by herself, pursuing them high up into the border mountains. He figured she'd only left him alive to make sure there would be someone left to tell her story. 'Had my crossbow aimed right at her,' he repeated over and over. 'But those eyes . . . Gods of sea and sky – one look and I just couldn't bring myself to fire.'

There's something particularly pathetic about a man awaiting execution bewitched by the beauty of the marshal who's sent him to the gallows.

But when Torian Libri flashes that smile at you . . . When those high cheekbones rise even higher and that long black hair shimmers like onyx as it drapes down a neck so smooth you could stare at it all day long even when you weren't contemplating how much you'd like to throttle her . . . ?

And yeah . . . Those eyes.

'Like sapphires,' Reichis purred.

It's worth noting that squirrel cats don't purr.

Lieutenant Libri gave the six marshals escorting me a curt nod and they left me in her charge. No back-up, no handcuffs. That's because Torian liked to remind me that she was faster on the draw than I was and could easily bury one of those finger-length throwing knives she favoured in my throat before my hands ever reached my powder holsters.

'We can't keep meeting like this, card player,' she began, sliding her arm through mine to lead me through the grand foyer as though I were her escort to a royal ball rather than a prisoner headed for the palace dungeons. She leaned her head against my shoulder. 'People are going to start thinking we're sweet on each other.'

Her absurdly affectionate behaviour drew the attention of nobles and courtiers cockroaching their way around the palace in search of opportunities to advance their interests and frustrate those of their rivals. Reichis, convinced by all the stares that people were admiring him, shook himself, causing his fur to change colour from its natural brown to a rich silver accented with blue stripes almost the hue of Torian's eyes.

'Well now,' she laughed. 'Aren't you the handsome rogue?'

A blush of pink bloomed across the silver of Reichis's coat. Nearby, a pair of Gitabrian merchant lords, looking especially splendid in their jaunty purple hats, went to the trouble of whispering loudly in the Jan'Tep tongue of my people to ensure their insult wouldn't be lost on me. 'Did you see the animal that just slunk into the royal palace?' the first asked. 'The filthy creature's coat is probably full of fleas.'

The other chuckled merrily. 'Indeed . . . Perhaps he should borrow the squirrel cat's instead!'

Almost a year I'd lived in this palace, and I swear every single person to walk these halls thinks they're the first to come up with that joke. There are variations, of course. *'What a beastly stench . . . And the squirrel cat doesn't smell much better!'* was a popular one. Sometimes it was my accent that amused them: *'What is that awful mewling the beast makes? Why, I do believe Her Majesty's tutor of cards has learned a new word!'*

40

My personal favourites were the heated debates over whether it was Reichis or myself who'd mated with the most barnyard animals. Reichis didn't mind the stares and sneers though, mostly because I was generally the butt of the jokes, but also because the insults helped him identify the targets for his next heist.

'Yep,' he grunted, scampering down my shoulder before landing on the marble floor. 'Gonna get me that purple hat.'

'You're a squirrel cat,' I reminded him. 'What could you possibly want with a hat?'

He glanced up to give me a snarl. 'You sayin' I wouldn't look good in a hat?' Without waiting for a reply he grumbled off to perform his latest feat of feline larceny. 'You know who looks dumb in a hat? *You* look dumb in a hat. Gonna poop in your hat, that's what I'm gonna do. Not that you'll notice.'

Torian smiled as she watched him go. She's got a soft spot for the squirrel cat, possibly due to a natural affinity for animals whose preferred means of resolving conflict involves maximum bloodshed.

She tugged my arm and resumed our march down the great hall. A hard right turn brought us to a set of stairs that led to the lower levels beneath the palace, where they kept the kitchens and storerooms.

And the dungeon, of course.

'The queen's going to hear about this,' I informed her as we descended.

'The queen loves me,' Torian countered.

That, regrettably, was true. Queen Ginevra had a thing for tough, determined young women, and they didn't come any tougher or more determined than Torian Libri. Except maybe the queen herself, of course.

41

We arrived at a row of six cells reserved for those prisoners the crown preferred to keep close by. Each cell was unusually well appointed, with red-and-gold velvet curtains behind the bars to provide warmth and a measure of privacy. A small reading desk and a sturdy chair were bolted beneath a plaque written in archaic Daroman for which I hadn't yet found the translation, but was fairly sure read, 'Yeah, you're screwed.'

The cot in the corner was narrow, but not uncomfortable. You got a decent night's sleep in these cells, as I'd discovered from spending rather more time in them than was customary for one of Her Majesty's royal tutors.

'The queen loves me too,' I reminded Torian.

This is usually the part where she unlocks the door and shoves me into one of the cells. Instead she turned on me, the sharp glare in her eyes catching the lantern light. 'Too bad you don't seem to feel the same about her, spellslinger.'

'What's that supposed to mean?'

Torian began circling me in the narrow passage, halting periodically to poke me with a sharp fingernail. 'It occurs to me that if you genuinely cared about Her Majesty, you'd stop pissing off her marshals service, who are, in case you've forgotten, responsible for her security. That's the first rule.'

Poke.

Don't take the bait, I reminded myself. *Just let her push you around a little and soon you'll be enjoying a nice, comfortable cell for the night.*

'The second rule is that you stick to your own job, which best as I can determine is to play cards with Her Majesty. Tell her jokes. Make her laugh. Occasionally strut around the palace with your tousled hair and pretty face, spouting Argosi frontier wisdom about "The Way of Water" so the

42

warmongering nobles of this gods-forsaken empire get just nervous enough to focus their murderous impulses on you instead of the queen.'

She took a quick breath before asking, 'Well, card player? You got anything to say for yourself?'

'You think I have a pretty face?'

Poke.

'I could ignore the rest of it, for *her* sake. But the third rule, spellslinger? That's the one neither I nor the people I work for can forgive.'

She tried to poke me again but my patience was wearing thin and this time I batted her hand out of the way. 'If you're planning on locking me up for the night, do it, but don't keep—'

'The third rule,' she went on, barrelling over me, 'is that should you ever stumble upon gossip that a Jan'Tep bounty mage has entered my territory, you always – *always* – come to me with the information first so that I can do *my* job.' She spun around now, addressing an audience that wasn't there. 'But what does the spellslinging Argosi card sharp do instead? He sneaks out of the palace to square off against a lord magus – a *lord magus* – all by his lonesome. Doesn't even bring along the damned squirrel cat, who, frankly, is starting to look like the brains of the operation.'

'You seem to have forgotten one thing, lieutenant.'

She turned back to me, instantly snaring me with that indigo gaze. One corner of her mouth rose, just a fraction, offering the hint of a smile. When she spoke, the words came out in a soft exhalation of breath as though she were reading aloud from a book of love poems. 'I forgot that you outsmarted the mage, didn't I?'

'Yeah,' I said, though at that precise moment I couldn't quite remember what I was agreeing to.

Strange as it sounds, I was fairly sure that Her Majesty Queen Ginevra the First of Darome had assigned Torian Libri to be my liaison to the marshals service – or 'babysitter' as Torian put it – out of some perverse desire to see us matched. We were both young, both unattached. Torian had an endless horde of suitors begging for her attention. I had . . . Well, I guess we didn't have all that much in common after all. Regardless, the queen seemed determined to pair us up.

And she wonders why so many of her subjects keep trying to assassinate her.

Torian tapped a finger against my chest. By sheer chance it snuck through a tear in my shirt. I felt the tingle of her skin against mine. 'Fooled him with one of those ingenious ploys of yours?' she asked, letting her fingertip linger there.

'It was kind of ingenious, now that you mention it. See, I hired an actor to—'

'I.' Poke. 'Don't.' Poke. 'Care.' Poke.

'Ow! That last one broke the skin!'

She held up her finger, showing me the single drop of blood clinging to the nail. 'Poor baby. Tell me something, card player. What happens to my queen on the day you run out of tricks?'

It was the second time I'd been asked that question. Normally that would've been cause for reflection on my part, but I was getting tired of being poked and prodded throughout a litany of grievances I'd heard a dozen times before. Despite my earlier determination not to aggravate my situation, I did something then that no sane person would ever do: I grabbed Lieutenant Torian Libri, perhaps the most feared marshal in

44

the entire service, by the lapels of her long leather coat and shoved her away from me.

Now, when it comes to reflexes and fighting techniques, there's no one I've ever met more dangerous than my mentor, Ferius Parfax. But Torian comes awfully close. She had my arm twisted behind my back and my face mashed between the bars of one of the cells before I could even screech like a lost little boy. That came shortly after.

'Did you seriously just try to lay hands on me, card player?'

Her lips were almost touching my earlobe, warm breath teasing the tiny hairs on my neck. There is no more awkward feeling in this life than being simultaneously terrified and aroused. Still, while my *arta forteize* is only so-so, I have excellent *arta valar*, or as Ferius calls it, 'swagger'.

'You'll want to clean that cut,' I said, my voice calm as still water despite the pain in my wrist where her grip was squeezing the bones together. 'Wouldn't want your poking finger to get infected.'

'What are you talking abou—' She pulled away suddenly, letting out a surprised gasp.

With my free hand I pushed myself away from the bars and turned. She was staring at the blood on her index finger with a bewildered expression. I flicked her throwing knife in the air and caught it neatly between my own thumb and forefinger. The delicate point glistened red. 'Nice balance,' I said, then flipped the short blade over again before offering her the blunt end. 'You should hang on to these.'

She didn't take it right away. You could tell she was working through what had just happened. 'You lifted the knife from my coat when you pushed me. Palmed it so that once my hand was locked around your wrist all it took was a twitch of your fingers to cut me.'

I nodded.

'Pretty smooth for someone who trips over his own feet whenever anyone asks him to dance.'

One time. *One* time.

'Now you know,' I said.

She tilted her head. 'Now I know what?'

I chose my next words carefully. For all the mistrust between us, I'd never doubted Torian's loyalty to the queen. A while back, with a different ill-tempered marshal, I'd failed to comprehend just how dangerous such devotion can be. My oversight had nearly destroyed all our lives. 'You asked what would happen to the queen once I ran out of tricks.'

She held up a bleeding finger. 'And a paper cut is your answer?'

'My answer is that I always have one more trick.' I took the risk of moving closer to her. 'You have my word, Lieutenant Libri, when I use that last trick up, when I finally run out of ways to outwit my enemies and those of the queen? I'll come to you. I'll tell you it's time and then I'll leave her service for good. I'll walk right out the city gates and I'll keep on walking till I'm long gone from your country.'

I held out a hand so we could shake on the bargain.

Those impossibly blue eyes of her went first to my outstretched hand and then back to me. For once, there was no taunting or scolding in her gaze, just a kind of sadness that caught me off-guard. 'I wish things could work that way, Kellen.'

Torian hardly ever calls me by my proper name. It's always 'card player' or 'swindler' or occasionally 'squirrel cat boy'.

The Argosi talent for eloquence – what we call *arta loquit* – teaches that every utterance of a person's name is meaningful, each unique inflection filled with signs waiting to be interpreted. Her use of my name just then told me that something was very, very wrong.

I looked down at my chest, through the little hole in my shirt where she'd poked me with her fingernail. Blood from the tiny, almost insignificant wound had already begun to coagulate, the sharp, burning sensation replaced by a tingling numbness. I tore open the shirt – clumsily, because my fingers were also becoming numb. There, just beneath the skin surrounding the red dot of dried blood, was a slowly blooming patch of the second-most beautiful azure I'd ever seen.

My vision began to blur. My eyes sought out Torian, but she wouldn't meet my gaze.

'You . . .'

I couldn't get the words out to ask why she'd gone to all the trouble of poisoning me just to lock me in a cell for the night when she knew perfectly well I'd put up with this token incarceration a dozen times before.

She's not putting me in a cell, I realised far too late. *This was all a ruse.*

My balance fled all at once. My legs crumpled beneath me. I'd've fallen to the hard stone floor had Torian not caught me and propped me up. The familiar echo of marshals' boot heels came down the passageway towards us. My head settled awkwardly against Torian's shoulder. 'This is the problem with tricks, Kellen,' she murmured. 'You're not the only one who uses them.'

4

Arta Forteize

Four men carried me on their shoulders, reminding me of the four deuces the old man had dealt me back in the saloon. Daroman card players call that particular hand an eight-legged horse: the beast upon whose back gamblers are borne to the underworld at the moment of their death.

Our path twisted and turned along unfamiliar passageways, heading deeper and deeper beneath the palace. We passed through one locked door after another until finally descending a set of stairs I hadn't known existed, which was troubling considering how carefully Reichis and I had cased this place.

'Where . . . ?'

No point in even trying. My tongue was a bloated sponge I couldn't spit out.

A hand I could barely feel touched my cheek. 'Don't speak,' Torian said, her voice little more than a distant echo. 'Don't do anything, okay? Just . . . Trust me.'

A phlegmy cough erupted from my throat, which I guess was me trying to laugh. I suppose if I were a lying, manipulative poisoner, I too would tell my victim, 'Don't worry, it only *seems* like I'm burying you alive. Really I'm secretly saving you, so just trust me, okay?'

Never hurts to give the poor sap a shred of optimism to carry with them into the afterlife.

Despite the fog filling my senses, I couldn't help but admire Torian's ploy. Had she sent me some seemingly innocuous invitation or made a show of seducing me, I'd've been on my guard. Instead she'd had me arrested, same as always. Escorted me down to the palace cells, as always. Offered the usual insults, made the same veiled threats. Repetition. Ritual.

That's why I'd let Reichis run off. In a few hours, he'd sneak down to the cells expecting to pick the lock and break me out like he always did. Had I suspected anything different, I would've signalled him to trail us instead. The moment I'd begun to succumb to the poison, he'd've ripped Torian's face off – 'purdy eyes' and all.

But the marshal had suckered me like a pro, and now I was screwed.

You know those old romantic adventure tales of the clever hero or heroine who just happens to have spent years building up an immunity to the specific poison his enemies had intended to paralyse him with?

Doesn't work.

Don't believe me? Just try it. Go ahead. Poison yourself with, say, a few leaves of weakweed or a pinch of winterbloom. Now . . . Well, now you're dead. Small doses of poison, taken over an extended period of time, tend to accumulate in your internal organs until enough builds up to kill you.

But let's say you manage to survive. Well done. Once you've recovered – assuming recovery is even possible and you haven't condemned yourself to spending the rest of your days in perpetual agony, trapped in a delirious, semi-conscious daze as you drool over yourself while desperately trying to find some way to communicate to your loved ones that you'd really much rather be dead, thank you very much – go out and try the poison a second time.

Whoops. Same result.

Now, it's true that there are some forms of liquor and smoke whose effects become less pronounced over time, but that's just the fun stuff, like getting drunk. The bad part? The gradual assault on your liver or lungs? That just keeps churning along until you eventually cough yourself into an early grave.

That's why '. . . and then they poisoned the young, would-be hero' is never the opening act to a daring escape.

Except . . .

Except that during our travels together, I'd witnessed Ferius Parfax shake off the effects of paralytics faster than anyone else alive.

'It's not fair,' I once told her, groggily stumbling around in between bouts of vomiting all over myself.

'That so?' she asked. Her hands shook just a little as she drew a smoking reed from inside her black leather waistcoat. She lit the reed with one of the matches she kept hidden in the cuff of her travelling shirt – next to her lock picks.

The rising blue smoke reawakened my nausea. 'Oh, ancestors, please don't . . .'

Ferius offered not one scrap of sympathy. 'Never could teach good taste to you Jan'Tep savages,' she said. On her second puff she let out an impressive pair of interlocking smoke rings. 'Besides, after all these months on the road together, gettin' jumped more times 'n either of us can count, you tellin' me that you're still moanin' about some fella

50

tryin' to poison us so's he can collect that bounty on your head not being "fair"?'

I spent the next few seconds trying to regain my bearings so I could pair my reply with a passably menacing glare. 'That's not what I meant and you know it.'

'What's troublin' you, kid?'

'You!' I blurted angrily. Regrettably, the blurting was immediately followed by spewing the last remnants of our overpriced – and, as it turned out, poisoned – stew. 'You're no bigger than I am. You ate the same food. So how come you always recover so much quicker than me?'

'Ah,' she said, letting out another puff of smoke. 'That.'

'Yeah. *That.*'

Ferius stared down at the smoking reed between her thumb and forefinger. For a moment I wondered if maybe that's where the answer lay – that somehow smoking those rancid sticks was actually good for something other than stinking up the air. When she finally spoke though, the words came out so soft I thought maybe she hadn't wanted me to hear them. 'Arta forteize.'

'The Argosi talent for resilience?'

The only reason I recognised those words was because a few months before, Rosie – also known as the Path of Thorns and Roses – had explained the seven Argosi talents to me. It's worth noting that until then, I'd never even known they existed, because my supposed mentor hadn't bothered to mention them.

'Guess the others do like to call it resilience,' Ferius said. 'Me, I just think of it as trust.'

'Trust?'

She walked over to me, upright and perfectly balanced in

contrast to the way I was shaking and shuddering like too little tree caught in too much wind. She closed her hand into a fist and showed it to me.

'Please don't hit me,' I said.

'Sorry, kid. Only way the lesson works.'

Ancestors, I hate her lessons sometimes.

She didn't hit me hard. In fact, at first she moved so slow I tried to turn in the direction of the blow. She sped up at the last instant to knock me in the jaw.

'Ow!' I swore. 'What kind of *maetri* punches her *teysan* right after he's been poisoned?'

Maetri is the word the Argosi use for teacher, and teysan means student. Ferius hates fancy terms like that, which is why I use them when she's pissing me off.

She raised an eyebrow. 'Want to learn arta forteize or not?'

I rubbed at my jaw. 'Some lesson.'

She patted my cheek. 'Poor baby.'

Wait . . . 'Poor baby'? *Ferius never used those words.*

Torian – it had been Torian who'd called me 'poor baby' after she'd poked me with her fingernail.

I managed to force my eyes open, just a little, taking in the hazy sight of what appeared to be a massive iron door at the end of a narrow passage. Torian placed a finger against the metal surface and began tracing a circle. After a couple of seconds I heard what could best be described as a shimmery tinkling, like the faint echo of distant bells or the chime you get from tracing the rim of a crystal goblet with a moistened finger. A moment later, a heavy click chased away the chimes, followed by the grinding of bolts sliding open.

'Leave him and go,' Torian commanded the four marshals carrying me.

I found myself propped up against the passage wall, held in place by Torian's grip on my shoulders.

'Lieutenant, shouldn't we . . . ?' one of the marshals began.

'You should get out of here right now.' There was ice in her voice, along with something else, out of place for her. Trepidation? 'Believe me, you don't want the men and women in that room to wonder if you might recognise their faces.'

The dull thud of boot heels against the passage floor marked a hurried cadence.

'Who—' I began to ask, but Torian silenced me with a stinging slap against my cheek.

No, hang on. Torian doesn't slap people, she pokes them. The slap had been Ferius.

'Pay attention to the lesson, kid,' my Argosi mentor warned. 'Might save your life some day.'

I batted her hand away, which felt a little rude on my part, but Ferius just grinned. 'There, see?'

'See what?'

She reached out again. 'Quit it!' I said, swatting her hand away a second time.

'There. You did it again. What's the lesson, kid?'

'Find a better teacher?'

For a third time she tried to slap my cheek, and for the third time I knocked her hand away.

'What's the lesson?' she asked again.

Moments like these, neither petulance nor belligerence gets you anywhere with Ferius Parfax. She'll just keep doing the same thing over and over until she gets the answer she wants. Or at least, the right question. 'Who cares if I batted your hand away?'

'What were you doing a minute ago?'

53

'Puking my guts out and trying very hard not to fall flat on my face!'

She nodded as if I'd just given the correct answer. 'And now?'

'Now I'm . . . Oh . . .'

She took another puff from her smoking reed. 'So what's the lesson, kid?'

Even after all that it took me a while to figure it out, but I got there eventually. 'The paralysis. I thought it was still there, but as soon as I shifted my focus, I got steadier.'

She snapped her smoking reed in two and held up both parts. 'One end of this burns and there ain't nothin' either of us can do about that. But the other end only burns if you believe it's on fire.' She dropped the two pieces to the ground and stamped out the smouldering one. 'Most things in life are like that. Part of it's in the body; part of it's in the mind. Ain't much you can do about the body, but the mind?' She beckoned to me. 'Come a little closer, kid.'

'You going to hit me again?'

She grinned. 'Only if you're slow.'

I took a step.

'Good,' she said. 'Now close your eyes and take another.'

I sighed. By this point I'd just about forgotten what lesson she was trying to teach me, but I complied nonetheless. I closed my eyes and took a step. My boot heel landed on a rock that slid out from me. A second later I was on my butt, swearing at her.

'Why'd you fall?' she asked.

I pushed myself back up to my feet. 'Because you made me close my eyes!'

'Did I put the rock there?'

'No, but you knew—'

'So did you, kid. You saw the ground and you saw the rock. But when you closed your eyes, all you saw was darkness. Why not see the ground and the rock?'

'Because that's not how vision works?'

She took my hand and held it up between us before placing a steel throwing card between my thumb and forefinger. 'You feel this?'

'Just barely.'

She pointed to the tree behind her. 'Reckon you can hit the knot in that tree?'

'No.'

'Why not? You've hit harder targets.'

I pinched the steel card tighter. I couldn't even be sure my muscles were working. 'Because the poison's still affecting my nerves. I can't feel the card to aim, just like my vision's too blurry to focus on the tree and my muscles are too weak to throw properly.'

Ferius snorted. 'Kid, that tree ain't but a few yards away. You know where it is, just like you know you're holdin' the card and you know your muscles can throw it.'

I took a step to the right so she wasn't in my way, then stared at the tree a second longer before pulling my arm back and hurling the card. It didn't even leave my hand at first because I'd been pinching it too hard. When it did, it just flopped to the ground at my feet.

'Again,' she said, handing me another card.

I handed it back to her. 'Show me first.'

Ferius sighed, then snatched the card from my hand and – without even turning to look at the target – flung it behind her. The steel edge buried itself dead centre in the knot of the tree trunk.

'How is that possible?' I asked.

She held up her hand in front of me, rubbing her fingers together. 'I can't feel 'em any better than you can right now. Can't hardly see neither. Arms feel like dead weights. That's the poison in the body.' She tapped my temple with her finger. 'The rest is in there, makin' you believe you can't throw the card because you can't feel it. Foolin' you into thinkin' you can't hit the tree just because you can't see it properly, even though you know – you *know* – that tree's right there waitin' for you.'

'So you just . . .'

'Trust,' she said. 'Resilience is just trustin' your body. Gettin' up even when your mind says you can't get up again. Fightin' back even when your fear tells you there's no hope.' She put one palm over my eyes and with the other placed another steel card in my hand. 'Trust your memory to tell you where the target is. Trust your hand to remember how to throw. And most of all, trust your heart to lead you straight.'

I felt her hand come away as she stepped aside. I kept my eyes closed though, and even though I couldn't feel my arm moving, I drew back and threw the card.

'Well?' she asked then. 'Ain't you gonna look to see if you hit the target?'

I turned away and went to get our packs so we could leave. 'Reckon I'll just trust I hit it,' I replied.

I could hear the smile in her voice as she followed me. 'Here endeth the lesson, kid.'

I came back to myself then, just barely aware of Torian Libri hauling me into the chamber where I would soon find myself at the mercy of whoever waited inside. I kept falling in and out of consciousness, trapped beneath the palace where no one who gave a damn about my life or death could find me. The paralytic coating the fingernail Torian had cut me with was so strong that I couldn't move a muscle – couldn't so much as feel my face. I could hear just fine though.

'Why is he smiling?' someone asked.

5

The Murmurers

I awoke to a blinding light, a deadly threat and a most unexpected rescue.

'We warned you, little Tori,' a woman's gravelly voice said, sounding like a disapproving vulture circling above a rotting carcass in the sand.

Heh. 'Little Tori'. Can't wait to call her that next time she has me arrested.

'And I told *you*,' Little Tori countered, her tone somewhere between a birdsong and a razor blade, 'that if you'd just let the spellslinger explain, none of this would be necessary.'

'That is not the council's way,' a deeper voice intoned. I imagined a self-important camel standing on its hind legs in the middle of the desert, about to begin a lengthy sermon on the noble nature of sand. 'Disturbing murmurs have come to us about this one.'

Odd choice of word. Almost sounded like he said . . . Oh, crap. The Murmurers!

For months I'd been hearing rumours of a collection of high-ranking generals, spies and marshals operating out of the imperial palace. Every scrap of intelligence regarding potential threats to the empire went through them first, to be sifted, debated and finally, eliminated. These twelve men and woman had, so far as I could tell, no formal legal authority – though I'd uncovered passing references in the royal accounts to something called 'The Imperial Council for Strategic Preparation'. Those in the know, however, referred to them as the Murmurers.

Every time I'd brought up the possible existence of this shadowy group to Torian, she'd laughed in my face.

'He's an idiot,' she now declared. 'A buffoon who trades in card tricks and clever quips. He's no threat to the queen.'

'The concern of this council goes beyond Ginevra's person,' barked a new voice, thin and reedy like that of an angry meerkat popping up from its hole in the sand. 'We serve the empire.'

'Quite right,' the camel agreed.

Why does this desert have to be so damned hot? I wondered. I kept wanting to roll over to get away from the six dancing suns in the sky overhead before they burned holes through my eyelids.

Those aren't suns, idiot. They must be lanterns, swaying from chains embedded in the ceiling. Pull yourself together. Use your arta forteize to shake off the poison like Ferius taught you, so you can get out of here!

Right. Good plan. Which one's arta forteize again?

'Enough!' squawked the vulture. 'There's no point stretching this out. If the witness is to be believed . . .'

There was a pause during which I got the sense she was referring to someone in the room.

'We've no reason to doubt his testimony,' the meerkat hissed.

'Even if we accept his evidence,' someone new – possibly

59

a cobra or a particularly sibilant crocodile – added, 'the danger to the empire is too great. We must act now, before the opportunity passes us by.'

The vulture took over again. 'Exactly. We all know the spellslinger is a wild card prone to making rash decisions based on his own petulant and dubious moral code. Worse, he's got too much influence over the queen. So either we kill him now, or we . . . Actually, I can't see an alternative.'

'I vote in favour of the execution warrant,' the meerkat said.

'Aye,' spat the camel.

A few others – possibly two otters and some sort of singing ostrich – concurred in quick succession.

Well, they all sound like fine, upstanding citizens, I thought. *Guess I'd better start killing them.*

For the next few minutes, I paid little attention to their words – they were pretty much just taking turns pontificating on the necessity of eliminating me. Instead I focused on what their voices revealed about the room I was in. Each time one of them spoke, the sound came from a different direction. They had to be either standing or sitting all around me.

My back was sore, so I was lying on something hard, but I distinctly remembered Torian catching me before I hit the floor. Also, I wasn't cold; stone robs heat from your body faster than a chill in the air, so I must be lying on some kind of wooden table, likely in the centre of the chamber.

They're seated all around me like gluttons waiting to carve up a roast pig.

Torian broke my concentration when she yelled loud enough to silence everyone else in the room. 'Next person to lecture me on the necessity of making hard choices for the empire is going to wake up with a broken jaw,' she announced. 'Nobody kills this idiot unless it's me doing the killing!'

I was touched. Sort of.

'A similar warrant could be placed on your own head, Lieutenant Libri, should you threaten this council a second time,' the camel warned.

Not a camel, I reminded myself. *A human being. One who might need blasting pretty soon.*

My brain was now functioning at least moderately close to its usual slow-witted pace, so I shifted my attention to my body. Subtly and methodically, I began to clench and unclench my muscles one after another, even though I couldn't feel them working. Numbing the nerves is one thing, but actually deadening the muscles for any length of time tends to lead to rapid respiratory failure. So either Torian had given me a fatal dose of poison, or I should soon be able to make my move.

Now I just needed a move to make.

Most of the palace was warded against Jan'Tep magic, so my blasting spell was likely to fail even if I could muster the dexterity required – which I probably couldn't. Similarly, castradazi magic calls for deftness in the fingers to make the coins dance. If I tried anything that complicated right now, I'd just end up dropping the coins all over the floor. Even my steel throwing cards required careful aim, no matter what Ferius might say.

One of these days I need to come up with a way of killing people that doesn't call for steady hands.

'Six of us have voted in favour of the execution warrant before the spellslinger's recklessness endangers both the crown and the empire,' the vulture who'd referred to Torian as 'Little Tori' said.

Ancestors, please let me live long enough to call her that at least once.

The vulture went on. 'Let's hear from the rest of the council. We need one more vote for the required majority, so let's hurry it up, people. We have more important business to discuss.'

Her voice was the one closest to my ear, just to my right side. A plan began to form in my mind. Not a particularly good one, but then, plans never are until they're successful.

Then they're bloody genius.

Here's a fun thing to try: imagine yourself rolling over as fast as you can and at the same time drawing a steel card from a leather pouch strapped to your right thigh. Doesn't sound too hard, right? Problem is, without any feeling in your arms and legs, you have no idea if you've executed the move perfectly or just flopped onto your belly like a dead fish.

Next, picture your free hand pressing down onto the table, pushing you to your knees. Better do it fast, otherwise someone in the room will have the chance to punch, stab or otherwise put a quick end to your daring escape.

Again though, since you can't feel anything, you've no idea if it worked.

But let's be optimists, shall we?

Get your feet under you and push off hard against the table – not too hard though, because then you'll wind up slamming inelegantly into the back wall. No, you've got to make the leap with just the right amount of force to land right behind a chair that you're only guessing exists.

Now, assuming you've moved at all and this hasn't been one last, desperate hallucination brought on by a paralytic that's now worked its way to your heart, spin around and place the steel card you drew – remember the card? Don't drop it! You've got to carefully set the sharp edge right up against the neck of the woman who seconds before called for your execution.

Oh, and one last thing: do it all with your eyes closed because you've been lying under a half-dozen lights so long that right now you're pretty much blind.

Sound hard? That's because it's downright impossible.

Then again, studying under a crazy Argosi who teaches you fighting by making you dance, languages by making you study music, and resilience by forcing you to 'trust yourself' does, very occasionally, pay off.

'Ta-da!' I announced to the room.

I opened my eyes to see what I'd done. That's when things got . . . complicated.

6

A Talent for Trouble

My blurry vision revealed a dozen throne-like wooden chairs surrounding a long oval table. Six brass lanterns hung from iron chains attached to the ceiling. One of them swung more than the others, which explained why one side of my head hurt. On the plus side, I was now standing just behind one of those oak thrones and the edge of my steel card was pressed against the soft wattle of a woman's throat. Now all I had to do was use her to get myself out of here in one piece.

My captive gradually came into focus. She was older than she'd sounded, with more silver than copper in the wiry hair tied back into a loose bun. But her posture was upright and relaxed. Rope-like muscles down the sides of her neck made me suspect that this was a woman who could handle herself just fine in a fight.

'*Arta eres?*' she asked, not bothering to look up at me.

'That's dancing,' I replied. '*Arta forteize* is resilience.'

She sighed. 'I hate the Argosi.'

'I get that a lot. I don't believe we've met properly. I'm Kellen.'

'Emelda.'

'Nice name.' I made the card quiver ever so slightly against her throat. 'Try not to make me nervous, Emelda, or, you know, piss me off in any way.'

'An impressive performance,' the camel observed. He was, in fact, a tall man with grey-white hair and an improbably long face. A slender, well-manicured finger reached for one of several small indentations set in a semicircle on the table in front of him. 'Alas, you'll find this room well protected.' He pressed down, and I heard a small click just before a thin bolt flew down from a hole in the ceiling to bury itself three inches deep into the centre of the table where I'd been lying just moments ago.

Okay, that's pretty cool, I admitted to myself. 'Let me guess,' I said aloud. 'This whole room was designed by Gitabrian contraptioneers, wasn't it? No, wait – don't tell me. *Dead* Gitabrian contraptioneers, right? I mean, you Murmurers are all about secrecy, aren't you?'

The long-faced man shifted his finger over to a second indentation. 'For someone so insightful, you're remarkably bad at making the obvious calculation regarding your own fate.'

I enjoyed a modicum of satisfaction over just how lousy his bluff was. 'Can I first just say that having a room constructed with hidden darts to kill your guests is creepy? Also, I'm kind of dubious that you'd have mechanical dart throwers aimed *behind* each of your own thrones.' I gave a sideways nod towards the other end of the table. 'Lastly, to the guy who's trained his own weapon on me? Pretty little thing, by the way. You should know that the instant you so much as twitch, I'll slice your colleague's throat open so fast you'll be spending the rest of this otherwise enchanting afternoon wiping her blood off this lovely table.'

It's worth mentioning that I couldn't see what anyone else was doing in their chairs, much less make out a weapon aimed in my direction. So how did I know there was one? Because in a room full of ruthless, conniving spies and assassins, there's always *somebody* preparing to kill you.

My captive groaned. 'Gods of fortune and failure,' she swore. 'Save me from the Argosi and their idiotic arta valar.'

'Hey, you got that one right!' I said encouragingly. I pressed the sharp edge of the steel card up just enough that Emelda could feel its bite. 'Now stand up so that you and I can leave this dank little chamber together. Then we'll take a pleasant stroll up to see the queen and maybe you can explain to Her Majesty why you just tried to murder her favourite tutor of cards.'

'You know how stupid that sounds, right?' Emelda asked.

I did, but the first rule of arta valar is: once you start swaggering, don't stop until the fighting starts.

'Enough theatrics,' hissed the fellow I thought of as the crocodile. When he leaned forward into the light, I now saw that *she* was actually a rather beautiful woman in her middle years. 'Put down the blade, boy, and we can discuss this sensibly.'

'Don't let her go,' Torian warned. 'Once the motion has been opened, they can complete the vote any time they want. You've got to make them formally overturn the motion to issue an execution warrant.'

Emelda looked mildly affronted by Torian's remark. 'You always were a disobedient child.'

Torian winked. 'And you were a terrible mother.'

'Your father and I taught you to protect yourself, Little Tori. You should be more appreciative.'

'You made me sleep in a nest of rattlesnakes until I was eight!'

66

'We defanged them first,' the old woman insisted. 'Besides, it's not our fault it took you so long to figure out how to charm a few simple reptiles.'

Wait . . . Did that mean . . . ? Was Torian really able to mesmerise people?

Legends abounded that a few of the marshals trained in ancient frontier magics – the kinds of skills suited to fugitive hunters. I'd always figured it was just gossip spread by the marshals themselves to enhance their fearsome reputations. Right now, though, I had more pressing concerns.

'I hate to interrupt a tender moment between mother and daughter,' I began, 'but I have places to be and Murmurers – I mean, very important people – whose deaths I need to plan.'

'Well, best you start with me then,' Emelda said. 'Because I'm not going anywhere with you, spellslinger.'

There was an odd tinge to her voice, like I'd done something to offend her. I mean, other than holding a razor-sharp piece of steel at her throat.

Overall my escape wasn't working out quite as I'd hoped. Granted, it had been a long shot in the first place, but in my rush not to die I'd forgotten that ruthless killers are often untroubled by the thought of their own demise. I guess committing murder on a frequent basis must make one sanguine about the afterlife.

'Annul the vote,' Torian urged the others. 'Declare the warrant void.'

'I wasn't so much worried about the voting part,' I said.

'You don't understand. Once the council decides on someone's death, they don't stop. They'll keep sending assassins after you until the job is done.' Again she turned to the others. 'Call off the vote. Now!'

'No!' Emelda said. 'We warned you before, Little Tori, that the spellslinger couldn't be trusted. We gave you months to rein him in and you failed.'

'You think I can't make trouble for you, Mother? Push me too far and I'll turn the marshals service onto the lot of you and—'

'And then there will be no more marshals service,' camel-voice said. 'The Murmurers have been protecting the empire since long before the marshals were first formed. We will remain long after history has forgotten you.'

What I need now, Ferius, I thought, wishing for about the hundredth time that I'd never left my Argosi mentor's side, *is one of those clever rescues of yours where you make a few funny comments and all of a sudden everyone puts down their weapons.*

Oddly, my lucky break did come, only not in the way I hoped.

Rescue came in the form of applause.

A figure rose from one of the wooden thrones to stand beneath the light of the swaying lanterns overhead. He was tall, powerfully built. Upon a head covered in thick, perfectly coiffed black hair rested a wooden crown, exquisitely carved and yet nowhere near as regal as the chiselled cut of his jaw. His features were both handsome enough to make any man jealous, and familiar enough to chill my soul.

'Hello, Father,' I said.

7

The Witness

'How wonderfully melodramatic.' Ke'heops, Mage Sovereign of
the Jan'Tep people, clapped his hands together as if my near
execution had been a performance for his benefit.

'The witness will retake his seat and shut the hells up,'
Emelda said. She still hadn't made any attempt to free herself
from the razor-sharp edge of my steel card, but a slight shift
in the muscles of her shoulders told me she was about to
make her move.

'Ah, ah, ah,' Ke'heops warned. He allowed the index and
ring fingers of his right hand to rise just a hair above the
others – something he'd never do unless he specifically wanted
everyone in that room to know he was preparing the somatic
form for a spell. 'As amusing as this little display of Daroman
intrigue has been, I'm afraid I can't allow you to threaten my
son any further.'

'Shake your fingers at us all you want, Mage Sovereign,' the
camel said. 'This chamber has the strongest wards against
Jan'Tep parlour tricks in the entire palace. One would've
thought a man in your position would be better informed.'

'How strange . . .' Ke'heops stared down at his hand as if
it belonged to someone else. 'I would've sworn that —' He

gave the tiniest flick of his fingertips as he intoned a single-syllable spell. A cascade of red sparks danced across his knuckles, prompting a gasp from the camel. My father's gaze swept across the others around the table. 'It appears the great and wise Council of Murmurers has been misled as to just how effective those wards you rely on are against a true lord magus.'

'Impossible!' the meerkat, who was in fact a whip-thin young man maybe five years my senior, declared. 'The palace wards have proven impenetrable for over a hundred years!'

'Times change,' Ke'heops said, closing his hand into a fist and extinguishing the lightning that it shouldn't have been possible to summon in the first place.

The meerkat, the camel, and several of the others looked to Emelda, who just shrugged in response. 'The Jan'Tep have known about our wards for ages. They were bound to find a way around them eventually.'

Ke'heops gave a little nod as if she'd just personally complimented him on his tremendous display of genius. Oddly, though all the evidence suggested the contrary and my father abhorred trickery, I would've sworn he'd just pulled a con on them.

'Put the card down now, Ke'helios,' he said. 'No one will hurt you.'

Ke'helios.

Months ago my sister Sha'maat had delivered my mage's name to me; a gift from my father, or so she'd claimed. I hadn't believed her. Ke'heops had always considered me a wretched disappointment, even before he and my mother had strapped me down to a table and counter-banded me. They'd stolen any chance I had to ever spark anything but my breath band. I'd always assumed a mage's name would be denied

70

me forever. To hear my father now, addressing me by that name . . .

'Call me Kellen,' I said.

He dismissed my petty act of rebellion with a wave of his hand. 'A child's name. Despite your current comportment, you are a man now. A son of the House of Ke. Your name is and always will be Ke'helios.' He leaned forward, pressing his hands against the table. The lantern light from above made the seven points of his crown gleam. 'Now put down that silly card of yours so that I can get on with the business that brought me here.'

'Don't let my mother go,' Torian warned. 'Not until the council voids the execution warrant against you.'

For a woman who'd deceived me, poisoned me and dragged me here in the first place, she seemed remarkably concerned with my long-term well-being.

'By the ancestors,' Ke'heops swore, a line of irritation furrowing his brow. He cast his gaze over the others seated around the table. 'Kindly call off this so-called "execution warrant" of yours so that we might press on with more urgent matters?' He raised a finger. 'Oh, and before any of you threaten *me* with such nonsense, consider that all of the clan princes of the Jan'Tep are aware of my mission here. Should I suffer any mysterious accidents or unforeseen ailments you will find every lord magus on the continent working to undermine the Daroman empire.' He sat back down. 'Given said empire currently hangs by a thread, that would present a significant inconvenience to those charged with ensuring its continuity, wouldn't you agree?'

'Well, dip me in honey and cover me with fire ants!' Emelda growled, pre-empting the huffing and puffing from the others.

'Yeah,' I said. 'He has that effect on me too.'

'Don't you start, Argosi. Ought to kill you here and now just on principle.'

Despite the distraction of my father's display of power, I'd been watching for Emelda to make a move against me. When she did, it still happened too fast for me to react. The unexpected sting of a fingernail piercing the skin on the back of my hand was followed by my fingers going limp as wet noodles. The card I was holding fell from my hands. Emelda caught it neatly in hers.

'Reckon I'll keep this as a souvenir,' she said, stuffing it into the pocket of her coat.

I shook my hand several times, trying to will the life back into my fingers. 'Is poisoning people the family business or something?'

'More of a hobby. Our business is eliminating threats to the throne.'

Torian took my side once again. 'And I've told you, the spellslinger's no—'

Emelda cut her off. 'That's enough out of you, missy.' She nodded to my father. 'The witness is right; we've got more pressing issues than one particularly annoying Argosi card sharp. I move we table the execution warrant against Ke'helios an—'

'Kellen,' I corrected.

'Whatever. The Council of Murmurs will waive the right to enact your execution.'

'For a period of no less than one year,' Torian added. She turned to me. 'Even if they rescind the warrant, one of them could just call for a new vote the moment it suited their perverse little hearts.'

72

Emelda gave her daughter a withering look. 'If your father were here . . .'

'You'll need a shovel if you want his opinion, Mother.'

The glib words struck a discordant note in Emelda. You could see it in her eyes. She buried her reaction quickly though. 'Fine. I hereby move we table the warrant on Kellen of the House of Ke for a period of no less than one year.'

A few grumbles and complaints rose up from the others, but they dissipated like smoke in a breeze soon enough. The Murmurers were apparently as efficient at pardoning a person as they were at condemning them in the first place.

Which made no sense . . .

'Good,' my father said, placing his hands flat on the table as if this were his personal sanctum and the rest of us here by his invitation. 'Let us now turn to—'

'Abide a moment,' I said.

My father raised an eyebrow. Torian gave me a shake of her head to warn me not to press the matter with the Murmurers. She was probably right. No sense poking the bear right after he's promised not to eat you.

'You sad, pathetic bunch of liars,' I said. 'You almost had me.'

Voices rose in outrage. Fists pounded the table. Renewed calls were made for my immediate execution. Only Emelda – the vulture – looked at me with something akin to amusement.

'Something on your mind, Argosi?'

The second rule of *arta precis*. Perception. All deception is theatre. A performance with actors, sets and props. See through the play and you uncover the intention beneath. I took a moment to unwind all the steps it had taken to bring us to

73

this point: my arrest, Torian's betrayal, the Murmurers' ridiculous 'trial', my father stepping in to save me . . .

'Did he pass the test?' I asked, pointing to my father.

'*Test?*' Ke'heops demanded. He usually keeps a tight rein on his composure, but the fury rising up in him was like watching dry brush on the verge of bursting into flames. His gaze was withering even when you didn't consider the fact that he knew at least two dozen spells that would turn a body to ash in the most painful manner possible. His glare went from me to Emelda. 'What is he talking about?'

She ignored him, chuckling as she turned to look up at me. 'Go on then, boy. If you're so clever, why don't you answer your own question: did your father pass our little test?'

'Not entirely,' I replied. 'But he assuaged a few of your suspicions.'

'Do *not* speak of me as if I weren't here!' Ke'heops growled. He sounded rather like Reichis for a moment. 'I am not some schoolchild to be tested by—'

'They wanted to gauge your reaction,' I said, interrupting him – never a good idea, but I was on a roll. I held up one arm, pulling up the sleeve to show the counter-banded sigils on my tattooed Jan'Tep bands. 'The Murmurers know about our . . . troubled relationship. They needed to assess whether your presence here was some kind of pretext.'

'Pretext for what?' he asked.

I shrugged. 'Either to get close enough to finally kill me or because our feud was in fact a long con designed to get me inside the Daroman court where I could then spy on the queen for you.'

I didn't mention that, in fact, my family had tried to use me in precisely that fashion.

My father's got something of an iron jaw. Watching it clench always looks a little painful. He glared at Emelda. 'And what, pray tell, have you decided?'

Again she gestured for me to speak.

'Had you been here to murder me, Father, you would've just sat back and let the Murmurers do the job for you. Had we been working together all this time, you would have intervened sooner and come up with some kind of rationale for them not to harm me.'

'Instead you waited, Mage Sovereign,' the camel noted, his head tilted in curiosity.

'No plan, not so much as a shred of self-awareness of his own motives,' Emelda said. Her gaze went to Torian. 'Nothing more than the instinctive reactions of a parent who loves their child.'

Ke'heops and I laughed at the same time.

'Like father, like son,' Emelda said. She rose to her feet. Though neither tall nor physically imposing in any other way, her presence was nonetheless commanding. Her eyes – green rather than blue – were just as arresting as those of her daughter.

'*Like emeralds . . .*' Reichis would've said.

'All right,' Emelda began. 'We've played our little games and we've had our fun. The pieces are all on the board and now it's time to hear from the witness.'

The assembled Murmurers – the camel, the crocodile, the meerkat, the otters and all the rest (I was going to have to learn their proper names so that Reichis and I could pay them each a midnight visit sometime soon) – turned their gazes to my father.

Ke'heops withdrew two small pouches from the folds of

his robes. He set one aside and upended the other. Glittering purple sand scattered over the surface of the table, sending dust up into the air like a fog that settled beneath the lantern light.

'What is this?' asked the meerkat. 'Some type of mystical powder?'

'Merely sand,' my father replied. 'From this very city, in fact.'

He held one hand palm down over the table. A shimmer of light flashed beneath his sleeves as two of his bands ignited. '*Saver'et'aeoch*,' he intoned softly.

The sand began to swirl as if caught in a strong breeze. At first it rose and fell in waves, but soon the grains began to join together in orderly groups, forming shapes on the table. Buildings. Streets. Canals. And, at their centre, this very palace.

'Impressive,' Emelda conceded. She whispered a question to me. 'Sand magic?'

I'm not sure why she expected any answers from me, but I saw no reason not to oblige. 'Iron and silk, I think.'

'Iron, silk *and* sand,' Ke'heops corrected. 'Time has a part to play in this.'

The rest of the Murmurers rose from their seats, leaning closer to examine the model carefully. It really was remarkable – almost a work of art. Every building and street appeared not only to be accurate, but alive somehow, as if the stray grains of sand gliding down the little avenues were people going about their daily business.

'Darome,' he said, 'a nation rich in resources and influence. A military power unlike any other. Five hundred years the empire has stood as the supreme political force on this continent.' His gaze swept across the assembled generals, spies and marshals staring back at him. 'This is your capital. Your home.'

He paused with all the theatrical gravitas of an actor about to deliver the final line of the play.

'And this is Darome six months from now.'

With a snap of his fingers, every building, every street, the palace itself, crumbled, becoming grains of sand scattered upon an otherwise empty table.

8

The Shine and the Hook

A good con comes in two parts. The first we call 'the shine'. It's called that because a good shine always looks expensive, and you always give it away for free. In the end it turns out to be worth even less than the mark paid for it. In this case, my father had put on a compelling show of transforming a bag of sand into a perfect replica of the Daroman capital, only to then return it to dust.

The second part? We call that 'the hook', because it's what you use to reel in the fish.

The Council of Murmurers were all staring down at the scattered purple sand on the table. Me? I was looking at the hook. 'What's in the second bag?' I asked, pointing at the leather pouch Ke'heops was still holding surreptitiously in his other hand.

The look that earned me was made up of equal parts irritation and something that, coming from any other father, might've been confused with parental pride. 'The enemy,' he said simply.

Emelda looked up at me even as she asked my father, 'And what will it cost us to glimpse this enemy, mighty Ke'heops, Mage Sovereign of the Jan'Tep people?'

At first I wondered why she'd go to the trouble of addressing him using a title that wasn't formally recognised by the Daroman throne. That, of course, was the answer: this was Emelda's opening bid.

Ke'heops dismissed the offer with a shake of his head. 'The intelligence I bring cost my people a great deal to obtain. My . . . emissary was lost in the mission.'

'We'll be sure to weep tears of gratitude at your agent's funeral,' Emelda said, waving the other Murmurers to silence with a flick of her hand.

Ke'heops withdrew a rolled-up parchment from the folds of his robes. It looked expensive, with a gold wax seal that glimmered as though alive. He tossed the scroll at Emelda.

'What's this?' she asked, catching it.

'Relations between the Daroman empire and the Jan'Tep arcanocracy are long overdue for . . . reconsideration. We will require certain assurances, concessions and . . . Let us call it an *evolution* of the diplomatic ties between our two peoples.'

Torian's outrage was so palpable you could practically feel the temperature in the room rise. 'Any such *reconsiderations* are the purview of the queen. *She* is the ruler of this empire, in case no one informed you.'

Ke'heops ignored her, his eyes still locked on Emelda's. 'We find it more expedient to deal with those who rule in fact rather than in name.'

For her part, Emelda struck me as utterly at ease in what should have been a tense and complex diplomatic situation. She cracked the seal, igniting a flash of sparks that looked as if they would set the scroll on fire but faded away almost immediately. The parchment appeared blank at first, but then shimmering golden letters appeared across its surface. Emelda rolled it back up without bothering to read it.

'The queen's a reasonable girl,' she said. 'I'm sure if what you've brought us is as vital to our interests as you claim, she'll be persuaded to give due consideration to Darome's most beloved ally.'

The Daroman empire and Jan'Tep arcanocracy by and large despised each other, each looking down on the other nation as barely civilised. Ke'heops, however, seemed perfectly satisfied with this vague and informal assurance. He swept a hand over the table, washing away the sand. When he upended the second pouch, what poured out was the far less impressive yellow-brown sand that for me brings back several unpleasant memories of getting horribly lost and nearly dying of thirst.

Ancestors, but I really hate the desert.

'Saver'et'aeoch,' my father said for the second time as his hands formed somatic shapes above the table. Once again the grains swirled and spun, taking on the shapes of a glittering, golden city in the desert. 'Behold the enemy who will destroy the Daroman empire and enslave its people.'

The man I'd thought of as the meerkat barked out a laugh. 'Berabesq? You expect us to fear a bunch of petulant viziers? These people can't even agree on which of six holy texts to follow, never mind unite behind a single ruler. The only reason the Berabesq people haven't already strung up their viziers from the tallest trees is that there aren't enough trees in the desert!'

That struck me as an ill-informed and somewhat bigoted view. First of all, deserts are home to far more diverse flora than people think, including some impressively tall trees. I knew this because I'd nearly been hanged from several of them during my unfortunate travels in that otherwise lovely and inviting country.

The woman I'd thought of as the crocodile spoke in a breezy whisper. 'The Berabesq are a spiritual people. More numerous than any other on the continent, and dangerous as well. The ones they call the Faithful are far more deadly than any warriors in our own armies.'

That much was true. I'd fought a couple of the Faithful in my time. The powers they'd exhibited would have given even a Jan'Tep war mage pause.

'But they are disunited,' the camel noted. 'Factions within factions, all disputing which of their six codices offers a glimpse at the true face of their god. Any vizier who rises too high in power and influence soon finds himself short of a head.'

Neither Emelda nor Torian had spoken in a while. My father just sat there watching, the subtle play of amusement on his features betraying his enjoyment at listening to the dreaded Daroman Murmurers debating trivialities. The best cons are the ones where you get the marks talking about the hook before you've even started reeling them in.

Me? I've seen plenty of con games. After a while even the most elegant become boring. 'Time to show them your magic trick, Father.'

Usually he gates my glib posturing, but this time he smiled. He intoned a new esoteric syllable under his breath and spread his hands. In response, the golden sands shifted and rearranged themselves, the centre of the desert city expanding outwards until almost the entire table was dominated by a temple that surrounded a tall spire. He stood up and traced a circle around the structure. As his fingers twitched, loose grains of sand became tiny people in the streets, gazing up at the spire. More and more of them appeared until it was like looking down from the clouds upon a mass of bodies worshipping something at the top of the spire. A soft roar rose from the grains rubbing together as the little sand shapes raised their arms and shook their fists. I could almost hear them chanting.

'Who do they cheer for?' Torian asked.

Ke'heops gave a final flutter of his fingers, very carefully, near the top of the spire where a balcony appeared, and a robed figure stepped out, holding a baby in his arms. 'One who will unite them,' Ke'heops replied. 'One for whom the largest army ever seen upon this continent will take the field. One who will lead them to the destruction of Darome.'

'A baby?' the camel asked. 'You expect us to fear a newborn child?'

'That was eleven months ago,' Ke'heops replied. He held out his palm, fingers curled as if were gripping the dial of a clock. He turned his hand a fraction. The sands changed again, and as the crowds cheered with even greater enthusiasm, a boy who looked no older than five was standing upon the spire's balcony.

'This was five months ago.'

His hand shifted again and the boy grew before our eyes, now at least eight years old.

The camel gasped. 'But how is this—'

Ke'heops turned his hand one last time. The crowds were now so densely packed that it felt claustrophobic just watching them. At the edges of the street surrounding the temple, new figures arose, running to join the others, their arms outstretched in religious ecstasy.

The boy on the balcony looked to be about twelve or thirteen.

'His birthday comes in thirty-three days,' Ke'heops said. 'The viziers have already announced their gift; they will present him with the severed head of the blasphemous Queen Ginevra of Darome.'

My fingers slipped into the powder holsters at my side – a pointless reflex given this kid, whoever he was, had to be a good thousand miles from here. I felt somewhat better when I saw Torian holding a pair of throwing knives in her hand.

Emelda was leaning against the table. She lifted one hand to reach out and touch the tip of her finger to the sandy figure who commanded such complete adoration from a notoriously divided people. 'Who is he?'

At first my father hesitated, but when he spoke I finally understood what had brought the mage sovereign of the Jan'Tep people to seek the aid of those he always thought of as insignificant barbarians.

'God.'

9

The Question

The Murmurers booted my father and me from the chamber pretty quickly after that. I suppose even ruthless spy councils deserve a little privacy after learning that a foreign god plans to strike down their entire civilisation.

A hundred questions assailed me as I strode down the passage after my father. His longer legs forced me into an awkward jog and his greater height required that I crane my neck to watch his expression.

'How did you pull off those spells inside a warded chamber?' I asked.

He cast me a mildly amused glance. 'After all that was revealed within the Chamber of Murmurers, *this* is your first question?'

'I like to start with the small stuff before I move onto existential threats of deities and genocides.'

My father finds glib remarks almost as distasteful as card tricks. A flash of irritation crossed his features. 'Given your predilection for parading your own cleverness, Ke'helios, perhaps you should provide the answer yourself.'

I'd been trying to puzzle that one out ever since those red ember sparks first appeared on his knuckles inside the

Chamber of Murmurs. Warding physical spaces against spell-craft is easier than you might think and over the last couple of hundred years the royal marshals service have turned it into something of an art.

Certain extrusions of copper wire, properly wound, disrupt the casting of spells – particularly ember magic, which is the sort most people fear because it produces such obviously destructive effects. Silver wire wrapped around an iron core can block silk magic, which is handy when you don't want mages stealing your thoughts or filling your head with visions so terrifying you start clawing out your own eyeballs. The scents emitted by hallucinogenic flowers can disrupt a mage's concentration, preventing them from casting spells, and there are even architectural designs – like the one to which the palace throne room was built – that confound the esoteric geometry required for spellcraft.

So if you know what you're doing, warding against magic isn't all that hard; that's why mages like my father don't simply declare themselves emperors of the world and subjugate everyone to their rule. Which meant there was only one way he could've cast spells inside the most secure chamber in all of Darome.

'You have someone on the inside,' I said.

Ke'heops gave a passable impression of someone who'd entirely forgotten the topic under discussion. 'Hmm?' he asked as he turned down another passageway that led towards the next set of stairs out of the palace dungeons.

'I'm pretty sure the Murmurers have the means to test their wards every time they enter that chamber,' I went on. 'Which means one of them disabled the wards *after* they'd begun the meeting.' My thoughts ran through each of the people

85

sitting around that table. 'Was it the camel? No . . . the meerkat?'

Ke'heops finally stopped, a faint smile on his lips. 'I suppose one of them *did* rather give off the impression of a meerkat, and the other certainly had the face of a camel. Your assumption that one of them is the infiltrator comes from some Argosi trick, I suppose? Arta precis, perhaps?'

That question took me by surprise. My father had never, to my knowledge, given more than five seconds' thought to the ways of the Argosi. As far as he was concerned, such things were of no more use to a lord magus than a rich knowledge of ditch digging or bonnet knitting. The fact that my father had clearly learned at least a little about the Argosi in recent years meant he was starting to take them seriously.

'Arta loquit, actually.'

His brow furrowed. 'I thought arta loquit was languages?'

'Arta loquit is *eloquence*, not just languages,' I explained. 'One of its first tenets is that every utterance serves a purpose. So when someone says something that doesn't need to be said, such as when the meerkat kept repeating the same concerns others had already raised, it signals his intent is something other than expressing his opinion.'

'That seems like rather a lot of conjecture.'

'Not really. The man's speech was too even. If he was genuinely worried the others around the table weren't sharing his concerns, the pitch in his voice would have risen when he was pounding the table. He was hiding something, I'm sure of it.' I caught my father's eyes. 'Just as you are right now.'

My father laughed off the accusation. 'And just what is it that your little deductions tell you *I'm* hiding?'

Like most men who prided themselves on their honour and forthrightness, my father was a natural schemer but a lousy poker player. 'That this is the longest conversation we've ever had without you calling me a weakling, a failure or a traitor to our house. What is it you need from me, Father?'

Ke'heops returned my stare. I wondered if he was even aware that he was gazing at me the way someone does when assessing a potential threat. 'Not here,' he said, and headed up the stairs.

I followed, noticing too late the somatic forms he made with his hands that were half-hidden by the shadows. I heard the last whispered syllable of an incantation I didn't recognise just as I reached the top of the stairs only to find myself looking up at what should have been the ceiling of the palace's grand foyer, but turned out to be a sky full of stars.

The air grew chill against my cheeks, and the stone floors beneath my boots gave way to soft sand. In the distance, the lights of a city caught my gaze. Mighty spires rose up from within its walls, reaching to touch the heavens, the moonlit shadows they cast reaching out towards us.

'*Makhan Mebab* . . .' I whispered. 'Capital of the Berabesq theocracy.'

'You've always wanted to play the hero, Ke'helios,' my father said. 'Now I'm giving you the perfect opportunity.' He gestured to the city. 'All you have to do is slip inside those walls and murder a god before he can destroy everything and everyone you've ever loved.'

10

The Mission

It's hard not to panic when your senses are screaming at you that you're a thousand miles from where you thought you were. The muscles in your lower body clench in preparation to flee even as your balance falters. Your hands shake and your tongue feels as if it's swelling to the taste of copper. The nausea's not much fun either.

Focus, I told myself. *Close your eyes. Ignore the outside world and trust what your insides are telling you.*

At times like these, Ferius Parfax likes to say, 'Breathe in emptiness, kid.'

I hate that phrase so much I almost wish it didn't work.

'Nice illusion,' I said finally, once the thumping in my chest had begun to subside. 'You should've worked a little harder on the breeze though.'

Ke'heops looked troubled by my critique. 'What are you talking about? The spell—'

I waved my hand gently back and forth in front of me. 'One's skin feels drier this far into the desert. The air pressure should also be heavier at these lower altitudes than it is in Darome.'

'Remarkable,' he said. I'm pretty sure that's the first time he ever used that word in reference to his son. 'Your mind should be filling in those omissions by itself.'

'Don't feel bad. I've spent more time fending off silk mages than most people.' I reached behind me. My sense of touch insisted there was nothing there, but the tension in the muscles of my hand and forearm told me I was pressing against a wall in the palace. 'What happens when someone walking through the halls bumps into us?'

'They'll avoid us without even being aware of our presence,' he replied, a little too pleased with himself. 'The spell creates a feeling of unease in anyone nearby – a compunction to avoid our location.'

'Clever,' I said.

My father hates that word. 'A contrivance of your sister's actually. She's become quite expert at constructing composite spell forms. A bit theatrical, of course, but the technique has its uses.'

My ears caught on the word *theatrical*. Ke'heops couldn't stand the thought of his daughter's abilities exceeding his own. 'Then maybe you should send Sha'maat to do your dirty work.'

He gave a twist of his fingers that nearly made me dive for the ground. Figures began to appear all around us, their bodies wrapped in desert linens, heads completely obscured save for their eyes, which gleamed with religious fervour. Half of them carried hook-bladed swords called *kaskhan*. Others wore *tiazkhan* – the razor-sharp steel claws over their fingertips that awoke painful memories belonging to the long-healed scars on my chest and back.

'The Faithful,' I breathed.

'Spiritual fanatics,' my father said dismissively, though his

89

tone failed to hide an anxious catch in his voice. 'Were we truly standing within their terrain, they would already have sensed the presence of my magic. They'd be hunting us even now.'

I'd encountered the Faithful once before, and had it not been for the ingenious trickery of Ferius Parfax – to say nothing of Reichis's ferocity – I'd never have survived that first meeting. I suppose it's worth mentioning that the guy responsible for those lunatics coming after me in the first place was standing right next to me.

'The Faithful have a new weapon in their spiritual arsenal,' Ke'heops went on. Again his fingers twitched; the linen-garbed warriors knelt down in the sand, praying together in a circle as blood began to drip from their eyes and ears. 'It is a kind of . . . curse.'

'A curse?'

In addition to gods, prayer and the merits of public art, my people don't believe in curses.

Trickles of blood sliding down the faces of the Faithful dripped onto the sand, becoming thin, sinewy rivers that slithered towards the centre of the circle, coming together there as a single crimson braid that reared up, hissing scarlet steam into the air before launching itself along the ground to come straight for me.

Don't flinch! It's just an illusion so don't flinch!

I flinched.

'We call it "the malediction",' Ke'heops said. 'Neither walls nor spells can shield its victims. The sickness it brings is slow, agonising and incurable.'

I guess that explains why he doesn't want to send his beloved daughter on this mission.

90

Ke'heops seemed to know my thoughts. 'You have an advantage no other mage of our clan possesses. The Faithful cannot track those whose magic is too weak to attract their notice.' He gestured negligently to the broad-brimmed frontier hat on my head. 'Those silver sigils on that preposterous hat of yours have also proven effective in masking your presence from those who seek you out using other means.'

That explained why my mother had mentioned having so much trouble scrying me. Even Nephenia, who was a pretty talented charmcaster, hadn't been able to figure out how the sigils on my hat worked.

With a flick of his hand Ke'heops made the apparitions of the Faithful fade away, leaving the two of us alone in the vast desert.

'So let me get this straight,' I said, pointing to the mirage of the luminous city in the distance. 'You expect me to travel a thousand miles to Makhan Mebab, evade the Berabesq armies, the viziers and the Faithful, then break into the most heavily guarded temple in the world and assassinate a god?'

'I do.'

'Then I think you've misunderstood our relationship, Father.' I fumbled in the pocket of my coat and handed him the cards my mother had sent me. 'When next you see Bene'maat, be sure to return these to her. I have no use for them.'

My father is rarely at a loss for words. He was staring at the cards in my hand, his expression as calm as still water, but the rage in his eyes made me reach for my powder holsters. Shalla had warned me that one day my glib tongue would push him too far.

Ancestors, let it not be today. I'm not ready.

I was about to pull powder when he backhanded me so hard I stumbled backwards. When I hit the wall the illusion of the desert made it appear as if I was being held up by the air itself. I couldn't recall the last time my father had struck me. When you have dozens of spells at your disposal by which to punish an errant child, such a brute physical response seems . . . crude.

Instincts developed during the past three years of facing off against enemies who sought to use violence to make me cower brought my arta valar back to me. I smiled up at the mage sovereign of the Jan'Tep people. 'Is today the day we dance, Father?'

Not bad, I thought. *You sound almost confident.*

Again he took me unawares, though this time with words that cut deeper than I would've thought possible. 'Can you even begin to conceive of how much Bene'maat loves you? She raised you, cared for you, bled magic every time she tried to heal you of the shadowblack.'

'And then she—'

'She made a mistake!' he shouted. '*I* made a mistake! No parent should ever have to witness the shadowblack growing upon their child's face, knowing that every day it brings him closer to the madness that overtook your grandmother and turned her so feral I had to kill her myself!'

His lips pressed together so tightly I knew he was holding himself back from hitting me again. 'We made a terrible mistake. Every day since, Bene'maat has searched for the means to restore your bands to you, even when our entire clan council forbade it. And for this you speak of her with such disdain?'

Three years of being an outcast, of being hunted by bounty

mages and hextrackers – some of whom my own father had sent to kill me – I really didn't think he had the ability to make me feel guilty any more.

Guess I was wrong.

'Keep the cards,' he said, handing them back to me. 'They are a gift. Your mother's way of trying to speak to you in . . . in your own language. You should treasure them.'

His shoulders slumped, which I'd never seen before. The proud lines of his cheeks and jaw seemed to sag with such genuine exhaustion that a kinder heart than mine would've ached with sympathy. But I couldn't show weakness. Too often my family had manipulated me to their own ends.

'I won't murder a child for you, Father.'

'You won't be doing it for me. You'll be doing it for *her*.' With another twist of his fingers he conjured up an apparition of Queen Ginevra, kneeling on the ground, terrified eyes reflecting the silhouette of a Berabesq warrior holding his kaskhan blade high. 'The viziers will bring their armies to Darome, and the first thing they'll do after they've shattered the gates of the palace will be to behead that little girl you seem to adore so much more than your own family. They'll offer her remains up as a gift to their god.'

A cold chill descended over me, but I refused to let my father's words and illusions cloud my thinking. 'Then I'll find some other way to protect her. The queen would never ask me to murder a child on her behalf. Besides, in case you hadn't noticed, the marshals and the Murmurers take a dim view of me doing their jobs for them. Why do you think they had Torian drug me and haul me into that room for that pointless trial, knowing I'd try to escape and just waiting to see if I could . . .'

The rest of that sentence died on my lips as the incongruity of my own words hit me.

Son of a bitch.

Ke'heops chuckled as he made Ginevra's image fade. 'For a card player, you do a poor job of keeping your hand hidden. Perhaps you should teach me to play that game that so fascinates gamblers one day . . . What do they call it? Poker?'

I ignored the jibe. I was too busying reliving every moment of my time inside the Chamber of Murmurs. 'They already knew about the Berabesq god, even before you arrived.'

What a stupid thing to say. Of *course* the Murmurers had to have known – or at least suspected something big was happening in Berabesq. They have spies all over the continent. Even if the viziers were hunting down foreign agents, some rumours must have gotten out of Makhan Mebab, which only made my father's evidence more valuable.

'They weren't testing you at all,' I said. 'They were testing me. Sneaking into the Berabesq lands and murdering a god would need someone knowledgeable about magic, but who can't be tracked by the Faithful. Someone with an unusual skill set of subterfuge and trickery. Someone loyal to the queen, who *isn't* Daroman – a known former criminal who can be easily disavowed when he's captured, because, succeed or fail, the Faithful aren't going to let him escape the Berabesq territories alive.'

My father looked down at me with something akin to empathy. 'You chose the life of an exile, Ke'helios. The path of an outlaw. You had to know there would be those who would seek to take advantage of you.'

And not all of them turned out to be my relatives.

94

'The queen would never countenance the murder of a child,' I insisted.

'Not even to save her people? The Berabesq outnumber the combined populations of Darome, Jan'Tep and Gitabria three times over. Only their fractious religious beliefs have kept them from dominating the entire continent. This god of theirs, real or otherwise, will unite them into an army such as the world has never seen. To the Berabesq viziers, the rest of us are heathens and blasphemers. They will destroy everything in their path.'

'But why me?' I asked, feeling myself losing the argument and sounding every bit the petulant child my father considered me. 'The world is full of trained spies and assassins. Why should I be the one to—'

'Because you're far more dangerous than any hired killer, Ke'helios. You're unpredictable. Your enemies come at you with swords and spells and you defeat them with playing cards and coin tricks. Bounty mages, hextrackers, lords magi . . . They've all met their ends at your hands. In a world filled with killers and connivers you keep finding ways to survive, learning from each confrontation, teaching yourself to become ever more dangerous to your foes, and all with nothing more than a simple breath incantation and exploding powders.' He gripped my shoulder, but his gaze became oddly gentle. 'It may not have been your intention, son, but you have made yourself into the most formidable assassin on the continent.'

Sadly that was the most complimentary thing my father had ever said to me.

Ke'heops made a somatic gesture with his fingers and the desert disappeared, leaving us standing in the grand foyer of the palace, surrounded by nobles and courtiers going about their business, entirely unaware of the events that would soon overtake their lives.

My father turned to leave me there, pausing only to say, 'Who but a trickster can hope to kill a god?'

11

Duty

The rank of royal tutor brings with it a number of privileges, few of which live up to their lofty-sounding titles. *Liberas Mandat*, for example, which is Daroman for 'Mandate of Free Reign', refers to the fact that a royal tutor cannot be prosecuted for any crime without the consent of four-fifths of the queen's court. This is because a monarch who can have her teachers locked up for assigning homework doesn't do the empire much good. Of course, this has never stopped the marshals service from arresting me (which, as Torian Libri likes to point out, is different from prosecuting me) every time I annoy them.

Similarly, *Consovi Mandat*, which grants a royal tutor audience with the queen on demand, doesn't technically prevent a dozen or so marshals from greeting said tutor outside the throne room and making it clear they're going to beat him to a pulp if he chooses to unwisely invoke that particular prerogative right now.

I understood the logic, of course. What the Murmurers – to say nothing of my father – were contemplating was a diplomatic crime of monumental proportions. If the queen never heard about the plan to assassinate the Berabesq god, then

97

it would be that much easier for the empire to deny culpability. That's why an hour later I found myself trudging along the upper gallery that led to what was informally known as the tutors' wing towards my private chambers – the one and only privilege of my position that lived up to its reputation.

The queen had, at last count, seven tutors. Mathematics, philosophy, natural sciences, politics, history, literature and, of course, card playing. Really you could throw out those first six; skill at poker serves you well enough in most situations.

Except when your political enemies are vastly better at this than you are.

'Now what's a no-good, lousy—'

'You used that one already,' I informed Torian Libri.

She was leaning against the gallery railing that overlooked the floors below, the easy smile on her lips letting me know there would be no tearful apologies for her having poisoned me. 'You didn't let me finish. I had several complimentary things to add to my list.'

'Why don't you write them down in a letter?' I suggested as I strode past her. 'Then do me a favour and burn it.'

Several things went wrong then, mostly having to do with reflexes. Torian, not used to being so casually dismissed, grabbed my arm. 'Now just wait a second, damn it!'

A lot of people had laid hands on me recently. I guess I'd had too many brushes with death mixed with too few hours of sleep, and I reacted out of instinct rather than forethought. I spun around to face her, brought my hand up over her forearm and drove my fingers into the crook of her elbow. There's a cluster of nerves there that hurt like seven screaming demons when you hit them just right. Torian winced.

'Hells,' I swore. 'I'm sorry, I didn't mean to—'

The problem with reflexes is that other people have them too. Without so much as an angry glare, Torian's left fist came up in a roundhouse that would've knocked me out cold had I not ducked underneath. As I came back up I tried to create some distance between us by shoving her away. She was too fast for me though, and twisted sideways so that my hands slid by her. She spun back to face me and wrapped both her arms around mine, trapping them to her sides. With just about the nastiest grin I'd ever seen she leaned back and then drove her forehead towards the bridge of my nose.

As an aside, I quite like my nose. I don't usually make a thing about it, but it's very straight, entirely proportional to my face, and, miraculously, has never been broken.

I threw my head to the right, letting hers crash into my collarbone. Before she could try a second time I clenched my arms around her back. We struggled for leverage and I had the unfortunate suspicion that we looked like a couple of very drunk and incompetent dancers trying to find the music.

'You guys can do that with your clothes on?' a chittering voice behind me asked.

'We're fighting,' I said, my desire not to get beaten to a pulp overcoming my embarrassment at Reichis seeing us like this.

'Oh, you'll know when we're fighting, card player,' Torian growled into my shoulder.

She tried a couple of tentative knees to my thighs. The pros don't go for the groin, which both men and women instinctively protect. But there's a spot on the inner thigh where you can cause just as much pain while also paralysing the leg.

'Truce?' I suggested after I'd narrowly dodged her third attempt.

Torian's muscles tensed even tighter for a second. I thought she was going to try to throw me, but finally she eased up and said, 'Truce.'

The two of us separated. I immediately ducked just in case she'd been setting me up for another roundhouse. Sure, I probably looked stupid, but I wasn't in a trusting mood.

'You two done mating yet?' Reichis inquired politely from behind me.

'That's *not* what mating looks like.'

Torian winked at me. 'Maybe you've been doing it wrong.'

You'd think after the kind of day I'd had that the last thing I'd be doing was blushing like some backwoods hick rolling in the hay barn for the first time, but that's just what happened.

Torian looked oddly charmed by my embarrassment. 'You know what I like about you, spellslinger? For a reckless, irresponsible, unimaginably awkward card sharp –' she reached out a hand and gently pinched my cheek – 'you have a very cute squirrel cat.'

She turned my chin so I'd look behind me. There, sitting on his haunches in the hallway, was Reichis, wearing a purple velvet Gitabrian merchant's cap several sizes too big for his fuzzy head.

'You look like an idiot,' I said.

Torian brushed past me. 'Don't listen to him, master squirrel cat.' She bent down to gaze at him admiringly. She's one of the few people in the palace other than the queen who recognises that Reichis is actually intelligent, as opposed to thinking I'm demented for believing he speaks to me. 'You,' Torian told him, wagging a finger at his muzzle, 'look entirely dashing. I think you should wear this hat as often as possible. Especially when you and the card player go to visit the queen.'

'So purdy . . .' Reichis said, tilting his head as he peered into her eyes. He reached a paw into his mouth and removed something that glittered even in the dim light of the gallery.

'Now what have you got there, little fella?' Torian asked. She reached a hand out to take it from his paw.

Despite my irritation with her, some last shred of chivalry prevailed. 'Don't!' I warned, trying to grab her before she lost her fingers.

Without even looking back, she batted my hand out of the way and put her own palm out to the squirrel cat. Reichis, betraying every instinct of his species, deposited the gleaming blue stone into Torian's hand.

'A sapphire?' she asked, holding it up to the light.

'Does she like it?' Reichis chittered. 'Ask her if she likes it.'

'You're a sap,' I said.

Torian grinned. 'Jealous?'

I was.

'Of course I'm not,' I replied. 'He brings me stuff like that all the time.'

He doesn't.

Torian reached out her free hand and scratched Reichis under the chin.

He hates that.

'Oh yeah . . .' he cooed.

'You're embarrassing us,' I informed him.

Also, squirrel cats don't coo.

101

'She ain't so bad,' he said, lifting his chin for more scratching. 'You know what I'd do if I were you?'

'Take off my trousers and dance for her?' I asked.

Torian looked so shocked that for just a second there I'd swear I saw a flush coming to her cheeks. She rose and faced me, holding up the sapphire next to her eye. 'What do you think? A good match in case I ever need a replacement?'

It's funny how disarming a gorgeous smile can be. It shouldn't work really. There's no link between beauty and decency. If anything, I'd noted a distinct *inverse* correlation lately. And yet there's something inside us that draws us towards beauty, a pull that on occasion – specifically occasions like these – feels just as strong as the shadowblack.

'Don't,' I said.

'Don't what?' she asked.

'I heard what your mother said in there about you learning to charm snakes as a child. I imagine that was just practice for humans later on, right?'

She shrugged. Even the shrug was endearing. 'Don't know. Is it working?'

'Better hope not. The last two people who seduced me ended up dead.'

She took a half-step closer to me, her lips parted a fraction as she said in a soft breath, 'Guess I'll have to rely on my marshal's magic to keep you on your toes.'

Keeping my eyes on hers I said, 'Put the knife back in your coat, Torian.'

Did she have a weapon in her hand? I had no way of knowing. I certainly had one of my steel cards hidden inside the cuff of my sleeve and a castradazi coin I like to call the *stinger* palmed in my other hand.

Her grin widened as she stepped back, showing no sign of the knife that I was now sure she'd been concealing.

I realised then the awful truth about our relationship: Torian loved this – the threats, the danger, the fights. I would too, I guess, if I'd lived a different life. But a year ago I'd killed the first woman I'd ever made love to only days after a vicious bastard called the white binder had taken control of me and nearly made me . . .

'Hey,' Torian said quietly, unexpected concern in her gaze. 'I'm sorry. I didn't mean to—'

I couldn't stand the pity in her eyes. 'Go back to your bosses, Torian. Tell them I'm not interested in murdering some poor kid who's probably no more a god than I am.'

Torian's voice carried an edge to it when she next spoke. 'They're not my bosses. I work for Queen Ginevra, same as you. I'm loyal to her, same as you.'

'Is that why you've got your marshals keeping me from seeing her?'

She groaned. 'Of course it is, you idiot! I keep trying to make you understand that protecting Ginevra is my job!'

'Then maybe you should be the one who goes and assassinates a foreign god for her.'

She grabbed my arm a second time, proving that she wasn't remotely troubled by the possibility of another physical altercation. 'You think I didn't offer? You think I didn't beg the Murmurers to let *me* do what has to be done?'

There was an anguished sincerity in her voice that gave me pause before I pulled away. 'You're the most famous marshal in all of Darome,' I said at last. 'The Berabesq would know you were working for the empire.'

She nodded.

'This is a job for an outlaw,' I said.

She nodded a second time.

I turned away from her, not wanting her to see the tears forming at the corners of my eyes. I always cry after a fight, once the threat of life and death has come and gone. That lord magus in the saloon would've been enough to send me whimpering to my bed even on a good day. I hadn't been ready to narrowly avoid getting myself executed by a shadowy group of generals and spies mere hours later. If I was being honest with myself though, neither of those events was what was making me tear up.

'Does she know?' I asked. 'Does she agree with this . . . plan?'

Torian did me the courtesy of not feigning ignorance. 'She's the queen, Kellen.'

'That's not an answer.'

The soft echo of Torian's footsteps followed her down the hall as she said, 'I think it is.'

12

The Messenger

'What now?' Reichis asked, scampering along beside me.

Probably a bunch of weeping and moaning, I thought, but didn't say aloud. Squirrel cats are not known for their appreciation for inconsolable melancholy.

'A very long bath,' I replied. 'Followed by clearing out the royal stores of butter biscuits, followed by us finding out if the queen we agreed to serve is or isn't the person we thought she was.'

He climbed up my leg and back before settling himself on my shoulder. 'You mean because she doesn't want to wait for a horde of religious nuts to show up and cut her head off? What do you think she hired you for? To play cards with her once a week and drink tea?'

Figures he'd take Torian's side.

The truth was, though, my life since entering the queen's employ had been filled with far less conflict than my outlaw days. I mean, sure, there was that royal coup back when I'd first started, but since then – not counting the weeks of watching the co-conspirators being marched either to the gallows, to prison or, in some rare cases, to be pardoned – things had settled into an admirably dull routine.

Once a week I played cards with Ginevra. Sometimes the game was just a game, other times she'd drop hints about political or military matters that concerned her and we'd play Argosi games, assigning people or issues to individual cards, laying them out in various ways and gleaning what we could from the patterns.

When I wasn't fulfilling my role as tutor of cards, I did a little spying here or there. Foreign diplomats often tried to bribe me to persuade the queen to agree to some request or other. I used these none-too-subtle conversations as ways to find out what I could about their true intentions. Sometimes, late at night, Reichis and I would pay them a little visit to see if we couldn't convince them to reconsider their plans.

The rest of the time? I kept an ear out for rumours of Ferius, always hoping she might pass through the Daroman territories and leave some disaster in her wake that would give me a clue as to her whereabouts. I missed her terribly.

Missing people ain't the Argosi way, she would've told me in that irritating frontier drawl of hers. *Can't walk your path if you're always looking backwards.*

I could though. I looked back all the time. Saw that smirk of hers as she pulled out a smoking reed from inside her waistcoat. Her voice as she dispensed some new piece of lyrical Argosi wisdom that made no sense at the time but ended up saving my life in the end.

Mostly, though, I missed the way she helped me see the world differently.

What would you tell me to do now, Ferius? I swore to protect the queen. Easiest way to do that would be to go off and kill this so-called god-king the Berabesq have conjured up. Stop their people and their armies from uniting and setting off a war that will likely destroy half the continent. Isn't that the Way of Thunder?

In any given situation, the Argosi consider the four ways: be like water, flowing around conflict. Follow the wind, letting it guide you to where you need to be. Stand firm like stone, holding to what you know is true. Or strike like thunder, without hesitation, without remorse.

Ferius was never big on thunder.

I walked up to the pair of double doors that led to the baths in the tutors' wing. Royal tutors are a big deal in Darome – especially when the monarch is only twelve years old. So each of our chambers had its own private bath, but Reichis preferred these ones, with their multitude of bathing opportunities and delicately arranged platters of biscuits.

'Think you can bathe yourself or should I ask for a servant to come and scrub your back?' I asked him.

Generally speaking the squirrel cat hates humans; there aren't many he allows to touch him without paying with a finger or possibly an eyeball. But he's developed a perverse fondness for being pampered.

'Well?' I asked. 'What's it going to be?'

It was only then that I noticed the soft, rattling snore coming from where he lay slumped on my shoulder.

'Reichis?'

I picked him up to see what was going on. He opened his eyes a fraction, gave me a bleary, unseeing stare, then went back to sleep.

Ah, crap.

Reichis is a tough little bastard, but he's vulnerable to Jan'Tep silk magic. Those mages who know about him will always open with a sleep spell to knock him out of the fight first. That's why I hadn't taken him with me to the saloon to deal with that lord magus. The guy knew way too much about us. The silver sigils on the frontier hat I wear protected me, but Reichis would've been unconscious the entire time. I didn't want him to be embarrassed.

Gently I set him down on the floor outside the doors to the baths. I flipped open the steel clips on the powder holsters at the sides of my belt and reached inside to take a pinch of the red and the black. 'You may as well reveal yourself,' I said. 'It's been hours since I killed anyone and people have given me plenty of reasons to want to.'

No one replied. The baths are just a few doors down from my room, which meant in all likelihood someone was waiting for me there. My chambers have wards on them, just like those of most of the rooms inside the palace. Some spells can get through, but most forms of aggressive magic won't work.

I padded silently down the hall towards my room, the powders in my hands already starting to make my skin itch. 'Last chance,' I said. 'Shalla, if this is you . . .'

I saw the shimmering traces of an obscurement spell just outside my door begin to break apart. I recognised the signature.

'Damn it, Shalla!' I swore even before she began to appear. 'You promised me you wouldn't do this any more. Maybe he's just a *nekhek* to you, but Reichis is my business partner, and you've got no right to . . .'

I fell silent as the obscurement faded and Sha'maat of the House of Ke, Jan'Tep ambassador to the Daroman court, appeared before me. I often wondered how many hours my little sister spent in front of a mirror before any given encounter, carefully arranging her blonde tresses just so,

spending ages picking the perfect gown, matching it to whatever locale she'd be standing in when she revealed herself, to
the particular light at that time of day.

She sat huddled against the door to my room, her simple
black gown bunched awkwardly around her, golden hair
strewn across her face. I couldn't see her eyes, but I knew
from the sobs that only now were becoming discernible as
the last remnants of the obscurement crumbled.

'Shalla?'

She turned her face towards me, a mask of misery and
despair so foreign to her features that I swear, for a moment,
I wasn't even sure if it was her.

I crouched down beside her, searching for wounds or signs
of some kind of assault, magical or otherwise. 'Shalla, what's
wrong? What's happened to you?'

Her next words came out in a broken, wracking cry so
wretched I had to wait until she repeated them before I could
make sense of what she'd said.

'Mother is dead.'

13

The Emissary

The instant you realise you've walked into an ambush, your body does its level best to protect you. The muscles in your stomach clench in preparation for the first blow, your shoulders rise to protect your neck. The mind rids itself of all thought, all contemplation and conjecture, leaving behind only two choices: claw or cower. This is, by and large, a useful instinct, meant to keep you alive. The problem comes when you're not actually being ambushed.

Even if it feels like you are.

'What did you say?' I asked, for what must've been the third time.

Shalla was still sitting there, crouched against the door to my chambers. Even through her tears I could tell she was worried I'd lost my senses. 'Bene'maat is gone. Our mother is gone.'

I couldn't seem to slow my breathing. My hands – usually steady in moments of danger from all the practice I'd had casting my powder spell in a fight – shook so badly it took me three tries to reach into my pocket and pull out the thirteen cards. 'She can't be dead! She gave me these just today! She—'

Shalla tried to grab hold of my hand, but my reflexes were those of someone expecting to be attacked. As I yanked my arm away, the cards went flying, triggering whatever spell Bene'maat had placed on them. Even as the cards fell to the floor they began to slide into position, surrounding me in a circle.

'She sent you those cards weeks ago,' Shalla said. 'Before the—'

'Stop, please!' I begged.

My head was splitting open. Questions formed in my mind, over and over, each one coming so fast there wasn't even time to ask the first before a new one appeared. I couldn't even turn them into words; they were more like pictures . . . Symbols, flashing before me, each one representing a gap in my knowledge. A sudden itch in my left eye made me blink over and over, then a tightening around it as if someone were pinching the skin. I could tell the markings of my shadow-black were slowly spinning like the discs of a combination lock.

'Brother, what's happening to you?' Shalla's voice was distant, a muffled echo that rose and fell in pitch like wind screaming through a canyon.

The enigmatism, some saner part of me realised as the circular markings around my left eye twisted and turned.

A while back, I'd travelled to the Ebony Abbey in search of the means to rid myself of the shadowblack. There I'd met dozens of others with the disease, only it turned out there were many, many forms of the shadowblack, some of which could be wielded almost like magic. Mine was different, of course, because it wasn't natural; my grandmother had banded me in shadow as a child. One side effect of my own markings

111

was that I was an enigmatist – someone who could see into the secrets of others. Problem was, it only worked if I knew the exact right thing to ask, which is a lot harder than it sounds.

Even in the chaos of questions flying through my mind, other voices tickled at the back of my skull. Memories. Echoes.

The first was my mother's: *'Forgive the awkward fashion in which our conversation must take place, but I've been unable to properly recreate your sister's wondrous spell for long-distance communication.'*

But why? Bene'maat was one of the most accomplished mages in our clan. Even if she couldn't reproduce Shalla's particular spell, why go to all the trouble of imbuing cards with messages instead of communicating some other way or coming to Darome herself?

I imagined a click as I felt the first ring of my shadowblack markings unlock.

Another memory, this time of Ke'heops in the Chamber of Murmurs . . . *'The intelligence I bring cost my people a great deal to obtain. My . . . emissary was lost in the mission.'*

That momentary pause, the stumble of switching words at the last moment. My father never fumbled his words.

Click.

'Bene'maat was the emissary,' I said aloud. 'She was the one who brought word of the god from the Berabesq lands.'

Shalla's voice came to me as a distant whisper that muted the urgency of her words. 'Brother, whatever you're doing, stop! Your eye is turning black on the inside!'

But there was one final piece, and again I heard my father speak as he had just hours ago inside the illusion of the desert he'd constructed for me.

112

'The Faithful have a new weapon in their spiritual arsenal . . . It is a kind of . . . curse.'

Click.

The last of the circular markings around my left eye twisted, unlocking my enigmatism, sending me tumbling into the land of shadows.

The hallways of the palace disappeared. The familiar sights, the sounds, the smells, all of them gone. Shalla was gone too. In their place a shadowblack realm, the sky above cut from ebony and the ground beneath me carved from onyx. All was black and yet I could see every detail of the landscape surrounding me with perfect clarity.

I soon wished I couldn't.

Bene'maat gallops across the shadowy desert. Her horse is wounded, covered in slashes from the kaskhan and tiazkhan blades of the Faithful chasing her. The horse stumbles, falls. My mother runs, limping towards the border. Someone is there, helping her, but I can't see them. Why? Why are they obscured from me?

You haven't asked the right question for that, a different voice tells me. It's familiar even though I don't recognise who it is.

My vision shifts. The Berabesq Faithful stop their pursuit. A sandstorm whirls all around them, preventing them from continuing the chase. They gather in a circle and . . .

One of them removes his linen garments, unwinding them in long strips until he is naked. He lies down on the ground in the circle of the others. The ones with the tiazkhan finger blades begin carving words onto his chest, his arms, his legs, his face. His moans of pain are muffled by the prayers chanted by his fellows. Blood seeps out of the words inscribed in his flesh, but still they continue to cut more and more of them as his body becomes a kind of scarlet scripture.

113

Elsewhere my mother screams.

'Neither walls nor spells can shield its victims,' my father had said. 'The sickness it brings is slow, agonising and completely incurable.'

Time moves ahead – days or weeks or months, I can't tell. The scene shifts and I find myself in a place I recognise. A place I haven't seen for more than two years and which makes me ache in ways I didn't think was still possible. My home.

Bene'maat is walking through the hall. She's beautiful, as she's always been, her grace conveying a kind of strength none of the rest of us possess. But something's wrong. Something is stilted in the way she walks, as if she's moving unnaturally slowly as she tries to force her steps to be smooth and precise. A vase on a nearby table falls and breaks. Her bare foot lands on a broken shard. She winces, and only then do a dozen other tiny, invisible wounds make themselves known to me.

There's a sprain in her wrist that came when she did nothing more than reach for a book on a high shelf; a small cut on her collarbone that appeared out of nowhere but is now infected and won't heal no matter how many spells she casts; when she walked by a fire, the flames crackled and a burning ember singed the back of her hand.

An endless stream of accidents, a rising tide of inexplicable misfortunes that tear at her will. She has trouble sparking her silk band now. Before that her iron band went dead. Piece by piece these tiny afflictions are destroying her.

'Brother, please,' I hear Shalla's voice coming back. The markings around my eye are slowly closing again, but not before they curse me with one more vision.

My mother stands before a mirror, putting ointment on the cut on her collarbone, but sees something beneath. She pulls open the

114

top of her robe. There on her skin is a word, inscribed in the Berabesq language. The scar looks old, almost healed, yet it wasn't there yesterday.

The black sun outside rises and falls, rises and falls. Each time it brings me back to Bene'maat standing before the mirror, witnessing a new word inscribed in scars across the canvas of her body, each one paired with a new accident, some new misfortune that brings her inexorably closer to her end.

The malediction, my father called it.

I try to shut my eyes to avoid seeing my mother this way, but the last traces of the enigmatism reveal the entirety of the text to me. I speak only a little Berabesq, but I can read enough to know that the sinewy lines slowly carving themselves on my mother's body are words of joy. A devotional. A prayer.

The shadow world faded from view and I was back in the Daroman palace, standing outside my chambers with my sister holding on to me to keep me from falling.

'He killed her,' I said aloud. 'The Faithful cast the malediction, but they invoked his power. They did it for him.'

'Who?' Shalla asked.

'God.'

Oatas Jan'Xan

City of Wonders

City of Wonders

Home is a feeling. The memory of a warm bed. The voice of your parents calling you to breakfast. Home isn't a roof or four walls. It's not a place at all.

Maybe that's why it's so hard to find again once you've been gone too long.

14

Tantrums

A mile-long caravan of carriages and supply wagons, along with hundreds of horses bearing soldiers, retainers and diplomats wound its way along the gleaming western imperial road with all the elegance of an armoured worm slithering through dirt. Every plodding step of my own horse was a jostling reminder that I was getting closer and closer to the home from which I'd long ago fled and had sworn never to return.

It takes nineteen days to ride from Emni Urbana, the Daroman capital, to Oatas Jan'Xan, the city of my birth. Not a long time, unless God's first birthday happens to be mere weeks away and the festivities include a declaration of war. So why was the queen – to say nothing of the Murmurers – risking such a lengthy delay just to attend the funeral of a woman none of them had ever met?

'It's nice, don't you think?' Shalla asked as she slowed her horse to ride alongside mine.

I'd taken to sticking to the tail end of the caravan, preferring to avoid the angry glares and muttered threats of the mages in my father's retinue. The queen was perpetually ensconced in private meetings in her own carriage, and her

121

advisors – which these days always included at least one of the Murmurers – were doing an admirable job of keeping me away from her.

'Nice?' I asked.

Shalla gestured to the endless line of horses and wagons ahead of us. 'The empire honours our mother with such a large delegation.'

I wondered if she genuinely believed that. My sister is extraordinarily astute about politics and intrigue, but she's always had a blind spot when it came to our family. Maybe that was why she couldn't see the obvious: you don't bring this many mounted soldiers and generals to pay tribute to the wife of a minor foreign sovereign. You bring this many because it's a convenient way to transfer several regiments of your elite troops closer to the Berabesq border without causing suspicion.

That was the first reason the Daroman crown was willing to use up so much valuable time when the Berabesq child god's birthday was fast approaching. The second reason? Well, that came down to simple arithmetic: Oatas Jan'Xan lies just eleven days' ride on a fast horse from Makhan Mebab, the capital of the Berabesq theocracy. By the time we'd finished laying my mother to rest, I'd have to either set out to commit my first political assassination or sit back and watch the entire continent go straight to hells.

'Brother?' Shalla asked.

I gestured down at Reichis, who was curled up in front of my saddle. In a minute or two he'd be letting out a rumbling stream of snores, which he'd later deny, and an occasional fart, for which he'd take excessive pride. 'Every time you come by, you put my business partner to sleep. He hates that.'

She rolled her eyes. 'You think I waste silk magic on a nekhek?'

'They prefer the term "squirrel cat",' I informed her. 'How come he turns into a dumb animal anytime you show up?'

'The answer is somewhat . . . complicated.'

My sister has a habit of forgetting that during our years as initiates I'd been just as diligent a student of magic as she was. I'd mastered all the verbal invocations, developed an outstanding command of esoteric geometries, and nobody could perform the complex somatic forms as precisely as I could. Really, I was as adept in spellcraft as any lord magus in our clan. Except for, you know, the actual magic part.

She caught my expression and sighed. 'Fine. All those spells you begged me to cast to keep the nekhek alive back when he was wounded in the desert and you were a captive of the Ebony Abbey? By necessity they involved the use of iron and blood binding spells which . . . I haven't been able to fully remove.'

'So every time you're near him . . .'

Shalla gazed down at the slumbering squirrel cat. 'I believe it's a form of mystical hibernation.' She held up her forearm to show me her tattooed blood band was glimmering. 'A portion of my own strength is drained, while that of the filthy little monster is restored.'

My ears pricked up at the uncharacteristic note of affection in the words 'filthy little monster'.

'Why, sister . . . is it possible you've developed a fondness for a dirty nekhek?'

Her cheeks reddened. 'Don't be ridiculous. His species are vile. Disgusting. Greedy. Vicious.'

She paused in her litany of faults and edged her horse

closer to mine. With a tentative hand she reached out to touch his fur. 'But I am glad that you found him, brother. I dislike the thought of you being alone.'

The unexpected and surprisingly compassionate sentiment was like a warm breeze shared between us. I counted the seconds until she ruined it.

'Which is why –' four seconds, if you're wondering – 'when this awful business with the Berabesq is completed, you must return to our family. Stop playing the bitter outcast and take your rightful place as protector of our house.'

I prided myself on always having a glib reply whenever Shalla brought up the subject of me returning to our clan, but she cut me off before I could try out any of my new ones. 'This isn't a joke, brother. I've been negotiating with Father and the councils of lords magi for months. They're offering a full pardon for your crimes.'

'Generous of them, sister, only I haven't decided if I'm ready to pardon them for theirs, so why would I care?'

The smug look in Shalla's eyes told me I'd cut her off before she'd finished making her offer. 'Because you're not the only outcast they're willing to pardon.'

Now *that* caught me off-guard.

'Nephenia?' I asked.

'*Neph'aria*,' my sister corrected. 'Yes, brother, your little mouse girl can come home too. The warrant against her for killing her father will be lifted.'

This was the first real concession Shalla had ever made in this ongoing debate of ours. She despised Nephenia, for reasons I'd never understood. The feeling was, I'd been assured, mutual.

I hadn't seen Neph in over a year, not since she'd come to rescue me from the Ebony Abbey and brought Reichis back

124

to me. The joy I'd felt at seeing her that day had been muted by the confusion of our subsequent parting.

'I think I love you, Kellen, but I won't know for sure until I meet the man you're going to be once you finally get tired of being the boy you once were.'

How can something so painful to hear sound inspiring at the same time?

Shalla misunderstood my look of uncertainty. 'I'm offering you a life, brother. A *real* life. Not this bizarre frontier folk tale you seem to be trying to enact.'

I nodded ahead of us to where, somewhere half a mile down the imperial road, the queen's carriage rolled along, with her discussing important matters of state with just about everybody but me. 'I already have a job, thanks.'

Shalla gave me one of those imperious, reprimanding looks only little sisters are capable of. 'Your skills – and yes, I'm admitting you have skills, brother – are owed to your family. Not wasted guarding some little barbarian queen who only keeps you around because you amuse her.'

Then she did something that froze the blood in my veins: she reached up and traced a finger around her left eye and said, 'Unless there's some other reason you're so loyal to this foreign queen.'

What did she mean by that? I searched frantically within those light, lilting, mocking words for the real meaning underneath. *Arta loquit*, I thought. *Where's my damned arta loquit when I need it?*

There were two possible interpretations of Shalla's jibe. The first was that she was ridiculing me for believing the Daroman court, with its armies of doctors and physicians, might one day be able to devise a cure for my shadowblack. The second was much, much worse: what if Shalla – and therefore my father – knew that Queen Ginevra herself had the same affliction?

When the queen turned thirteen, by bizarre Daroman custom she would have to appear naked before her people, not to mention every foreign dignitary on the continent. Unless she could either find a cure or a way to hide the disease – a gambit that would be sure to fail in the most cataclysmic way imaginable if my father chose to reveal the truth – it would be the end of her reign. To keep her secret, Ke'heops could blackmail her with just about anything he wanted.

Maybe he already had.

Was this why she was keeping me away?

'Brother?' Shalla asked. 'Are you quite well?'

Again I tried to sift through the syllables of her words, searching for notes of sarcasm. But I couldn't find any. Maybe she didn't know anything. Maybe it was just another of her games.

'I'm sorry, Shalla,' I said. 'I won't be a pawn for—'

'Sha'maat,' she corrected, cutting me off, her tone becoming strident. Angry. 'Our mother was Bene'*maat*. Our father is *Ke*'heops and you are *Ke*'helios. Why must you persist in taunting me with a child's name? Does it please you to imagine that I am not truly her daughter and you are not his son?'

'I don't know,' I admitted. 'I only know that no matter what happens, you'll always be my sister.'

It had sounded good in my head. Unfortunately, the sentiment struck entirely the wrong chord with Shalla. 'Then stop forcing me to choose between you and Father!'

Heads turned. People stared. I doubt I could've come up with a more uncomfortable phrase for my sister to shout at me in front of all these soldiers and marshals and retainers.

Shalla never swears. She considers profanity as much a sign of immaturity as my insistence on using our birth names. So I guess it really meant something that when she kicked her horse to ride away, she left me with, 'And stop being such a fucking child, Kellen.'

15

The Funeral

People say that when you return to the place of your birth after a long time away, everything looks smaller. Once you've visited faraway empires, strolled the avenues of magnificent capital cities, trekked across majestic landscapes and experienced cultures far different to your own, home becomes a quaint little word that can stand for any number of different things, but mostly youthful nostalgia.

Sometimes I wonder who the idiots are who come up with these sayings.

Oatas Jan'Xan, the city where I'd spent the first sixteen years of my life until one night I'd left with nothing but a sleeping squirrel cat and a cocky attitude, wasn't quaint. The sight of the seven gleaming columns surrounding the oasis didn't fill me with sentimental longing for my youth. The perfectly still silver sands and the low stone pool filled with the raw, shimmering magic my ancestors first named the *Jan* pulled at my soul with all the raging force of a dozen horses.

You'll never hear one of my people admit it, but magic is a drug.

'Do you feel it?' my sister had asked as we'd entered the

city. The exultant smile on her lips, the almost wide-eyed delight, reminded me that I wasn't the only addict. No wonder exile is considered almost as harsh a punishment as death among the Jan'Tep.

Hours later, standing among the throng as Bene'maat's funeral rites were being performed, my skin still tingled with the simple proximity to the oasis. My boots practically vibrated from the rapturous power in the veins of ore winding under the ground beneath my feet. From these raw metals came the inks used to tattoo the sigils of the six fundamental forms of magic around my people's forearms, the means by which Jan'Tep initiates learn to cast the spells that define us.

Those of us who haven't been counter-banded by our parents, of course.

'Duty is the lesson Bene'maat sought to teach all of us,' Ke'heops intoned. He was standing over my mother's perfectly preserved body – tastefully attired in two diaphanous strips of purple silk that granted the barest modicum of modesty. One of the perks of blood and iron magic is that the flesh doesn't decay as quickly as it should. The skin hardens instead into a lustrous marble-like sheath. That Bene'maat's corpse was so perfectly preserved even a month after her death was a testament to her strength as a mage and my father's arrogance in wanting to make sure everyone saw her like this.

I was distracted by Reichis sniffing the air for the fifth time since we'd arrived.

'What are you doing?' I asked quietly.

'Can't smell any other squirrel cats.'

'Were you expecting any?'

129

His furry shoulders rose and fell in his rendition of a shrug. 'Would've figured they'd have taken over this lousy city by now. You know, snuck in one night and murdered all your people in their sleep on account of that time a bunch of these skinbags tried to burn everyone in my tribe with fire spells?' He raised his snout and sniffed again. 'Talk about a lack of leadership.'

'You don't think a full-scale massacre is a little excessive?'

'I think it's our gods-damned duty.'

'Duty to family,' Ke'heops droned on. 'Duty to her people.' He spread his arms wide, performing the somatic gestures he'd used with me back at the palace. The sky above us, clear and bright from the early afternoon sun only seconds before, darkened even as it filled with stars. 'And at the end,' he said in a whisper that somehow we all heard, 'duty to the entire world.'

Far above us, the stars shifted and moved, taking on the shapes of places and people, retelling the story of how Bene'maat had travelled deep into Berabesq territory, where she had uncovered the existence of their new god and the monstrous plans of the viziers, and brought them at the cost of her own life back to us.

'Cool trick,' Reichis chittered from his perch on my shoulder as he leaned back to gaze up at the sky, apparently having completely forgotten his plan for the utter destruction of my clan. 'You should learn that spell. Then you could put on little magic shows detailing my exploits.'

'Silence the nekhek, traitor,' a voice muttered behind me. 'Or I'll burn the filthy creature alive.'

Even before I turned to face him, I'd plastered a big grin on my face. 'Is that my old pal Tennat I hear?'

'I am Ra'ennat now,' he said, eyes blazing. 'A true Jan'Tep mage.'

Back when we were both initiates, Tennat had been just about the cruellest, most despicable bully I'd ever known. He was standing between his two brothers, Ra'fan and Ra'dir, who were just as bad. Of course, since they were all sons of Ra'meth, the man who'd tried to kill my family and frame the Sha'Tep for it all, I suppose that was only natural.

'Right, right,' I said, pushing Reichis's face back with my right hand to stop him from leaping at Tennat. The little monster was snarling up a storm. Nobody else was paying attention to us, thankfully, because I was about to do something stupid. I extended my free hand to Tennat. 'My name is Ke'helios.'

Tennat – *Ra'ennat*, I suppose I should say – spat on my palm. 'You're no mage, just an outcast spellslinger with a few tricks.'

I wiped the spittle on my trouser leg. 'True, but then . . . Eleven.'

'Eleven?' Ra'fan asked. 'Eleven what?'

'Eleven lords magi,' I replied. 'That's how many I've beaten, battered and left for dead across the continent.' I leaned closer and whispered, 'So unless one of you would like to be number twelve, I'd suggest you back the hells off.'

Reichis chuckled then, relaxing on my shoulder. Nothing calms him like a good death threat. 'Nice one. Bag me his eyeballs when you're done with him.'

It was something of an empty threat. Duelling at a funeral? In front of hundreds of foreign barbarians come to pay tribute to the wife of the mage sovereign? That would be a death sentence in and of itself. Still, Tennat looked like he was considering it.

131

So was I.

Maybe it's dangerous to renew childhood acquaintances after you've spent as much time learning to fight mages as I have. The pulsing desire to punch your former tormentors in the face is almost as enthralling as the taste of magic.

'Enough,' growled a new voice. This one I recognised immediately.

Panahsi had been my best friend growing up. The heavyset, often mocked boy who'd followed me around as if I were someone worth knowing was different now, leaner, with the firm jaw and stern gaze of a war mage. He was called Pan'erath these days, but I'd come to know him as the red mage when he'd beaten me nearly to death a while back. I could've forgiven that more easily than the way he'd let his family come perilously close to pressuring Nephenia into marriage with him. The scarlet silk garments he'd been wearing during our last encounter were still strapped tightly around muscles he'd not had as a boy, and that were certainly far more impressive than my own.

'Hey, Pan,' I said.

His eyes flared. I wasn't scared though. One thing about Panahsi is he always follows the rules. He turned to Ra'ennat and the others. 'Go stand somewhere else. I'll not see these proceedings denigrated by any of you.'

Is it odd that I felt a kind of pride at watching the scions of the House of Ra, who'd all mocked Panahsi back when we were initiates, skulking away at his command?

'Thanks,' I said.

Behind us various delegates of the councils of lords magi were taking their turns singing my mother's praises. Not literally of course. My people don't think much of singing.

132

For his part, Panahsi was staring at me with a gaze that could've pierced through a steel door.

'They say you're the one chosen to end the threat of the Berabesq god,' he said.

'That's what they tell me.'

'Will you do it? Will you fulfil your mission?'

You didn't need training in arta precis to see the tentative, almost desperate hopefulness in Pan's eyes. He wanted me to say yes, to speak the same words of duty and loyalty as my father had done. He wanted to believe I'd changed – that I was now the Kellen he'd assumed I would become, back when we were boys and would endlessly recite to each other the stories of the great heroic mages of the past. He wanted us to be friends again. Until that moment I hadn't had any idea just how much I missed him.

'I don't know, Pan,' I said softly.

'They killed your mother.'

'Will she come back to life if I murder their god?'

His gaze hardened. My people don't appreciate a glib tongue. 'That's not how duty works.'

Abruptly the spell my father had been using to turn the sky into his own personal canvas faded and the afternoon sun returned, the light seeming far harsher now than it had before. A different spell broke too, as Panahsi's expression hardened and he turned away to leave me standing there alone. 'Why must you always betray your own kind, Kellen?'

16

The Eulogy

The official ceremony came to a close with my father delivering a flag-waving speech about fidelity and courage that ended with all the mages in the audience raising their fists and sparking their tattooed bands, the eruption of raw magic creating a boorish light show that was lacking only a Zhubanese marching band to bring the whole tawdry affair to a patriotic climax. All of this was entirely in line with Jan'Tep funerary custom and yet felt subtly off-key to me, as if these displays of national pride only served to accentuate how small a people we really were.

Only after the principal rites had been completed were foreign dignitaries invited to approach the dais and deliver their eulogies. Queen Ginevra's was the best, I thought, striking a nice balance between mournful acceptance of loss and cautious optimism about the future. The phrase 'our two peoples' came up a lot. The Gitabrian delegate spoke of peace a great deal, while making a number of not-so-subtle references to advanced military equipment they could provide in the interests of a quick resolution to any conflict – at a price, naturally. This was, of course, directed at the queen. My people don't debase themselves with weapons when going about the business of killing people.

The Zhuban delegate managed to politely blame my mother's death on a failure of our nation to follow the ways of philosophy so obviously laid out for all to see in various astronomical phenomena that it really was a shame the rest of us were so stupid. A few others spoke as well, representatives of tiny self-proclaimed nations from the far north and south of the continent. Nobody paid much attention to them. But it was the final speaker who caused me the greatest surprise: a well-spoken young woman come to represent the Seven Sands. She was my age with pale blonde hair and a winding scar around her right eye so faint I doubted anyone but me even noticed it.

'Seneira?' I said aloud.

'Who's she?' Reichis asked, half-asleep on my shoulder.

'The girl we met in the Seven Sands,' I whispered. 'The one we thought had the shadowblack but it was actually an onyx worm that had been implanted into her eye?'

He peered towards the girl speaking on the dais. 'Not ringing any bells.'

Squirrel cat recollections of humans tend to be a little vague once they're done with them.

'Her father was Beren Thrane, founder of the Academy of the Seven Sands,' I said. Sometimes Reichis has a better memory for places and events over people. 'The gigantic tower? The arsehole spellslinger, Dexan Videris? The conspiracy to infect all the students so they could be used as assassins against their own families? We nearly died, remember?'

'I recall something about a crocodile,' he acknowledged, then extended a paw towards the dais. 'But who's she?'

I sighed. There was only one way to go about this. 'You had your first bath at her house and she gave you butter

135

biscuits.' And she was the second girl I ever kissed, but I didn't mention that.

'Oooh . . .' He perked up. 'And then later, after I'd murdered the crocodile and saved everyone from the onyx worms, Beren Thrane offered us a job and served up some of that delectable amber hootch of his!' He started sniffing at the air. 'You think anybody around here's got some? I could use a drink.'

As doubtful as it was that anyone attending a funeral was carrying around a flask of pazione liqueur, the last thing I needed was a drunken nekhek stumbling around challenging lords magi to a fight. 'Maybe later.'

He turned his nose up at me. 'Bath first. You stink.'

'We've been on the road for over two weeks – what do you expect?' He stank worse, by the way.

Seneira's eulogy was brief, with most of the Jan'Tep in the crowd turning away as she spoke. The Seven Sands isn't considered a legitimate country by the nations bordering it. The Jan'Tep, Berabesq and Daroman see it as a kind of no man's land whose primary function is to create a buffer between them and, occasionally, a place to wage war. Nonetheless she spoke in that clear, almost haughty way of hers I'd come to know during our time together a couple of years ago.

'We have known a great many wars in the Seven Sands,' she said, coming to the end of her speech. 'It is on our lands where the great powers have always chosen to fight. It is beneath our ground where the bones of hundreds of thousands of combatants rest next to those of our own people who never asked for war. As witnesses to so much bloodshed, we have a saying: "The greatest debt in any battle is owed to the last soldier who died fighting it." Wouldn't it be the highest honour we could pay to Bene'maat if she were the only casualty of this war?'

Like all the eulogies, Seneira's was filled with kind and admiring words, but underneath it a simple message brought in the interests of her own people. In her case, that message was: 'Wage war if you must, but fight your battles away from our lands. We're tired of picking up the bodies.'

Standing next to the dais, Ke'heops appeared to listen patiently, but his eyes were on me. The look my father gave me carried its own message: Bene'maat couldn't be the last casualty in this conflict. One more corpse was needed to stop the bloodshed, and it was up to me to provide it.

17

An Overdue Bath

Seven pale shafts of light rose from the clan palace in the centre of the city. The massive heptagonal edifice with its sloped walls rising up to end in a roof smaller than its foundations had always given the impression of a place better suited to incarcerating one's enemies than housing one's monarch. Maybe that's why my father had graciously turned the entire palace over to Queen Ginevra and her retinue for the duration of our stay.

'What a dump,' Reichis said as we wandered the halls with a set of purloined towels in my arms.

I should point out that, by any reasonable standard, the traditional residence of the clan prince was still luxurious beyond the dreams of mere mortals. The squirrel cat had been spoiled by the opulence of the royal palace in Darome – not so much by the furnishings as the number of servants.

'If you think I'm going to dry off my own fur, you've got another thing coming,' he warned.

Having never been inside the home of the clan prince before, it took me a while to find the baths.

'Maybe there's a better one somewhere else?' Reichis suggested.

The chamber was, to my uneducated eyes, perfectly suited to our needs. There were seven different sunken baths. (In case I've never mentioned it before, my people have a thing about the number seven.) Each tub was surrounded by an elaborate tiled mosaic depicting the tale of a great Jan'Tep victory over an enemy either mundane or supernatural. The tubs were spelled each morning by charmcasters to ensure the water inside remained perfectly clean, and heated to a particular temperature ranging from tepid to scalding. Reichis, for all his pretensions at ruggedness, insists on a very precise temperature for his baths, one that seems to change daily. I had to stand there waiting as he dipped his tail into each tub before finally narrowing it down to two options.

'Which one do you want?' he asked.

I picked the one I least wanted. He then demanded the other one and waited expectantly for me to haul one of the narrow wooden benches over and place it inside the tub for him.

'Butter biscuits,' he demanded as he began to settle himself inside.

'You ate them all on the way here,' I reminded him.

'What about the ones you hid in that leather bag strapped behind the saddle bags?'

'You found those.'

Reichis's growl carried the promise of a thousand mortal wounds, hideous mutilations and certain death. The black markings on the fur around his left eye began to swirl and turn. His paws clawed at the air, fangs clacking together as he instinctively mimed the punishments he envisioned for a world that dared deny him his preferred bathing delicacy. All of this would have been slightly more frightening had he not been lying on his back on the bench in the pool, half-submerged in the water. He can be a petulant little bastard at times.

I reached a hand out of the bath to the towel, inside which I'd hidden a small cloth bundle just big enough to hold a half-dozen butter biscuits. I'd had to pay a rather confused-looking servant to carry these all the way from Darome for me. Fumbling with the cords to open it, I took out one of the sugary morsels and tossed it at Reichis. Despite the lack of warning, the squirrel cat still managed to snatch it out of the air with a greedy paw. He began devouring it immediately, pausing only long enough to say, 'You can live, I guess,' sending a small shower of crumbs falling around his muzzle into the water. Squirrel cats' jaws are meant for rending flesh, not nibbling on dainty pastries.

We sat there in companionable silence before he spoke again. 'Kellen?'

'Yeah?'

'Sorry about your mom.'

'Thanks.'

'Did you . . . ?' He hesitated, looking rather as if he were in danger of vomiting into the pool. 'Did you want to talk about it?'

Squirrel cats don't discuss the dead. To them it's pointless. Death should be followed by swift, murderous revenge and then left in the past. I felt oddly touched that Reichis would offer to listen to me moan and whimper about my mother.

'Thanks,' I said again. 'I guess I'm still trying to figure out what it is I'm feeling. It's like there's this empty part inside of me, but it's so cold I can't seem to—'

'Ugh . . .' He groaned. After a few seconds he looked over at me. 'It's okay. I can take it. Tell me more about your . . . feelings.'

This is what happens when an innately selfish creature entirely incapable of sympathy attempts to change its nature.

'Do you ever . . . ?' I began, then thought better of it.

'What?' he asked.

'Do you ever miss your mother?'

It was Chitra who had bound Reichis and me together. *'You must be his caution,'* she'd told me, that night she lay dying at my side, *'as he will be your courage. You will teach him when to flee and he will teach you when to fight.'*

I had never imagined in that moment, as a madman rained fire upon her tribe, that Chitra had given me the greatest gift I would ever know in my life. Reichis was more than just a friend. He was my business partner. Granted, one who mostly tended to bite me and steal my stuff, but still . . .

Reichis snarled and it took only a second for me to realise it wasn't at me. Before I even knew who was in the room with us, I'd leaped out of the bath and rolled on the floor to grab my deck of steel throwing cards. I sent a pair of them spinning in the air at the figure near the door.

Please let that not be some over-zealous and remarkably quiet servant who just happened to unlock the door without either Reichis or me . . . Nah. Has to be an assassin.

The grey-haired woman who called herself Emelda but whom I still thought of as the vulture shielded herself behind what looked like a thin wooden case about three feet wide by two feet high. The two steel cards embedded themselves in the wood.

'Knew there was a reason I brought this with me,' she said.

Should've known one of the Murmurers would come for me sooner or later, I thought as I mapped out my next move. By now I had my castradazi coins in one hand and a towel in the other. It's almost impossible to use my powders when my fingers are wet, so I'd need to use one of the coins to distract her while I dried my hands, then grab my holsters and blast her from existence.

'You always this homicidal when you're naked?' she asked, lowering the case.

I don't know why I looked down. I really wish I hadn't.

'No wonder my daughter fancies you,' Emelda said as she pried the steel cards from the wood. 'Likes them feisty, she does.'

I grabbed a bigger towel. And my powder holsters. Just because someone makes fun of your nakedness doesn't mean they're not planning to kill you. 'Something I can help you with, ma'am?' I asked.

She walked over to us, apparently no more troubled by Reichis growling at her than she was by either my nudity or blast powders. When the squirrel cat started stalking towards her, she locked eyes with him and a made a kind of breathy whistling with her lips.

'Don't waste your so-called "marshal's magic" on us,' I said. 'Me and Reichis aren't . . .'

I glanced over and watched helplessly as the squirrel cat went from baring his teeth to resting back on his haunches as he gazed up longingly at her. 'So purdy . . . like emeralds,' he chittered softly, drooling butter-biscuit crumbs all over his furry chest.

'You're hopeless.'

Emelda chuckled as she set the case down on a stool and undid the latches on one side.

'Slowly,' I warned.

142

'Couldn't kill you even if I wanted to, son. Little Tori went and forced the council to agree to bring no harm to you for at least a year.'

'You'll forgive me if I don't take your word for it?'

She stepped back. 'Go ahead and open it yourself then.'

Realising I could just as easily have set myself up, but unwilling to look like even more of a fool, I knelt down and very carefully opened the case. I've got a pretty good feel for the tension caused by springs and trip-wires, but my fingers couldn't detect anything amiss. With the lid open, I saw what appeared to be a coiled rope made of some kind of ancient braided strands. At one end was a grip wrapped in leather that looked almost as old.

'You brought me a whip?'

'Technically it's called a scourge,' she said. 'But yeah. It's a kind of whip.'

'And what am I supposed to do with it?'

Emelda reached inside the case and removed the scourge. Some charmed objects give off the sensation of heat or cold, but this was different. It wasn't so much a vibration in the air as an uncomfortable stillness. 'You know much about Daroman magic, Kellen?'

'Only that you don't have any.'

She laughed. 'Well, I suppose that's true. Magic's never been something we needed, I suppose, what with our superior military might and vastly more civilised natures. But we've always been good at collecting things.'

Stealing them, more like. The museums of Darome were filled with the artefacts of conquered nations.

'Anyway, we've never been much for spells and such, but our explorers know items of power when they come across

143

them.' She held up the scourge to me. 'And this here? Well, this may just be the most powerful artefact on the entire continent.'

She was waiting for me to ask for more, but I've never liked being strung along. I examined the whip more closely. To say it looked ancient was putting it mildly. It looked as if the strands came from long, thin strips of some kind of dessicated tree bark, all braided together. I doubted it would hurt much if someone used it on you. On the other hand, I was absolutely positive Emelda hadn't gone to all this trouble for a practical joke.

'This wood,' I said, pointing at the braided strips. 'It's from a *baojara* tree, isn't it? The kind that sometimes grows in the Berabesq desert?'

'Good eye. Care to be more specific?'

What's more specific than the type of tree? I wondered. *The exact sub-species? The precise geographic location?*

No, I realised then. *She means something else.*

'The Berabesq have six different holy books,' I said, watching her eyes to see if I was on the right track. She gave me nothing in return, but that, too, is a clue at times like these. 'Six different codices that each argue a different one of the six faces of God is the true one.'

'If you're going to give me a lesson in theology, son, I'd appreciate it if you put on some trousers first.'

I ignored the jibe. 'Six different versions of Berabesq history, with just one thing common to all of them: the Baojara Scourge. The whip made from strands of the first tree God ever made grow in what had once been the most desolate desert in the world.'

Reichis came up and sniffed at it. 'Stinks like dead skinbag,'

144

he said, and went off to eat more butter biscuits.

He wasn't wrong about the stench of death on it. According to the Berabesq codices, the desert peoples of those ancient times came to fear the power of their god, and had made the scourge from his first tree in the belief that his own primal creation was the one thing that could hurt him. So in secret, as God slept, they'd stripped bark from the first baojara tree and made the scourge.

You'd think an all-knowing, all-powerful deity would just, you know, smite them, but expecting religion to make sense is like asking a squirrel cat not to steal your stuff when you're asleep.

'You really believe this is it?' I asked. 'The instrument that can make a god scream?'

Emelda shrugged. 'Can't say for sure, but every expert we've been able to find swears this is a holy artefact. Even had a few Jan'Tep mages examine it. They pretty much ran off whimpering in a corner after taking one look. Now these . . .' She reached into the case and removed something I'd missed before – a tiny bag made of purple felt that she tossed to me. I caught it and opened it up.

'Dice?'

'Made from the same tree, or so my sources tell me. Figured they suited your chosen profession.'

'You want me to gamble the Berabesq god to death?'

She chuckled at that. 'Dice are a funny thing, don't you think? Never know what number they'll turn up. Their very existence implies the universe is filled with random events. You know what the opposite of randomness is?'

'Destiny?'

'God.' She reached out a finger and tapped one of the

145

dice in my hand. 'Passages in several of the Berabesq holy texts claim that if you roll these in God's presence, his dominion over the world will be suspended until they come to a stop.'

'Seriously?'

'Well, hard to say if it's meant to be interpreted literally. The prose gets a little flowery at times. Could be they just make him laugh and then he incinerates your soul.' She held the scourge out to me. 'That's why you'd best get this wrapped around his neck as quickly as possible.'

When I didn't take it, she carefully placed it back in its case and closed the metal clasps. 'Don't blame you for believing you can walk away from fate,' she said. 'But take it from an old dog who's seen more than her share of ugliness – we all do what we have to when it comes to protecting the ones we love. Even when the deeds are more foul than our souls can bear.'

Something about the way she said those words, the mixture of weariness and determination in her craggy features reminded me of someone. Someone I'd met when I'd first arrived in Darome. Someone who'd distrusted me as instinctively as Emelda did. Someone I'd killed.

Oh, ancestors . . . Please let me be wrong about this.

The queen had made sure no one knew the truth about his death – any one of a thousand loyal outraged marshals would've murdered me for sure if they'd found out the truth. Only I guess she was wrong about that, because Emelda hadn't killed me yet.

'Does Torian know?' I asked.

'Know what?'

I hate it when shrewd people act dumb. It tells you they don't respect your intelligence.

'That I killed her father.'

Jed Colfax had been a legend among the queen's marshals service. An old man when I met him, he could still take down the toughest outlaws on the continent, and had a reputation for pursuing fugitives no matter how long it took to bring them to justice. Looking back now, I felt kind of stupid for not realising Torian had to be his daughter. Given she'd changed her last name, I guess it was one of those open secrets everyone knew but nobody talked about.

I have to hand it to Emelda: she didn't flinch when I brought up killing her husband. Didn't so much as blink. We might as well have been talking about the weather. She turned and walked to the door, but not before saying, 'My daughter believes what the rest of Darome believes: Andreas Martius and his band of would-be tyrants murdered her father. That's why every last one of them is dead and you're still standing there like an idiot in a towel, debating whether or not to do the one thing that can save this world from blood and fire. The only thing by my reckoning that gives you any right to live at all.'

I stayed there, staring at the gnarled wooden case for a long time after she left. Eventually Reichis came over and chittered, 'You know what we ought to do?'

'What's that?'

'Open that case back up and light the whip on fire, then leave the ashes outside that old bird's door tonight. Bet she won't feel so smart then.'

Never in my life have I been more tempted to follow a squirrel cat's advice. Problem was, that would pretty much guarantee we spent the rest of our lives with the marshals service chasing us across whatever parts of the world weren't

147

already filled with Berabesq zealots hunting blaspheming spellslingers.

'Come on,' I said, reaching for my clothes.

'Where're we goin'?'

'To find the queen. Past time she gave us some answers.'

But Reichis sat back on his haunches. 'Umm . . . Kellen?'

'Yeah?'

He pawed pathetically at the fur on his chest. 'You're gonna need to brush me. Lot of butter-biscuit crumbs in that pool. Must've been left there by somebody else.'

I sighed. 'Fine,' I said as I went to grab one of the brushes from the grooming area at the edge of the baths. 'But there's one condition.'

Squirrel cats, while unable to comprehend any number of human concepts, understand negotiations just fine. 'Well, not sure I need to be brushed *that* much. I mean, it's just a couple of crumbs, really, and it's not like anyone's going to notice and . . . Okay, what're your terms?'

I pointed to the jaunty purple merchant's cap sitting on the damp floor near Reichis that he still insisted on wearing whenever I wore my frontier hat. 'You promise not to wear that thing in front of the queen.'

'Deal!' Reichis chittered victoriously. 'I was done with the hat anyway.' He looked up at me with the squirrel cat equivalent of an evil grin. 'Sucker.'

18

The Letter

Even for a royal tutor with the traditional right of Consovi Mandat, it's not as easy as one might hope to get a private audience with the Queen of Darome. Turns out monarchs have more important things to do than subject themselves to the irate complaints of their tutor of cards.

'I can get you in next week,' Arex said, standing outside the entrance to the sanctum.

A Jan'Tep palace has no actual throne room, but that didn't stop the queen's entourage from keeping up appearances. The moment my father had turned over the palace to her use, dozens of retainers and servants had set to hauling in various furnishings brought with us on the journey to ensure her temporary accommodations conveyed all the trappings of imperial power. This included various gilded pennants, jewel-encrusted sceptres and the actual Daroman throne, which weighs a little over a ton. Her royal accessories also included Arex Nerren, the man who was currently keeping me from seeing her.

Arex was, technically speaking, the queen's social secretary. This came with a rather wider range of powers and privileges than one would normally associate with such a position, not the least of which was to be a huge pain in my arse anytime he felt the urge. Occasionally even when it was someone else's urge.

'Let me guess,' I said. 'Torian got to you too.'

He gave me a sideways grin. 'The lieutenant's got a lot of clout. Would've thought you'd have figured how these things work by now, kid.'

Reichis, sitting atop my shoulder, gave Arex a snarl that would've wilted an oak tree. This wasn't on my behalf, you understand. He's just never liked the man.

Arex is one of the few people in the world other than Ferius who manages to get away with calling me kid. Despite the somewhat obsequious-sounding title of 'social secretary', he stands six and a half feet tall, could probably wrestle a bear and really, really enjoys pummelling people who try to get past him.

On the other hand, a year or so ago, during the attempted coup, he'd gotten stabbed several times and come perilously close to bleeding out all over the floor of the Daroman palace. I knew the precise location of every one of those wounds and which ones to strike in the event we ever came to blows.

I quite like Arex Nerren. He's funny, astute and fundamentally decent. His devotion to the queen is beyond question and I trust him implicitly. Unfortunately I tend to be a terrible judge of character, so these days I balance out my trusting nature with careful contemplation of how best to murder just about every individual in the Daroman court should the need arise.

And yeah, I have a plan for how to kill Torian Libri too.

Maybe my father had been right about me. My moral compass didn't seem to be working very well lately. On the other hand, considering Ke'heops – along with the queen's own strategic council – expected me to kill a boy younger than me, I was having my doubts about how finely tuned anyone else's moral compass was these days.

Where are you, Ferius? The world isn't making any kind of sense any more.

That thought made me chuckle aloud. Ferius Parfax had never made any sense to me either.

'You okay, kid?' Arex asked.

'I'm fine. Just . . .'

I sighed. I really needed to see the queen, but I wasn't ready to get into another fight right now, especially with someone I actually respected. Fortunately, not all of my ruses involve homicide.

'Want me to rip his face off?' Reichis offered. 'Might make him more accommodating.'

'Forget it,' I said, and turned to leave the sanctum's foyer. I made a show of stopping as if I'd just remembered something. 'Actually, could you let the queen know I won't be able to make our poker lesson next week?'

Arex's tone conveyed just the right amount of confusion and suspicion. 'I guess. She'll want to know why you cancelled – what with that being your only job.'

'Good point.' I removed a small, sealed envelope from my coat and turned to hand it to him.

'What's this?' he asked, examining the envelope.

'My resignation as her royal tutor of cards.'

He gave me a cock-eyed look. 'Seriously?'

'You can read it if you like. I had it notarised by a magistrate and everything.'

I counted six steps before he called out to me. 'Gods of

151

sea and sky. Fine, you can see her now. She wasn't doing anything important – just reviewing a seven-hundred-page treaty she's supposed to sign in front of a thousand of your fellow Jan'Tep tomorrow. If we end up in the wrong war by morning it'll be on your head.'

I reached out for the envelope. 'Nice doing business with you, Arex.'

He let me tug on it for a second without letting go. 'How long've you been keeping this resignation letter in your pocket to blackmail me with?'

'Wrote it the day after I took the job.'

He chuckled and released the envelope. I stuffed it back into the pocket of my coat.

As I walked past him he snagged me by the shoulder. 'That trick's only going to work once, you get that, right?'

Truth be told, I hadn't been sure it would work this time. 'They only ever work once,' I said as I entered the sanctum and prepared to confront the queen. 'That's why I need so many of them.'

19

The Sanctum

There are actually three chambers you must pass through to enter the palace sanctum, each one with its own set of double doors. There are various esoteric and meditational reasons for this, most of which were pretty much defeated by the presence of a small detachment of marshals polluting the otherwise pristine environment with their maces, crossbows and determined readiness to use them. Guarding the monarch used to be the province of the First Royal Regiment of the Imperial Army, but, well, a whole bunch of them had to be executed last year as punishment for having supported an attempted coup against Queen Ginevra.

The marshals are more irritable than the soldiers used to be. Fugitive hunters aren't trained to stand there doing nothing for hours at a time. When it comes to foul dispositions though, not even they could hold a candle to the aging canker sore known as the royal herald.

'Tutor Kellen,' he said, managing to turn both words into insults.

'Cerreck. It's been a while.'

'Has it?' he asked, conveying a distinct weariness with both my presence and my mere existence.

I gestured to the final set of doors leading into the sanctum. 'Care to announce me? If you're too tired, of course, I'd be happy to . . .'

He gave me the long, withering stare I no doubt deserved before finally, in an act of sublime defeat, pushing open the double doors.

Jan'Tep sanctums are lit by glow-glass balls, which shed light only in proportion to the magical abilities of those nearby. I tried pushing my will into them and got barely a flicker. Some enterprising soul had mounted oil lanterns to each of the seven columns in the centre of the sanctum, but they barely dented the darkness permeating the massive chamber, making the throne set in the middle of the room look smaller somehow. On each arm were stacks of papers piled high, and between them, the very weary-looking twelve-year-old monarch of the Daroman empire.

'Yes?' she asked, without looking up from her papers.

'Ahem,' Cerreck coughed. 'His Most Excellent Royal Tutor of Cards, Kellen Argos.'

The herald, thinking his duty done, began to back away, until Reichis looked up from the floor and gave him a stare that had induced heart failure in many, many rabbits.

'You better just do it,' I said to the old man quietly.

A look of spiritual dismay passed over his features. 'The whole thing?'

'You know what he's like. You really want to risk it?'

Cerreck took in a deep breath. 'And His Most Murderous Lord, Slayer of Mages, Killer of Crocodiles, Destroyer of Dragons – Even the Stupid Metal Ones – Most Beloved of All Sixteen Squirrel Cat God—'

'Twenty-nine,' Reichis corrected.

154

I translated for him.

'Really?' the herald asked. 'I would've sworn last week it was sixteen.'

'Just roll with it,' I advised.

Cerreck sighed. 'Most Beloved of All *Twenty-Nine* Squirrel Cat Gods, and Bearer of. . . "The Coolest Shadowblack Markings Ever", Reichis The Terrible!'

For the first time the queen looked up from her papers and smiled. She was a beautiful girl, though not in the conventional way favoured by Daroman painters. Her features were flatter than those of the majority of her subjects – more like those of the Zhuban in the north than the lighter-skinned people who inhabit the traditional Daroman lands. Her black hair fell in ringlets either side of a round, almost chubby face meant for laughter, but which too often wore the strains of her rank.

'Master squirrel cat,' she said with a brief nod. 'I understood we were overdue for an important meeting, but I was unaware you'd be bringing your assistant.'

Reichis chuckled. This was the kind of joke the two of them always enjoyed, mostly because I didn't.

'Your Majesty,' I began.

She went on as if I hadn't spoken. 'I'm especially surprised to see the royal tutor of cards here this evening as I believe he attempted to resign just minutes ago.'

Ancestors, I swore silently. *How could she know?*

'Your Majesty, are we alone?'

She looked back at me with a raised eyebrow.

There's no such thing as being 'alone' with the Queen of Darome. There's an actual law that makes it a crime for the queen's security services to leave her unattended. Specifically,

155

anyone *in teretro* – which literally means 'tethered to' the monarch but in practice refers to being one of the six people on duty at that time as part of her *custodia regita corpora* ('guards of the royal body') – found more than twelve paces away from her can be hanged as a deserter.

Most places, like her bedroom or the private study where she meets with her tutors, the guards can be outside the door while still within twelve paces of her. But the clan prince's sanctum was huge, so even if she'd overriden her own laws to demand privacy, at least two designated guardians had to be here somewhere, standing in the shadows on either side where I couldn't see them. Of course, anyone guarding her is always sworn to absolute secrecy, never to reveal even under torture anything they had seen or heard in the throne room.

'We are as alone as we need to be,' the queen replied at last.

Which means I know at least one of the two people watching us.

A year ago, the queen had – against my protestations – slid down the top of her gown to reveal the shadowblack markings she'd kept hidden from almost everyone. I hadn't known it at the time, but even then there had been two marshals in the room. One of those had been Torian Libri; the other a man who, devoutly believing that this revelation of the queen's defect made her ineligible to hold the throne, tried to persuade Torian that they had a duty to inform their superiors.

I'm told you can still find pieces of his corpse in all four corners of the country.

So who was the second person in the room with us now,

standing in the shadowy alcove at the back of the sanctum? The queen almost certainly knew why I'd come here. She wouldn't allow anyone to observe us unless she completely trusted them.

I still wondered how she knew I'd pull the resignation gambit.

'I'm rather busy,' the queen said, fingers rifling through one of the stacks of paper resting on the arm of her throne, 'and unlikely to see my bed before morning. So if you've come to yell at me about my many failings as monarch, master card player, it would be helpful if you could give me a little warning so that I might prepare myself for the experience.'

It's . . . possible that I haven't always displayed the courtesy expected of a servant of the crown.

'Oh, you're going to get yelled at,' Reichis chittered as he sauntered over to hop up onto her lap.

'I rather expected as much,' she said.

The queen is the only person other than myself who seems to be able to understand the things Reichis says. Whether this is because she really is the two-thousand-year-old spirit of the royal line inside the body of a twelve-year-old or because both of us are actually deranged has never been clear to me.

'Actually, I came with a simple question, Your Majesty.'

'Go on,' she said, suspicion evident in her tone.

'Are you ordering me to assassinate the boy living in the great temple of Berabesq?'

'Have I issued any such order?'

'Your Murmurers are clearly intent on forcing me to do it, and apparently they can command just about anything they want. I'm having trouble believing they would be operating without your consent.'

She gave me an arch look. 'You'd be surprised what my subjects do without seeking my consent. For example, one nearly threw away his life just a few weeks ago trying to outwit a lord magus in a tavern.'

I was getting tired of people throwing that in my face. 'I see. Well, thanks for your time, Your Majesty. I'll leave you to your paperwork.'

I turned and started to walk away. Turning your back on the monarch is also a crime in Darome, though not necessarily one punishable by death.

'Bow before you leave, card player,' Torian Libri bellowed.

Damn it.

'Calm yourself, lieutenant,' the queen instructed. 'My tutor of cards meant no offence to me.'

'He didn't?' the marshal asked, stepping out of the shadows.

'No. He was trying to provoke my other guest into revealing themselves. Isn't that right, master card player?'

I turned back to face her. 'I've been set up enough times in my life – most recently by your own loyal servants, Your Majesty – to warrant a certain amount of caution. I've also been ordered to commit a murder on the grounds that I'm both the easiest person to disavow if things go wrong and the most likely to get through the Berabesq border because of how weak and irrelevant I am. Oh, and my mother died not too long ago – you may have gleaned that from the funeral? Turns out she caught a rather fatal curse after my father sent her to spy on a god. So I apologise if my manners are lacking, but I'm feeling a little pissed off right now!'

Queen Ginevra gently lifted Reichis from her lap and set

him on top of one of the stacks of papers before rising from her throne, but she didn't approach me – just gazed back at me with so much sorrow and compassion that I instantly felt horrible about how I'd behaved.

'I'm sorry, Kellen,' she said. 'I hadn't meant for our encounter to go like this. I'm just . . . The things that are troubling you are troubling me as well, and when you walked in with that angry swagger of yours—'

A cough came from the second alcove.

A flash of irritation crossed the queen's young features. 'I'm getting to it.'

'Not hardly fast enough,' said a female – but not typically *feminine* – voice.

Jan'Tep sanctums are designed with unusual acoustic properties meant to enhance the harmonic frequencies of reverberations. This is particularly useful when practising complex incantations, but also has the effect of lending an eerie, preternatural quality to the echoes within. Maybe that's why, for those first couple of seconds, I wondered if my ears were playing tricks on me.

Please, I thought, *ancestors, please let it be her.*

The scratch of a fingernail against a match. The flicker of orange flame. The rise of a beautiful, blessed blue-black smoke which, until that moment, I hadn't realised I'd missed so badly.

I was running to her, practically falling over my feet, even before she stepped out of the alcove to reveal herself.

Ferius Parfax.

20

Royal Commands

An inexplicable feeling of shame knifed its way through my joy at seeing Ferius again. I was eighteen years old. A grown man. I'd killed people, saved people, seen and done things most never would. You'd think I'd've hardened a little in the process. But I was still soft. A boy.

'It's okay, kid,' Ferius whispered, still holding tight to me, keeping me from drifting away.

I thought I'd never see you again, I wanted to say, but that would've led to blubbering, which was a bridge I wouldn't cross. I hadn't cried for my mother, and the confusion and guilt that left me with surely made weeping at my mentor's unexpected arrival a kind of crime.

'What are you doing here?' I asked instead.

'Oh, you know, walkin' the path of the wild daisy.' Ferius let go of me, pressing her hands to my shoulders to hold me at arms' length. 'You look fine, kid. Real fine.'

I suddenly felt awkward and pretentious in my idiotically shiny silver court shirt and dark blue leather trousers fitted to me by the royal tailor.

'Put some meat on your bones too,' Ferius went on, evidently unaware of how much she was embarrassing me.

'Kellen has adapted well to court life,' the queen said, a little too proudly for my taste.

She couldn't know how oddly unpleasant that sounded to my ears, nor could I have explained why, but it did.

Ferius was staring at me. 'Nah,' she said at last.

'"*Nah*"?' the queen repeated.

'He ain't adapted at all,' Ferius said. She tapped me in the chest. 'Not here.' Her fingers rose to tap me in the centre of my forehead. 'Not here neither.' She leaned in to peer into my eyes. 'I can see it plain as day.'

'See what?' the queen asked.

'The Path of Endless Stars.'

Sometimes – albeit incredibly rarely and with no predictable pattern – Ferius says just the right thing to save your soul. She grinned at me as if she knew exactly what I was feeling. Maybe she did know. Maybe she didn't.

'They want me to kill a boy,' I said. 'They say it's the only way to protect the queen and stop the Berabesq from starting a war.'

Ferius nodded but said nothing.

'Is that why you've come? To stop me?'

'Do you want me to stop you?'

I thought about that for all of a quarter of a second. 'Yes, very much.'

'You know I can't though, right?'

I'd known she was going to say that. '*Ain't the Argosi way. Can't mess with another's path*,' or some other such nonsense.

'We should talk,' the queen said, rising from the throne and stepping outside of the ring of columns to walk towards one of the tables beneath the gallery that ran the right-hand length of the sanctum. 'All of us,' she added, and Torian Libri finally stepped out of the darkened alcove where she'd been standing guard.

Once the four of us were seated, the queen quickly took hold of the conversation. 'While I do not condone the methods demonstrated in recent times by the Council of Murmurers –' she glanced at me with just enough guilt in her expression to take some of the edge off my anger over that particular experience – 'and certainly there will be . . . adjustments to their remit within my court, nonetheless, the threat is real.'

'Which threat is that?' Ferius asked.

Torian Libri took offence at the question. 'The Berabesq have a population three times the size of the rest of the continent, with hundreds of separate household militias – well trained and disciplined. If they should unite, they could field an army larger than any the world has ever seen. They could sweep through Darome like—'

'Army that big ain't gonna fall apart just cos one kid gets killed.'

'That's why we can't let it form in the first place,' Queen Ginevra said quietly. Uncertainty played across her features, making her seem all too young to be facing such a dilemma. 'And while I appreciate the irony of the situation, we cannot treat the target as a "kid". He is, for all intents and purposes, their god. Whether we believe it or no, it is their faith in that which now binds them, and leads them to war.'

Ferius shook her head and stamped out her smoking reed on the surface of the table. Torian Libri didn't appear to like that particular display of disrespect for the throne.

'Stare all you want, girl,' Ferius said. 'That snake-charmin'' of yours ain't gonna get you nowhere with me. Won't work on the kid neither.' She snorted, 'Parlour tricks for simple minds,' and absently gestured to a spot about four feet away where Reichis was now seated on the floor gazing up at Torian longingly.

'Gonna eat that stupid tongue of yours, Argosi,' he muttered dreamily, still entranced by the marshal's eyes.

But Ferius and Torian weren't done posturing, apparently. My mentor leaned in closer. 'And the answer to the question I see written all over your face is: no.'

'"No" what?' Torian asked.

'No, you can't take me. Couldn't have taken the kid either, if it weren't for him lettin' you take advantage of his trustin' nature.'

How had she known about that?

Ferius gave me a sideways grin, somehow knowing that would be the question on my mind. 'Marshals love to brag, kid. Especially about one of their own beating a famous outlaw in a fair fight.'

'It wasn't a—'

She turned back to Torian. 'Now listen up, girl. Either you slide that little knife of yours back in its sheath or I'm gonna whup you up and down this throne room until you start singin' the Argosi anthem note for note.'

'There's an Argosi anthem?' I asked.

'I'll write one for the occasion.'

Before Torian could reply, the queen rose. 'That will be enough, both of you. This gathering was clearly a mistake. Leave us now, Lieutenant Libri, Lady Ferius.'

'I ain't no la—' Ferius stopped and swore in a language I didn't recognise. 'You did that on purpose.'

163

The queen kept a smile from her lips, but not very convincingly. 'Something your arta loquit would have told you were you not a little too hot under the collar, which is why I wish to speak with Kellen in private now.'

'Your Majesty,' Torian began, 'the law forbids—'

'There's an antechamber at the back of the sanctum with refreshments. I will summon you both when I have further need of you, assuming either of you is still alive by then.'

Neither of them looked particularly happy about the situation, but they complied nonetheless.

Once the queen and I were alone – at least as alone as we were ever going to be – she took my hands in hers. 'I'm sorry about your mother, Kellen.'

I stiffened. 'That's kind of you, Your Majesty.'

'What's wrong?'

'Nothing,' I said. 'Could we . . . ? That is, it seems there are more urgent matters we need to discuss.'

She held my gaze awhile, but eventually nodded. One of the things I've always liked about the queen is that she never shirks her duty, no matter how unpleasant. 'Kellen Argos, it is my royal command that you travel to the Berabesq lands, sneak into their capital and then use whatever tricks or ruses are available to you in order to break into their most sacred temple. You will find this young god of theirs, Kellen.'

'And when I do?'

Back when a group of nobles had tried to take the throne from her, in the midst of all the chaos and bloodshed, when a particularly nasty fellow who called himself a white binder was controlling me through the shadowblack, it was Queen Ginevra who'd found a way to free my soul. She'd told me not long after that she didn't want me killing for her.

She squeezed my hands tightly. 'Do what must be done, Kellen. Do the right thing.'

'What's that supposed to mean?'

'Exactly what I said.' She held my gaze a moment longer than was natural. 'Do you understand?'

Arta loquit is more than the skill of eloquence. It's the art of listening. In this way it is closest to arta precis – the Argosi talent for perception. *Do you understand?* The queen had asked, and in that question had encoded much more than the words themselves would allow.

I spoke quietly then. 'If I refuse to go, or if you fail to command me to go, the Murmurers will simply send someone else – someone who would get the job done.'

She nodded.

I glanced towards the antechamber. 'Torian.'

'She would be an obvious choice. Certainly more likely to follow through on their orders.'

'But they like the idea of sending me because I'm far easier to disavow than any other imperial agent. I'm not even Daroman, after all, and I'm a former outlaw to boot.' Something darker occurred to me then. 'I imagine it helps everyone's cause that the Berabesq appear to have murdered my mother.'

'I would never use th—'

'None of that is why you want me in particular to go, because I think we both know I'm . . . unreliable as assassins go.'

'Entirely unreliable,' she said, a small smile breaking through her composure. 'But you have other virtues.'

'Torian says I have a pretty face. Is that what you meant?'

'Don't make me laugh!' she hissed. 'And you know that's not what I meant, so stop teasing me.'

165

I did, in fact, know exactly what she meant. She was sending me because she was convinced I was the only person she could trust to find out the truth before I committed a murder on her behalf, and just maybe find a way through this mess that didn't involve assassination.

All this time, the queen had still been squeezing my hands so tightly I was surprised at her strength. Tears had begun to form in the corners of her eyes. It took me a moment to understand why.

The Argosi say that no one can ever see all the paths in front of them – that there's always one more than you believe. But right now every road I could envision led away from the queen. If I refused the mission, I'd have to leave. The Murmurers would never allow me to stay in her service. If I went to Makhan Mebab – and odds were pretty good I'd get caught long before I even made it past the Berabesq border – if I actually managed to sneak into that temple and somehow murder their god, I'd be the most reviled man in the history of the Berabesq theocracy. I could never set foot in Darome again or would risk starting up a whole new war. Of course, the most likely outcome was that I'd die long before that would happen.

And if somehow I survived all of this?

'I can never come back,' I said at last. 'Whatever happens, people will be hunting me and Reichis all over this continent. I'll never be able to set foot in Darome again.'

The queen was silent, but even she couldn't hide the tears sliding down her cheeks. 'What about Torian? You and she—'

'Twelve years of age is perhaps a bit young to be playing matchmaker, Your Majesty.'

My attempt to lighten her mood provoked the opposite

response. 'Oh, because your extra years have brought you so much wisdom in matters of love? Pining away for that charm-caster girl from your clan? How convenient this must all be for you, tutor of cards, that you now have the perfect excuse to abandon my service the moment the Berabesq matter is resolved so that you can go off in search of this "Nephenia" who has such a tight rein on your heart, despite clearly having better things to do than be with you!'

It was an impressive display of outrage, and the closest thing to a temper tantrum I'd ever seen from her. She almost reminded me of Shalla for a moment there, which made sense, because my sister only ever talked this way when she was afraid of losing me.

'My entire life I've felt inadequate, Your Majesty. Weaker and less clever than my sister, nowhere near as wise and determined as my mother. Even as a young boy I knew I'd never be half the man my father was.' I brought Ginevra's hand to my lips. 'Until I entered your service and, for a little while, I found looking in the mirror every morning wasn't so bad after all.'

'Then come back to us!' she cried, pulling me to her. 'No matter what happens out there, I'll protect you. I'm the queen, remember?'

I gave no reply, just kept my arms around the twelve-year-old girl with the two-thousand-year-old spirit and the freshly broken heart. One of the things Ferius had taught me is that fighting sorrow is like boxing your shadow. No matter how hard you hit it, the heartache keeps coming back for more. I glanced over to the far end of the sanctum and the open door to the antechamber. Torian Libri was there, keeping an eye on us from afar. Somehow even in the disapproval of her

167

gaze I saw that the queen had been right about us. If I'd stayed here, we would have ended up a couple, even if we'd likely never fall in love, just as I'd likely live out my days in Ginevra's palace, even though it would never be my home.

I guess this is how you find these things out.

Very gently I pulled away from the queen's embrace and gave a subtle twitch of my fingers to signal to Reichis that it was time to go. He ambled over and hopped up onto the queen's lap for just a moment, allowing her to stroke his fur before I picked him up and put him on my shoulder.

I reached into the pocket of my coat and retrieved the envelope I'd so cavalierly held out to Arex earlier. I left it on the table in front of the queen and, as I'd breached just about every other rule of royal protocol already, I leaned down and kissed the top of Ginevra's head. 'Farewell, Your Majesty,' I said.

21

The Summons

I left the throne room shaken, unsettled at what I was leaving behind, almost ashamed over the joy I felt at seeing Ferius Parfax again.

'Argosi don't collect nothin' but dust and scars,' she said, watching me closely.

The late hour had emptied the palace halls of the infestation of visiting nobles and courtiers, who'd now moved onto whatever nightly intrigues were in fashion this season. It was only the faint pinch in Ferius's voice that drew my attention to the limp she'd been trying to hide.

'Don't start on me, kid,' she said.

'What happened?'

'Just had a run of bad luck is all.' She stopped to reach into her waistcoat in search of a smoking reed that apparently wasn't there. 'Say, kid, you don't suppose anybody in this fine city of yours would have—'

'The Jan'Tep don't smoke.'

She glanced around the empty hall with a pained yet hopeful expression. 'Maybe one of them fancy courtiers travellin' with the queen?'

'Pipes are the fashion in the Daroman court these days, I'm afraid.'

Ferius sighed. 'Barbarians. Everywhere I go, kid, nothing but barbarians.'

Her glib tone only served to remind me of the precariousness of her situation in this city. Years ago Ferius had beaten the hells out of Tennat and his brothers – to say nothing of the inconvenience she'd caused their father. The entire house of Ra would be after her the second they found out she was here.

'What are you doing in the Jan'Tep territories, Ferius?'

Her reply was a little too smooth. 'Oh, you know. Following the Way of Wind like always. Reckoned I'd pay my respects to your mama.'

I reached into my pocket for the cards Bene'maat had sent me, curious what Ferius would make of them, but the sound of footsteps alerted us to a Sha'Tep servant walking down the long hallway towards us. I didn't recognise him, despite noting the sigils of my own house on the shoulder of his long clerk's coat. That wasn't in itself surprising – after my uncle's rebellion years ago, my father would have had to replace any number of his household servants.

Without so much as a bow the clerk said to me, 'You have been summoned by the mage sovereign.' He handed me a folded note that repeated exactly what he'd just said.

Reichis snarled at him. The squirrel cat has an unsympathetic relationship with servants. First, because he can't seem to tell the difference between servitude and slavery, and second, because he considers murdering anyone who calls himself your master to be a moral imperative.

My people don't typically rely on servants to deliver messages. Given the number of spells one can use for communication

170

within a city like ours, having somebody walk around with a piece of paper searching for its intended recipient is a waste of time. However, casting spells within the house of a guest is considered poor form. I suppose my father was showing respect to Queen Ginevra – which told me he was far more keen on this alliance than he pretended.

Ferius positively beamed at the clerk. 'You mean my old buddy Ke'heops?' She made a show of glancing around the hallway. 'Where's he at? Me and him have a wagon-load of catching up to do!'

I wondered if it were a sign of the Sha'Tep's receiving better treatment these days that the clerk felt comfortable looking down his nose at Ferius. 'You are not invited, Argosi. Only Ke'helios.'

'Ke-what-now?' she asked, looking at me.

'Long story,' I replied, then noticed the twitch in Ferius's grin. 'Which you already know, apparently.'

She chuckled. 'Don't give me that look, kid. Gotta let a body have fun where it can.'

'The mage sovereign awaits,' the clerk reminded us.

While I don't share Reichis's disdain for those forced into lives of service by chains, economics or societal convention, neither did I appreciate the way this guy kept sneering at Ferius. 'Tell Ke'heops I'll wander by in an hour or so.'

'Your presence is not requested in an hour. It is expected now.'

I patted him on the shoulder. 'Don't worry. My father is accustomed to me disappointing him.'

The clerk spun on his heel and managed to stomp down the hall with remarkable aplomb.

'Why do you suppose your daddy's so fired up to see you this late at night?' Ferius asked.

171

'Tradition,' I replied. 'After a Jan'Tep funeral the family assembles to grieve privately and fulfil any last requests of the deceased.'

'Sounds innocent enough. Sweet almost.'

'Yeah.'

'So probably a trap then?'

'Yep.'

22

The Athenaeum

There's a tavern that serves foreigners not far from my family's ancestral home. I left Ferius there with Reichis. While she doesn't speak squirrel cat, she has a reliable intuition about what he means to say. For his part, Reichis loves to gamble, and one of his many aspirations in life – after killing off the Jan'Tep, ridding the world of crocodiles and one day becoming a giant, skinbag-devouring demon – is to finally beat Ferius at cards.

'Cheater!' he accused in an angry chitter. His paws, though extremely dextrous, aren't all that good for holding cards. His frustration sent his hand flying across the table. The other patrons in the tavern's common room glanced over nervously. Watching an Argosi and a squirrel cat play cards is funny only up to the point where the beast starts snarling in a way that reminds any Jan'Tep in the room why nekhek are considered demon spawn.

'He just accuse me of cheatin'?' Ferius asked.

'What else?'

I motioned for the nervous waiter to bring the platter of food I'd ordered for the two of them. Reichis immediately snatched the biggest piece of lamb between his two paws and started chewing noisily while giving Ferius dirty looks.

She made a show of being affronted. 'I'll have you know, sir, that I'm as honest as the day is long. Double-dealin' *ain't* the way of the Argosi!'

She proceeded to deliver an extremely conspicuous wink.

'Did you see that?' Reichis demanded, dropping the hunk of lamb from his jaws. 'She just winked! The Argosi's lying!'

'He thinks you winked,' I informed her.

'Me? I did no such thing.'

She winked again, even more atrociously this time.

'There!' Reichis insisted. 'She did it again! She's been cheating this whole time, Kellen!'

I translated the accusation, though it was hardly necessary.

'Well now,' Ferius began, leaning in to whisper conspiratorially to Reichis, 'maybe it's time I taught you how the professionals do it, squirrel cat.'

For a second Reichis just stared at her, entranced by her words. Finally a nasty squirrel cat grin appeared on his muzzle. 'Oh yeah?'

Abruptly he looked away, towards the window at the far end of the tavern, and sniffed at the air. He'd been doing it a lot since we returned to my city.

'What is it?' I asked.

'Nothing.'

'That's like the eighteenth time you've reacted like you smelled something important.'

'Just thought I caught the scent of another . . . It was nothing.' He went back to peering intently at his cards – his way of telling me to drop it.

'I'm out of here,' I declared, heading for the door. 'My loving family will be expecting me.'

Ferius looked over at Reichis. 'What time you reckon me and you oughta go rescue him?'

The squirrel cat chuckled, delighted to be in on the joke.

I was going to say something caustic, but it occurred to me that there really was a decent chance I'd need to be rescued soon, so I left them to their cards and cheating lesson. 'Maybe give it an hour?' I suggested.

Ferius shuffled the deck of cards. 'Sure, kid. See you in thirty minutes.'

'You're late,' Shalla said, greeting me in the arched doorway outside our family home. She wore a red satin grieving gown – a Daroman tradition uncommon to our own people and distinctly at odds with her longstanding belief that the customs of foreigners were by nature uncivilised. Perhaps spending the past year as head diplomat of the Jan'Tep arcanocracy to the royal court of Darome had given her a more cosmopolitan outlook.

'I informed Father's clerk I'd be here in an hour,' I said.

'You're still late.' The slim fingers of her right hand played at the glittering gemstones sewn along the neckline of her gown. Grieving gowns are meant to be modest garments that convey sorrow and solemnity, not low-cut affairs that accentuate the wearer's curves. The preposterously expensive fabric Shalla had chosen shimmered under the glow-glass lanterns overhead. The soft light cast a halo around the golden hair arrayed about her face in an elaborate arrangement of curls and tresses designed to draw attention to her cheekbones.

Life in Darome hasn't changed you at all, has it, sister?

Shalla, the girl who disdained outsiders as fools, had simply grown into Sha'maat, the woman who used them as puppets in her petty political schemes.

Often as not, I was the puppet in question.

'Oh, go ahead, brother,' she said with a sigh, noting my gaze. 'Make some snide little comment about my appearance if it makes you feel better about your own shabby state.'

That last jibe was unnecessarily cruel, though I supposed I'd earned it when I'd intentionally gone to the trouble of changing out of my proper court clothes before coming here. Still, I'd worn my good travelling shirt – the one with only a single hole in the right sleeve. And the knee of my trousers was freshly patched. I'd even brushed my hat. 'I did have a nice metaphor about excessively expensive frames around cheap paintings all set to go,' I admitted. 'But you've taken the fun out of it, so maybe I should just ask why, for the memorial of our mother's passing, you're dressed like a comfort artisan in a low-rent saloon.'

'We're not here for a memorial,' she said, and pushed open the door. 'Now are you coming inside or are you going to stand there all night glaring at me?'

I gestured for her to go through first. She rolled her eyes and led the way.

I paused beneath the archway to check my powder holsters, throwing cards and castradazi coins. The reason I'd been late was because I'd spent the past half-hour skulking in the shadows across the street. I'd told myself this was because I'd been – very prudently – casing the place to figure out if an ambush awaited me. That was a lie of course. Whatever traps awaited me here were more likely familial than supernatural. The simple truth was that, despite my frequent stays in various jails, prisons and dungeons all across the continent, nothing scared me more than the prospect of stepping inside my childhood home.

When I was a boy, I'd always assumed ours had been a comfortable, though not extravagant lifestyle. A few years wandering the long roads and seeing how other people lived had quickly cured me of that misapprehension.

The humblest thing you could say about my father's house was that it was a touch too small to be a palace. After all, a dozen servants was barely a sufficient number to run the household of a family of four. How could anyone get by with only two high-ceilinged libraries, the walls lined with shelves stacked with expensive books and glass cases filled with rare scrolls? Of course, that wasn't counting the expansive athenaeum used exclusively for the housing of our ancestral records.

My parents, quite naturally, each required their own marble-floored sanctum for meditation, these in addition to their private studies specially designed to suit their personal interests in astronomy, healing and military strategy.

As for the mansion's exterior? Well, when you've already got two walled gardens, what's one more? You've got to put those statues of your less renowned ancestors *somewhere*.

'Are you quite all right, brother?' Shalla asked, staring up at me as we walked through the wide central hallway of the main floor.

'I'm fine. Why?'

'Your hands are shaking.'

I guess I forgot to mention the one special chamber on the top floor – the one with copper- and silver-lined walls where my father practises his most complex spellwork, the one with the heavy oak table to which I'd once been strapped for days while he and my mother used molten metallic inks to inscribe counter-sigils into the tattooed bands on my fore-arms. The burns had been the least painful part of the process.

Breathe in emptiness, I told myself.

Shalla led me to the family athenaeum. The circular room, modest in size – which is to say, not much bigger than a Sha'Tep family's entire house – was ringed by sandstone statues of those of our ancestors no doubt too important to be kept outside. At the centre was a large marble table with a short lectern built into each of its four sides to facilitate the careful reading of fragile texts. In my entire childhood I'd never been allowed in this room.

'You came,' Ke'heops said, looming over one of the lecterns, fingers turning the yellowed pages of a worn, cloth-bound book. In contrast to Shalla, he was dressed in austere grey robes of the sort mages wear during meditation and struck me as remarkably plain given the ostentatious surroundings. Still he projected a kingly demeanour, as if destiny was a glow that emanated from beneath his skin.

Maybe some people really are born to rule.

'You've got fifteen minutes,' I said.

He didn't bother to look up. 'You'll stay the night. You and I both owe your mother's memory that much courtesy at least.'

'I'm afraid we may have very different estimations of any debts I might owe this family, Father.'

I'd have expected him to turn his considerable capacity for ire on me, but it was Shalla who bore the brunt of his outrage. 'You see now, daughter?' he asked, glaring at her. 'Always you cajole and beg me to reconcile with him, just as your mother did. "A father's duty", the two of you insisted over and over.' His forefinger jabbed towards me with such force my hands instinctively went to the clasps of my powder holsters. 'What about *his* duty? Not once has Ke'helios shown the slightest concern for the interests of our house.'

'That's not entirely fair,' I said casually. 'I've made every reasonable effort to undermine them wherever possible, Father.'

The three Jan'Tep bands on each of his forearms flared to life. 'Because I permitted it. Bene'maat insisted I give you the freedom to tramp your way through the world, that I allow you to pretend at being an Argosi or an outlaw or whatever clownish games you chose to play. That ends tonight.'

I flipped open the flaps of my holsters.

Well, this got real ugly real fast.

'Father, please . . .' Shalla said.

She starts that sentence a lot, I've noticed, but never seems to finish it. Her eyes went to me, pleading for me to be sensible and back down. Maybe she was right. One thing I've learned during my travels is that the world is never quite big enough to get away from your family. That doesn't mean you shouldn't try though.

I bowed deeply to my father then my sister. 'Well, it's been a delight as always, Ke'heops, Sha'maat. I'll bid you both a good night now.'

I turned to leave, but when I reached for the doorknob, my hand missed. I tried a second time. A third. No matter which angle I tried or even if I attempted to overshoot the knob in any given direction, all I got for my efforts was to keep smacking the ends of my fingers into the hard surface of the door. My father usually goes for iron binding spells, so his use of silk magic was aimed at making me lose my temper.

'Drop the bewilderment spell, Father.'

I heard the tell-tale hum of a shield spell behind me. Ke'heops was now simultaneously holding a silk confounding spell *and* summoning an ember cocoon around himself. Not one in a hundred mages can do that. This was his way of telling me that no matter how many tricks I'd learned in my travels, no matter how cunning I considered myself, he could still take me down, and would always be able to do so.

He's waiting for you to try to blast him with your powders, the cold, calculating part of my mind warned me. *To him you're just a petulant child about to throw a tantrum.*

My father had miscalculated though. His choice of the ancestral athenaeum for this little reunion had been a mistake. The instant I tossed my red and black powders in the air and formed the somatic shapes with my fingers, I'd aim the spell not at him, but at the glass cases that held our family's most precious texts. A man obsessed with his own lineage couldn't stand to witness the obliteration of his ancestors' artefacts. He'd have no choice but to extend his ember shield to cover half the room, and that would force him to drop the silk bewilderment spell.

'Brother, no!' Shalla shouted, no doubt guessing that whatever trick I had up my sleeve was unlikely to improve relations between us. 'Our people are in danger! We have to think like a family now!'

'Thanks, but I prefer my own,' I said, taking advantage of the interruption to surreptitiously pass a hand across the hidden pocket in the hem of my shirt and get my castradazi coins ready. 'You may remember them. The lunatic Argosi who loves taking down Jan'Tep arseholes and the

180

two-foot furry one who likes to eat their eyeballs afterwards? Probably best for all of us if I leave before they come looking for me.'

I turned to go, but the silk confounding spell in the air between me and the door was as strong as ever.

'Is this the day we dance then, Father?' I asked.

First the feint with the powders, I thought. *Then throw a half-dozen of the steel cards. Go for the eyes. He'll protect them with his shield, but that'll give you time to pull the coins. He's never seen me use those. Blind him with the luminary coin, then bind the fugitive coin to the rest of my cards, toss it, and use the chaos of razor-sharp pieces of steel flying through the air to—*

'See how he scowls at me?' Ke'heops demanded of my sister. 'How am I to trust him with our people's future when his only desire is to prove he can beat me?'

'Tell him!' Shalla shouted. I wasn't sure who she was talking to until she grabbed my father's arm – an absolutely insane thing to do when the two of us were squaring off like this. 'Stop trying to control your son and explain to him what's happening to us!'

She's given me the advantage, I thought. *He's off-guard. If I time it just right, I can take him.*

I hesitated, which is suicide for a spellslinger facing off against a lord magus. But Shalla wasn't done with him. 'Now, Father,' she said, a rare defiance suffusing her words, 'tell your son the truth, or I swear that I too will leave this place behind.'

Was she even aware of the way the tattooed metallic bands around her forearms were blazing so bright that Ke'heops and I were being drowned in the multitude of colours? That much raw magic being drawn into the air was breaking apart his

181

shield spell, to say nothing of the headaches that threatened to have both of us bleeding from the eyes and ears.

Just how powerful are you, sister?

'Enough,' Ke'heops said at last, putting up his hands and banishing his own spells. He waited for Shalla to draw back her magic before locking eyes with me. 'Let him hear the truth then, and we shall see whether your brother intends to save our people, or by his wilful disregard make himself the cause of our destruction.'

182

23

The Riddle

My father is a big man. Tall, powerfully built. The unbendable iron in his stance makes it impossible to be in a room with him and not feel small by comparison. Yet now he slumped, eyes downcast, and for the first time reduced to mere mortality. 'I . . . I'm not entirely sure how to begin,' he said. The deep baritone that used to rattle the windows of my room when I'd disobeyed him was barely more than a whisper. 'Perhaps it is easier to show you.'

He stepped behind the table and drew from his robes a small leather bag like the ones he'd brought with him to the Chamber of Murmurs.

'I've already seen this trick, Father,' I reminded him.

'This is neither an illusion nor a confounding spell.' He poured pale blue sand onto the table, the grains spreading across the white marble surface, making it appear as if I were staring up into the sky on a cloudy day.

Sand magic – which only occasionally involves actual sand – is the fundamental force used in the manipulation of time. Its workings are incredibly complex, but even a first-year initiate learns that prediction, prognostication and the like are nothing more than superstitious nonsense.

'You must really have a low opinion of my knowledge of magic to expect me to believe you can divine the future now, Father.'

The bands on his arms first glistened then glowed. His hands weaved back and forth above the table as his fingers formed a series of complex somatic shapes. 'Divination implies foretelling events through insight into the unknowable. This spell operates within the mind of the mage, taking his awareness of the past and present to infer the future. It bends the pathways of his thoughts to calculate possibilities and probabilities, deducing the inevitable outcomes that will come to pass unless the historical forces shaping them are opposed.'

I would've pointed out that none of that sounded any more credible than pulling out the guts of a dead sheep and looking for auguries within its entrails, except for the fact that what my father had just described was distressingly similar to the underlying theory of an Argosi deck: by painting each card to reflect the hierarchies of power and influence within a civilisation, the Argosi attempt to extrapolate the most likely effects of those structures on the lives of its citizens.

Sweat appeared on Ke'heops's brow as he uttered each syllable of the invocation. It was like watching someone trying to walk through waist-high mud in a hurricane. Finally the grains of sand began to move, swirling around one another until they settled, forming miniature cities that spread out across the table. Seven cities for the seven clans of the Jan'Tep.

'Imagine a paradox,' Ke'heops began. 'A secret kept by all yet unknown to any.'

'Riddles, Father?' I asked. 'That's not like you.'

184

In addition to card tricks, actors and his son, my father's never had much patience for riddles. This was the kind of gibberish I'd expect from Ferius – something that sounded ridiculous until you realised it somehow made perfect –

'Wait,' I said before Ke'heops could explain. 'A secret kept by all – you mean something known only to the councils of lords magi, right?'

Ke'heops shook his head as more shapes appeared, men and women in the elaborate robes of clan princes. 'Not even them. Only the seven princes and their closest advisors.'

Even on a good day my arta precis isn't the best, but I'd been getting a lot of practice lately. 'A discovery made by each prince separately, but because they never shared it with their fellow rulers, none of them realised it was happening to all of them. A *secret kept by all yet unknown to any.*'

'Correct.'

'It must have been something that shamed or weakened them,' I went on, gazing at each of the little blue princes on the table as they turned away from the others. 'Something they couldn't share for fear the information would be used against them by their rivals.'

My father gave me a weary smile. 'Shall I show you the rest, or do you intend to deduce it all yourself?'

'Show me.'

He snapped his fingers and the figures broke apart. He whispered and the grains of sand swirled together again until they began to form new shapes. An oasis rose up from the centre of the table, the fount of raw magic ringed by seven columns marked in the sigils of iron, ember, breath, blood, silk, sand and shadow.

Ke'heops raised his hands even higher, hovering them above

185

like a puppet master pulling invisible strings. Thousands of grains of sand followed, coming together into the effigy of a man, his limbs outstretched, strands of raw magic winding around his forearms.

'A mage is forged by three forces,' Ke'heops said. 'Years of exposure to the oasis, careful training of the mind and natural talent – which cannot be learned, but must arise in the blood.'

'The difference between Jan'Tep and Sha'Tep,' I said. 'Between those who rule and those who serve.'

A flash of my father's customary irritation flashed across his features. 'Between those who serve our people with their magic and those who serve through their labours. We all serve, Ke'helios. Every one of us.'

'Our numbers are small, brother,' Shalla said, stepping in as always to calm the tensions between me and our father. 'The Jan'Tep way of life is preserved not through military might but through our magic – that which makes us unique. Special.'

'Powerful,' my father corrected. 'It is by virtue of the strength of our spells that other nations think twice before seeking to take from us that which is ours.'

I didn't bother bringing up the fact that the oases originally belonged to the Mahdek, until our ancestors massacred them. My people are touchy on that subject.

My father brought one hand low then high again, causing a gust of sand to fly up to form the shape of a second mage – a woman – who stood next to the first as they joined hands. 'The wedding of magical bloodlines,' Ke'heops said. 'The essence of Jan'Tep society. For three hundred years we believed the survival of our people lay in the careful cultivation of such

186

unions.' He clapped his hands together and the sand couple fell apart. 'We were wrong.'

Something caught in my throat. My father's casual dismissal had just contradicted the fundamental premise our parents had imbued into Shalla and me since we were born. 'You were *wrong*?' I demanded, surprising even myself by the vehemence in my voice. Almost my entire life I'd believed my weakness at magic was due to a fault in my own character. 'Wrong how, exactly?'

My father spread his hands wide again, and the air above the table filled with hundreds of tiny sand figures. Men and women, boys and girls, and those who chose neither definition. 'The talent for magic lies in the blood,' he said, as a paltry few of the figures began to glow while the majority remained dull and lifeless. 'But this gift is a . . . a selfish thing, it seems.'

He rotated his hand clockwise as if turning the dial of a lock. The sand figures began whirling in the air, pairing up together. When one with the talent was matched with one without, about half the time the combined form still retained the same glow of magic. But when both showed the talent, the combination was dimmer. Weaker.

'You're telling me that breeding those with the greatest talent actually *weakens* the magic of their offspring,' I whispered; disbelief had taken the very air from my lungs.

'There are exceptions, of course.' Ke'heops nodded to Shalla. 'It is a question of probabilities and thus difficult to measure with precision. When I became mage sovereign over all the clans, I demanded all the archives of house lineages so that I could better plan for the future of the great houses.'

That my father would believe it his right to dictate the

marriages of every citizen for the good of his people was barely a surprise. I glanced over at the plain bound book he'd been reading when Shalla had first brought me into the athenaeum. 'You calculated the change in the number of bands sparked by the offspring of each generation?'

He nodded. 'The contamination of the blood is slow, of course. The trend manifests only across many generations. That's why none of us understood what was happening until it was too late.'

Unite the strong with the strong, the weak to the weak. It was such a pattern of Jan'Tep life that when I was first approaching my mage's trials and my magic had begun to fade, I took consolation in watching Nephenia struggle with her own spells. A small, petty part knew that the worse she did, the better my chances of one day convincing her to marry me.

Yeah, I know. I was a lousy kid, all right? In case you haven't noticed, I come from a pretty lousy people.

'Change the pattern,' I said, the idea striking me like blast of ember. 'When mages first travelled to this continent in search of a new source of raw magic, they came from many different nations. Jan'Tep civilisation has never been based on ethnicity, but our shared culture. Open the schools of magic to foreigners again! Seek out those in Darome, Gitabria, Zhuban and everywhere else who show an aptitude for magic, and bring them here!'

The answer felt so obvious to me now, so right, you'd almost think I cared about the future of my people.

'We can't,' Shalla said. 'Outsiders can't—'

'Oh, for the sake of our ancestors,' I swore, 'let go of your prejudice for once and—'

'Shut up!' she shouted, fists clenched, angry flares of magic sparking across her bands. 'You idiot! You think Father hasn't thought of that already? You think such an obvious solution somehow eluded everyone but you?'

'Then why not do it?' I asked.

It was my father who answered, speaking in the dull, flat tones of a soldier surrendering the battlefield. 'Because war is coming. I have had to sign a treaty with Darome to supplement their armies with our mages lest the Berabesq overrun us all. Once the battle begins . . .' He began flicking his fingers in the air. One by one the tiny glowing figures dimmed, their magic disappearing as they fell apart into grains of sand once again, the brilliant blue draining away as they fell as motes of dust upon the table. 'There will be too few of us left to hold our own territories.'

'Those with the talent, like me, will be forced to marry the scions of powerful foreign houses,' Shalla said, 'so that their family lines will produce mages loyal to their own nations. We will be absorbed into their societies. Magic will continue to exist on this continent, but the Jan'Tep culture, our way of life, will be no more.'

All this time my father had avoided my gaze, but at last our eyes met across the table. He didn't speak, didn't utter a word, yet in that moment I knew why Shalla had brought me here. And just how badly I'd been suckered.

'All this,' I said, slapping a hand across the dust-covered surface of the table, sending up a dirty brown cloud between us, 'this dark prophecy of our people's future, all to give me one more push to sneak off into Berabesq and murder a child?'

'To save our people,' he replied, but he was talking to Shalla

189

now. 'Look in his eyes, daughter. Tell me you find something in there beyond disdain and distrust. He has not an ounce of duty inside him, not one shred of love for his people.'

He stepped out from behind the table. My hands drifted to my powder holsters.

'Can you not see?' Ke'heops demanded of his daughter. 'Even now his twisted thoughts turn to murder. But does he seek the blood of our enemies? Never! Only the death of his father.'

He came closer and I had to step back to keep enough distance to use my weapons. His own hands were loose at his sides, ready to cast any number of spells for which I'd have no counter. A quick, brutal first strike was my only hope.

'And what crime did we commit that was so heinous as to justify these endless retaliations?' he asked. 'We counterbanded him. We sought to end the threat of the shadowblack that will one day eat his soul. And for that he would sacrifice the future of every other Jan'Tep.'

I took a pinch of the red and black powders, my eyes locked on my father's hands. The moment they so much as twitched, I would fire the spell.

'Kellen, don't,' Shalla warned. Now the bands around her forearms were gleaming too.

'Ke'helios,' my father corrected, seemingly more angered by this than the fact that I was about to blast him. 'I have named him Ke'helios. He is a son of the House of Ke, and by the blood and magic of my ancestors, this is the day he begins acting like it!'

I backed up again, nearly tripping on the threshold of the doorway out of the athenaeum. 'I'm walking out of here,

Father. I don't think Mother would want me to kill you on the day of her funeral.'

He sneered at me. 'You have no idea what your mother wanted, you craven boy. You wouldn't believe me if I told you.'

'Father, stop,' Shalla said. 'Just tell him. It's not too late to—'

But it was too late, and she knew it, because my father's lips had already begun to form the first syllable of a spell that would either incapacitate or kill me, and I wasn't going to let either happen. My powders were already in the air as my hands formed the somatic shapes of my own spell.

But nothing happened.

In the periphery of my vision, I could see my sister whispering syllables that echoed around the athenaeum over and over, becoming neither louder nor softer, but filling the air like an ocean of breath. The spell materialising on my father's fingertips froze like a candle-flame trapped in ice.

I watched, paralysed as she made quick, subtle movements with her fingers in the air, tweaking the effects of the spell piece by piece. I found myself able to speak again, but not move. 'Let me go, Shalla.'

'Sha'maat,' she said, almost sadly. 'How many times have I told you? My name is Sha'maat now.'

She made another adjustment, and my father was released from her spell. 'Say nothing,' he warned her before leaving the room. 'We do this my way.'

'Sister,' I said, fear rising up from the pit of my stomach like a worm slithering through my lungs, sticking in my throat.

'Just try to relax, brother,' she said. 'This . . . This is for the best, I promise.'

191

No good has ever come from those words.

My father came back into the room, bringing with him a large wooden tray laden with a set of burning braziers upon which small ceramic dishes bubbled with molten metals. A set of needles were arrayed alongside them. All my arta valar, all those times I'd faced down bounty mages and hired killers, fled as I recognised those instruments.

'No,' I said, but I doubt anyone heard me.

'He'll never forgive me for counter-banding him,' my father said to Sha'maat as he brought the tray closer. 'For spite and revenge, he'll always make himself a threat to my plans. I can't allow that any more.'

'Please,' Shalla begged, seeing the terror in my eyes. 'Just explain to him wh—'

'No!' My father's bellow reverberated along the walls of the athenaeum. 'I am Ke'heops of the House of Ke, Mage Sovereign of the Jan'Tep people! I am done explaining myself to children!'

My sister looked at me with a mute apology in her eyes, proving once again that while she loved us both, she would always obey our father's commands.

I screamed then, a thousand pleas that I knew would not move my father one inch, but which were loud enough that Shalla looked pained when she passed her hand across my face and put me to sleep, my last thought a question I could never seem to answer.

Why do I keep trusting my sister?

24

The Banding

I dreamed of a crowded room, with a dozen faces staring down at me, waiting expectantly as if I were a performer who'd entered the stage only to forget my lines in front of the entire audience.

There was a pressure on my chest. A warm, oddly fuzzy weight that turned out to be Reichis. He was delivering a long, slow growl at everyone around me. Ferius was there too, standing at my left shoulder. Shalla was on the opposite side, glaring at my Argosi mentor. Queen Ginevra watched me with an anxious gaze, ringed by a rather large entourage of guards and marshals, including Torian Libri, who looked very much as if she'd come here in hopes of killing a few people and had thus far been stymied. The mesmerising blue of her eyes was what made me realise I wasn't dreaming.

I was lying on my back on the hard surface of the athen-aeum's central table. At the end, leaning against one of the columns a couple of feet away, was my father. His face was paler than usual. Lines furrowed his brow, making him appear older than I'd ever seen him before.

'You're all right, Kellen,' the queen said, glancing from my father to me. 'We're here for you.'

'My brother will be disoriented for some time yet,' Shalla said, attempting to take control of the situation. 'All of you standing around here gawking at him accomplishes nothing.'

Well, that much was true anyway. My head was so buried in fog it took all my concentration just to separate all the strange sights and sounds that surrounded me like buzzards waiting over a dying deer. 'Keep it down for a second, okay, partner?' I asked Reichis.

'Fine,' he grumbled, settling himself on my chest. 'But if I don't get to kill somebody before this is done, I'm gonna get real irritable.'

'Rest, brother,' Shalla said to me. 'You won't be able to think clearly for a few more hours.'

A familiar chuckle over my left shoulder, like the opening notes of a jaunty tune or perhaps the irritating morning crowing of a rooster, turned my attention to Ferius.

'Show 'em who we are, kid,' she said. 'Show 'em *precisely* who we are.'

Sometimes I love the sound of that voice. But the way she'd said that one word, almost as if were pronounced *pre-cease-ly*, tickled at the back of my brain.

Sounds like 'precis', I thought. *Arta precis.*

Perception.

I propped myself up on my elbows and waited for the dizziness to pass. 'Ferius and Reichis came to rescue me,' I began. 'Only th—'

'*Rescue you?*' my sister demanded. 'From your *family?*'

Though my sister is far cleverer than I am in most ways, irony is frequently lost on her, particularly as it applies to having imprisoned your brother with silk magic only to then be perturbed at accusations of wrong-doing.

194

'When Ferius and Reichis couldn't breach the spells around the house, they went to the queen . . . No, wait.' I nodded at Torian. 'She went to you, didn't she? Because Ferius wouldn't be able to get in to see the queen in the middle of the night by herself.'

'Reckon I could if I set my mind to it,' Ferius said, sounding a little offended.

'Yeah, but that would take too long. Torian doesn't like you, but you knew she'd likely feel guilty over having suckered me into nearly getting executed by the Murmurers back in Darome.'

'The who?' Shalla asked.

'And he wonders why we keep state secrets from mouthy card sharps,' Torian said, but I could tell by the look in her face I was right.

Good to know you've got a conscience in there somewhere, lieutenant.

'You brought a detachment of marshals,' I said, nodding to the men and women surrounding her. 'Only you know enough about magic that I'm guessing at least one of them is a foreign mage disguised as a guard.'

Faces turned towards the marshals' entourage, no doubt trying to guess who the hidden mage was.

'Somebody, please, shut him up,' Torian swore.

Ferius chuckled at that.

'What purpose does this game serve, Argosi?' Shalla asked.

It was a fair question, but Ferius ignored her. 'Go on, kid,' she encouraged me. 'You're doin' just fine.'

'You decided you had to go get Queen Ginevra,' I said. 'You knew even my father wouldn't dare refuse a foreign monarch searching for one of her royal tutors. It would be a diplomatic nightmare.' I glanced over at Torian, who turned away. 'The lieutenant refused at first. She'd never let the queen walk into a dangerous situation like this. I imagine she had her marshals surround you.' I took them in properly for the first time, and saw more than a couple of bruises blooming around their faces and cuts on their hands that looked a lot like the kind you get when a razor-sharp steel card hits you.

A slow rumbling on my chest told me Reichis was getting irritated.

'So you distracted the marshals while Reichis slipped past them to get to the queen.'

'Finally,' the squirrel cat growled. 'I *did* save your life, you know.'

'This is all nonsense,' my sister declared. Her gaze kept going to my father.

She doesn't want him embarrassed like this in public, I thought. *Tough luck, sister.*

'Ke'heops granted the queen entry, of course, though I suppose that means he'd already done what he came to do.'

'What is the point of all this?' Shalla demanded. 'If he wants to know wh—'

'He ain't the one who needs to know, girl,' Ferius said. 'You do. You all do.'

Queen Ginevra stepped forward. 'Forgive me, Path of the Wild Daisy, but I too am somewhat confounded by this . . . demonstration.'

Reflexively, Ferius reached into her waistcoat for a smoking reed, only to come away disappointed. 'Like bein' stranded in the desert without a drop of water.' She turned her attention back to the others. 'All of you have been pushin' the kid here to go do your dirty work, out there in the Berabesq lands where your worst fears are coming true. But you act like he's an arrow you can just aim and fire and wait to see what damage it does to your enemies. That ain't the Argosi way. It ain't Kellen's way.'

'Great,' Torian muttered. 'Another speech about the Argosi.'

Reichis giggled at that.

Ferius ignored them both. 'The boy ain't like all o' you. Ain't like me neither. But we're all gonna have to trust him when the time comes. Just reckoned it might help for you to see that he ain't half as dumb as he seems, which makes him twice as smart as you lot.'

I was still trying to figure out whether she'd just insulted me, complimented me, insulted everyone else in the room or actually said nothing at all. Some puzzles even arta precis can't solve.

I started to scratch at my right arm, which I now realised was stinging like seven devils. When my parents had counter-banded me, Reichis had rescued me before they could destroy my breath band. It had been my last connection to the magic of my people, and now . . .

Ferius pressed a hand down on my shoulder, preventing me from raising my forearm to see what had been done to it. 'We don't get to decide our fates,' she said quietly. 'Only what meaning we give them.'

It was a warning of sorts. But I already knew the answer. Despite all the incredible things Ferius had taught me, magic still mattered to me a great deal. I raised up my right arm, turning it this way and that to find the source of the stinging.

My breath band was intact. No counter-sigils had been

inscribed to block my access to the magic of air, of communication and the guiding of forces. The Jan'Tep consider breath the weakest and least useful form of magic, but I'd come to adore it in its way. While it could do little on its own, breath, when combined with other things could be useful. Surprising. A trickster's magic.

Ancestors, thank you.

I had just started to breathe a sigh of relief when I noticed something odd on the back of my forearm below the breath band. A small, complex configuration of tattooed copper lines wound inside one of the ugly counter-sigils that had destroyed my ember band. There was a kind of bizarre, twisted geometry about the way these new copper lines interacted with the counter-sigils and the original ones beneath. I kept trying to find the beginnings and endings of lines but the longer I looked, the more confused I became.

'Do not stare at it too long,' Ke'heops warned. 'It can be dangerous to the mind.'

But why would he have needed to inscribe new forms to reinforce the counter-sigils? Unless . . .

'You . . . You didn't bring me here to counter-band me?' I asked.

When my father didn't reply, I forced hopefulness back down. Hope, like despair, only pollutes will, and what I needed right now was a great deal of will.

I sent the first, tentative urgings into my ember band. In the past when I'd tried this, a sickening nausea would overtake me. The harder I pushed, the worse it became, until finally blood would spill from my nose and I would pass out from the pain.

Now, though, something was different. The nausea was still

198

there, but it was weaker . . . Incomplete somehow. I pushed more and more of my strength into the ember band, willing it to spark.

'Don't drive yourself too hard,' Shalla warned. 'Your will has never been all that—'

'Silence, daughter,' Ke'heops said, watching me closely from the end of the table.

Sweat dripped into my eyes, blinding me. I ignored the discomfort, ignored the crowd of people watching me, ignored everything but the copper-coloured sigils on my ember band.

Slowly, ever so slowly, I felt a tingle, like the metallic ink in the tattoos was shifting between icy cold and burning hot, back and forth. The tiniest, briefest flicker of orange-red light shimmered across the one sigil where my father had inscribed over the counter-banding.

I shaped my right hand into the somatic form for the simplest ember spell I'd learned as an initiate – a cantrip really. With any luck, it would ignite a flicker of flame at the end of my fingertip. '*Ure'feres*,' I intoned.

The new sigil of my ember band sparked for an instant, then faded back to a flat, lifeless copper colour.

'I have only corrected the first sigil,' my father said, taking a step closer. 'It will take much time to repair the others, but it is a start.' He looked down on me with a weary smile that spoke of a kind of pride I hadn't seen in him before. 'It is a good start.'

Then my father collapsed on top of me.

199

25

The Price

Strange as it sounds, my first thought was that this was the closest I'd been to my father since before I'd left home. I'm not talking about him poking me with needles dripping with molten-hot metallic inks or casting spells on me, but the simple warmth of one person's skin touching that of another.

I wondered if perhaps he was dead.

'Everyone out!' Sha'maat said.

'We could summon the court physicians,' one of the queen's attendants began.

Raw magic billowed around my sister with a rage that terrified even me. Queen Ginevra, ever protective of her subjects but not entirely of sound mind, stepped in front of the others. 'That will suffice, Sha'maat of the House of Ke.'

My sister's eyes flashed with something more than just irritation at this twelve-year-old girl – monarch or not – defying her. Some part of her knew she could kill everyone in that room with a thought. I'm pretty sure some part of her wanted to.

'Don't,' Ferius said quietly, her hand on my shoulder. My hands had drifted into the powder holsters at my side. 'You're gonna have to trust her one day, kid.'

An odd thing to say. Of course I trusted my sister – almost as far as I could throw her.

The raging fires of Sha'maat's magic settled themselves, first into a pulsating glow of shifting colours, then finally containing themselves once more within the six sparking bands around her forearms, shimmering with the promise of violence should they be awakened once more.

'We will leave you now,' the queen said, signalling for the athenaeum to clear. 'Should you require any assistance—'

'We won't,' Sha'maat said.

The queen nodded as she left. 'As you say.'

Ferius gave my arm a final squeeze, then picked up Reichis and placed him on her shoulder. I'd kind of wondered why the squirrel cat had remained silent throughout Shalla's mystical tantrum. Now I saw all his fur sticking straight out as if he'd been caught up in the static charge of a lightning storm.

'Crazy Jan'Tep skinbag,' he muttered, then added, 'Of all the times for her to *not* put me to sleep . . .'

The crowded chamber emptied out, leaving only myself, my father and Sha'maat.

'Help me get him to his room,' she commanded.

I was still weak from the effects of the banding so it took all my strength just to roll my father off my legs. I had to sit there a while before Shalla and I were able to support his weight between us up to one of the nearby guest rooms. Tall and broad-shouldered, muscled like a soldier, carrying him was like hauling a slab of stone.

'Why not simply use iron magic to make him float?' I asked her.

'You wouldn't understand.'

That was becoming a frequent refrain from my sister. The pinched skin at the corners of her eyes, the slight tremble of her jaw when she'd admonished me, those gave the answer.

She can't focus enough to cast a spell properly, I realised. That show of magic she'd made before the others had been posturing, the growling of a cornered animal. She could summon all the magic she wanted, but in her panicked state she couldn't have cast so much as an initiate's cantrip properly.

Useful information to know for the future.

A petty thought? Maybe, but people have been trying to kill me for pettier reasons lately.

'Lay him on the bed,' she instructed.

We settled him down on the mattress and stretched him out. Sha'maat began murmuring incantations longer and more complex than any I'd learned in all my years as an initiate. The bands for blood and silk on her forearms ignited sporadically at first, sputtering with red and purple sparks.

'What are you doing?' I asked.

She didn't answer – just kept up the steady, uncommonly long incantation, the fingers of her right hand shifting through dozens of somatic forms I didn't recognise.

Colour began to return to our father's face, and his stern features settled into a kind of peacefulness.

'We must give him time to recover,' she said, and bade me follow her out of the room.

'What happened to him?' I asked once we were back in the central foyer of her chambers. 'Is it a . . . malediction like Mother's?'

Shalla gave a short, sharp and very bitter laugh. 'A kind of malediction, I suppose.' Her gaze as she stared at me was

202

damning. 'Do you have any conception of the raw magical force it takes to interweave new pathways within a counter-banded sigil? The unimaginable, maddening complexity of the esoteric geometries that must be envisioned?'

I didn't. So far as I knew, no one else did either.

Every Jan'Tep initiate knows you can't unwind a counter-banding. No spellmaster has ever written of any discoveries that could make it possible, and believe me, I've looked. In the nearly three years since I'd left my home, in between searching for cures for the shadowblack, I'd hunted for any hint of a way to restore my connection to the raw magical forces of iron, ember, silk, sand and blood.

I raised up my forearm and stared at the one restored sigil on my ember band. 'How did he do it?'

'It was Mother,' Sha'maat replied, barely holding back tears.

'Mother?'

She nodded. 'Ever since the day you walked out on us, she searched for ways to undo the counter-banding, to give you a reason to come home. Father too. Even as he fought his own battles against those who sought to keep him from becoming mage sovereign, he worked tirelessly with Mother to find a way to restore your bands.'

I had trouble imagining my father and mother sitting there in her study, exchanging theories, frantically scribbling down formulae and designs of new sigils, all the while reminding each other how terribly important it was to bring weak, disloyal Kellen back into their loving embrace.

'They fought, Kellen,' my sister said as she saw the dubiousness in my expression. 'Not just against our enemies, not just against the problem of your bands, but with each other. Night and day, sometimes weeks at a time. Resentment built

203

up between them, both blaming the other for failing to find a way to make you whole.'

Make me whole. I felt my own stab of resentment at that. I wanted to tell her that I was fine as I was. I was Kellen Argos, the Path of Endless Stars. An outlaw who'd survived dozens of duels. I was the queen's spellslinger. I didn't need or want to ever be Jan'Tep again.

Only . . . I did.

My eyes went to the bands on my forearms, so ugly and distorted from the counter-sigils, all except my breath band and that one beautiful copper sigil on the ember band. Even after all this time, some part of me yearned to be a true mage. Like my mother. Like my father.

'What happens now?' I asked.

My sister nodded as if we'd made some kind of bargain. 'The process will be long and difficult. Each counter-sigil takes a great deal of time and power to unwind.' She took hold of my wrist and held up my forearm. 'It's taken nearly two years to find the solution just for this one sigil.'

Two years. There were nine sigils on the ember band. Sixteen on silk. The band for blood magic had twenty-seven separate sigils. I'd be a doddering old man long before I could become a true mage.

'The first one will have been the hardest,' she said, seeing my deflation. 'We couldn't even be sure it was possible.' She let go of my hand and wrapped her arms around me. 'But now that we know the method works, brother, with all of us working together, once you've dealt with the threat of the Berabesq god and returned home . . .'

There was that word again. *Home.*

She must've seen something in my expression. Shalla's

always known me better than anyone else. Only she's never quite understood me. She opened her mouth – no doubt to berate me as always about family and duty, but then stopped. A weariness seemed to overcome her as she shook her head like an old woman with a palsy. 'I just don't know, Kellen,' she said at last.

'You don't know what?'

Again she hesitated. 'I . . . I don't know what to do about you. I keep thinking there's something I could say, some gift I could give you or some action I could take that would bring you back. Something that would make you stop hating us.'

Somehow those words cut me deeper than any rebuke.

'I don't hate *you*, sister,' I said, reaching for her hand. 'I love you.'

Her eyes met mine, and a kind of sorrowful smirk appeared at the corners of her mouth. 'You love me. And you hate me. Sometimes I'm your beloved sister, other times your reviled nemesis. You go back and forth so often and so quickly I sometimes wonder if even you know what you feel.'

With a gesture of her hand, the door of the athenaeum opened, signalling I was being dismissed.

As I turned to go, I heard a sob as Sha'maat said, 'I'm not sure how much more of it I can take, brother.'

26

The Enigmatist

I found Ferius waiting for me outside. Somehow, in a city where such things are unheard of, she'd managed to find a smoking reed. She looked remarkably pleased with herself.

'Where's Reichis?' I asked.

She held up the reed, the smouldering end a dot of red light against the backdrop of night. 'Doesn't appreciate the finer things. Said he had some huntin' to do, though I expect it involves pastries and liqueurs more than rabbits.'

We set off down the street. It was a long walk back to the palace, which was why even she couldn't hide that something was wrong.

'That leg of yours is hurting worse than you're letting on,' I said.

'What, this?' she asked, slapping it with her hand and doing a piss-poor job of not wincing. 'You tellin' me you've never taken a crossbow bolt in the leg?'

Notice that she didn't say *she* had taken a crossbow bolt.

'What about you?' she asked, pointing the burning end of her reed at the ember sigil on my forearm. 'That had to sting somethin' fierce.' She chuckled then. 'Mind you, probably no more than havin' your pappy tell you off like I imagine he did. You make peace with your sister before you left?'

'Ferius . . .'

'Family's important to you, kid, no matter how hard you try to—'

I put a hand on her arm and made her come to a stop. 'You know this routine doesn't work on me any more, right?'

She looked down at my hand. Ferius doesn't much like people grabbing her. 'What *routine* would that be, kid?'

'The one where you change the subject to keep me from asking questions you don't want to answer. What happened to your leg, Ferius?'

'Didn't I tell you not to worry abou—'

'I've never seen you without a supply of *oleus regia*, which would take care of a simple flesh wound. Assuming you'd run out, I'm willing to bet the moment the queen saw you she'd've called for a physician to bring you *aquae sulfex*, which is even more potent. Hells, I wouldn't be surprised if she'd ordered the nearest marshals to round up every Jan'Tep healer lurking around the clan prince's palace just to fix you up.'

'Told 'em to search the entire city, as a matter of fact,' Ferius said with a wry smile. 'Told her not to bother though. Ain't met a mage yet who could do half as much good as a decent bottle of whisky.'

I stared at my old mentor, searching for signs of some more pervasive illness – something *oleus regia* or *aquae sulfex* couldn't heal. Potent as those concoctions were, they wouldn't halt the progression of a disease. If Reichis were here, he'd've walked up to her and sniffed her leg. I don't have his nose, but I leaned in anyway. Putrefaction's easy enough to smell.

'I ain't rottin' from the inside out, if that's what you're wonderin,' Ferius said, pushing me away.

'Then what's the matter with you?'

She crossed her arms. 'You tellin' me I spent all those months teachin' you arta precis and the best you can do is badger an answer out of me?'

I resented that, mostly because a small, nagging sensation in the back of my head told me she was right.

The Argosi talent of perception is subtle. Oh, there are a few tricks here and there – mostly ways of envisioning relationships between seemingly unrelated pieces of information. The way Argosi play cards together, mixing their decks and laying out different hands over and over to find patterns in world events that might otherwise go unnoticed was a good example of arta precis. But the one Ferius always harped on about? It was recognising that most truths are right there in front of us, even when our fear blinds us to them.

A *run of bad luck*, she'd called it.

A knot tightened in my stomach. 'You were in Berabesq recently, weren't you?'

'Askin' questions when you already know the answer is the least courteous form of arta loquit, kid.'

The glib answer woke a vicious anger in me. 'And what do you call a damned *malediction* when you know that's what killed my—'

'This ain't nothin' to do with—'

'Don't lie to me!' I shouted.

She put up her hands. 'Okay, kid. Okay. I won't lie to you. Just ask the question.'

I couldn't though, because the words wouldn't come. They were there though, pounding at the insides of my skull, clawing to get out. Dozens and dozens of tiny connections between disparate pieces of information. Ferius's reference earlier that night to a run of bad luck; the thirteen cards still sitting in the pocket of my trousers, a massive spire in a faraway land; men and women in the desert, pausing their hunt to carve lines into the body of one of their own; a woman screaming . . .

'Kid?' Ferius asked. 'Something's happenin' to that crazy shadowblack of yours.'

The skin of my left eye pinched as if someone were twisting the markings.

'Kid, snap out of it,' Ferius called out, but she sounded far away now.

I could see her right there in front of me, but it was as if she were behind a dark veil, watching helplessly as the shadow-black lines on my face turned like the dials of a lock.

Click.

New shapes appeared in the space between us, all of them made from that strange shadowy material I saw whenever my enigmatism took hold. Fearsome warriors wielding curved blades with wicked hooked points, their limbs wrapped in the pale linens of the Berabesq Faithful. Blood dripping down their forearms, but not from injuries – these were careful incisions made by their own sharpened fingernails, unleashing the blood magic they attributed to their god's will. One of their number lay on the sand, his chest covered in bleeding cuts while the others chased a woman across the desert.

I'd seen all this before.

Click.

The picture was different now, as if I were watching it from further away. That's how I was able to see a second woman

209

a dozen paces behind the first, holding the pursuers at bay. I knew her from her frontier hat and the way she danced as she fought.

Ferius. She had been there with Bene'maat!

'Kellen!' the other Ferius – the one standing in the street with me – shook me by the shoulders.

It's funny how people only ever seem to use my name when they think I'm about to die.

In the haze between us, I watched as the shadow Ferius sent steel cards spinning through the air at her enemies before running to lift up the fallen woman and haul her over her shoulder.

'You *were* in Berabesq,' I said aloud.

'We can talk about it later, kid. For now just—'

'Following the Way of Wind,' I said, repeating her own words from earlier. 'You were following the rumours of their living god, weren't you?' I asked.

She said something in reply, but I didn't hear it. Instead I watched in horror as the shadow Ferius stumbled, her feet barely able to keep her steady in the shifting sands while carrying the other woman. The Berabesq Faithful had almost caught up to her. She was outnumbered, out of tricks, fighting for her life in the worst possible conditions for a lone Argosi.

How did you survive?

Fractured onyx lines exploded in my vision, bolts of lightning shattering the air. My hands rose up instinctively to protect my ears from the thunderclaps. There, a dozen yards away, a lone woman in a long coat held a metal box out in front of her. The raging storm was coming from inside it. There was an animal by her side . . . A dog? No. A hyena.

'Nephenia was there! She saved you.'

'Yeah,' Ferius admitted, though she sounded none too pleased about it.

If Ferius Parfax has one weakness, it's that she can't stand being saved by anyone else. If she has one fear, it's that someone she cares about will sacrifice themselves for her.

In the shadowy desert floating in the air before me, the Berabesq Faithful pulled back, unable to face the onslaught of Nephenia's caged lightning charm. She dropped the box and reached into the pocket of her coat before hurling what looked like a dozen tiny metal spiders onto the sand. She uttered a single word and the spiders came to life, skittering along the desert floor towards the pursuing warriors.

'Guess you could say I got myself into a bit of a jam,' Ferius confessed.

That sparked something inside me. *You did, only you're never the one to get into trouble. You're too slippery, too skilled a tactician. So why would the incomparably clever Ferius Parfax, the Way of the Wild Daisy, get herself in such an impossible situation?*

Click.

I felt the last of my shadowblack markings turn, the final dial unlocking the secret being kept from me. Nephenia and Ferius each slung one arm of the unconscious Bene'maat over their shoulders, carrying her between them as they raced across the desert while the Berabesq Faithful struggled to escape a web of lightning and spiders.

The pursuers fell back. For a moment it appeared as if the three women had got away, but then the Faithful's leader nodded to one of the others, who then removed their clothes and laid down in the sand so that the ritual could be repeated again.

The second scream came from Ferius, as the Faithful, drawing on the love of their newly born god, infused the hundreds of invisible tendrils of an unbreakable curse inside her.

The malediction.

Ferius Parfax had tried to save my mother's life, and for that kindness a god had condemned her to death.

27

The Malediction

All at once the enigmatism faded and I was left staring at Ferius Parfax, who I'd never seen cry before but now watched helplessly as tears came sliding down her cheeks. 'I'm sorry, Kellen.'

I was so dazed from the visions that I couldn't make sense of her words.

'Sorry?' I asked.

Ferius wiped the linen sleeve of her travelling shirt across her eyes. 'I tried to save your mamma for you, kid. Tried as hard as I could.'

'But . . . How could you have known she was in the Berabesq territories? Why were you the one trying to save her? My father must have had other agents in the territories. They should've—'

Anger flashed across her features. 'What've I told you about askin' me to make sense of the foolishness of boys and men?' She held up a hand to keep me from asking any more questions and took in a long, slow breath before speaking again. 'I was in Makhan Mebab on account of I'd been given a discordance card by a gal I might've mentioned to you before. Calls herself the Path of Whispering Willows – stupid name, if you ask me. Anyway, she'd painted a pretty picture of this new god of theirs, all decked out in the rays of the sun, but behind him was a figure hiding in the shadows. So I followed the trail to see what I could see.'

I was having trouble making sense of what she was saying. The blood in my veins felt cold, the way it does when panic and terror start to overtake me. But there was something else too, something dark and dangerous deep inside my chest that was beginning to smoulder at the thought of what the Faithful had done to Ferius.

'What did you find out about their god?' I asked.

'Never got that far. Caught wind of some gossip about a high-powered foreign mage captured by the viziers who they reckoned could bring down the entire Jan'Tep arcanocracy. They were bringing in inquisitors from across the territories to see if they could torture her into concocting a binding spell – said it would let 'em kill the mage sovereign himself. Well, you know how little attention I pay to Jan'Tep magic, but it wasn't hard to guess that their captive had to have some powerful connection to your daddy. At first I figured they must have that sister of yours – precocious little monster that she is. But then, well, then it turned out to be your mom.'

'You rescued her? Even though it meant abandoning your mission for the Argosi?'

Ferius shrugged. 'Lady was kind enough to me, for a Jan'Tep anyway. Loved you somethin' fierce. Reckoned that was reason enough.' She took one of my hands in hers. 'The malediction they put on her – there wasn't nothin' I could do about that. I'm sorry, Kellen.'

I nodded, still choking on grief and confusion. 'You and Nephenia were hit with the malediction too, weren't you?'

214

'Girl's all right,' Ferius said. 'Had some silly charm or other on her that she said deflected the curse. She'd offered me one ages ago, but, well, I told her it wasn't my way.'

'Why must you always do that?!' I snapped. 'You mock magic as superstition, as if it's all some game the rest of us are playing. Magic is real, Ferius! It kills people. It killed my mother. It's killing . . .'

She reached out a hand and with her thumb wiped away a tear I hadn't even known was starting down my cheek. 'Old Ferius don't go down so easy, kid. You know that.' She grinned. 'Not for some superstitious nonsense anyways.'

'We have to get you help,' I said, already turning to run back to my family home. 'My father can command every healer in the city to—'

Ferius caught hold of me. 'Don't you think if this thing could be cured with magic, your daddy would've gotten all his little mages together to save your mother?' She let me go and smiled as she smoothed the hair away from my eyes. 'Got me a different plan, kid.'

'What plan?' I asked. 'How do you stop a malediction?'

'Well, near as I can tell, the way it works is, every time you fix one thing, a new problem comes along. An inexplicable sprain starts up in your wrist? You go get it fixed and then the next day you break a toe. Bandage up the toe? Suddenly you burn your finger. Douse that in *oleus regia*? You wake up in the morning to the worst cold of your life. Over time the curse just sort of wears the body out until it can't fight no more.'

Which was what had happened to my mother. One of the most powerful healers our clan had ever seen, and she couldn't save herself.

'But then I had a thought,' Ferius went on. 'I asked myself, "Ferius, what do you suppose happens if you *don't* fix a problem?"'

'You mean just keep suffering with one thing and don't try to heal the injury?'

She spread her hand in a kind of mock surrender. 'Life is suffering, I've heard it said.' She looked down at her right thigh. 'Got you trapped in there, don't I? Little rat bastard. Yeah, you go on an' give me a limp all you want. Ache all day and all night, but old Ferius has you in a cage now, don't she?'

'I really don't think the malediction has a consciousness,' I said.

'Oh? You some kinda expert now? Way I see it, this thing's gotta be some kind of spirit, bit like that sasutzei you had hanging around you a while back.' Ferius peered into my right eye. 'She still living in there?'

'Left months ago.'

Ferius sighed. 'Too bad. Figured she mighta chased this one outta me.'

A thought came to me. 'Maybe a whisper witch could remove the malediction. We could find Mamma Whispers in the Seven Sands and—'

'Already tried that, kid. Found me a whisperer on my way north. She told me the only way this thing is gettin' out of me is to starve the source of its power.' She chuckled. 'Don't reckon that Berabesq god's gettin' any weaker any time soon. In the meantime, though, I got me a continent to save.'

She set off down the street, flinching every time she took a step.

I caught up with her and stopped her.

'What's the matter, kid?' she asked. 'You don't think my arta forteize can handle a little pain? Didn't I teach you better than that?'

'What you taught me,' I said, pulling her arm across my shoulder, 'is that it never hurts to lean on your friends once in a while.'

Ferius smiled at that.

What I didn't tell her was that my path had finally become clear, as though my every future footstep was glowing right there on the street before me. All the uncertainty that had plagued me – my father's manipulations, the Murmurers' machinations, Torian's appeal to duty and even my desperate desire to protect the queen – all of them fled me in the face of a profound conviction that the Argosi call the Way of Stone.

For a long time I had thought maybe I'd never see Ferius Parfax again. The woman who had taken a broken, selfish boy and given him the chance to become . . . Well, I wasn't quite sure what, but something better than destiny had intended. Now she was right here in front of me, making all her clever quips about tricking the curse that had killed my mother and was now killing her. But no amount of arta valar can break the curse of a living god.

That was my job.

Shalla had it right all along. In the end, duty isn't about grand dynasties or ethical debates. Duty is about family.

I was going to Berabesq.

I was going to kill God.

The Penitent Army

City of Soldiers

City of Soldiers

What do soldiers fight for if not their nation, their city, their home? Yet to defend these things they must often leave them behind, sometimes forever. So must soldiers carry their homes with them, in their hearts and on their backs, lest one day they wake to discover that they are truly lost.

28

The Outskirts

We set out for Makhan Mebab that night. No goodbyes, no farewells, just like the first time I'd left my home. Reichis kept pivoting on our horse's neck, looking back as though expecting someone to be following us. Oddly he seemed disappointed to find only the empty road. Turned out he was looking in the wrong direction.

Almost three years to the day, my sister had stood defiantly at the outskirts of the city, armed with tears and ultimatums to keep me from leaving. This time a different yellow-haired girl awaited me.

'Seneira?'

The heir to the famed Academy of the Seven Sands was still dressed in her diplomat's finery, though with a long black riding coat to keep out the night's chill. 'You left without saying goodbye last time too,' she said.

I slid off my horse's saddle and into a hug with more genuine affection than I'd have expected. A couple of years back the two of us had gotten mixed up in a plot involving onyx worms, shadowy conspirators and a particularly unscrupulous spellslinger by the name of Dexan Videris. Seneira had nearly lost her soul to one of the worms and Reichis had almost been eaten by a crocodile. Me? I got a nice hat out of the deal.

'What are you doing out here in the middle of the night?' I asked, after Seneira let go of me.

She ignored the question and walked past me. 'Lady Ferius,' she said with a short bow.

'Ain't no lady, kid, it's just . . .' She caught Seneira's grin and grunted in return. 'Ain't nice to mess with your elders.'

'Forgive my impertinence, Path of the Wild Daisy. Perhaps you will allow me to follow the Way of Water and make restitution?' Seneira reached into her coat and took out a thin roll of leather.

Ferius accepted it in both hands as though it were a priceless artefact. She held it up to her nose and inhaled deeply before letting out a sigh of blissful anticipation. 'Teleidan brightleaf . . .'

'Finest smoking reeds in the Seven Sands. I'd intended to give them to Kellen to pass on to you, but I'm pleased to be able to deliver this small token of our gratitude to you in person.'

Ferius's vocal mannerisms shifted in that effortless way of hers to take on a more formal style of speech as she bowed low. 'A thousand gifts have you given me then, daughter of the Seven Sands, for in every waft of the smoke from these reeds will I be reminded of the endless beauty of your homeland and its people.'

Seneira was taken aback by the unexpected, almost ceremonial declaration.

'What about me?' grunted a tubby ball of fur, shaking himself off as he trundled over. He's never fond of other people receiving gifts without him getting any. 'I'm the one that did all the hard work on that job! Nearly got my hide chewed off by a gods-damned crocodile!'

Seneira had no way of knowing what he'd said, yet she smiled as if she'd expected it all, and again reached into her coat, retrieving a small case covered in a greenish, heavily textured hide. Crocodile hide, as it turned out. 'You may not remember the beast that attacked us in Dexan Videris's lair,' she said to me, 'but in the Sands we waste nothing, so I had this made as a reminder of your business partner's daring victory.'

She handed me the case, which was strikingly beautiful. When I opened the clasp and raised the lid, Reichis nearly lost his mind clambering up my side to grab at its contents.

'My father's recipe,' Seneira said. 'When I told him I was travelling here to pay our respects to the mage sovereign, he insisted I bring some of his butter biscuits just in case.'

I snapped the lid shut to keep Reichis from devouring them all at once. He groaned in obscene ecstasy as he chewed the one he'd snatched in his paws, then hopped from my shoulder to hers and rubbed his crumb-covered muzzle in her hair. 'Always liked this girl,' he purred.

I didn't bother reminding him that earlier he couldn't even remember her name.

Seneira smiled at him before politely asking, 'Brave and handsome hunter of the treetops, might I have a minute's privacy with your . . . sidekick?'

Reichis laughed uproariously, repeating her words for my benefit a couple of times before demanding another biscuit and sauntering off to devour it in private.

Seneira and I walked a little way down the road together. 'I'm afraid this gift isn't for you either,' she said as she handed me a thin blue glass bottle. 'My father asked me to bring you this. It's from his private supply of pazione liqueur. However I suspect someone else will end up drinking it.'

I accepted the bottle gratefully. 'Hey, having the means to get Reichis passed-out drunk next time he's irritable is gift enough for me.'

'I have something else as well,' she said, opening her right hand.

I looked down to see a tiny pendant attached to a thin silver chain resting on her palm. The pendant was shaped like a tall tower that I recognised as a replica of the Academy of the Seven Sands, its surface a kind of mosaic decorated in the colours of each of the different terrains of the region.

'The students wear these as passes to prove their right to enter the Academy,' she said. 'And many continue to wear them throughout their lives as a remembrance of their time there.' She held the pendant by the chain. 'May I?'

I removed my hand and bent down so she could slip it around my neck.

'Thank you,' I said. 'It is a lovely gift.'

'The pendant isn't the gift, Kellen.' She hesitated a moment before going on. 'I saw you when I was speaking at your mother's funeral. Even before those young mages came over to harass you, you looked so . . . I don't even know how to put it.'

'Out of place?' I suggested.

She shook her head. 'I want to say unhomed, though I'm not even sure that's a word.'

Yet it perfectly described how I'd felt, and I said as much to her.

Seneira took my hands in hers. 'Let this be my gift to you

then, Kellen. No matter how far you travel, know that there is always a place for you in the Seven Sands. The Academy offers a dozen different paths to its students. If you grow weary of violence, join us and become a physician. If you tire of breaking things, become a contraptioneer and build instead.' She grinned up at me. 'That Gitabrian girl, Cressia – we've become close friends these past two years – claims you're a passable philosopher at times.'

I reached up to hold the pendant in my hand. Admission to the Academy was exorbitantly expensive and offered only to those who showed outstanding promise, making this a princely gift in more ways than one. Before I could thank her, Seneira stood on her tiptoes and kissed me on the cheek. 'Remember this one thing always, Kellen: you have friends, and our love for you far outstrips the malice of your enemies.'

For the life of me I couldn't think of a reply to the startling depth of her generosity. My rhetorical skills lean towards sarcastic quips, and for once I was smart enough to keep my mouth shut.

She kissed me on the other cheek before she turned and walked back up the road, leaving me standing there contemplating the dreams of a hundred futures I would never see, feeling nonetheless grateful for all of them.

29

The Road

There's always a rhythm to the road. Iron-shod hoofs clomping against cobblestones or tromping down dirt trails produce a hypnotising cadence that makes the hours come and go without notice. Days and nights drift by one after another. The repetition of making camp, of unpacking supplies and measuring out what can and can't be afforded based on how long it's been since you last bought or hunted food, trudging around in search of wood for a fire, setting up bedrolls only to pack them up again before the sun rises and beginning the process all over again. After a while the scenery before you fades from your thoughts and all you have to mark time with are the memories of what you left behind.

I kept finding myself staring at the new ember sigil on my forearm. There wasn't a lot it could do except remind me that I hadn't said goodbye to my father. No doubt he'd see that as another example of my ongoing disloyalty to our family. Sha'maat would lie and say I'd left her with any number of tearful apologies to convey to him. I hadn't said goodbye to Torian either, though really, how much could that matter? She'd poisoned me and fed me to the Murmurers – it's not like she had the high ground when it came to etiquette.

None of that was what really bothered me though. The problem was my saddle bags.

'No butter biscuits?' Reichis complained, rifling through the second one. He'd already made a mess of the first.

'Would you quit digging around in there?' I asked. 'I told you, you ate all the ones Seneira brought already.'

He started swearing then, using words so foul I was honestly curious where he'd learned them. Apparently too much time sneaking around court had corrupted his once delicate vocabulary.

I actually still had a few left, wrapped in cheesecloth and secreted inside the pocket of my coat for a special occasion. I'd hidden them away the night Reichis had demanded a sip of the pazione and promptly grabbed the blue flask out of my hands and run off with it. He'd shown up the next morning with a headache, an empty flask and an improbable story about a coven of bewitching flying rabbits.

As to the saddlebags? Other than the scourge and dice Emelda had given me, all I had in them was what I'd brought with me to the Daroman court over a year ago. No more, no less. All that time living in the queen's palace and, other than a few trinkets for Reichis, I hadn't accumulated a thing. In fact, I'd kept most of my stuff in the saddlebags themselves. Packing had been a matter of stuffing two shirts, two pairs of trousers and a few underclothes into the bags and then walking out the door.

'Told you before, kid,' Ferius said after I'd mentioned feeling unmoored from that life now, 'Argosi don't collect much but dust and scars.'

Dust and scars.

I'd certainly acquired my share of both. Not even nineteen, and my body was a patchwork of knife wounds, badly healed burns and the kinds of bizarre-looking patterns of skin discolouration that you can only get from magic. 'How's the leg?' I asked Ferius, reminding myself that she had it worse than I did and yet managed not to complain all the time.

'You know, it don't feel quite so bad this morning,' she said, sounding a little surprised. She pounded her fist lightly against her thigh and chuckled. 'Maybe that cursed malediction's gotten tired of me and moved on.'

'Maybe it just doesn't like the scenery,' I suggested. 'Though I doubt maledictions are too particular about such things.'

There are any number of routes that will take you to Berabesq. The southern trade route is a particularly nice one, fitted with cobblestones, mile markers and the occasional saloon. Ferius had instead chosen to lead us through the patchwork of trails that criss-crossed the most barren terrain in all of the Jan'Tep territories. Nothing to see but dirt and scrub. Worst of all was the wind that came and went in gusts, swirling dust and grit into the air, brewing a pale brown haze that stung the eyes and aggravated the lungs.

Ferius gave a cough. 'Reckon you're right about the . . .'

She coughed a second time. Something strained in her voice made me turn around. Her customary grin was gone. The lines on her face, usually so faint as to make her ageless, appeared more pronounced. Her brow was furrowed as if she were trying to remember a joke but the punchline wouldn't come. I followed her gaze down to the thin trail of blood dripping like a winding creek along her white

230

linen shirt where the head of an arrow protruded from her chest.

'Reckon you're right about maledictions, kid,' she said as she fell from her horse.

30

The Wound

'Reichis, scatter!' I said.

The squirrel cat leaped from our horse, his fur changing colour in mid-air to match the dust and dirt all around us. He wasn't invisible, but close enough that as he tore off I lost track of him almost immediately.

I tumbled off my own horse – not because it threw me but because, well, it turns out that's pretty much the fastest way for me to dismount. I turned the fall into a shoulder roll as best I could and used the momentum to get back on my feet so I could run to where Ferius lay on the ground.

'Where's your *oleus regia*?' I asked, rifling through her saddle-bags much the same way as Reichis had done with ours.

'You crazy, kid? Get out of here before you get hit too!'

I ignored her. She wasn't thinking this through. A passable archer using a 120-pound pull bow could fire roughly fifteen arrows a minute with decent accuracy. That's one every four seconds. Since this particular archer had nailed Ferius on a moving horse on the first shot in a windstorm, it was safe to say they were better than passable.

So why wasn't there an arrow sticking out of me yet?

I let my fingers do the searching through Ferius's saddlebags as I scanned the area, but there was nothing to see other than the winding trail ahead of us, and the patchy scrub and occasional outcropping of rock on either side.

They could be hiding behind one of those outcroppings, I thought, my fingers still fumbling through the inner pockets of the saddlebag. *If so, they're a lot better at camouflaging themselves than I am at spotting them.*

Finally my fingers found a little round jar made of rough glass. I pulled it out and checked the continents. *Oleas regia.* Not quite worth its weight in gold, but damned close. I scrambled back to Ferius on my hands and knees.

A piercing growl cut through the wind. 'Reichis?' I called out.

Stupid. Don't make him draw attention to his location.

But the squirrel cat answered back anyway. 'I'm snared, Kellen. Some kinda lousy skinbag trap.'

How could there be a snare lying in wait just where Reichis would go?

Because there's only a couple of good places to hide around here, I realised then. Which meant whoever'd attacked us knew about Reichis and had known where we'd be. Only that was just about impossible, given how many different roads there are going south from the capital. *So they must've been following us for days, then once we were on this trail, rode ahead of us and set a trap.*

'Yeah,' Ferius said, looking up at me. 'It's somebody who knows us.'

'Don't talk,' I said.

'You know talkin' don't actually make you die any quicker, right?'

'It does if you keep distracting me.'

233

First problem: getting the arrow out. She'd managed to fall on her side, which had kept the shaft from bending and doing further damage inside her. It had struck her high up in the back, a little to the right of dead centre. That meant it hadn't hit her heart, but might well have pierced a lung.

Ferius reached up with a hand to the arrowhead. 'Just give me a second to . . . get this thing . . . out.'

'Stop it,' I said, batting her hand out of the way.

I needed to cut off the arrowhead so I could pull the shaft out the back. The *oleus regia* would do a decent job of staunching any bleeding and keeping her alive, but it couldn't do much with the shaft inside her, so I had to take it out without doing further damage. A knife would do it, but I hadn't sharpened mine and hadn't found Ferius's.

I flipped open my holsters and took a minuscule pinch of each of the powders. 'I'll try not to miss,' I said.

'Mighty courteous of you. They been teachin' you manners in that big old palace?'

'Not nearly enough,' I replied, glancing around us once more, trying to pick out where our assailant was hiding, but now I was almost positive there was no one there.

Ferius wounded, me out of commission trying to save her, and a snare for Reichis to keep from tracking them until it's too late to catch them.

The moment the wind died down, I moved Ferius's arm out of the way so I'd have a clean shot before I tossed the red and black powders in the air, forming the somatic shapes with my hands. Fore and middle fingers aimed at the target for direction, ring and little fingers pressed into my palms in the sign of restraint, and thumbs pointing to the sky, the sign of . . . *Ancestors, please don't let me kill my friend.*

'*Carath*,' I intoned.

The powders ignited on contact, the explosion instantly caught in the channelling force of the spell like a rush of water forced down a narrow tube. A blast of red and black fire shot clean through the shaft just below the arrowhead.

'Nice shot, kid. Hardly felt a thing.'

I wished that could've been true of this next part.

The instinct, when extracting a long thin piece of wood from someone you care about, is to draw it out as quickly as possible – keep the pain sharp and short. That's a terrible idea, as I'd learned about a year ago, after a highwayman had shot me through the thigh with a crossbow bolt. The problem is that it doesn't really want to come out straight, so if you just yank it, you risk tearing something important. In Ferius's case, there were way too many important things I could damage.

'Slow and steady,' she said, gritting her teeth in a smile.

Don't know why she does that – smile, I mean. Doubt it makes it feel any better. But I guess she takes this Path of the Wild Daisy thing pretty seriously. *Joy shines brightest in the darkness*, she'd once told me, along with a thousand other nonsense sayings.

'Any time now, kid.'

I gave one last glance around to make sure no one was creeping towards us. Once I started, I needed to do this all the way.

'Sorry about this,' I said, and slowly, methodically and excruciatingly painfully, drew the arrow out of her body. Ferius let out a scream that would've made the dead rise.

I tossed the shaft away. It was slick and soaked with her blood.

'Damn, but that don't get any less painful with practice,' Ferius said.

I grabbed for the little jar of *oleus regia*. 'This won't feel much better, I'm afraid.'

After I'd slathered a small fortune's worth of ointment over the entry and exit wounds left behind by the arrow and freed Reichis from the snare, I built up a small fire. I spent that night watching over Ferius, convinced with each stuttering rise and fall of her chest that she was about to move no more. Only when her eyes finally fluttered open and a weary, broken smile appeared on her lips did I feel I could breathe again.

'Hey, kid?' she asked.

I offered her water, but she shook her head. 'Yeah, Ferius?'

'I love you somethin' fierce, but you bring the worst luck with you I ever seen.'

I let out what could charitably be called an awkward chuckle but sounded more like a sob.

'Hey,' she said, grabbing hold of my wrist, 'don't let guilt make you stupid. You know what this was, right?'

Yeah, I knew what this was.

Someone with a bow takes out one of your party with a perfect shot, camouflaged somewhere they'd have to have been waiting for hours to catch you – which meant they knew you were coming – and yet doesn't kill both right there and then? That's not brigandry. It's not even an assassination attempt.

It was a message.

Someone didn't want Ferius Parfax returning to Berabesq.

31

The Oath

The smart thing to do after your mentor's narrowly avoided being mortally wounded and you now realise someone's out to get you would be to hole up somewhere safe, bide your time and come up with a brilliant plan to outwit your opponents.

Ferius, Reichis and I had set out again that morning. Hard as it would be to sneak into Berabesq under our current circumstances, the situation would get a lot worse once their god's birthday had come and the combined armies of the largest peoples on the continent set out to wage war on every heathen they could find.

When your luck is as lousy as mine you start wondering if maybe the religious fanatics aren't quite as crazy as you thought.

'Are you okay?' I asked Ferius.

She didn't reply at first, just kept her horse trotting along. Her skin had always been pale, but for days now it had been more grey than pink. 'One hundred and twenty-one,' she said finally.

'One hundred and twenty-two,' Reichis chittered from his perch atop our horse's neck, then rolled onto his back to resume snoring.

'What'd he say?' Ferius asked.

'He said I've only asked two or three times. So, *are* you okay?'

'One hundred and twenty . . .' Reichis went back to dozing before he could finish.

'You know, kid,' Ferius said, pulling on the reins to halt her horse, 'for someone who gets all fired up about knowing the truth, you sure do seem to want people to lie to you all the time.'

I stopped my own horse. We were about a day's ride from the Berabesq border. You could tell we were getting closer from the way the sand was changing colour from dull brown to a more golden hue. Soon we'd be entering more populated areas, and that's when our real troubles would begin. 'I just meant—'

'I'm dying, kid. You know it, I know it. So quit askin' about it.' She coughed. Blood stained the back of her hand when she wiped her mouth. 'Damned thing's moved again. Now it wants my lungs.'

Where the oleus regia *can't help*, I thought.

Healing the hole the arrow had left in her chest had also, it turned out, cured the pain in her leg. The malediction was shifting its unpredictable attacks on an almost daily basis. Ferius was the strongest, most resilient, orneriest person I'd ever met, but even she was coming apart piece by piece as this damned curse played with her like a cat with a wounded bird, letting it flutter its wings only to catch it again before it could fly away.

Ever since we'd left the Jan'Tep territories, I'd spent every waking hour trying to understand the malediction and its workings. A typical disease attacks either a part of the body, like the liver, or some continuous system like the blood. But the malediction was different. It could go after the victim in a hundred different ways – as often as not appearing as dumb bad luck. A strange rash might appear over Ferius's body one day, then the next by sheer accident she'd slip and fall, spraining an ankle that wouldn't seem to heal or getting a cut that almost instantly became infected. However we tried to compensate for one problem – taking more care whenever she moved, for example – some new problem always came along.

Each day I watched her, trying to make sense of this curse by turning over its properties in my mind. By this point there were only two possible explanations I could come up with: either the malediction was some kind of spirit or supernatural force that haunted her, or it was a disease that affected both body *and* mind, causing her to produce her own injuries whenever she tried to mitigate against other ones.

Either way, though, how was I supposed to put a stop to it?

If it was some kind of spirit, it had eluded my pathetic whisper magic skills thus far. I'd only ever been able to communicate with one particular wind spirit called a sasutzei who'd once taken up residence in my right eye, but Suzy, as I liked to call her, had left me long ago.

And if the malediction was a mystical disease of the mind, causing its victim to create their own symptoms? Ferius had the most indomitable will I'd ever known, and she couldn't fight it.

Which left only one solution.

'You just have to hold on,' I said to her. 'Once we reach the Berabesq capital, we'll find a way to reverse it.'

'Once we reach the capital,' she said, nudging her horse back into a walk, 'we'll be figuring out how to stop a war, not worryin' about a little cough.'

239

She'd dismissed the conversation this way every other time too. She'd remind me that the world had bigger problems to worry about than the life of one itinerant gambler, and that the Way of the Argosi was about preventing the big, unsolvable calamities by dealing with the little, fixable ones that led to them, not letting the world go to hells for the sake of one person.

'I'm sorry,' I said as we rode side by side.

'It's all right, kid. I know you mean well.'

'No, I mean I'm sorry because I know, despite all the crap you talk about walking the Path of the Wild Daisy and making light of things that happen to you, that what you're really looking for is a noble death.'

'Since when is—'

I cut her off. 'That's not going to happen, Ferius. I won't let it happen.'

She raised an eyebrow. 'And just who are you supposed to be now, Kellen of the House of Ke?'

She always called me that when I was starting to sound pompous.

'Nobody,' I replied. 'Not a proper mage, not a proper Argosi, not a proper anything. It's like you always say: I'm a kid.' I spurred my horse on to a trot. 'I'm the kid who's going to figure out how to sneak into a foreign country, find their god and stop him from starting the war to end all wars. And while I'm doing that, I'm also going to be beating the hells out of said god until he cures you of the malediction. *That's* who I am.'

From his perch atop our horse's neck, eyes still closed as he snoozed on his back, Reichis said, 'Damned straight.'

32

The Border

'We're all gonna die,' Reichis chittered.

The three of us were crouched low on a ridge overlooking a wide flood-plain. I always think of Berabesq as a desert nation, but that's not entirely true. Two massive rivers pass through their territory, one of which lay about an eighth of a mile to the right of us, its currents enriching the soil so that crops of wheat and barley could grow in abundance, and with them, the Berabesq people themselves.

'There's so many of them,' the squirrel cat added.

I'd never heard him sound quite so uncomfortable before. Then again, this was the first time we'd actually found ourselves facing an entire army. Column after column of soldiers in glittering golden breastplates, their curved swords and javelins carefully laid at their sides, knelt upon the plain. Thick leather bands covered their forearms, providing protection from cuts while still allowing them the freedom to move with fluidity and grace. They weaved their hands in the air in perfect unison, almost as if they were casting a spell, all the while intoning soft, almost musical chants.

'What are they doing?' I asked.

'Praying,' Ferius replied.

241

I'd been to Berabesq before – twice, in fact. I'd seen them pray, and I didn't recall it looking anything like this. When I pointed that out to Ferius, she said, 'You ever notice how the Berabesq refer to their deity just as "God", but everyone outside the country calls him "the six-faced god"?'

'I guess.' In fact I'd never actually paid attention to that distinction. Until recently I'd just assumed all gods were superstitious nonsense.

'The Berabesq are monotheistic. They believe there can be only one true god. Problem is, they have six different holy books.' She lowered the brim of her hat to counter the glare from the rising sun. 'Depending on which one you read, "God" is either a ruthless warrior, a meticulous gardener, a silent hermit, a tender healer, an obsessed clockmaker, or a penitent prisoner who forever holds the world close to the sun so that his people don't die of cold.'

'How did they end up with six holy books?'

'No one knows for sure. They started out with one.' The corner of Ferius's mouth rose in the hint of a smirk. 'Then a couple of hundred years ago, five more codices were . . . discovered.'

That look on her face got me thinking. 'Ferius, is it at all possible that the Argosi just happened to come up with altered versions of the original Berabesq codex – ones different enough to split them into six, disunited religious sects?'

'More likely them other stories already existed and some concerned citizens just made sure they didn't disappear on account of never being written down.' She winked at me. 'Now a wise teysan might wonder why the Argosi would go to all that trouble.'

'Because it would allow the Berabesq to live in peace, but stop them from launching a massive holy crusade against the rest of the continent. Anytime one sect tried to start something, one of the others would get into a theological dispute with them and that would be that.'

'Well now, all that just from a few old books? Sure does make the Argosi sound clever, don't it? Right admirable, I'd say.'

Admirable wasn't necessarily the first word that came to mind. 'Ferius . . .' I wasn't even sure how to broach the topic. 'How often have the Argosi interfered with the development of nations?'

'Just often enough to keep 'em from killing each other,' she replied. She dug her hand into the soil and lifted it up, letting the grains of dirt fall between her fingers. 'This place, it's nobody's home, kid. Folks came here from the old continents, searching for new lands, for magic, for power of all kinds. Didn't have millennia to learn how to get along. Just started conquering whatever they could.'

'So the Argosi . . .'

'We try to keep the peace, when such a thing is possible.'

'And when it's not? When, say, one country thinks their god has arrived on earth and is going to use that as an excuse to start a continental war?'

She ignored my question entirely. Instead she pointed to the thousands of armoured men and women praying below us. 'We're gonna need to find a way past all those folks.'

'Just sneak around 'em,' Reichis advised.

I translated for Ferius. She shook her head. 'Army this big – and by the way, this ain't a tenth of what a united Berabesq army will look like – they'll have scouts for miles around,

243

not to mention a few holy men and women with their own kind of magic looking for spies.'

'So what do we do?' I asked, my eyes constantly drawn back to the fluid movements and melodic chants of their prayers. 'Which face of their god do they pray to?'

'The penitent prisoner.'

'Is that good for us?'

Ferius rubbed at her jaw. 'Could be. Could be. His followers ain't the worst anyway.'

'Who are the worst? The ones who worship the brutal warrior face of their god?'

'Nope. The healer.'

'The healer? Why? I would've thought—'

'You remember them Faithful we came across a couple of years ago?'

I did. They were some of the deadliest fighters I'd ever encountered. Crusaders determined to drown the desert sand in the blood of blasphemers. 'I'm guessing the one being "healed" in this case isn't the patient?'

She nodded. 'Them as follows the healer believe it's their job to rid the world of the disease of blasphemy.'

'You two gonna jaw all morning?' Reichis asked nervously.

'What's gotten into you?' I asked him.

'Don't like armies. Don't like religious nuts. Don't like armies of religious nuts.'

I couldn't fault his logic.

Ferius made a choking sound. She was having another coughing fit, trying in vain to stifle it. I handed her a hand-kerchief. Usually she refused it, but this time she accepted. It came away smeared with even more blood and bile than usual.

244

'We've got to get past this army and find an apothecary who can concoct something to hold off the symptoms,' I said.

She wiped at her lips with the kerchief again. 'Ain't no apothecary gonna fix this, kid. Might as well ask the six-faced . . .'

'Ferius?'

Despite the ashen pallor, the trickster's grin that came to her face made Ferius look like her old self again. 'Reckon I got a plan to get us through the army.'

Something about the way she looked at me got me worrying. 'How exactly?'

She clapped me on the shoulder and rose to her feet, exposing us to the army below. 'When's the last time you got beat up good and proper, kid?'

33

The Penitents

Nothing good has ever come of the question 'When's the last time you got beat up good and proper?' In this particular case, Ferius insisted it was a necessary lesson in *arta siva*.

The Argosi talent for persuasion was one I'd always been keen to learn. Who wouldn't want to master the art of being charming? However, the Argosi have some peculiar notions about what types of things people actually find endearing, and one of them turns out to be the unique charm of watching someone get beaten up.

'Back on your feet, kid,' Ferius said. 'Can't dodge when yo—'

'"Can't dodge when you're flat on your back",' I finished for her. 'I know. You taught me that two years ago, when I was getting my arse handed to me by that kid in the Seven Sands.'

A punch to the nose brought me back to the fight. Well, the beating, anyway.

'Seems you ain't learned the lesson yet,' Ferius observed.

Allow me to set the scene properly: three Berabesq cavalry troopers were taking turns punching, kicking and occasionally kneeing me in various tender spots on my body. Interspersed with this was a good deal of insults, ranging from questioning my manhood to . . . questioning my manhood in other ways.

246

This was made only slightly more embarrassing by the fact that all three soldiers happened to be women. In between the violence and verbal chicanery, they amused themselves by spitting on me. I was squirming on the ground when one of the soldiers decided on a truly ambitious way to wrap up our little exchange: she began to hike down her trousers in preparation for urinating on me.

'You just gonna lie there and take it?' Reichis asked in disgust. Here's something interesting about squirrel cats: they consider urinating on an opponent to be the ultimate dismissal of said opponent as unworthy of being killed, because even a squirrel cat won't bite something that's covered in piss.

Am I going to lie here and take it? I asked myself.

Ferius's theory was that our best bet for getting safe passage past the encampment was for us to act as penitents – our story was that she was travelling in search of God's blessing to cure her disease and that I was offering myself to be his sword, smiting his enemies and generally bringing glory to his name. If that sounds arrogant beyond belief, well, that was the point.

'You pathetic little mouse!' the soldier pulling down her trousers spat. 'You think God wants *you* for a sword?'

One of the others chuckled as she egged on her comrade. 'More likely God wants him for a piss bucket.'

The plan – if you can use that term for something this ill-conceived – was that my earnest commitment and willingness to get beaten senseless by anyone who doubted 'the devotion of a foreigner inspired by God's sovereign will' would cause the soldiers' commanders to find me first amusing and then – and this is Ferius's term for it – adorable. The problem, of course, is you can only be so pathetic before people stop finding it entertaining. Also, while instinct and necessity have led me to allow myself to suffer more indignities than most, even I have to draw the line on humiliation somewhere.

That line was being pissed on by a smug Berabesq half-wit soldier.

Just as she tilted her hips in preparation for urinating on top of me, I rolled onto my left side, getting in closer to her and swinging my right foot over her hip. I hooked my leg behind hers and pulled hard. This had the effect of changing the angle of her – quite impressive – stream of urine, such that instead of hitting me, she hit her comrade.

'Stupid cow!' the other woman growled. I think it was cow anyway. I always confuse the Berabesq words for 'cow' and 'camel'.

The woman's soaking prompted laughter in their third comrade, who slapped her on the shoulder. 'Now who's God's piss bucket?'

The second swore and grabbed the rather confused first soldier by the shoulders, pushing her towards me, but by now I'd rolled myself over my back, coming up on the balls of my feet. Still crouching low, I ran around them in a tight circle, which prompted the first soldier to spin like a top in search of me, resulting in her falling onto her comrades and peeing on them more as they shouted obscenities at both of us.

'Enough!' roared a new voice.

Two of the three soldiers instantly stood rigidly at attention. The third, thankfully, hiked her trousers back up.

Me? I took a long, slow breath to ready myself for what came next.

'You want me to handle this, kid?' Ferius asked quietly.

'I got it.'

A commander – I've never figured out Berabesq military ranks, which make no sense to me – strode towards us, the crowd of onlooking soldiers parting for him to pass. He had a thick barrel chest covered in an ornate bronze breastplate. Berabesq soldiers have a tradition of spending their off-hours decorating their breastplates using a slow and painstaking art form called *hamitshani*, in which small, precise hammers and special awls are used to engrave designs into the metal. The designs tend to be religious scenes from one of the Berabesq codices that are of particular inspiration or significance to the soldier in question.

In this particular case, the commander's breastplate depicted a sinner, his arms bound and stretched to breaking point, having his entrails lifted out by an angelic being who was holding them up to the ray of sun shining down from above.

'What heresy is this?' he demanded of his trio of soldiers.

'Spies, *quadan*,' one of them assayed.

Quadan meant 'guiding hand' – a high-ranking division commander, if I recalled correctly.

The commander cast a dubious expression at her, but stepped forward to tower over me, idly fingering the coiled barbed whip at his side. 'To whom belong your eyes?'

It took me a second to translate the odd phrase. *He's asking who I spy for.*

I pointed a finger to the sky.

The implication that I was spying for God drew a chuckle from some of the onlookers, but not the commander. He uncoiled his whip. 'With this I can strip the skin off a man within a single minute.' He let me see the barbs. 'It takes even less time when I dislike the man, and I dislike spies very much.'

'I am no spy,' I said. I gestured to Ferius. 'My aunt and I are penitents, come to serve the living god.'

'He is not your god,' the woman who'd tried to piss on me said in a rage.

I gave her a belligerent snort. 'Does not Vizier Ossodif write, "A god is god of all, or god of none"?'

The commander eyed me warily. 'I have not read this Ossodif.'

Me neither.

I shrugged. 'As Vizier Ossodif says, "The truth of God needs no author, for the words themselves are recognised in the heart of every believer."'

The commander gave that due consideration. 'There is wisdom in this, but as Vizier Calipho sagely wrote, "Faith lies in deeds, not words."'

I'd never heard of a Vizier Calipho before either, but then again, I really didn't know much about Berabesq theology. When you've spent your life growing up in a culture that considers god-worship to be superstitious nonsense, you don't exactly spend a lot of time studying it. So now I was trying to figure out whether there really was a Vizier Calipho or whether the commander was screwing with me. I decided to put faith in this possibly non-existent vizier.

'My faith is proven in my deeds,' I said.

'And what deeds are those?' the commander asked.

At last the conversation had wound itself to the place I needed it to go: to where I could deliver my joke.

According to Ferius, arta loquit – the Argosi talent for eloquence – places a rather high value on humour. Of course,

250

she might've been kidding. Still, this particular joke was a key part of my plan, and I had my erstwhile urinator to thank for it.

'The deeds of a mighty warrior,' I replied with a straight face.

The three soldiers sneered in remarkable unison. 'Mighty warrior? He fell without landing a single blow!'

'Indeed,' I said, as if she'd made my case for me.

The commander, who seemed to be finding this increasingly amusing, gestured to the bruises and cuts on my face, which I'd gotten at the hands of his solders, 'Explain, oh mighty warrior.'

'It's simple, noble quadan. Who but a mighty warrior could, by virtue only of his intimidating presence –' I gestured to the trio of cavalry troopers who'd beaten me to a pulp – 'cause hardened soldiers to piss themselves?'

There was silence for a moment as the crowds of onlooking solders waited to see who would be slicing me into pieces first. Then . . . thunder. Booming laughter that made me feel as if the earth itself was shaking beneath me. 'Bold!' he chortled, thumping a hand against my shoulder. I wondered how much of that I could take before I'd end up hammered into the ground like a tent peg.

The rest of the crowd picked up his mirth, laughing among themselves as the joke spread throughout the columns of soldiers. Even the three who'd given me the beating began to snicker. Guess they'd decided I was 'cute'.

Damn. I really thought this time Ferius would turn out to be wrong.

It was only then that I noticed the commander himself had gradually settled, his gaze threatening to pierce my deceptive manner. His hand settled on my shoulder, fingers gripping as tight as an iron vice. 'Now, oh mighty warrior,' he said, leaning in, 'you have five seconds to tell me your true purpose before I see if you are even funnier on the inside.'

I nodded. This, too, we'd expected. The point of my latest public humiliation hadn't been to convince the commander of a lie, but to make him like us enough that he'd accept a piece of the truth. 'My teacher,' I said, pointing to Ferius, 'she has a sickness that no healer among our people can cure. Word came to us that the Berabesq god is real, that he resides in your capital and performs miracles. I hoped . . .'

This next part was tricky, because honesty isn't something that comes naturally to me. I let my gaze linger on Ferius. My mentor. My friend. The person who'd saved my life a hundred times and who'd taken a miserable, self-involved boy who saw no value in anything but magic and opened his eyes to all the things that really mattered in the world. I remembered with perfect clarity the day I'd first met her, the sight of those laughing green eyes, that maddening smirk, and the wild kindness written in every part of her face after she'd forced air back into my lungs and made my heart start again.

Now she was dying. Slowly, painfully, inexorably.

'If he is God, then I will make him save her.'

It wasn't the appropriate way to say it. Nobody likes it when you talk as if you can force their deity to do your bidding. But it was true, and every once in a while something as seemingly futile as the truth can be compelling.

The commander's jaw tightened, but then his features softened. 'I would normally beat a man black and blue for such blasphemy,' he said. He brought his hand back as if to strike me, but I've been hit enough times to know a feint when I see it. I stood there without flinching as he brought his palm to my cheek, gently holding it there. 'Vizier Calipho writes that courage comes from God.' He took his hand away and began coiling his whip. 'Yours has earned you passage to the capital.'

34

The Quadan

The commander's name was Keliesh, a Berabesq variant, it turned out, of my own name. Somewhere deep in antiquity, some ancient common language had provided the root for both the words Keliesh, which meant 'bright and eager child' in the Berabesq tongue, and Kellen, which – according to my sister Shalla's purported research on the subject when we were kids – meant 'clumsy, idiotic, stubborn boy who thinks being clever is the same thing as being smart'.

It's possible something was lost in her translation.

'You have a fine hand for the board,' Quadan Keliesh said, grinning as he picked up one of his tiny wooden spearmen and knocked over my vizier with it. 'But the game of shujan takes a lifetime to master.'

Shujan was a variant – Keliesh would say the originator – of a type of military strategy game I'd seen played in several countries on the continent, primarily Gitabria and Darome. The most notable Berabesq innovation was to play on a six-sided board rather than four.

'Allows for flanking,' Keliesh had explained. 'No two armies ever fought by hurling themselves at each other in a straight line.'

I'd wondered aloud whether perhaps the six sides were related to the Berabesq six-faced god. This earned me a cuff across the head that, while irritating and somewhat painful, had no doubt saved me from worse, given the way some of the soldiers nearby had glared at me for suggesting something so blasphemous.

'God has one face, which is the one he gave his children,' Keliesh had said.

'But we all have different faces,' I argued.

This might have seemed a stupid thing to do, given their religious fervour, but I'd noticed Keliesh quite enjoyed correcting me, especially if it made me the butt of a joke.

'Have you never seen a picture of God?' he asked.

'I'd understood that to be frowned upon.'

His brow furrowed. '"Frowned upon"? Why should God fear his own image? The only prohibition is in making false images of him.' He reached back into his pack. 'In fact, every soldier keeps a picture of God nearby, lest he forget his true commander.'

Keliesh handed me a small bronze disc, like a Daroman cameo only flatter and less adorned. I spotted a tiny clasp and prised the two sides apart to reveal the image. When I looked at it, the face I saw was young, lean and weather-tanned from travel, and rather confused. 'It's a mirror,' I said.

Keliesh cuffed me again. 'See how foolish these foreigners are?' he asked his soldiers. 'They cannot even recognise God when they see His face!'

There was considerable laughter at that, followed by Keliesh giving me a lengthy explanation that we all shared God's face, and it was only our vanity that made us believe any one of us looked different from each other.

255

'Ours is a religion of unity,' he explained.

'That has six holy books?'

I really shouldn't have kept pushing my luck, but I really was curious to understand the nature of their god, especially given there was a decent chance I was going to attempt to murder him. Also, for all their warnings against blasphemy, once you get them talking, Berabesq soldiers love debating religion.

'There is but one true codex, just as there is but one true god,' Keliesh said sternly, resetting the shujan board by arranging two sets of six pieces on each of the six sides.

'How do you know your god – the penitent – is the one?' I asked, already contemplating an opening move with one of my faithful pieces. These were warriors who could attack in any direction when at least two spaces away from a vizier. Next to a vizier they couldn't attack, but also couldn't be killed, which was why the usual Berabesq strategy was to keep them close. I, however, used them a little recklessly, possibly because I'd nearly been killed by a squad of Faithful once, and now rather enjoyed watching them die.

'We know ours is the true god because all the signs make it clear,' Keliesh said, moving one of his spearmen.

'But you're soldiers. Why not believe that God is a warrior? You personally command thousands of soldiers, carefully deciding their precise movements the way a clockmaker must. Why not believe God is like you?'

He gestured to himself and then the others sitting nearby, cleaning their armour or sewing patches onto worn clothing. 'Look at how we live, boy. Far from the comforts of home, here under the hot desert sun, our lives ones of hardship and bloodshed. Who but a penitent would accept such a life?'

Bloodthirsty killers? I considered suggesting, but Keliesh wasn't done. He pointed to the south, towards the capital. 'Three hundred miles from here, God awaits, alone in his great temple, never leaving its spire, though he could claim the entire world as his own. Now what does that sound like?'

It was getting late, and I was ready to seek out my bed, so I conceded, 'Like a penitent in a prison of his own making?'

Keliesh smiled and held his hands palm up to the sky. 'See, my lord? Even the lowliest among the heathens can be brought into the faith!'

I was dubious about that one, but not eager to continue the debate. Keliesh, though, reached out a hand and gripped my shoulder before I could rise. 'You see the truth, Kellen, even if you try to close your eyes to it. Do you know why?'

'Because even the lowliest of heathens can—'

'Because you are a penitent yourself,' he said, his voice quieter now. He nodded towards the other side of the encampment, where I'd left Ferius sleeping fitfully in a tent they'd granted us. 'It is your guilt that drives you.'

'I didn't have anything to do wi—'

Again he cut me off. 'The heathen culture from which you come no doubt sees guilt as a flaw. A weakness. But you and I know the truth. Guilt is conscience. Penitence is not merely the coin by which we pay for our sins, but also the means for us to right the world's wrongs.'

There was a strange gentleness in this big, brutish warrior who, but for a good joke, might have had us hung for spies. Perhaps these little acts of kindness he showed me – playing shujan with me, allowing me to question his faith – were part of his personal penitence. I wondered how he'd feel when he learned the price of my own redemption might be the death of his god.

'Go to bed, Kellen,' he said. 'Even the penitent must rest.'

Despite my efforts to be silent as I entered our tent, Ferius woke almost immediately. I noticed her fingers trembling as they reached for a pair of the razor-sharp steel cards she kept under her pillow.

'Kid?' she asked. Her gaze was blurry, her skin so pale it was as if I could see the bones of her skull underneath.

'Go back to sleep,' I said. 'Unless . . . Is there anything you need?'

She shook her head. 'Just dozin' a little. Where's the squirrel cat?'

'Out hunting, I think.'

Ferius chuckled. 'Thievin's more likely.'

Actually he was perched in a tree outside our tent, making sure anyone who dared come too close knew that there would be a price to pay for disturbing Ferius's rest. I didn't tell her that though. She hates being protected.

'Funny how he's stuck around this long, don't you think?' she asked.

The question took me by surprise. 'What do you mean? We're busine—'

She waved me off. 'You're business partners, I get it. But he's a squirrel cat. Don't you think he wants to . . .' She looked up at me with bleary eyes. Something she saw in my expression made her hesitate.

'What is it?'

'Hmm? Nothin'. Just tired is all.' She reached out a finger

258

to feebly poke the back of my hand. 'So, you spent the evenin' with that crazy quadan again?'

'He's actually a lot kinder than he lets on.'

'He's a religious nut. Nobody said they can't be nice folks.'

'I don't know,' I said, unwinding my bedroll. 'Once you see it from his perspective, there's a kind of logic to his faith. Maybe even something noble about it.'

Ferius laughed then, catching herself only when she started coughing and had to spit on the ground. A trace of blood in the trail of spittle looked like it was trying to slither back towards her. Ferius reached out and took my chin to stop me staring at it. 'So this Keliesh ain't so bad then?'

I knew she was trying to distract me, but I went along anyway. 'I think he's trying to convert me though.'

'Seems like he's doin' a fair job of it so far.'

'It's not like that. I just . . . There's more to these people than I first thought, that's all.'

Again she laughed. 'That's what I love about you, kid. No matter where we go, no matter how strange the people, if I leave you with 'em long enough, you'll start to see things their way.'

'I guess that makes me gullible then.'

She shook her head, suddenly serious. 'No, kid, it's what makes you Argosi.'

Ferius rarely complimented me, and when she did, it was usually in a snarky way that made it hard to tell how genuine the sentiment was. But every once in a while she'd say something so simple, so utterly without artifice, that I'd suddenly find myself struggling to keep back the tears.

Her eyes had closed and her breathing had become so quiet I couldn't be sure if she was alive. 'Ferius?' I said.

'Yeah, kid,' she wheezed.

'I'm going to get you help. I know you don't like people looking out for you, and I'm sorry about that, but I'm not letting this stupid malediction take you. Somewhere in Berabesq, whether with their god or some vizier, somebody has a cure. I'm going to make them give it to us. I don't care about the price or what I have to do, but that's just how it's going to be.'

'I know, kid,' she said, eyes still closed, reaching for my hand but not quite making it this time. 'That's what makes you Kellen.'

35

The Capital

One of the virtues of travelling with an army is that it makes it vastly easier to push your way into all kinds of places that might otherwise prove inaccessible, such as, for example, a city so bursting with people that it made the overcrowded capital of Darome look like a ghost town.

'Under God's loving eye,' Quadan Keliesh swore as he gazed at the sweating, churning city. The Berabesq language suffers from a notable lack of profanity. 'I do not know whether to find this magnificent or maddening.'

'Haven't you been here before?' I asked.

He shook his head vigorously. 'As Vizier Pheybas instructs, the comforts of the hearth are bars that cage the soul of the true penitent.'

Makhan Mebab was actually two cities, one encircling the other. *Makhan*, which meant 'glorious', was a tiny walled district of gleaming spires overlooking temples and palaces. Surrounding it was *Mebab*, which can mean either 'worshipful' or 'kneeling', depending on your translation. Here glittering streets of a white stone that sparkled in the sun were paved in perfect geometric patterns that made you wonder if perhaps the city really had been designed by a god. It certainly wasn't designed for people.

'This place stinks,' Reichis sneered, his mouth hanging open so he wouldn't have to breathe through his nostrils.

Large as Mebab was, it had been built to hold thirty thousand souls, but now had swollen to accommodate as many as a million. Clerics in white and gold robes led their own armies of lurching, limping men and women in rags in their wake, penitents in search of miracles. Wealthy merchants and artisans had squads of armoured guards holding the line to keep beggars and other undesirables from their establishments. The less well-to-do were forced to stand sentinel in front of their own shops or rely on their families. I saw more than one boy or girl aged barely ten hovering by a small market stall with a club in their hands and a nervous look in their eyes.

Yet even through the stench of sweat and too many bodies, there was a vivid excitement in the air, almost a glow about these armies of soldiers and pilgrims, fuelled by faith that here, in this place, they would see that which no one before them had ever seen: their god.

Keliesh shared that joyous anticipation, though I noted he'd balanced hope and optimism with a dozen soldiers at his back. The rest he'd left encamped outside the city with the other armies. Merchants and other wealthier citizens, seeing his red quadan's cloak, shouted at him as we passed, demanding to know why the city was filling with riff-raff.

'It is as Vizier Calipho warns,' the commander said to me as we walked. '"Some gaze upon God and yet still see only their own face, and so are filled with misery instead of ecstasy."'

'You ever read Vizier Sipha?' Ferius asked.

Keliesh, usually delighted to compare religious theologies, frowned. 'The rantings of a *female* vizier, unordained by the great councils, are not considered law within the canons of our faith.'

'Is it only when men say so that words convey wisdom?'

The quadan nodded with a wry smile as he brought his palms together and turned them out – his way of showing temporary surrender in such debates. 'I await the wisdom of Sipha then.'

'She wrote, "In all things must moderation be embraced, for should every soul upon the earth in righteous fervour shout God's name, then would all be rendered deaf."'

Despite his apparent biases, Keliesh really did adore a neat axiom, and pondered this one before asking, 'What is one to glean from this observation?'

Ferius gestured to the teeming streets, the men and women begging for food, the press of body against body everywhere we looked. 'Place like this ain't built for so many. Gonna see disease run like wildfire through these streets before long. Gonna see blood spill soon after that.'

A sudden hue and cry caught our attention. A fight of some kind had broken out further up the street. Meanwhile, a contingent of two dozen helmeted men in strapped leather armour, short-hafted spears in hand, pushed through the crowds, walking *away* from the screams.

'Clerical guards,' Ferius said. 'Aren't they supposed to enforce law and order in the city?' she asked Keliesh.

He didn't reply, but stepped in front of the other commander. 'You appear to be facing the wrong direction, guardsman.'

With surprising fluidity – and temerity – two dozen spears

lowered to direct their points at Keliesh's belly. His own men, however, didn't make a move.

'They will wait for my command,' Keliesh told the commander of the clerical guards.

'No soldier of the profane armies may draw a weapon in the sacred city,' the other said. 'Should even one of them do so, all will be excommunicated, they and their families hunted down and given blasphemers' deaths.'

Keliesh showed no sign of fear. 'That seems . . . extreme.' He turned to Ferius. 'Perhaps I should read this Vizier Sipha after all.' To the guard commander he said, 'I still hear screams ahead. If you won't see to it, then step away and I will.'

'All proceeds as it should,' the guard commander sneered. 'Run along now, *penitent*.' His eyes lingered on the religious scene of Keliesh's breastplate.

'Most of the clerical guards follow the clockmaker's codex,' Ferius explained quietly. 'Don't have much time for those who believe God's a penitent.'

Ancestors, I thought. *How does a theocracy function if people resent each other's interpretations of God?*

More sounds of violence reached us; people were racing past, trying to get away.

'Reichis, go find out what's happening.'

The squirrel cat sniffed. 'But these two nutjobs are gonna start killing each other soon, I don't want to mi—'

I pointed to the crowded street ahead of us. 'There's probably worse things happening up ahead.'

'Good point.'

The squirrel cat launched himself from my shoulder, landing on the wooden awning of a shop before scrambling up to the single-storey roof. He took off along the roof, leaping into the air, fuzzy glide flaps spread wide to catch the breeze. Soon he was flying above all our heads, making his way to the source of the cacophony.

The commander of the clerical guards took note of Reichis's flight. 'Now even wild beasts infest our city.' He gestured for one of his subordinates. 'Begin drawing up plans for a city-wide extermination campaign. I'll not see the sacred temples covered in the droppings of filthy animals.'

Well, if I hadn't already disliked this guy, he was making it easier by the minute.

The commander must've caught my expression, because he started paying attention to Ferius and me for the first time, and said to Keliesh, 'Why do you bring foreigners into the city?'

'They are pilgrims, and it is right to allow them in Makhan Mebab. Does not Vizier Calipho say, with his customary piercing sagacity, "The poorest pilgrim, stumbling from a foreign land, is the truest citizen of the city of God"?'

The commander of the clerical guards took that like a slap in the face. 'You would bleat the ravings of a penitent preacher at me?'

Keliesh made a show of whispering to me, loud enough for all to hear, 'Calipho also warns that, to a fool, words of wisdom are as the bleating of sheep.'

Why is he picking a fight with this guy? I wondered.

'I have no cause to detain members of the army,' the commander of the clerical guard said. He motioned for two of his own men, spears held out, to come forward. 'The foreigners come with us to be interrogated. I'll have no spies in my city.'

'Then we have a problem,' Keliesh replied. 'Because these

265

two are my guests, come to witness the glory of God, and –'
he gestured to Ferius, who was now having to lean on me
from standing so long – 'to seek admission within the temple
walls to find healing in His presence.'

'It is not for foreigners to find succour in Makhan.' The
commander raised a finger. 'And if you quote one more time
from the nonsense of the penitent codex, I will arrest you
for creating a public disturbance.' He smiled then. 'The council
of viziers holds a conclave even now, quadan. God's presence
necessitates once and for all the distinction of the true holy
texts from the false ones. It is time to purge the faith of chaff.'

Keliesh smiled back at him. I noted the subtlest twitch in
his fingers and a change came over the dozen soldiers who'd
accompanied him. 'I could not agree more, guardsman.' Keliesh
then turned to me. 'The great temple awaits in the centre of
the city. Take your companion there and pray outside the
walls for God's grace.'

'Arrest the foreigners!' the commander shouted. 'And the
traitor who brought them!'

'Go!' Keliesh told me. Even before he'd turned back to face
the clerical guards, he'd drawn his sword in one smooth
motion and brought its point to the other man's throat.

'C'mon, kid,' Ferius said, pulling at my arm. 'The man's
given us a gift. We'd be poor guests not to make use of it.'

I felt an odd sort of guilt wash over me as I helped Ferius
stumble through the crowded streets. Keliesh was a military
man and a religious zealot, two things I despised both on
instinct and by upbringing. Yet he had spent every night
since we met playing shujan with me, teaching me the axioms
of his faith and listening to me counter them. Debating,
arguing and, just as often, laughing out loud together. Now

he was putting his life and those of a dozen of his soldiers at risk for me, simply on the central principle of his beliefs: a penitent pilgrim must be allowed the chance at redemption before God.

The irony was that, in doing so, he was giving me the chance I needed to murder his god.

'Dirty business,' Ferius said, noting my expression.

A dirty business indeed.

36

The Entrance

There's an art to casing a joint, as Ferius would put it. Reichis would agree. It involves the two Argosi talents at which I'm the least adept: arta precis – perception – and arta tuco – subtlety.

'What're you seein', kid?' Ferius asked.

'Six entrances on the ground floor,' I replied as we continued our awkward stroll around the low circular wall surrounding the tiny temple city of Makhan. The spire of the great temple at its centre rose high above the other houses of prayer and palaces that housed the high viziers. Only by following the circumference of the surrounding wall could one periodically see through gaps between the other buildings to the lower floors of the great temple itself. Each of the six sides of the huge hexagonal structure bore a phrase in archaic Berabesq, which Ferius translated into a welcome for those who worshiped that particular 'face' – or in this case, codex – of God.

I'd tried to convince her to stay behind and rest, but in a city already bulging with pilgrims, you'd be lucky to find space to sit on the pavement, never mind a proper room in an inn.

"'Enter boldly, those with courage in their hearts and steel in their hands,'" she read aloud, squinting as she peered over the low curtain wall at the inscription above the arched doorway on the third face of the temple.

'. . . and then get your head cut off,' I added, noting the contingent of guards barring entry to the warrior's door, just as there had been at those of the clockmaker and the gardener.

Apparently Makhan was usually open to travelling viziers, who would bring their flocks with them not only to pray within the temple, but to converse and debate peacefully with those of other sects. There was an optimism to that idea that appealed to me – that this place was so grand, so beautiful and so imposing that those of contrary views would feel both the impetus to champion their view of the Berabesq god and yet never dare turn to violence within.

Now though?

My gaze went up, high up past the hexagonal walls that formed the base of the temple, up the massive spire at its centre, as tall as any tower, taller even than the central tower of the Academy of the Seven Sands, which until now had been the biggest building I'd ever seen. Somewhere inside, near the top, perhaps even now looking down on us from one of the tall, narrow windows, was the Berabesq god. I kept wondering when lightning would strike me down from one of those windows.

A fight broke out in front of us between two groups of pilgrims. Berabesq is a funny language – I can *kind of* understand what people are saying most of the time, but when they get angry they talk so fast the words start to tumble out like a raging waterfall and I become lost in it.

269

Ferius and I slipped out of the way, pulling back a few yards to resume our route around the circumference of the tiny walled city.

'So, six doors on the ground floor,' I said. 'Every one of them too thick to blast through and barred from the inside, so no locks to pick.' I glanced up again. 'Windows too high to reach, walls too sheer to scale.'

Normally none of this would've been a problem. My usual technique for getting into a place is to let Reichis glide in through a window – sometimes a chimney, which makes for some hilarious moments as he stumbles out covered in soot, right up until he starts biting me for laughing at him – and then unlock the door from the inside to let me in. Problem here was, the bars were made from solid iron and it took two guards to move them.

'I think I *might* be able to lift one,' the squirrel cat said, perched on my shoulder. A vizier was being allowed past the guards through the clockmaker's door, which allowed us to see the heavy bar inside.

A hundred squirrel cats all working together – something that, so far as I can tell, is an impossibility – wouldn't be able to budge one of those bars. I didn't bother pointing that out though.

'Best we find another way inside,' I suggested.

'Six doors,' Ferius said. 'That's all you see?'

Most of the time we'd been casing the temple, Ferius hadn't even bothered to look at it, which made me find it hard to believe she'd spotted a seventh entrance that I'd missed. 'You see another one?' I asked.

She shook her head. 'Nope.'

'Then how—'

270

'What's the third lesson I taught you in arta precis, kid?'

'Was it, "Go get me another beer"? Because as I recall, those were the fourth, fifth, sixth and seventh lessons you taught me in arta precis.'

Like all things Ferius, as absurd and frustrating as the experience had been, there had been a point to it: she'd wanted me to notice that the bartender was refilling the glass higher each time, because I'd flashed too valuable a coin and he'd decided to get us drunk and then have a few of his serving staff mug us when we tried to leave. By the last refill, I'd spotted him putting drops of something black and viscous into our drinks.

'The third lesson of arta precis,' Ferius said, leaning on me to steady herself, 'is never look where everyone else is looking.'

'Even when you're trying to case the entrances to an otherwise impregnable temple?'

'*Especially* then.'

I looked around the packed courtyard that surrounded the temple. 'So what have you been looking at?'

Ferius pointed behind us, down one of the streets that radiated outwards from the temple grounds. A man in exquisite vizier's robes was walking away, accompanied by a smaller man who looked like some sort of assistant and four guards in glittering armour with designs on their cloaks that matched those on the robes of the vizier.

'Tell me about him,' Ferius said.

He was already a good way away from us, but I'd seen enough to have an impression. 'Rich. Dresses to show it. Doesn't trouble himself to look at any of the pilgrims. Doesn't seem bothered by any of the suffering around him.'

271

'Didn't ask you to judge the man. Where you reckon he's headed?'

'No idea. Into the city, I guess.'

'Fair enough. Where's he coming from then?'

'How should I . . . ?'

It occurred to me then that, of course, he had to have come from inside the temple. Only something was bothering me about that very logical inference.

'Which door did he walk out of?' Ferius asked.

Every time a vizier had come out of one of the doors and then through the gates in Makhan's surrounding wall, there was a great hue and cry from pilgrims rushing up to them, begging for blessings or miracles or pelting them with questions about the god within the temple. Even accompanied by guards, by the time they'd gotten past the crowds, they'd all ended up looking like they'd narrowly escaped being lynched.

'His robes weren't rumpled,' I said quietly.

'What's that?'

'His robes – they were perfectly orderly. And the way he walked was relaxed. Calm. Not the gait of someone who's just had to press their way through a mob.'

'And where did he come from again?' Ferius asked.

I turned back to stare past the wall at the great temple. There were six doors. In my travels I've been to some pretty strange places, seen all kinds of bizarre architecture, including doors that have no handles and almost no visible seam around them. This building only had six doors. I was sure of that.

'Is it magic?' Reichis asked. He started sniffing the air all around us – he claims he can smell magic, though that doesn't explain how we've been ambushed by mages so many times.

'Why're you starin' at that ugly old building, kid?' Ferius asked.

Because that's where we want to go, I thought. *Because that's where everybody's looking.*

Ferius's third lesson of arta precis: never look where everyone else is looking.

My eyes went to the sandstone courtyard beneath our feet, searching for any signs, but of course I wouldn't be able to find them.

'What're you lookin' for now, kid?'

I glanced back at the vizier disappearing into the city with his entourage, the man with the unrumpled robes and casual stride. 'There's a tunnel,' I said. 'A tunnel beneath our feet that lets the most powerful viziers enter and exit the temple unseen.'

Ferius clapped me on the shoulder. 'See, kid? Knew you'd get there eventually.'

Her smile stayed intact even as the last drop of colour drained from her skin and she collapsed into my arms.

37

The Wrong Direction

Crowds of men, women and children buffeted us like ocean currents too powerful and capricious for such a feeble vessel as that which carried Ferius Parfax. Life at the royal palace of Darome had afforded me a period of steady meals and decent rest that had given me a little more muscle than I used to have, but already my arms were near exhaustion and we'd barely made it two blocks away from where Ferius had fainted.

'Get out of the damn way!' I shouted at people, so angry and terrified that I realised I was speaking in Jan'Tep and not the language they would understand. It didn't matter. When they caught sight of my eyes they pressed aside regardless.

'Where we goin'?' Reichis asked.

'We have to find a travellers' saloon.'

They called them 'pilgrim's respites' in Berabesq of course, but travellers' saloons were dotted all over the continent. Places where Argosi and others in the know could meet in secret, trade information, barter for some of the more exotic supplies, and recuperate in peace and safety from whatever ailed them. We wouldn't find a cure for the malediction there, but at least Ferius would be protected while I went and figured out how to blackmail a god into saving her life.

Only problem now? How to find the damned place.

'Ferius?' I said, shifting her weight in my arms as I leaned against the outer wall of a shop to give myself a moment's rest. 'Ferius, wake up. You need to tell me where the travellers' saloon is!'

Damn me. I should've made her take us there the second we'd entered Makhan Mebab. But she'd insisted we case the temple first.

'Ferius?'

'She's unconscious,' Reichis said, craning his head down from my shoulder to sniff at her. 'Deep.'

'Ferius, wake up,' I repeated, panicking now. 'You've got to tell me—'

Her eyes fluttered, only to close again.

'Ferius, please!'

Her lips parted, just a little. She mumbled something I couldn't hear over the noise of the crowds. I leaned in closer. 'Say it again, Ferius. Tell me how to find the travellers' saloon.'

Like the whisper of a fading breeze, she said, 'Arta precis, kid. Always . . . arta precis.'

'She's out again,' Reichis said.

'No!' I shouted, practically screaming into her unconscious face. 'Not another stupid test! Not now!'

But it was no good. Ferius was alive, breathing, but nothing more. I had to find the travellers' saloon without her.

Arta precis.

Ancestors, but I was even more exhausted from trying to be 'perceptive' all the time than I was from carrying Ferius in my shaking arms. Why couldn't the Argosi ever just answer a simple question? Why was everything a mystery? Was it really so hard to just help a person when they asked?

275

Only . . . I hadn't asked.

Arta precis. Look where others aren't looking. Ask the question no one else is asking.

Here we were, in the city where a god waited high up in the spire of a great temple, his rapidly approaching birthday the spark that would set off generations of war and strife. The Argosi didn't like war. If they had any purpose in the world that I could discern, it was to prevent them from starting.

So, the question nobody was asking: how likely was it that Ferius would be the only Argosi in Makhan Mebab right now?

I pushed my shoulder against the wall to get myself upright again, then turned around and walked back the other way.

'Where are we going?' Reichis asked. 'Why are we headed back inside?'

It was hard to talk while carrying Ferius and pushing through the crowds. 'Because we weren't the only ones casing the temple.'

38

Criminal Elements

There had to be at least fifty thousand people in the circular courtyard that surrounded the walled city of Makhan. They spilled out into the nearby streets, clambered up on the single-storey buildings of Mebab just to have a vantage point from which to peer up at the spire.

In the short time since I'd tried to get Ferius away from here, the crowds must have doubled. The temple had no bells, but the pilgrims carried their own little ones with them, shaking them almost feverishly. Those without simply banged one tin begging cup against another over and over.

'What's going on?' I asked a pock-faced man next to me.

'God!' he said, religious ecstasy oozing from him like pus from his wounds. 'Word has come from the temple; He will visit another miracle upon us!'

Great. Of all the times for Him to make an appearance, why now when I needed to track down whatever other Argosi were in the area and get them to help me take Ferius to a travellers' saloon?

'Is she dead?' the man asked, reaching out his hand like a scavenger's paw to see if there might be easy meat.

'Touch her again and you'll *really* need a miracle from your damned god,' I growled.

Blasphemy aside, my reaction was enough to make him slink away, slipping deeper into the mass of souls all around us.

'Heh,' Reichis said, after repeating my threat to himself. 'I like that one.'

I had to squat down, supporting Ferius on my knees to give my arms a rest. How was I supposed to find another Argosi in the middle of these hordes of bodies? Ferius had never taught me any sort of Argosi distress code to gain the attention of others. It was always just 'find a travellers' saloon' or 'paint a card' or something equally slow. No wonder there were so few of them; they probably all ended up dead on account of never getting help from any of the others when they needed it.

'Reichis, can you get airborne and spot any other Argosi?'

He gave a nervous snarl. 'In an open area like this, with all those temple guards? Somebody'll get it in their head to shoot me down with a crossbow bolt. Besides, how would I tell who's an Argosi and who's just another useless skinbag?'

He had a point. It's not like there was an Argosi uniform.

Different looks. Different paths. Half the time they don't even use the same words to describe the Argosi ways. They're all so . . . individualistic.

A joyous roar began to build from the crowds, reaching a crescendo as I felt the swell of bodies begin to push forward, pressing even tighter around the temple walls. I had to stand back up to avoid being trampled.

'My God!' a woman next to me sang out in desperate

278

fervour. 'Do You see me, God? Please, it is I, Ahame. Please, turn Your eyes to me!'

Above us all, on a shallow balcony near the top of the spire, a pair of curved double doors slowly swung open. A figure stepped out in plain white robes. A boy, perhaps twelve or thirteen, but with his shaved head and rake-thin frame he looked even younger.

'*That's* the skinbag idea of a god?' Reichis snorted. There were so many people pressed up against us now that he wasn't even bothering to stick to my shoulder, clambering onto their heads to get a better view. 'Squirrel cat gods are giants, their teeth as long as that spire there. And the claws, so sharp they—'

'Not now,' I said.

All around us, men, women and children screamed at the spire, all of them with some variation of the first woman's plea. They begged with desperate urgency for God to glance their way.

Is this all we want from our gods? To be noticed by them? To know they're watching over us? Not the big, collective mass of humanity, but just us personally?

Seemed to me the last thing I needed in my life was to live under the scrutiny of some deity. I had enough problems with guilt already.

Not to mention with exhaustion.

I couldn't set Ferius down for fear she'd get crushed, but my arms were ready to give out. She's wasn't very big, but was a lot heavier than she looked. Or I was weaker than I thought. Either way, my whole body was starting to shake with the effort.

'Your friend comes for God's blessing?' another woman

279

next to me asked in a Berabesq accent so strong I could barely make out her words.

I nodded.

'I will share your burden,' the woman offered.

She was covered head to toe in a gauzy beige linen fabric, even her face hidden from the world. There were a number of illnesses that required such covering. I'd seen men and women whose skin and muscle – even their very bones – were slowly melting away from a wasting disease. The very thought repulsed me.

Despite that, I nodded again and thanked her as she took Ferius's legs and helped me hold her there, protected from the crowds around us. The removal of so much strain on my arms almost made me cry out with relief. 'Thank you,' I said.

The woman's head tilted down. At first I thought it was a small bow, but then I realised she was staring at Ferius. 'Your friend is very ill. Let us pray God hears her even though her pleas are silent.'

I looked back up to the balcony atop the spire. The boy hadn't moved an inch. He just stood there, gazing down at his followers packed like fishes in a net. The heat had become sweltering, and sweat dripped down my face in sheets. When the drops landed on the skin of my collarbone, even they felt hot.

I heard a groan behind me, and turned to see an old man collapse to the ground. One person knelt down to help him, only to nearly get trampled as others just stepped over him to get closer to the wall.

What kind of god allows his people to suffer for no better purpose than to watch them adore him? I wondered.

Just then, I saw the boy's arms spread out wide. He turned his hands palms down, the fingers wiggling playfully. What I thought was more of my own sweat sliding down my face turned out to be drops of rain, cool and gentle on my skin.

The crowds chanted, *'Dabhra, dabhra!' Thank you, thank you!*

This soon ended as men and women once again began shouting to the boy to see them, to hear them, to heal the ills of their lives. A deafening cacophony of entreaties filled the air. They begged for the easing of a sickness, or for wealth, or even for love. 'I am so lonely, God!' one elderly woman in front of me cried. 'Send someone to me! Man or woman, I care not! Do not let me end my days alone!'

In fact, most of the cries weren't for supernatural aid at all. They were for those simple things human beings were supposed to give one another anyway. The sharing of wealth, of food and shelter. Medicine to cure suffering. Companionship to ease loneliness.

What odd miracles we ask for, I thought.

And what miracle have you come in search of, Kellen of the House of Ke? Kellen Argos, Path of Endless Stars. The spellslinger. The outlaw. The God slayer.

I looked around to see who had spoken. It wasn't the voice of the woman helping me with Ferius, and no one else nearby was looking at me. The voice had been so close though, as if they were whispering in my ear or coming from inside my . . .

My gaze rose above the heads of the crowd, higher and higher until it reached the top of the spire. Though it must've looked to all those in the temple grounds as if the child

281

god was looking at them, I knew then that they were all wrong.

He was looking at me.

Well, Kellen? God asked, his young voice like a bell inside my head. *Have you come to kill me or not?*

39

The Voice of God

Rain was now falling not in drops but in great sheets that drenched the crowds amassed outside the temple city's walls. Berabesq has never been entirely arid, not even its deserts, but this much precipitation in such a short time was unprecedented. Impossible. A miracle.

But then . . . a simple ember spell can appear as a miracle to someone who's never before seen magic performed.

You doubt me? God asked. He didn't sound particularly angry, but then he didn't sound too pleased either.

The men, women and children crowding the streets began to dance in the rain, twirling about joyously as they tumbled into one another, their arms raised to the sky in religious ecstasy.

'You seem like you have more than enough admirers already,' I said quietly.

One presumes that if he was a god, he didn't need me to shout.

But these are my followers. They have spent their lives in prayer almost from birth. The first words they learn to read are from their family codex. When a child takes her first step, her parents cry out, 'God gives her strength!' again and again, until neighbours all along the street chant it with them.

'In my business we don't call those followers,' I said. 'We call them marks.'

'Who are you talkin' to?' Reichis asked. His fur was soaked all the way through and starting to smell a little dank – a refreshing reminder of things more mundane than the voice of a deity in my head.

I meant only that devotion comes easily to my people, he said. 'And belief in miracles.'

And belief. A pause. *But faith is foreign to you, isn't it?*

'An apt choice of words. My people don't believe in gods.'

Yet they share such profound conviction that only magic defines them. A Jan'Tep house is no more than the sum of the power of its bloodlines. A man is measured solely by the spells he can cast. Do you believe that, Kellen of the House of Ke?

The woman next to me in her linen wrappings ignored the frenzied dancing all around us, her gaze locked on me. Blessedly – if that's the right word – she was still helping me carry Ferius.

'Shouldn't gods have better things to do than worry about whether a lone foreigner worships them?' I asked.

Another pause, longer this time.

But how is one a god if he is only worshipped by his people?

A good question, if one was even the slightest bit interested in theological quandaries.

Are you here to kill me, Kellen? he asked again.

I strained my weary muscles to lift Ferius a little higher. 'Save my friend,' I said softly. 'Save her and I'll leave here tonight. I'll leave you to—'

What of your mission? What of the people whose lives your employers fear will be destroyed by war if I live?

'They're not my problem!' I shouted, unable to stop myself.

284

I gazed down at Ferius, her features so pale under the sheen of rain coating her skin. She looked like a corpse freshly pulled from a river. 'Berabesq magic comes from worship, from their faith, from you. That means this damnable curse, this *malediction*, it comes from *you*!'

Then you accept my godhood?

'You stupid, vain son of a bitch! You think I give a shit whether you're really . . . Whether you're . . .'

A long time ago, sitting in some lousy saloon, I'd watched Ferius drinking herself into a stupor. One shot of Gitabrian whisky after another. I'd asked her what was wrong, what she hoped to accomplish.

'Accomplish?' she'd asked with a snort. 'I aim to get mighty drunk, kid.'

'But why?'

She held the little glass tumbler up to her eye, the dark, smoky liquid inside distorting my view of her. 'Fifth lesson of arta precis, kid. Sometimes to see a thing truly, you have to stop trying to see through it.'

'What's that supposed to mean?'

She rose to her feet, the legs of her battered chair creaking in complaint. 'It means that every once in a while when somebody smiles at you, it ain't a sign they're plannin' to knife you in the belly. They're just happy. Sometimes a body cries just cos they happen to be sad, not to manipulate you.' She picked up several of the little whisky tumblers on the table, carrying them awkwardly against her chest as she turned to go. 'And on occasion a respectable woman just feels a hankerin' to get good and drunk.'

I don't know why that memory came back to me just then, but I looked down at Ferius's pale features, searching desperately for a glimmer of that customary smirk of hers – the one she used to tell me that everything was going to be okay, no matter how much the evidence suggested otherwise. All I found was a very sick woman whose eyes were clenched so tightly in pain that I wondered if they would ever open again.

Sometimes to see a thing truly, you have to stop trying to see through it.

I looked back up at the spire, at the god standing there, performing miracles even as he seemed so determined to question my belief in him.

Yet what did I really see?

A boy looking down at me, asking if I believed he was God.

'Ancestors,' I whispered. 'You aren't sure, are you?'

What?

'You don't know if you truly are God.'

Just like that, the rain stopped falling. The crowds stopped dancing, looking at each other in confusion. Once again they all turned to look up at the boy on the spire, waiting for his next miracle. But he just turned and walked back inside, the doors closing behind him of their own accord.

Perhaps we will find out together, when you come to kill me.

286

40

The Path of Winding Roads

At the boy's abrupt departure, a great wail rose up from the crowds outside the temple. 'Come back! Come back!' they cried, hands gesticulating manically in the air as they formed the religious signs of their various sects. It was like watching thousands upon thousands of spellcasters discover their magic had suddenly fled them.

'Interesting,' said the woman in the beige linen wrappings, still holding on to Ferius's legs to help me carry her. 'I suggest we leave this place now. There will be increasing . . . consternation among the pilgrims when they realise their god will not be returning today.'

'*Their*' god. She wasn't one of them.

Her voice and accent had changed too. Strangely, Reichis recognised her before I did.

'Ugh,' he groaned. 'Of all the stinkin' Argosi in the world, why did they send us *her*?'

The gauzy fabric covering the lower half of her face shifted just a little – enough for me to detect the hint of a smile. 'Does the squirrel cat suffer from an upset stomach? Or is it perhaps that he recalls that last time our paths crossed he absconded with a number of my possessions?'

'Tell the skinbag she ain't gettin' none of her stuff back, Kellen,' he snarled in warning.

'Come,' she said, shifting her grip to take Ferius from me. It was mildly embarrassing how easily she was able to bear the weight, but then I recalled that she was a lot stronger than she looked.

'It's good to see you again, Rosie,' I said.

Even as she turned to carry Ferius from the temple grounds, I saw the tell-tale stiffening in her shoulders. 'I am the Path of Thorns and Roses. I have walked the length and breadth of this continent, fought duels against soldiers and mages, rescued villages from plagues and turned away armies with nothing more than the cards in my deck. You, *teysan*,' she said, emphasising the Argosi term for a lowly student, 'will address me with the proper respect.'

'Anything you say, Rosie.'

Reichis liked that one too.

Rosie led the way, navigating effortlessly through the endless crowds of people frantically discussing, debating or simply bewailing the god's disappearance. There was something both dizzying and faintly blasphemous about the winding route we followed, defying the geometric perfection of the city's arrangement of streets and alleys with sudden hard turns left and right in no pattern I could discern. Despite the fact that it was Rosie who carried Ferius all by herself, it was all I could do just to keep up.

For his part, Reichis seemed to enjoy the unpredictability. He would suddenly leap from my shoulder to bounce off the sides of one building and then land on the shop awning of another. He'd clamber up to a rooftop in order to launch himself into the air, spreading his limbs so that the furry flaps between them would billow out and catch the breeze, allowing him to fly above the crowds. As often as not he'd end up having to land on the street and scramble back to catch up with us when the Path of Thorns and Roses had once again made one of her unexpected turns.

'Where are you taking us?' I asked.

'A strange question,' she replied.

'It seems a perfectly obvious one to me.'

'Exactly.'

The urgency driving me to get help for Ferius warred with my irritation at Rosie's imperturbable and needlessly inscrutable behaviour. It had been a while since I'd run into another Argosi, and I'd forgotten that most of them are smug arseholes.

'How long has it been since last our paths crossed?' Rosie asked, turning another corner onto a wider avenue filled with street carts bearing fruits, vegetables and other foods, along with signs that showed prices crossed out and much higher ones hastily marked in their place.

'A couple of years, I guess,' I replied. 'Since that mess with the shadowblack plague in the Seven Sands.'

Her eyes glanced up at a small polished mirror mounted on a pole one of the merchants had attached to their cart in order to spot thieves. 'Have you travelled in that time, teysan? Seen new places?'

'Well, yeah, but—'

'Consider then all the places I have travelled. All the things I must have seen and done since last we met. Ponder on how many battles I have survived, what secrets I have unearthed.'

'What's your point?'

She changed the subject as unexpectedly as she switched sides of the street. 'Walk next to me and flip a coin, please.'

'What?'

'A coin. A shiny one. Do you have such a coin?'

I had any number of coins of course. In this case I chose my castradazi luminary coin, not for its mystical properties, but because it was the one that somehow always stayed cleanest and so was always shiny. I pulled it from the slot I'd sewn into the hem of my shirt and tossed it in the air. It landed tails up in my palm.

'Once more, if you please,' Rosie said.

I would've asked why, but since I knew I wouldn't get a proper answer, I let myself be guided by the severity in Rosie's tone and flipped the coin a second time. Tails again.

'Good,' she said.

'What was that for?'

She turned back a few yards, and so did the conversation. 'You asked where I was leading you.'

'Yeah, and . . . ?'

She seemed irritated by my obtuseness. She hoisted up Ferius a little more in her arms, showing that despite her strength and stamina, she was getting exhausted too. '*And*, given all the things each of us have done since last we saw each other, all the vital knowledge and information we might know, it is strange that your first question to me would be one to which you already know the answer.'

'A travellers' saloon? That's where you're taking us?'

She strode ahead, narrowly avoiding a cart being pushed along the alley by a man who seemed determined to crash into someone. 'Obviously.'

'Then why are we taking such a winding route?' I asked, more annoyed than ever. 'There's no possible way it can be this complicated to reach a place in a city made up of completely regular arrangements of streets and avenues.' I glanced around us. 'In fact, I'm pretty sure we've been down this road already.'

Rosie gave me a raised eyebrow to convey her disapproval. 'We've passed this corner three times already. Has the Path of the Wild Daisy not taught you arta loquit?'

For some reason, I always hated the way she seemed to refuse to call Ferius by her name, insisting on referring to her by her path instead. 'What has the Argosi talent for eloquence got to do with walking through a city?'

'Because *eloquence* does not refer only to languages and music. Arta loquit is for navigation, whether what is being navigated is a conversation, a culture, or a city; it is all the same.'

'Those are three completely different things actually,' I muttered, but on some level her observation made sense to me. The words of a language had to be memorised to speak it, but they also had to be understood in terms of their relationship to each other, just like places on a map. There were many ways to express any given idea, each with nuances and complications that would affect the outcome, just as there were many ways to go from one place to another, each with their own benefits and dangers.

'Do not reproach yourself,' Rosie said. 'Your maetri's way of teaching is as . . . unconventional as her path.'

Her implied criticism of Ferius got my back up. 'My *friend* is dying, and you're bouncing us all over this gods-damned city like a drunk searching for her coin purse. So do you think I care one bit about whether I kept track of the exact number of times you've walked us past this same corner?'

'A fair point,' Rosie conceded, then resumed walking. 'To answer your question, we have taken this route so that I could ascertain the number and nature of our pursuers.'

'Pursuers?'

All of a sudden I understood the strange little quirks of Rosie's behaviour as we'd travelled through the city. The way she'd glanced up in the mirror near the merchant's cart. Her request that I flip a shiny coin in the air twice in front of her. *She'd been using those things to see behind us without being noticed, to secretly observe whoever's following us.*

I spun around, my mind immediately filled with visions of armoured warriors, feral crowds and angry viziers come to carve my heart from my chest as punishment for some act or other of heresy. Given my conversation with the god back at the temple grounds, the very least I was guilty of was blasphemy.

'Arta tuco, teysan,' Rosie said, her tone a mixture of amusement and disappointment. 'An Argosi must learn arta tu—'

'I know what arta tuco means,' I snapped angrily.

'Then perhaps you could display some of it now,' she suggested.

She had a point. While subtlety wasn't one of my strong suits, I usually had the sense to keep a low profile. Thing was, at that precise moment I didn't give a damn about being subtle. I unclipped the flaps of the powder holsters at my sides. 'If someone's following us, just tell me where they are and I'll go blast them out of existence.'

'Now you're talkin'!' Reichis chittered from above us where

he was running along the rain gutter of a shop roof. His fur shifted colours, changing from the subdued tones of the sandstone buildings to take on a fiery red. 'Been hours since I ate a skinbag's eyes.'

I couldn't imagine when in the last day he could possibly have had occasion to consume a human eyeball. I decided not to ask.

'Arta eres is a skill best used judiciously and infrequently,' Rosie said. 'Save the fight for when the only path forward is the Way of Thunder.'

'Would you stop trying to teach me and just get Ferius to the damned travellers' saloon?'

Rosie stopped and handed her to me. For a second I was afraid I'd gone too far and our only ally was about to abandon us. Instead, once I was holding Ferius, Rosie reached out a hand to brush my cheek, her fingers soft as rose petals. The gentle sensation was so at odds with the hardness I associated with her that it was as if she'd become a completely different person. 'You are filled with fear for Ferius.'

'She's sick. She needs—'

'You are right to fear for her. The Path of the Wild Daisy has been a long one. Improbably, impressively long. But I fear it comes soon to its final destination, as all our paths must.'

I looked down at Ferius. 'You mean she's dying?'

Rosie lifted my chin. 'Argosi are not long-lived. Our paths are dangerous by design. One can be lucky only so many times. It is through skill and ruse that we survive, and eventually –' she took Ferius back from me – 'even the best of us runs out of cards to play.'

Once again I looked around for any sign of pursuit. 'You're

right,' I conceded. 'Let's just lose whoever's left and get Ferius help.'

Rosie nodded as though I'd just given her an order and turned to resume her march through the city. 'As you command, Path of Endless Stars, so it will be.'

41

The Travellers' Saloon

We finally stopped at a plain wooden door indistinguishable from the eight others that similarly fronted the row of attached single-storey buildings in this narrow alleyway.

'Didn't we pass this place twice already?' I asked.

'Good,' Rosie said in reply, then stopped herself. 'No, not quite good, but better. There were still two sets of spies following us when last we came by here.'

I glanced back again, and saw no one. 'And now?'

'We left them behind three streets back. This is as safe a time to enter as we're likely to find.'

I moved to go ahead of her and open the door, but Rosie, still bearing Ferius in her arms, raised a foot and pushed it open. She wasted no time in entering the building, which turned out to be vastly larger than it had appeared from the outside. What must once have been a row of individual terraced homes had had the walls between them removed, leaving space for a huge common room filled with tables. Only a few of the men and women crowding the place looked to be Berabesq. I wondered how many of them were Argosi.

'What happens if you enter through one of the other doors?' I asked.

'They are locked,' Rosie replied.

'And if someone notices that no one ever goes in or comes out and decides there might be something inside worth stealing?'

'Burglary is punishable by death in the Berabesq territories. We Argosi follow the laws of the lands in which we find ourselves.'

The faces of the men and women around the room suddenly struck me as much more dangerous than when we'd entered. I'd grown so accustomed to Ferius's preference for avoiding violence. She wasn't one to follow the Way of Thunder unless there was no other choice.

'Come,' Rosie said, moving across the room towards the bar.

People looked up, but no one barred our way and no one spoke to us, except the bartender, who barely glanced up from pouring ale into mugs to say, 'Times like these, it's best to stay indoors.'

Rosie walked right past the end of the bar towards another door. 'Times like these, it's safest underground,' she said.

This wasn't the usual passphrase I'd encountered in other travellers' saloons. I wondered if the change was for this particular place or for the times we were in. Perhaps the usual phrase was too commonly known, so in times of war those in the know used the other one? I considered asking, but the Path of Thorns and Roses had never shown herself to be forthcoming about such matters.

She pushed through the door at the end of the bar and waited for me to come behind her. As soon as the door closed, we found ourselves shrouded in complete darkness. 'Count your steps,' she said.

'It's not my first time,' I said irritably.

I imagined her shrugging. 'I find myself often baffled by what things you know and what things you don't, teysan. It was many years into my training before my maetri first brought me to a *hosta pilgri*.'

'Ferius does things differently,' I said, not bothering to mention that she'd never told me the Argosi referred to travellers' saloons as 'hosta pilgri'.

Twenty-seven steps down the carved stone stairs we reached the end, and Rosie pushed open a final door that led us into what I'd come to think of as the real travellers' saloon, the upstairs being little more than a front.

From what I'd gleaned during my travels with Ferius, these sanctuaries could be found everywhere on the continent, from Gitabria in the south-east to Zhuban in the far north. Who had first built them, and to what purpose, was a mystery I doubted even the Argosi could answer. This one was much like the others I'd visited: a cavernous space below ground, carved into a stone chamber big enough that you could hide a small army down here. Lanterns hung from chains mounted into twenty-foot-high ceilings, lighting mismatched sets of tables and chairs, but leaving many a shadowy nook for secret conversations to take place and to mask the two or three exits that would lead to tunnels that provided escape, should the place get invaded. Far to the back were curtained-off sections – alcoves really – where greater privacy could be found, along with the occasional comfort artisan.

Unlike the crowded common room above, only two tables down here were occupied. The first by a man sitting alone, boots up on the wooden table, his eyes hidden beneath a frontier hat much like the one I was wearing. It didn't hide

297

his smile though, or his resemblance to Dexan Videris – a fellow spellslinger and outlaw who had almost as much cause to kill me as I had him. Fortunately, when he raised the brim of his hat enough to reveal his face, I saw he was a little younger than Dexan, though just as irritatingly handsome. He made a gesture of tipping his hat towards me before reaching over to grab his mug to take a drink.

Now that I could relax enough to remove my hands from my powder holsters, I noticed Rosie was leading us towards the second occupied table. A man and a woman sat there, leaning in close as they spoke quietly. When they saw us coming, they turned, and even in the dim light I recognised them: a grey-haired, grouchy-faced fellow by the name of Durral and a woman of the same years but considerably more gracious bearing, named Enna. Ferius's foster parents.

'Bring her to the couches,' Enna said, pulling a leather case from under the table as she rose to take charge of the situation.

Durral came over to us, his arms out. 'Give her to me, Rosie.'

'I am the Path of Thorns and Roses,' she said as she gave over Ferius.

'Yeah, well today I'm the Path of I Do Not Give A Crap.' He carried his foster daughter to one of the curtained booths and laid her on a couch there.

'Heh,' Reichis chittered at Durral's comment. 'Gotta remember that one.'

Enna opened up her leather case and pulled out an elegantly carved object that appeared to be made of two different polished woods. A dark one, almost mahogany black, shaped like a tiny bowl or jar, and, attached to it, a tubular stem

298

made from what appeared to be cherrywood. It took me a second to understand what it was.

'A pipe?'

'Don't get too close,' Enna warned as she set down the pipe and removed a tiny satchel from inside the case. 'Breathe too much of this in without the requisite preparation and you're liable to end up running through the streets of Makhan Mebab flapping your arms like a bird and wondering why you can't fly.'

She pulled the top of the satchel open and began tapping out a portion of its contents into the pipe's bowl. I counted four different kinds of powdered leaves inside. Two were green, though different textures. A third was brown the shade of manure – it might have been manure for all I knew. The fourth looked as if it was made from tiny, translucent shards of some kind of blue-green crystal. She carefully fished out one of the shards with a fingernail, depositing it back in the satchel and muttering, 'Don't want too much of that,' as she pulled the drawstring tight. 'Gonna need you to light this for me,' she said.

'Me? You want me to light a pipe with a spell that's got a decent chance of blowing up the pipe, your hand and half your face?'

'Need a little of your magic,' she said calmly, though I was sure I noticed the pipe quivering in her hand. 'The herbs, see, they're a . . . conduit, of sorts.'

'A conduit for what?'

Durral gave a grunt. 'You an expert on healin' ways now, kid? Reckon we need your approval before we try to save our daughter?'

'Don't bite the boy's head off, Durral,' Enna scolded. To me she said, 'It's a little complicated, Kellen, and truth be told, none of us can be sure exactly what pieces of the puzzle work and which don't make no difference at all. But the long and the short of it is, this malediction those viziers put on Ferius can't be fought off with regular medicine. It takes . . . Well, I guess you'd say it takes spirit.'

'Spirit?'

'I expect that must sound a little strange to a former Jan'Tep initiate.'

Strange? The idea was bizarre, superstitious and almost childish. To my people, magic was science. Forms of raw power existed everywhere in the world. The dangerous ores that clustered together underground beneath an oasis provided the means for an initiate to be banded in them. With the right training and talent, a Jan'Tep then used the language of somatic forms, esoteric geometry and syllabic intonations to channel those forces into a spell.

What Enna was describing? Nonsense.

Even whisper magic made more sense: disembodied but conscious spirits occupying planes close to ours but invisible to us could be communicated with, and, should they choose, they might perform various tasks that worked upon the laws of their planes and manifested as magical effects in ours.

'Sometimes you've got to trust a little, Kellen,' Enna said gently.

I reached into my powder holsters, taking out infinitesimally small pinches of the red and black powders. 'So, just light the herbs inside the pipe bowl?'

'You'll need to focus your will.'

'I always have to focus my will,' I replied testily. 'Can't cast the spell without it.'

300

'I mean you need to do that *and* think about Ferius. It's like . . . It's like you're calling out to her. Like she's buried behind a rock fall, and the breath magic in your spell is a tiny straw passing through the rubble. You need to call to Ferius through that straw.'

I felt Durral's thick fingers clamp down on my shoulder. 'And not miss.'

Reichis gave him a growl on my behalf.

'You think I ain't wrastled a squirrel cat or two in my time?' the old man asked.

'The Path of the Rambling Thistle grows prickly in its old age,' Rosie said.

Her jibe brought back her earlier words about the Argosi not being long-lived. From the set of his jaw, Durral didn't much appreciate the reminder of his advancing years.

'Don't you get him started,' Enna warned. She waved them all off. 'Go on, the three of you, shoo. This is between me and Kellen and Ferius.'

Reluctantly, Durral and Rosie took a few steps back. Reichis gave them each an extra snarl to make it clear to all concerned that he had won the stand-off, then hopped off my shoulder and set off towards the other occupied table. 'Gonna go pick that guy's pockets.'

Enna reached out a hand and placed it on my forearm. 'It's okay, Kellen. You don't have to believe. This business of maledictions and curses is its own kind of mess.'

'Will this save Ferius? I mean, if we get it right?'

She gave a weary shake of her head. 'No, son, it won't. But it'll ease the symptoms. Give her a little strength so she can fight the malediction off awhile longer.'

She took away her hand and I looked down at my fingertips.

I had only a few grains of the red and black powders on the callouses of my thumbs and forefingers – just enough to cast the spell and send flame into the bowl of the pipe. I'd have to snap my fingers just right to get the grains to collide in the air between them and then channel the fires just right – all the while somehow pushing my own will into the spell to call out to Ferius.

A straw through the rubble.

I had to take another step back. It's harder to aim when you're too close to the target. Once I was sure I had the angles right, I snapped my fingers. The instant before the powders touched I shifted my hands into the somatic shapes and uttered the one-word incantation.

'Carath.'

Two thin threads of fire, red and black, spun around each other as they shot out. I realised too late my angle had been just a fraction off. Somehow Enna saw this in time and moved the pipe the half-inch needed so the flame struck the contents of the pipe bowl.

'Back away now,' Enna said. 'Don't want you breathing this in.'

Even with that warning, I stood there like a stump until I felt Rosie haul me back to where she and Durral had taken refuge from the ugly black smoke emanating from the pipe. Enna took in a long, slow drag – cautious, like she was creeping up on a rattlesnake. Her cheeks bulged out, but she held the smoke there as she carefully set the pipe down and took out a second instrument that tamped down the flame. Then she looked back at me, her eyes wet with tears. I couldn't tell whether the smoke was to blame or her fear for her daughter's life.

She reached over and pinched Ferius's nostrils closed with the thumb and forefinger of her left hand. With her right, she gently tugged at Ferius's chin to open her mouth. With aching slowness, Enna breathed out a thin trail of the black smoke, her lips working the whole time, like she was using whisper magic. The smoke entered her daughter's mouth only to sit there, swirling, as if trapped inside a glass bowl.

'Come on, girl,' Durral said behind me. 'Your momma's callin' you. For once in your life, listen.'

A sudden wracking cough emerged from Ferius, though instead of expelling the smoke, it seemed to suck it deep into her lungs.

'That's it, my darling,' Durral said. The old man's voice cracked. 'No damned curse is gonna keep my girl down.'

More coughing, thick, rasping, hacking. Blood oozed from the corner of Ferius's mouth, a thread of black slithering inside it like oil in water. Her hands came up, trying to block the smoke, but Enna held her down and kept up that slow exhalation until every bit of it had entered Ferius's lungs.

She settled after a while, and her eyes blinked open. 'Momma?' she asked.

Enna smiled. 'Who else?'

'Wasn't sure I'd ever see you again.'

'One last time,' her mother said. 'Told you we'd meet one last time.'

'But never again?'

'Can't rightly see the paths ahead. Never could. But I think this time's our last, baby girl.'

The notion of anyone referring to Ferius Parfax as 'baby girl' seemed absurd. But Ferius wiped a tear away with the back of her hand. Her head turned then, and her eyes sought me out. 'That you, kid?' she asked.

I came close and knelt beside her. 'I figured you were dead,' I said, taking her hand, trying not to bawl like a lost child.

'Thought about it,' she said. She reached clumsily for my hand. I clasped hers between mine. 'Then I remembered you were way too stubborn to let me die.'

'She's going to need rest,' her mother said, pulling jars and bottles from her leather case and laying them out carefully. 'Leave her with me a few hours so I can give her what medicines I can to lend her strength.'

'Only one medicine can cure what's ailin' me right now,' Ferius said. 'And I can't imagine anyone had the courtesy to bring some.'

'Oh, really?' Enna asked, raising one eyebrow.

Ferius's eyes went wide. 'Momma, you didn't . . .'

Enna reached into the inside pocket of her coat and removed something long, thin and instantly recognisable to me.

'You brought me a smoking reed!' Ferius said, the enthusiasm in her tone at odds with the weary paleness of her features. 'But you and poppa hate smoking.'

Durral came over and put a hand on his daughter's shoulder. 'It's a foul habit, girl. Gonna kill you one of these days. But your momma carries 'em with her everywhere. Just in case.'

I got up and stepped back, removing myself from what felt like a moment for family.

'You did well,' Rosie said to me.

I couldn't tell if she was serious or just being nice. Then I remembered that Rosie's never nice. 'Thanks,' I said.

'Come with me now,' she said, first going over to close the

curtain and provide Ferius and her parents with privacy, and then walking towards a set of stone stairs carved into the long side of the cavern that led up to a gallery looking down on the chamber. 'The others will be coming down momentarily.'

'The other who?'

She tilted her head as if she were trying to ascertain if I was just playing dumb or was *actually* dumb. Then she nodded as if I'd provided the answer. 'The other Argosi. They've been awaiting us.'

'Awaiting us for what?'

Rosie's version of a smile came to her face – a kind of pressing of the lips together in a not entirely unpleasant way but which nonetheless sent a chill down my spine. 'To play cards, of course.'

42

The Card Game

During my travels with Ferius Parfax I'd learned a hundred different card games. Simple ones based largely on chance, like Farmer's Harvest, in which each player started with two long rows of cards face down and could call out either the suit or a number and get points based on how close they got. Complex ones like Wayward Stars, that required tremendous amounts of strategy – not to mention memorisation (Ferius could remember the position of every card in the deck once they'd been fanned out for her). She'd even taught me bizarre games like Forgetful Troubadour, in which each player began with a single card from which they spun a tale to which the other player added with one of their cards. With each pass – or 'verse' as it was called – the story became more and more elaborate, and a set of narrative rules evolved to which the players had to fit the cards in their hands. In the end, winning became as much a matter of applying these unsteady rules to tell the best story as it was of having the right cards.

So, yeah. I knew a lot of card games.

'What the hells are they doing?' I asked, standing with Rosie atop the gallery.

Below us, nearly fifty men and women, each looking as different from one other as they did from the Berabesq in the city above, had arranged themselves around tables lit by beaten brass lanterns where they sat in perfect silence as they played cards. I'd once seen Ferius and Rosie do this, so I understood the general principle: pairs of Argosi would lay out patterns of cards using their respective decks – the ones they'd each painted to represent the various cultures of the continent as they saw them – to show each other what they'd learned about the state of the world. Then they'd each begin moving the other's cards, as if to say, 'Maybe you got it wrong – perhaps it's more like this?' and the first player might agree, or reverse the change, or alter the pattern in an entirely new way, some-times using the other player's painted cards.

'The Path of the Wild Daisy never taught you the game, did she?' Rosie asked.

I wasn't surprised by the question so much as the lack of either disdain, disbelief or general disappointment in her voice. 'No, she didn't.'

Rosie nodded, apparently satisfied with my response.

I wasn't though. 'Why did Ferius never teach me the Argosi ways properly?' I asked, a treasonously plaintive note insinu-ating itself into my voice. 'It was always dancing instead of defence, music instead of eloquence. Why did every single one of her lessons have to be so . . .'

'Gods-damned unfathomable?'

The light-hearted response was so at odds with the hardened woman I knew that I laughed despite myself.

Rosie looked towards the far end of the cavern, and the closed curtain behind which Ferius rested under the watchful eyes of her parents. 'My sister is unlike any of the rest of us.'

Her gaze swept across the mismatched tribe of misfits playing cards below us. She sighed. 'Which, I suppose, makes her exactly the same as all of us.'

That raised a question I'd been wondering about for a long time – one I knew Ferius would never give a straight answer to. 'Why are the Argosi so different from one another? So . . . disorganised. With the talents you all have, you could be . . .'

'An army?' Rosie suggested.

'I suppose so.'

'An army of card-playing wandering gamblers,' she said, almost wistfully. 'We would surely be the terror of the continent.' She turned to me, leaning her back against the wooden railing embedded into the stone walls of the gallery. She held up one hand, the fingers wiggling. 'What do you see?'

'Your hand.'

She shook her head even as she closed her hand into a fist aimed at my chest. 'An army. Efficient. Cohesive. Perfectly formed to its purpose.'

'War?'

'Perhaps war. Perhaps simply control.' She brought her fist closer to me. 'Can you resist the control of my army?'

I formed my own fist, but then uncurled my fingers and used both hands to wrap around hers.

Another small smile. 'You have captured my army.' The smile disappeared. 'Unless . . .'

I hadn't even noticed her other hand move, but now I found the short, sharp point of her fingernail at the corner of my eye. 'Argosi.'

'Cool,' Reichis said quietly from the railing. I hadn't even noticed him there. 'I think she's going to pop your eyeball right out, Kellen. Can I have it?'

308

I let go of Rosie's fist and she pulled her finger away from my eye. 'Is this the Way of the Argosi then?' I asked. 'To become a kind of warrior meant to evade, outwit and defeat armies?'

She turned back around to lean her hands against the railing and watch the players below. 'It is *my* way. My path has always been that of roses and thorns. To seek out that which is beautiful in the world, that which is gentle, and defend it without hesitation. Without mercy.'

'Ferius isn't like that,' I snapped, resentful at what sounded to my ears like criticism of my mentor.

Rosie ignored my outburst. 'Nor are most of the others. Each of us follows our own path, never certain if it is the right one, always hoping that somewhere out there another Argosi has found the path we all seek.'

'Which path is that?'

Without turning back to look at me, she raised her fist in the air again. 'The one which will keep the armies of this world from destroying themselves and everything they are meant to protect.'

I joined her at the railing then, and watched the dozens of card games unfolding below us. Each deck was hand-painted by its owner, reflecting not only their personal artistic style but their individual insights – their unique perspectives on the civilisations of this continent. And yet, no matter how different the cards appeared or what arrangement the players placed them in, when I looked at the spreads, the same pattern emerged over and over.

'What do you see?' Rosie asked me. I hadn't noticed her turning to look at me.

'It's . . . It's as if no matter how they move the cards, the result always looks like armies about to clash.'

'And why is that, do you suppose?'

I knew the answer – or at least it was rattling around in my brain – but I couldn't seem to put it into words. 'It's something to do with the cards themselves,' I began. 'But why? Why can they only ever form one—'

A sharp pain in my left eye took my breath away. The skin around my shadowblack markings pinched as the lines twisted and turned like the dials of a lock. First one, then the second, and finally the third.

The enigmatism was coming over me more often now, blindsiding me out of nowhere. This time as my vision blurred it seemed to fill the entire cavern in a green-black mist. The cards on the tables floated up into the air, arraying themselves before me. Every suit came to life – shields for the Daroman empire, chalices for the Berabesq theocracy, spells for the Jan'Tep, contraptions for the Gitabrians, wheels for the Zhuban, and others representing cultures I'd never visited in the furthest northern and southern reaches of the continent.

The frames around the cards shattered like glass, freeing the images within. The seven of chalices became a cleric leading his flock in prayer. The two of shields spread apart to reveal a pair of young warriors training with wooden swords. Upon the spinning six of wheels a group of Zhuban artisans wove straps of leather into sturdy yet flexible armour. Each card, each facet of life within a culture, went about its business. The lives they depicted seemed perfectly natural, noble even, yet brought together like this, those lives all led towards . . .

'Kellen?' Rosie asked.

'The suits,' I whispered. 'It's in the suits themselves.'

Saying the answer out loud caused the vision to unwind itself. The people and places scattered across the cavern froze, encased once again by the borders of the cards. They drifted back down to the tables from which, in truth, they'd never left. The shadowblack markings around my left eye turned back, locking closed once again.

'Are you ill?' Rosie asked.

Already the insight the enigmatism had offered me was beginning to fade, so I spoke quickly, forcing out the words while I still could. 'The game is rigged. The suits, the cultures they represent . . . When you see them all together, every card from every suit can only fit together in such a way that no matter how you choose to play them, the result is war.'

Rosie was watching me silently.

'Is that what all human civilisation leads to?' I asked. 'Are we destined for nothing more than endless wars and bloodshed?'

'The Argosi do not believe in fate,' she replied, steel in her voice, but then her shoulders sagged and a sigh escaped her lips. 'And yet, here on this continent, all paths appear to lead to the same end. We travel to every nation, visit every culture, always seeking to better understand their people and refine our decks to more perfectly represent them. But when we lay out the cards, always they tell the same tale of a long, steady march to war.'

I understood then why the Argosi were the way they were. Why Ferius was so different from Rosie, and she different from all the others. They weren't simply gamblers; they were the gamble itself. The unpredictable shuffle of the cards that sought to produce the one hand that could prevent war from

311

overtaking the continent. And yet, no matter how many times they shuffled the deck, the result was the same.

'It's the game,' I said again. 'The game itself is rigged.'

Rosie opened her mouth to speak, but I didn't hear what she said. A different voice had appeared in my head.

Will you come play a game with me now, Kellen?

The voice of a young boy.

The voice of God.

43

The Deck

'The Berabesq god *wants* you to go kill him?' asked the Path of Mountain Storms. He was the tall man in the frontier hat who'd been sitting by himself in the cavern when Rosie and I had first brought Ferius to the saloon.

'I'm not sure,' I replied. 'His exact phrasing was, *Will you come play a game with me now, Kellen?*'

A short, compact woman with the blackest hair I'd ever seen, who'd introduced herself as the Path of Emerald Steps, tilted her head as though she were trying to hear something hidden in my words. 'Such an overture might signal that he seeks to test you,' she suggested.

'A test?' The Zhubanese girl a couple of years my junior who stood next to Emerald snorted. 'More likely the little bastard wants to lure the spellslinger to his temple so as to kill him. I say we take the artefacts – this "scourge" and these ridiculous "dice" or whatever they are – and turn the tables on this so-called "God".'

The Zhuban have even less respect for religion – and gambling – than my people do.

'Always you see things too bluntly, my teysan,' Emerald sighed.

'Perhaps I just see them plainly, maetri,' the girl countered.

Several of the other Argosi piped in with their own thoughts, some uttering poetic aphorisms like how one must never mistake the players for the game pieces, while others suggested such nuanced solutions as, 'Let's just blow the temple doors and kill him.'

Reichis was so enthused with that last one that I thought maybe he was going to sign up to be the guy's teysan, but then he raised his muzzle in the air and sniffed. 'Somethin' stinks,' he said.

'Like what?' I asked.

Without giving me an answer he scampered out of the cavern and up the stairs that led to the common room above, leaving me to deal with the fifty or so Argosi who were currently debating my future.

Ferius's mother Enna once told me that to be Argosi is to choose your own unique path in life, and while that path might sometimes cross with that of another, each one is meant to be walked alone. Listening to all of them argue with no end in sight, I realised she'd missed the point. The real problem was that anytime you get more than two Argosi in a room, they can't so much as agree on the time of day, never mind what to do about a possibly homicidal god.

'Well now,' boomed a voice over the rest, bringing everyone to a stunned silence.

Ferius, leaning shakily on a wooden cane, shuffled awkwardly towards me as the others stepped aside to make room for her. Durral, her father, kept his arm hovering about her shoulder, ready to grab hold of her if she collapsed.

She laughed at the assembly of Argosi. 'Guess we all know why all our maetri taught us to play cards with our mouths shut.'

314

'A strange observation, sister,' Rosie noted drily, 'coming from one who has barely allowed a moment's silence during our own games.'

Ferius grinned at her, a faint ray of light trying to push through a thick blanket of grey clouds.

She looks so . . . old, I thought helplessly.

'Quit givin' me them puppy-dog eyes, kid,' she said, limping her way over to me. 'Haven't I told you before there ain't no use in you takin' a fancy to me? I mean, you're pretty and all, but my tastes lean in a slightly different direction.'

Some of the others laughed at that, the tension momentarily leaking out of the room. In the periphery of my vision I noticed a barely perceptible movement at the corner of Rosie's mouth. A smile, this one different from the others she'd guardedly revealed in the past, and meant only for Ferius.

Ancestors, I thought. *Were the two of them a couple at some point?*

Every time they'd been within striking distance of each other back in the Seven Sands they'd looked like they were about to duel – or 'wrastle' as Ferius called it.

'You planning on getting better any time soon?' I asked, noting her unsteady grip on the cane. 'Or am I going to have to rescue your sorry arse again?'

She leaned all her weight on the cane and with her free hand touched my cheek. 'Always, kid. Always.'

The Path of Emerald Steps clucked disapprovingly. 'Sentimentality will not stay a god's hand if he seeks the conquest of this continent.'

'Neither will tryin' to whip him into submission with some ratty piece of old rope,' Ferius replied. She turned to the others. 'Listen up, people. We Argosi don't got no generals. We don't follow no rulers. Ain't got no books of laws and never needed any either.' She took her hand away from my cheek and clapped it on my shoulder in a companionable gesture, but I could tell right away she was trying to hide the fact that she needed to lean on someone. 'Now the kid here is the only one this "god" seems interested in talkin' to. His path, winding as any I've ever seen, has taken him from the Jan'Tep territories to everywhere from Gitabria to Darome and even to the Ebony Abbey. Everywhere he's gone, he's found some connection to whatever it is that's been setting this continent on the path to war.'

A prickling itch around my left eye made Ferius's words more ominous. She was right; every disturbing discovery I'd made in the three years since leaving my homeland seemed to be connected: the onyx worms she and I had encountered at the Academy of the Seven Sands, the mysterious abilities wielded by the monks of the Ebony Abbey, the power of the white binder who'd taken control of me in Darome. My fingers reached up to trace the winding lines that began just above my left cheek, banded upon me by my own grandmother when I was just a child.

It's like I'm staring down at the pieces of a puzzle but I can't make out the picture because one is still missing.

'What's your point?' the Zhuban girl next to Emerald asked, ignoring her mentor's frown.

Ferius gave her a friendly grin. 'My point, sweetheart, is that the kid here's gonna be the one who decides what path he has to follow now to get us all out of this mess. Anyone has the notion to get in his way is gonna have to wrastle me first.'

This elicited a light-hearted chuckling that began as respect and ended as acquiescence. Unfortunately the sentiment wasn't shared by everyone.

'Who are you to decide the future of the Berabesq nation?' asked a thick-set woman whose colouring and hawk-like features hinted she herself came from this region. 'The scourge is an ancient artefact of *my* people. The god, real or not, is of *my* people.'

Ferius rolled her eyes. 'Yeah, and right now *your* people are lookin' to spill everybody *else's* blood. Besides, you stopped bein' Berabesq the day you chose the Argosi ways, Lily.'

'Path of Floating Lilies,' the other woman corrected, the edge to her voice making my powder fingers twitch. 'Not "Lily", not "sweethcart", not any of your other nonsense.'

Ferius gave no sign of even noticing the threat. 'Whatever, buttercup. You want to return to your people? Go find yourself a copy of the clockmaker's codex or the warrior's or whichever one suits you best. There's a path right there waiting for you, all laid out in them pretty verses.'

The Path of Floating Lilies approached us, her movements as fluid as water gliding over river rocks, and more unnerving to behold than a rattlesnake slithering along the sand towards you. 'It is not *my* choices that are in question, so perhaps I should simply "wrastle" you instead, Path of the Wild Daisy.'

A chorus of mutters rose up from the other Argosi, some arguing for peaceful discourse, others already stepping aside to make room for the two women to duel. All of it came to an abrupt halt when a deafening explosion boomed through the cavern. A burst of red and black flames scorched the stone floor an inch from the Path of Floating Lilies.

I flipped closed the clasps of my powder holsters and did

my best not to let anyone see how badly my hands were shaking.

'You threaten me, teysan?' the Path of Floating Lilies asked.

Despite all the duels I've fought against mages, marshals, soldiers, spies and the occasional flying snake, I've never actually had to face off against an Argosi – someone who knew more about defeating an opponent through trickery than I ever would. I didn't like my chances.

'Ferius is my friend,' I declared, loud enough for everyone to hear. 'She's my family. So yeah, *Lily*, take that first shot as a warning, cos it's the only one you're gonna get.'

Arta valar. My best Argosi talent. I was pretty sure it was going to get me killed one day.

'You're sweet, kid,' Ferius whispered to me. 'But you know I can take care of myself just fine, right?'

'You can barely stand,' I whispered back. 'So unless you're planning to fall and squash her to death, just leave it to—'

I caught the subtle flick of Lily's right wrist. A weapon hidden in the cuff of her sleeve slid down to her palm. With the toe of her boot she rubbed away the scorch marks on the floor in front of her. 'The first principle of the Way of Thunder teaches never to reveal your most powerful weapon until you actually intend to use it, teysan. It is a fine thing to want to protect others, Kellen of the Jan'Tep, but this city is filled with soldiers, the temple is guarded by the Faithful and the spire within by viziers whose abilities rival that of your own people's lords magi. Who will protect you from them?' I heard a click come from the metal object hidden in her hand. 'Who will protect you from me?'

I wasn't sure what weapon she was holding, but I was willing to bet she could take me out with it before I could pull powder a second time. I guess that's why she looked almost as surprised as I was by the second explosion that was so loud it kept reverberating throughout the cavern even after it had left the smell of lightning in the air and a crack in the stone floor at Lily's feet.

The Path of Floating Lilies gazed at me, eyes narrowed as she tried to figure out how I'd pulled off the spell without her seeing. I was wondering that too, since I hadn't even touched my holsters.

Someone else had fired the blast.

'That would be my job,' a voice called out from behind me.

I was so deafened by the blast I couldn't make out who had spoken. Everyone else was looking up at the gallery, so I turned to follow their gaze, and there she was.

Happiness, it turns out, is the sight of a dust-covered woman in a long blue travelling coat so caked in brown and gold sand she might as well be wearing the desert itself. The three fingers of each hand were closing the lid of a small iron box that hissed and sparked from the caged storm contained inside.

Nephenia, the errant charmcaster whom I was pretty sure I'd loved long before I had any real comprehension of what that word meant, caught my beguiled stare and winked.

'Miss me?' she asked.

44

The Protector

Nephenia descended the stairs from the gallery, unhurried steps testifying that she had no intention of rushing for anyone. Ishak, her hyena companion, followed behind, stubby tail held high and looking very dignified apart from the fact that a scruffy squirrel cat was sitting atop him as if he were a pony.

'For future reference, Kellen,' Reichis said, 'that's how you make an entrance.'

'Ferius is right,' Nephenia said as she reached the bottom of the stairs. 'Whatever's waiting at the top of that spire, Kellen's path leads there. I'll get him inside the temple.'

Ishak offered up a rather stern yip. Nephenia reached down and patted his head. 'We will get him inside the temple.'

Reichis made a series of growls at her. I decided not to translate, but she smiled. 'With the invaluable assistance of a certain devilishly handsome squirrel cat, I meant to say.'

While the rest of the Argosi seemed at least open to the idea, the Path of Floating Lilies didn't appear impressed. She turned to the others. 'Two starry-eyed, barely trained teysani and a pair of unruly animals? *That* is who the Path of the Wild Daisy would have us send to face a god?'

'If he's really a god,' Ferius said, 'that's *exactly* who I'd send.'

'As would I,' the diminutive woman with the jet-black hair added. The Path of Emerald Steps began to walk around Nephenia, Ishak, Reichis and me, as if the four of us were some kind of experimental contraption. 'A little power, a little trickery and something else – something unpredictable.'

'The word you're looking for is friendship,' I said.

It had never occurred to me before, but the Argosi don't really make friends. Even Ferius, affable as she was, kept a kind of distance between herself and the rest of the world. I found myself catching her gaze, and being more aware than ever of how precious and unexpected the friendship between us had been.

The Path of Floating Lilies glanced around the room. I guess she was taking stock of where the others were in terms of what would happen next. Finally she threw up her hands. 'So be it. Let us put our hopes on the Path of Endless Stars. The worst that can happen at this point is that he dies and then the rest of us can find some other way forward.'

The place cleared out pretty quick after that. I tried to get a moment alone with Nephenia, but she and Ishak had other business first.

'I haven't bathed in weeks,' she said, then abruptly jabbed a finger at Reichis. 'And no comments from you, mister.' The squirrel cat looked so shocked he actually stayed silent for once. She pressed her hands against my chest. 'I know we haven't seen each other for a long time, Kellen, and this is awkward and . . . Oh, the hells for it.' She reached behind my head and pulled me into a kiss.

She did that sometimes. Just kissed me out of the blue with no warning, no explanation and definitely no promises.

She used to be such a shy girl back when we were both Jan'Tep initiates. I found myself entirely supportive of her more recent demeanour.

Someone behind me coughed, which at that precise moment constituted a hanging offence to my way of thinking.

'Forgive me,' said the tall, unpleasantly handsome fellow who called himself the Path of Mountain Storms. 'I was hoping the Path of Endless Stars and I could talk.'

Nephenia gave me a peck on the cheek. 'I'll see you in an hour. As soon as it's full dark we should be on our way.'

And with that she was gone again.

'Sorry about the interruption,' the Path of Mountain Storms said, doing a poor job of hiding his smirk.

'What can I do for you, Stormy?' I asked, gesturing for him to join me at one of the tables.

He winced at the nickname. 'Guess I had that coming.' He reached into the inside pocket of his coat and removed a playing card. 'You're going to need this.'

'A discordance?' I asked.

He slid the card across the table to me. 'Not exactly.'

I flipped over the card and found an elaborate drawing made up of six circles, each a little smaller than the other and filled with intricate lines that turned this way and that, almost like a maze. It took me a second to figure out what I was looking at. 'You have a map of the temple spire?'

'In theory.'

I looked across the table to see if he was joking.

'The spire hasn't been open to worshippers for centuries,' he said. 'Only the high viziers and their Asabli – those are the blind servants who carry their holy texts and turn the pages for them.'

322

I'd forgotten the viziers were forbidden from touching the pages of their own codexes for fear of defiling them. 'Aren't the Asabli recruited from those Berabesq who are born mute as well as blind?' I asked.

Stormy nodded, then grinned. 'But they sure do like to drink, and while you couldn't say their tongues wag when they do, the Asabli have a language all their own.'

His fingers twitched in a series of subtle gesticulations that had my own hands reaching for my powder holsters until I realised he wasn't casting a spell.

'So you found a servant of the viziers willing to betray the secrets of their most sacred temple?' I asked.

Stormy laughed at that. 'You think it took only one? Kellen, each vizier is only allowed entry to one of the floors, and if I'd tried to get even that much out of one of the Asabli, he'd've figured out what I was doing.'

'So how did you—'

'I've been at this for almost two years now. Different disguises, different contacts.' He reached over and tapped the card. 'Sometimes I'd spend weeks just trying to discover a fraction of a fragment of a detail. Even then, it's not like anyone would intentionally reveal the location of a hallway or passage. I had to get them talking about their duties. Every time they'd describe one, their heads would turn just slightly in the direction of whichever corridor or hallway they had to go through.' He leaned back in his chair. 'Worst assignment the Path of the Wild Daisy ever gave me.'

'Ferius was your maetri?'

He tilted his head quizzically. 'She never mentioned me? I was her teysan before you.'

I felt that familiar stab of resentment whenever I discovered another piece of Ferius Parfax's past that she'd made sure to keep from me. I pushed it aside though. When you owe a person as much as I owed Ferius, you have to accept the limits they choose to place on that friendship.

Reichis sauntered over and hopped up onto the table before sniffing at my face. 'Ugh. Jealousy *again*?'

'Shut up, Reichis.'

He leaned closer and chittered conspiratorially – even though, of course, no one but me would know what he was saying anyway. 'Don't feel bad, partner. I already got revenge on him for you.' The squirrel cat opened his mouth wider to reveal a slick, wet silver coin with a tiny ruby at its centre. 'This has got to be worth something, right?' he mumbled.

Reichis having stolen something from the Path of Mountain Storms should not in any way have made me feel better. But it did.

'Okay,' I said, pocketing the card with the dubious maps of the spire. 'Guess I better gather up Nephenia and Ishak and go. Can't imagine God likes to be kept waiting.'

Stormy grabbed my wrist. Reichis snarled at him, but the Argosi ignored him, eyes locked on mine. 'What are you going to do when you get there?'

'What do you mean?'

There were six good ways I could get him to let go of me. I was leaning towards the one that involved Reichis ripping off a piece of his arm when Stormy abruptly let go. 'I'm sorry,' he said. 'I just . . .' He glanced back at the curtained-off area of the cavern where Ferius's parents had taken her to rest. 'She's going to die, Kellen. You know it and I know it. Just like we both know she'd never want us to kill for her.'

'What would you do in my place?'

He shook his head. 'There's a reason I wasn't one of the people arguing over who should deal with this Berabesq god tonight.' He looked down at the table as if he were suddenly too ashamed to hold my gaze. 'But if it were down to me? If I were carrying that Daroman artefact the Murmurers gave you? I'd forget everything Ferius ever taught me, give up any claim I would ever have to call her my friend and go kill whoever I had to in order to save her life.'

There was a bitter taste in my mouth. Something about those words, no matter how loyal and determined they sounded, no matter how close they were to the ones I'd said myself just a couple of weeks ago, struck me as cowardly. If Ferius had taught me anything, it was that courage meant seeking the right path no matter how high the cost. Duty could excuse all kinds of atrocities if you let it deafen your conscience.

'What are you going to do, Kellen?' he asked again.

I rose from the table. The legs of the chair screeched against the rough stone floor. 'Assuming I don't get knifed in the street by some zealot on the way to the temple? Assuming I find the underground tunnel to get inside? That I can even reach the spire before a hundred guards cut me down? And even if I *do* get inside, that your maps are somehow accurate and none of those guys you talked to just had a nervous condition that made his head twitch? And then, of course, assuming the god doesn't just strike me down the second I get near him?'

My fellow teysan looked faintly apologetic. 'Yeah, assuming all that.'

I didn't have an answer. The needle of whatever compass exists inside our hearts to guide our choices was spinning in every direction right now. So I did what I figured Ferius would do at a time like this: I stuck my palm out just below Reichis's mouth and tickled his chin until, after giving me a suitably dirty look, he coughed up the coin. I flipped it in the air as I turned to go. 'Reckon I'll flip a coin.'

Makhan Mebab

City of Miracles

City of Miracles

Beware those who worship their home as though it were made for them by the gods themselves. Deities almost always make poor landlords.

45

The Luminary

It occurred to me, as Nephenia, Ishak, Reichis and I raced through the streets of Mebab, trying and failing to ditch the pursuers who'd picked up our trail within minutes of our leaving the travellers' saloon, that I wouldn't make a very good assassin. Self-criticism isn't the most helpful activity while trying to elude one's enemies, of course, but it's still better than being castigated by a squirrel cat and a hyena.

'You're not very stealthy,' Reichis observed, looking behind us while perched on my shoulder so he could spot the shadowy figures chasing us while I did the actual running.

'I know that,' I said.

Ishak, loping alongside Nephenia, gave a little yip.

'Ishak says you're also kind of slow,' Reichis informed me, before adding, 'Kellen, these guys are gonna box us in pretty quick if you don't—'

'I know, Reichis.'

The hyena yipped at me again. Nephenia shushed him.

'What did he say?' I asked.

'Nothing,' she replied.

Reichis was delighted to translate. 'He says your last shot

missed that guy by quite a lot and wonders if maybe you should practise your aim a little more?'

In fact, my powder blast had missed our pursuers by a mile, in no small part due to the dull numbness in my right shoulder where the blow dart had stuck me.

Blow darts.

Who uses blow darts? They're not nearly as accurate as arrows or crossbow bolts. Don't have the range either. Also, you've got to hit the target just right if you want to pierce anything useful like an artery in the neck or maybe an eye. You know the real reason people use blow darts? Poison. Blow darts are really good for dipping in poison and then killing your prey before they know what hit them.

So why wasn't I dead?

The trio chasing us weren't wearing the customary pale linen wrappings of the Faithful, but instead the traditional black and silver of Berabesq temple guards. Since we hadn't even attempted to breach Mahkan's walls yet, I had no idea why they'd be on our tail. Odder still, they'd hit me three times with the darts already. The first was in the shoulder, messing with my aim and preventing me from retaliating with my powder spell effectively, the second in my left leg, which had given me a stumbling limp that was slowing us all down.

And the third? The third one had hit me in the arse. That one I'm certain was just spite.

'Turn right,' Nephenia called out as we approached the end of an alleyway. The voice coming out of her ironcloth mask sounded strange, a mixture of menacing whispers and distant echoes that fit perfectly with the demonic lines adorning the red lacquer features concealing her face. They made it hard to look at her, which might explain why she hadn't been struck by any blow darts.

The real question was, why hadn't our pursuers just hit me in the neck and put an end to me? For that matter, why was the poison so mild? I was pretty sure it wasn't killing me. In fact, it seemed to be wearing off quickly.

They've been sent to capture, not kill. But why?

'There's another one coming along the roof!' Reichis warned.

I glanced up to see the silhouette of a short woman running nimbly along the rooftop above us. She raised a thin tube the length of her forearm up to her lips.

'I've got her,' Nephenia said, digging into one of the pockets of her coat for what would no doubt be a devilishly clever charm that would quickly dispatch our assailant.

'Oh no you don't,' I shouted back. I pulled one of the castradazi coins from the hem of my shirt.

The problem with Nephenia's charms is that most of them only work once, and we would need every weapon in her arsenal just to get inside the temple. It wasn't at all because I was irrationally annoyed by getting hit with blow darts all the time and tired of looking like a clumsy idiot.

The art of coin dancing involves a lot of subtle and precise movements – something not suited to running down an alley with one numb shoulder and a limp. But I'd had a lot of practice over the past couple of years, and besides, the *lomo-castra* – or 'luminary' as I'd come to call it – was the easiest to work with. Actually, I'm not sure if lomocastra was its proper name. The guy who'd gifted me with these five coins had never bothered to tell me their names or – and this was the more inconvenient part – how they worked. After a lot of trial and error, I'd figured out a few tricks with them and given each one a name. The warden's coin, for example, when flipped just right, could bind itself magnetically to an apparatus and then be used to manipulate it. That made it excellent for picking locks. Conversely, the fugitive coin could be bound to an object in such a way that if I threw the coin, the other object would be yanked along with it.

I'd considered trying to use the fugitive coin to tear that blowpipe away from my pursuer, but the problem with coins like the fugitive and the warden is that it's incredibly tricky to make the actual binding work – you have to flip them over and over until you find the exact right motion and angle that aligns it to the target. The luminary didn't need any of that. Instead, when flipped quickly enough, it would react to light in a rather impressive way.

The steel tip of a dart clattered against the cobblestones at my feet.

'She's takin' aim again,' Reichis chittered. 'And there're two more closin' in behind us.'

'I'm on it,' I said.

Ever tried running with a limp while flipping a coin? It's exactly as hard as it sounds.

I tossed the luminary in the air once, twice, thrice, searching for that strange buoyant sensation that signalled it was coming back down slower than it went up, pirouetting in the graceful way that told me the coin was ready to dance.

Come on . . . Come on . . .

The luminary, already the shiniest of the five coins, began to glimmer as it reflected the moonlight from above.

There!

I had to come to a stop because now the coin was resisting returning to earth, briefly floating in the air every time I flipped it. I gave it one more toss, higher this time, and as it spun free I pulled powder from the holsters at my side. My toss was clumsy, thanks to my numb right shoulder, but the powders collided and I managed the somatic shapes and incantation in time to spark the spell. Twin red and black flames shot through the air.

They missed the coin of course – if I'd been able to achieve that level of accuracy in that moment I'd've just blasted my pursuers. Fortunately all the luminary needed was the flash of light.

'Close your eyes!' I warned Nephenia and the others as I shut my own tightly.

Even through closed eyelids, the shattering, disorienting explosion of light was blinding. I'd given the luminary its name on account of the way it not only reflected light while dancing, but amplified it back a hundredfold.

I heard grunts and groans behind me. When I opened my eyes and glanced back, I saw two of our pursuers stumbling blindly in the dark. Up on the rooftop, the woman with the blowpipe missed a step and tumbled over the side. Luckily for her, she bounced off the awning above a shop before hitting the ground at our feet. The loud crack as she landed on her side didn't sound pleasant though.

'Heh,' Reichis chittered, squinting down at the unconscious woman. 'That's gonna hurt when she wakes up.'

The luminary coin fell back down to land in the palm of my hand. I pressed it there so it would stick and held my hand out in front of me. Even now the coin was bright enough to use as a lantern, sending a clear beam of light ahead of us wherever I aimed it.

'How long's that going to glow like that?' Nephenia asked

as we left our temporarily sightless and confused pursuers several streets behind us.

'Hard to say exactly,' I replied, finally coming to a stop on the narrow, sloping avenue I'd been searching for since we left the saloon. 'The luminary reacts differently to various kinds of light. If I leave it exposed to the sun all day, it'll shine most of the night. We'll get at least an hour out of it from my powder blast, which should give us enough time to find the entrance to the tunnel that runs beneath Mebab and past Makhan's outer walls.'

'Fascinating,' Nephenia said, catching her breath. 'There doesn't appear to be a charm attached to the coin itself, but rather some innate property of its metallic composition.' She glanced around the innocuous collection of shuttered shops and alley entrances around us. 'And you're positive there's a tunnel here?'

'Positive's a strong word, but yeah, I'm positive.'

I figured locating the entrance to the tunnel was just a matter of backtracking to the exact spot where Ferius had first pointed out the vizier who had clearly come from inside the temple and yet hadn't exited from any of the doors. The only problem was, now that we were here, all I could see was a long row of decrepit single-storey sandstone buildings with white painted doors that all looked the same. I didn't fancy the idea of picking the lock on some unsuspecting Berabesq family's door, only to have to explain why two Jan'Tep spies and a pair of wild animals had just busted into their home.

Ishak and Reichis began sniffing their way along the avenue, the squirrel cat taking great pains to express his lack of optimism about finding anything worth stealing here, the hyena giving little barks of agreement.

'Don't suppose one of your castradazi coins can show us the way to the tunnel?' Nephenia asked.

I reached into the hidden hem of my shirt. Aside from the luminary, I had a warden's coin, a fugitive, one I called the watcher for its eye – open on one side and closed on the other but which I had no idea how to use – and finally the stinger – so named because it stung the hells out of me every time I tried to figure out how to use it. I couldn't see how any of them could help with this particular task.

Ishak, who'd been sniffing around at each of the doors in turn, gave a series of yips.

'What did he say?' I asked.

Before Nephenia could translate, Reichis chittered, 'The hyena's wondering why we don't just try the door with the dead guy behind it.'

46

The Corpse

I've been around a fair number of dead bodies in my time. It's an occupational hazard, given my profession mostly involves having people try to kill me on a regular basis. But I don't think I'd ever seen this much blood come out of one person before. The front of the vizier's white penitent's robes were scarlet from the deluge of his own blood.

'Why slit his throat and hold him here until he bled out?' Nephenia asked, sounding more than a little ill. She generally manages to get through life without witnessing as many murders as I do. 'Was this some kind of ceremonial killing?'

'More likely the killer wanted to keep him from calling for help.'

I swallowed my own revulsion at the grizzly scene and knelt down to see what else I could find. Usually to slit someone's throat, you grab them from behind. Given the lack of any spray of blood on the narrow walls of the passageway in the direction the vizier was facing, that suggested he'd been attacked just after the door had closed behind him.

So had someone been waiting for him? No, because this wasn't an ideal spot for an ambush. Too easy to be spotted as soon as the victim opened the door. 'I think whoever did this was looking for the same tunnel we are. They followed the vizier until he led them to it, then killed him.'

'How long has he been dead?'

I gestured for Reichis to come closer. The squirrel cat sniffed at the corpse a couple of times before scrunching up his muzzle. 'Four hours.'

Ishak wandered over and inspected the body for a moment before giving a terse yip.

'Four,' Reichis insisted.

'What did he say?' I asked.

'Doesn't matter. He's a stupid hyena.'

'Six hours,' Nephenia translated.

Reichis scowled at her. He gets a little jealous of Ishak's superior olfactory abilities sometimes.

'Okay,' I said, trying to make sense of the scene before us. I could make out several sets of footprints smearing the vizier's blood, all of them headed towards the outer door. Much harder to discern was the fact that one set of boot marks went in both directions – stepping in the blood on the way out, but avoiding it on the path leading deeper into the tunnel.

'What are you seeing?' Nephenia asked.

'After the vizier died, the killer led those temple guards we ran into on a merry chase through the streets of Mebab – probably near enough the saloon that, after they lost him, they waited around for him to reappear.'

'Which is why they chased the first foreigner they saw leaving the saloon, which happened to be you.'

I nodded. 'Only by then the real killer had already circled back to enter the tunnel.'

She looked down the darkened passageway ahead of us. 'So there's a new player on the board. What do they want?'

My gaze went to the body on the ground. Most killings are sloppy; even professionals make little mistakes here and there. Yet the assassination of the vizier and subsequent infiltration of the tunnels had been masterfully executed. How many of those Argosi back at the saloon had wanted to take the scourge from me and go end the threat of the Berabesq god once and for all? The words spoken by the Path of Mountain Storms came back to me: *'If it were down to me? I'd forget everything Ferius ever taught me, give up any claim I would ever have to call her my friend and go kill whoever I had to in order to save her life.'*

'Come on,' I said, turning to the sloping passage that would take us underneath the walls protecting the temple city of Makhan. I held up my luminary coin and followed its beam to begin the descent down slippery stones into the darkness.

'Wait,' Nephenia said as we reached the first bend in the passage. 'Where are Reichis and Ishak?'

She started to turn back, but I took her arm and led on down the tunnel. I was pretty sure I knew what the squirrel cat was up to anyway. 'They'll be along in a minute,' I said. 'You probably don't want to see what they're doing.'

'Don't put this on me,' the squirrel cat called down from the entrance to the tunnel, mangling his words as he chewed noisily. 'If somebody had fed us back at the saloon, we wouldn't need a snack now.'

As it turned out, the lack of appropriate snacks turned out to be the least of Reichis's gripes.

'Never thought I'd end my days stuck in a maze,' he grumbled up at me. 'Had a more noble death planned, you know?'

'Yeah? Like what?' I asked, shining the rapidly diminishing

340

light of the luminary coin ahead into yet another dank passageway.

Ferius and I had been wrong about there being a simple tunnel to the temple. Beneath the meticulously designed streets of Mebab were the remnants of a much older city whose citizens had no doubt died from starvation after getting lost in the labyrinthine avenues that seemed to turn back on themselves every few blocks. Worse, with everything in ruins, we'd get a few dozen yards down one passage, only to find the way blocked by wreckage. We'd turn back in search of a way around it, only to hit yet another dead end.

'Gonna die here,' Reichis mumbled.

Ishak gave a perky yip.

'Shut up,' the squirrel cat replied, then added, 'stupid hyena.'

I pulled out the card the Path of Mountain Storms had given me, hoping that somewhere on his intricate little map there might be some clue as to where the secret passage entered the temple, but nothing in those tiny lines suggested a hidden entrance.

'Kellen, are you okay?' Nephenia asked. 'You're sweating.'

'I'm fine. Great, really. Having the time of my life.'

Shortly before I'd left my home three years ago, I'd found myself in the mine shafts beneath our city's oasis. That's when I first discovered that I really, really hate enclosed spaces.

'Them walls don't look stable,' Reichis said, scratching at one with his claws. 'Won't be long before one of 'em falls on us.'

'Stop doing that,' I said.

He inhaled noisily. 'Air's stale down here. We'll probably suffocate first.'

'Shut up, Reichis.'

He sniffed again. 'Pretty sure I smell rats. Lots of them. Bet they've got crocodiles down here too.'

One of Ishak's stranger attributes is his ability to mimic anything he hears. He chose to display it now by perfectly repeating, 'They've got crocodiles down here too.'

Reichis jumped as if a pair of fang-filled jaws was snapping at his tail. By the time he landed again, all his fur was sticking straight up.

'You're really not helping,' Nephenia chided the hyena.

Ishak responded by making a series of laughing yip-yip sounds as he paraded around Reichis.

'Could everyone please be quiet?' I asked, wiping more sweat from my brow. 'I'm trying to find a way into the temple.'

I kept staring at the card, scrutinising it again and again for something I was already pretty sure wasn't there. My vision was blurry and my lungs had to work harder than they should to draw in breath. The others seemed fine though, which meant it was just my claustrophobia getting the better of me. Unfortunately, when I get like this, Reichis gets confused and starts looking for reasons to explain my anxiety.

'Stinks of rot too. Stinks of skinbags. Stinks of sewa—'

'Would you stop?' I whispered furiously. 'I'm trying to figure out a way to find the route those other "skinbags" took when they—'

'What is it?' Reichis asked, unnerved by the look of surprise on my face. 'Did you see somethin'? Was it a crocodile?' The squirrel cat's head spun left and right, convinced he was about to be snapped in half.

'What's wrong with Reichis?' Nephenia asked.

I knelt down and grabbed him by the scruff of the neck

to get him to pay attention to me. 'You said you smelled skinbags, right? How many?'

The squirrel cat snarled at me, then gave a shrug. 'Just the remnants of a couple of scents. Guess they don't have too many that come down . . .' His beady little eyes seemed to light up as a grin came over his fuzzy brown muzzle. 'Say, Kellen?'

'Yeah?'

'I've just devised a brilliant plan.'

'Is it to use your keen squirrel cat sense of smell to follow the freshest trail of skinbag stench until it leads us right into the temple?'

'No, dummy. Squirrel cat noses are way too refined to track skinbags with all this stench around.' He sauntered over and hopped up onto Ishak's back. 'But hyenas don't mind the stink.'

47

The Maze

The luminary coin had lost all its light before we found the entrance to the temple. Reichis was riding on Ishak's back, and the hyena's sense of smell guided them unerringly past the obstacles all around us. The two of them had the advantage of being lower to the ground. Nephenia and I, on the other hand, having neither light nor particularly useful noses, kept bashing our heads repeatedly into low-hanging beams from the broken-down buildings of the ancient city. This, I thought, provided an excellent excuse for me to hold Nephenia's hand and take the lead. For Reichis, my chivalrous impulse was a source of great mirth.

'Heh,' the squirrel cat chuckled each time he heard the dull thud of my skull banging into something painfully solid.

He did that every single time. After a while we'd settled into a pattern; Ishak would make a turn, followed by Reichis saying, 'This way, quick!'

Thud. I'd hit my head.

'Heh.'

'Okay, now this way.'

Thud.

'Heh.'

Nephenia had charmed candles in her coat that would've lit our way, but both Reichis and Ishak insisted that the smoke would interfere with their sense of smell. I'm not sure I believed them. Nonetheless, sometime just shy of when I began contemplating the potential culinary merits of roasted squirrel cat and sautéed hyena, we came upon a heavy iron door.

'It's locked,' Reichis said.

'You can tell that just by smell?' I asked.

'No, but who has a secret door into their most sacred temple without putting a lock on it?'

'Good point.'

In fact, he was right. Usually if a lock is big and heavy but relatively simple I can pick it. The smaller, more intricate ones, Reichis handles – the little monster is a genius at picking locks. The problem comes in when you have a big lock with parts that are too stiff for the squirrel cat to turn, but the mechanism is too complicated for me to pick. That's the sort of lock you put on a secret door into your temple.

'We could just hide out here until another vizier comes along,' Reichis suggested. 'As soon as he unlocks the door, we jump him, rip his throat out. I can pop out his eyeballs while you cut off his ears. Maybe you could get the tongue too. It's always so squishy I have trouble tearing them out.'

'Or we could just use my warden's coin,' I said, pulling it from its slot in the hem of my shirt.

He looked up at me quizzically, his whiskers twitching. 'How's that going to get us any eyeballs?'

'It's not,' I replied, flipping the coin over and over, adjusting the angle, height and motion until I felt it binding to the

345

lock inside the door. 'We're trying to sneak into a sacred temple to prevent a god from starting a war here, remember?'

'Oh, right.' His muzzle went down, making him look a little crestfallen. Somehow that made me feel guilty.

'Maybe the god has eyeballs?' I suggested.

His fuzzy little head tilted as he looked up, his feline upper lip curling into an extremely nasty smile. 'Oh yeah . . .'

Ancestors, I swore silently. A loud click signalled my warden's coin had bested the lock. The iron door swung open, beckoning us into the holiest site in all of Berabesq, where my business partner was now looking forward to the prospect of eating a god's corpse. *When did my life get this messed up?*

Despite my rather disreputable history and the general paucity of my purse – and not just because of Reichis pilfering it at regular intervals – I've visited a number of architectural marvels during my wayward travels. Cazaran, the capital of Gitabria, for instance, boasts eight spectacular bridges connecting the two halves of the city across a massive gorge. The Imperial Palace of Darome is no slouch when it comes to ostentatiousness either. The Ebony Abbey, with its unnaturally beautiful towers erected from the mystical material of pure shadowblack, had been just as impressive before my father and his posse of war mages had destroyed it. But for raw, awe-inspiring resplendence? None of them held a candle to the holy spire of the Great Temple of Makhan.

'God,' Reichis murmured as we slinked through one of the glittering passages.

'Which one?' I asked. 'Every time you bring up squirrel cat gods it seems there are more of them.'

346

He looked up at me as if we'd suddenly lost the ability to understand each other. 'What? No, idjit, I said "gold".' He gave a shake of his fur, causing his coat to change colour to match the lustrous walls all around us.

'Do you two always talk this much when you're supposed to be infiltrating the most protected temple on the continent?' Nephenia hissed.

'She's got a point,' Reichis said. 'Best if you shut up, Kellen.'

I took the card that the Path of Mountain Storms had given me and tried once again to orient myself on the little circular map representing this floor of the spire. I had no clue whether I could trust any of it any more, but so far it had turned out to be exactly as accurate as you'd expect, given the diagrams were based on the faint head movements of drunken blind servants who weren't even aware they might be revealing the temple's design, which is to say, not much at all. On the other hand, while places on the map were often mismatched left to right or front to back, most of the actual rooms and passageways described on the card did, at least, exist.

'There should be a prayer room on each floor,' I said quietly. 'We should probably stay away from those.'

'Agreed,' Nephenia said. 'Also, you might want to remind the squirrel cat about the purpose of our mission here.'

I glanced around, but Reichis had disappeared again. I crept down the corridor and turned a corner to find him scratching his claws against one of the gold-painted walls in an attempt to extract as much of the valuable ore as he could.

'What in all the hells are you doing?' I asked.

'Shh,' he snarled back at me. 'Can't you see I'm workin' here?'

There are times when my furry business partner's avarice has to be handled delicately. 'But if we load up on gold, how will we carry the gems?'

'Gems?'

'Haven't you heard the stories? The treasure room in the spire is rumoured to contain the largest collection of precious stones on the continent.' I began counting off on my fingers. 'Diamonds, rubies, emeralds, sapphires . . .'

'Sapphires?'

'Buckets of them.'

He stopped scratching at the walls, though his claws glinted with gold flecks as he sauntered back to me. 'Those buckets will be a big help when you're carrying my gems back to the saloon.'

Glancing once again at the map, I tried to reason out which hallway would most likely lead to the staircase to the floor above. We made painfully slow progress those next few minutes. The gleaming, polished floors felt almost like sheets of gold beneath our boots, our every tiptoed step echoing down the halls and threatening to summon the temple guards who patrolled the spire. Blessedly, there weren't as many of them as I would've expected.

'Why is this place so poorly protected?' Nephenia asked quietly. I recognised from the soft way she spoke the same techniques Ferius had tried to teach me for making yourself heard by those next to you without your voice carrying any further.

'I don't know,' I replied, cringing at how my own whispers seemed to reverberate all around us.

'This place is giving me the creeps,' Reichis chittered.

Ishak concurred with a quiet yip.

I gestured for both of them to keep silent, though I couldn't dispute their assessment; the further we travelled along the opulent corridors, the more bizarre the contrasts we discovered. Opposite a hospital room laden with shelves stacked with medicines and instruments of healing we found a second door, inside which awaited a veritable torture chamber filled with devices I could only assume were designed for the extraction of confessions from captured blasphemers. A library boasting more books than I'd seen in the entire Imperial Palace of Darome on one side of the corridor faced an anteroom equipped for the ritual destruction of unholy texts. The endless contradictions of Berabesq's six religious sects appeared to coexist in discordant harmony within a single temple.

At last we found the first set of stairs and began the laborious process of ascending through the levels of the spire one by one. Just as the card in my hand described, no single staircase united all the floors, which meant we had to cover almost every part of the spire as we made our way to the top.

The only consistent architectural features of the spire were the prayer rooms located at the end of the corridor that led off to the right at the top of each flight of stairs. Ceilings painted with the constellations of the night sky looked down upon parquet floors where carved wooden kneeling discs awaited those wishing to pray in comfort. It was while sneaking past the third of these vast chambers that we learned why the temple seemed so empty.

'What are the temple guards doing in there?' Nephenia asked in a whisper.

We soon realised that it was the same on every floor: a

prayer room filled with dozens of black-and-silver garbed sentries who should've been performing regular rounds of the spire but were instead on their knees, heads bowed as a vizier standing on a raised platform led them in worshipful chants to one of the six faces of the Berabesq god. The entrance to each of the chambers was protected by sturdy iron bars, which would have made sense if you wanted to prevent unauthorised entry, but these gates were locked from the outside.

I motioned for the others to stay back as I crept around the corner from one of the prayer rooms and climbed a latticed wall to the gap above the ceiling where uncovered wooden beams spanned the chamber to allow air to circulate throughout the spire. From there I got a closer look at the men and women below.

The temple guards, viziers and other holy functionaries were indeed deep in prayer, but something still didn't look quite right. The guards seemed jittery – visibly uncomfortable at just sitting there. Their heads would turn towards the door as if the empty corridors beyond troubled them. When one started to rise, the vizier leading the prayer shouted at him. The guard knelt back down on the prayer disc and resumed his chanting.

Why would the viziers be keeping the temple guards inside the prayer rooms? I wondered, not expecting to find an answer, of course, which was why I nearly fell off the beam when one appeared.

Strange, isn't it? A young boy's voice appeared in my mind. He sounded different than before, his words strained, thin, as if scraped from the throat of someone holding back tremendous pain. *It's almost as if they're waiting for you to kill me.*

350

48

The Torment

The screams weren't the worst of it. Even as those heart-rending wails drew Nephenia, Ishak, Reichis and me inexorably along the circular passageways of the spire's summit, our steps taking us in a spiral towards whatever awaited us at its centre, the four of us shivered, not from cold, but from the strange buzzing permeating the air all around us. The closer we got, the more the walls seemed to buckle and warp, as though the stones behind the golden surfaces were shuddering in revulsion. Something terrible was happening here. Something unnatural. The black markings around my left eye felt as if they were starting to bubble.

We were nearing the centre when Ishak, who had been pacing ahead of us, abruptly turned and bared his teeth, growling at Nephenia.

'He wants us to turn back,' she said.

'Damned straight,' Reichis grunted, the colour of his fur shifting from black to grey to blood-red and back again. 'I want out of here.'

'Get a hold of yourself, partner,' I said. I've learned the hard way that comforting him when he's scared results in nasty bite marks.

Nephenia shook her head, fingers pressing into her temples. The tattooed bands on her forearms weren't shimmering the way they normally did. Instead, the sigils glistened as if the metallic inks were slowly turning liquid. 'I'm getting sick, Kellen.'

I wasn't feeling great myself, but I was nowhere near as bad as she was, which was odd. Usually I'm the first to get nauseous.

You and I have something in common, the voice in my head said, even as the boy's screams echoed down the passage towards us. *Something that makes this less . . . unfamiliar to your senses.*

What? I asked silently. I figured a god who can put thoughts in your head can probably hear them too.

Come and see.

I forced myself onward. The others gritted their teeth and followed. Before long we reached the end of the winding passage and found ourselves hiding just outside an open doorway as we peered inside to a massive circular room maybe fifty feet across. Cheerfully coloured draperies depicting desert flora and fauna hung from floor to ceiling. Toys of all shapes and sizes were strewn about, some simple stuffed animals of the kind given to babies in their cribs, others complex wind-up mechanical contraptions suited to much older children. There were games too; illustrated boards with carved wooden pieces in the shapes of soldiers and siege engines. In one corner of the room sat a small student's desk, its surface buried beneath sheaves of rough paper covered in ink marks and scratched-out words.

Shattering the image of a rich child's bedroom was the waist-high block of stone at the centre, where six viziers in ornate brocade robes stood over the bound body of a boy whose dark skin had turned ashen from pain. Blind Asabli servants held out leather-bound books that the viziers turned back to again and again before inscribing sigils onto the boy's limbs with pens that ended in sharpened bronze tips. Each stroke left behind an angry red welt on the boy's flesh, the ridges between filled in with lines of ink so pure and unrelenting in its darkness that I couldn't stop myself from whispering its name out loud.

'Shadowblack.'

The breath froze in my lungs even as my mind began sorting through tricks and tactics, tracing the lines of attack and ruses I would need to stop the viziers. Nephenia pulled me out of the way before one of them might have glanced over at the doorway and seen me.

'Kellen, wait,' she whispered. She needn't have worried; the combination of the boy's screaming and the viziers' chanting would've drowned out an invading army. 'You can't fight them.'

I couldn't quite make sense of her words. The image of the boy, strapped down on that table . . . It was like watching myself three years ago, when my mother and father had dripped molten inks on the skin of my forearms, forever imprinting upon them the counter-bands that would deny me access to the magic that defined my people.

'What are you talking about?' I asked quietly. 'We faced worse odds when we fought the monks at the Ebony Abbey.'

'You see those gold designs down the arms of their robes?'

I nodded. They were incredibly intricate, almost like spiralling lines of script in a language I couldn't recognise. The time and effort to embroider such garments would be enormous.

'You won't find anything like that on the habits of regular viziers,' Nephenia went on. 'Nor even on the warrior vestments of the Faithful. Those men in there are the Arcanists.'

'The what now?' Reichis asked, his ears flattened against his skull.

I've never made much of a study of the Berabesq theocracy, other than looking for ways to avoid it. Nephenia could tell from my expression that I had no idea what she was talking about. 'The Arcanists,' she repeated, wincing from whatever phantom pains this place was inflicting on her mind before she explained. 'You remember a couple of years ago when we fought that squad of Faithful in the desert? The ones who could use their own blood to create mystical shields? Those abilities are imprinted on them by the Arcanists.'

'So they're charmcasters like you, only they can embed spells into human beings?'

'I suppose so, but I'm nowhere near as powerful. I doubt even a lord magus could hold their own against an Arcanist.'

I've spent a lot of time in the past few years devising plans for defeating the innumerable people out there who want to kill me. I had no tactics for taking on six of anything as powerful as a lord magus, mostly because such a feat was impossible.

Heed your friend's warning, the voice in my head said. *Should you meddle in their affairs, the Arcanists will destroy you and your companions in ways that will leave your spirits howling in agony long after your bodies have grown cold.*

Like they're doing to you? I asked.

It is not the same. The pain is significant, yes, but such sacrifices are necessary.

Necessary for what?

Another scream erupted from the boy's throat.

This, Kellen of the Jan'Tep, is how a god is made.

49

The Ritual

We crouched in the shadows like cowards and waited as they tortured the boy for another hour. Nephenia didn't dare use one of her charms to conceal our presence, for fear the Arcanists would sense the use of Jan'Tep magic. Theirs was a different kind of mysticism than that of my people, with abilities inscribed onto their skin just as they carved miracles into the flesh of the boy they were turning into a god.

Almost like the malediction, I thought, my fists clenched so tight my fingernails were digging into the flesh of my palms.

'There's something strange about this,' Nephenia said in a hushed whisper. 'There have been rumours about the secret techniques of the Arcanists since the birth of the Berabesq theocracy, but not one of the tales speaks of them working with the shadowblack.'

The chanting died out abruptly. The screams took a while longer. Several heavy thumps of leather-bound books closing was followed by soft, almost gentle words spoken by the Arcanists to the boy as they unbuckled the restraints holding him to the table. When they finally began trudging out of the room, I feared they might spot us in the shadows, but the stooping of their shoulders and the shuffling of their feet spoke of a bone-deep exhaustion that hid us from them as utterly as any obscurement spell. Soon the six Arcanists and their blind attendants had passed us by without notice.

Experience had taught me to wait in case one of them came back, but a pinched, reedy voice called out from the chamber, 'Have no fear. It will be many hours before they return.'

I rose from my hiding place. Before entering the room, I carefully and methodically unwound the ancient scourge rope coiled around my right arm, then removed the roughly carved dice Emelda had given me from their decaying felt bag in my pocket. Nephenia already had two of her charms ready: her box of caged storms and a pair of tiny mechanical spiders. Reichis and Ishak had their teeth and claws on display, along with their attitudes.

'Down on the floor, skinbag!' Reichis snarled, leaping into the room, his fur transformed to pure black with red stripes. Ishak followed just as quickly, mimicking Reichis's words, which sounded even more disturbing coming from the jaws of a hyena.

The sight of the god took me aback. You couldn't call him a boy, not any more. He stood as tall as me, though he can't have weighed half as much. He wasn't just thin . . . He was distended. He looked as through someone had aged him by stretching his limbs on a rack until his entire body relented, giving up years of life in mere hours. Yet when he saw Reichis and Ishak, he laughed as joyously as any child. 'They're beautiful!'

His innocent mirth was contradicted by the rows upon rows of black sigils inscribed into the skin of his torso that made me clench the dice even tighter. He fell into embarrassed silence when he caught my stare. Awkwardly, and with obvious

356

effort, he pulled his own plain white robes over his still-bleeding body.

I decided it was best to start with something simple. 'How old are you?'

'I'm not sure,' he replied.

Nephenia stepped closer, peering at his robes where the blood was already seeping through. 'Do you know when you were born?'

'Almost a year ago,' he replied, then seemed to reconsider. 'Though possibly when the world began.'

'You're going to have to pick one or the other,' I said.

A faint, almost forgiving smile came to his weary face. 'Because if I'm a child, caught up in the machinations of others, you will refuse to kill me, no matter the consequences my existence brings upon the world.' His eyes went to my closed fist. 'Yet if I am truly God, you'll roll those dice my people crafted from the ruins of the first baojara tree to bind me, then wrap the scourge made from its bark around my neck and strangle me without a second thought.' He shook his head. 'No, my friend, I will not free you from the burden of your own conscience quite so easily. Besides, does not the queen you serve claim to be both a twelve-year-old girl and the embodiment of her people's two-thousand-year-old royal lineage? Why is she allowed such a paradox and not I?'

Reichis looked up at me. 'Well, I don't know if this kid's a god or not, but he's already puttin' me in a killin' mood. Can we just throttle him and get it over with?'

'There's a third option,' I said, keeping a careful grip on the dice and the scourge as I approached him. The god looked nothing so much as a sickly, emaciated young man incapable

357

of harming anyone, but I wasn't fooled. 'You could heal my friend and promise to leave this place, go wherever it is gods go when they're not meddling in human affairs. Do that and we'll call it square.'

That seemed to amuse him, though I noticed he stepped back. 'You begin with the Way of Water, do you not?' He gestured to the little desk covered in books and marked-up pieces of paper. 'My attendants require that I read extensively about the affairs of this world. I find the Argosi most intriguing.'

'Why does a god need books to learn about anything?' Nephenia asked.

'Why not?' was his reply.

'If you know the Argosi ways,' I began, my hand clenching the scourge tighter, 'then you know that when the Way of Water fails, it's not long before we get to the Way of Thunder. So I suggest you take the deal.'

He tried to hide it, but I could tell he was genuinely afraid of what I might do. 'This friend of yours,' he said, 'your threats imply her life is of greater consequence to you than those of all the others that might be lost should war come. Who is this virtuous paragon of whom you speak?'

'Her name is Ferius Parfax,' I replied, more angrily than I intended because I wasn't sure if he was screwing with me. 'While you and I are standing here, one of your so-called miracles is killing her!'

He looked confused. 'Such a dastardly conjuration hardly sounds like a miracle.'

'The malediction,' Nephenia explained. 'A band of your Faithful cast it upon her.'

'Ah,' said the god, 'I understand now, though that is not

358

our word for the ritual. To us it is a form of consecration, meant to—'

I cut him off. 'I don't care what name you give it. Can you put a stop to it or not?'

'There is a way, I suppose,' he replied. 'Yes, I can save this Ferius Parfax's life, or rather, *we* can save her life.'

'How?'

He pointed to the scourge in my right hand. 'You have merely to wrap that around my neck, twist it very tight, and keep hold until I asphyxiate.'

'Killing you is the only way?'

He nodded. Long, unnaturally thin fingers reached up to pull at the neck of his robes, revealing the tops of the markings etched into his skin. 'What you call the malediction is not one of my miracles, though its power comes from me, even as mine comes from the sacred words upon my flesh. I am both the vessel and the wine, so to speak.'

'Is that what it means to be a god then?' Nephenia asked. 'To be nothing more than a . . . a collection of miraculous events?'

He shrugged, seemingly unconcerned by that contradiction, but I saw the gesture for what it was: a boyish evasion.

'He doesn't know,' I said. His words from yesterday came back to me and I decided to voice my speculations. 'His handlers tell him he's a god, but he has no memory or conception of becoming one. They give him lessons in Berabesq theology, tell him what to believe, but he senses something is missing. That's why he spoke to me, an outsider, because he thinks this strange connection between us might uncover the truth of who or what he is.'

Something I hadn't noticed before caught my attention: a

359

small wooden-floored area in the opposite corner of the room, with a single prayer disc about a foot in diameter. The sight of it made me chuckle.

'Why do you laugh?' he asked.

I pointed to the wooden kneeling disc. 'Who do you pray to?'

'I pray for wisdom.'

'Yes, but wisdom from whom?'

He considered my question, then walked to a different corner of the room, occupied by two chairs and a small hexagonal table upon which rested a shujan board with all its pieces. 'Play with me?'

An innocuous request, but I became distinctly aware of the scourge in my hand. It was vibrating like the tail of a rattlesnake, almost begging me to strike first. The 'helpless kid caught in unfortunate circumstances' act was all well and good, but this guy's very existence threatened an entire continent, not to mention Ferius.

If I do it now, I thought, feeling the strange comforting roughness of the rope in my hand, *if I just . . . forget myself for a moment and do the job I was sent to do, this will all be over. All the confusion, the danger of armies slaughtering each other on the battlefield, the fear of what will happen to the queen if the wrong side wins, the uncertainty of what will happen to the Berabesq if they lose. Ferius growing weaker every day until, like my mother, she just . . . stops.*

'What are you doing?' the boy asked.

It took me a moment to formulate a reply. 'Praying for wisdom, I suppose.'

He gestured once again to the two chairs. Unsure of what to do, I looked to Nephenia, but she was now nose-deep

360

inside one of the books we'd seen the Asabli holding for their Arcanists. Ishak and Reichis were sniffing around the room, probably in search of loot.

Maybe Nephenia can find a way to stop the malediction in one of those books, I thought.

I placed the scourge and the dice on the floor a few feet from the table, then sat down on one of the chairs. God took the other.

'You said you were praying just now,' he said. 'May I ask to whom?'

'I don't know. No one, I suppose. I'm not very religious.'

The boy leaned forward over the shujan board and whispered conspiratorially. 'Neither am I.'

When I didn't say anything, he leaned back and asked, 'Was that not funny? I was trying to make a joke.'

'Tell him it was lame,' Reichis said. The squirrel cat was sniffing everything in the room *except* the Berabesq god. 'And ask him where he keeps his sapphires.'

'What did your squirrel cat say?' the boy asked.

'Don't you know?' Nephenia asked, looking up from another of the leather-bound tomes. 'You're supposed to be the six-faced god of Berabesq. You've been speaking to Kellen through his thoughts. Surely a deity sees inside the minds of mere mortals?'

'I . . .' He hesitated, brow furrowing in confusion. 'I'm not sure how it all works.'

'How what works?' I asked.

This, he said, speaking inside my head. *It is not one of my miracles.*

'Do you communicate in such a manner with anyone else?' I asked.

'Only one other.'

361

'Who?'

His young brow furrowed. 'I am not sure. He . . . advises me.'

'Like a vizier?'

He laughed then. 'Oh, my viziers advise me too. They advise me on when to wake, when to sleep. They tell me what to eat and drink, which medicines to consume no matter how foul the taste . . .'

'Medicines? What does a god need with medicine?'

He sidestepped the question. 'Let us return to our earlier conundrum. You asked to whom a god prays, and I asked to whom *you* were praying when you sought wisdom.'

'Yes, but in my case I wasn't really looking outside myself for the answer.'

'Because whatever answer exists, it awaits inside you, yes?'

I nodded.

He spread his hands. 'Then perhaps it is the same with me. The wisdom I seek, the god to whom I pray –' he tapped his chest – 'awaits in here.'

Ishak looked over and barked twice. Reichis grunted in agreement. 'The hyena says if this guy doesn't stop with the philosophical claptrap pretty soon, he's going chew his head off.'

I decided not to relay that piece of information to the god. 'Why am I here?' I asked. Before he could speak, I held up a hand. 'No more clever prevarications. No more metaphysical pronouncements. Just the simple truth.'

For once he gave a straight answer, though it wasn't one that reassured me. 'I need you to help me decide whether or not I am God, and if I am, whether it is better that I live or that I die.'

'And how precisely are we to do that?'

He pointed to the shadowblack lines around my left eye. 'Those markings. They have a meaning, do they not?'

I was about to make a joke about how what they mean is that everyone and their dog is allowed to attack me without provocation, but then I finally understood why I was here. 'The enigmatism,' I breathed. 'The shadowblack ability to see inside the secrets of others. That's why you wanted me to come. That's why you haven't just blasted me out of existence already – because I'm an enigmatist.'

He didn't speak, but by then I didn't need him to.

'You believe that with my shadowblack I can see inside you and reveal whether you're really a god!'

'Can you do that?' Nephenia asked, looking up from yet another of the books. 'How does it work?'

'I . . . It's complicated. The enigmatism isn't something I can turn on and off like a glow-glass lantern. It requires finding exactly the right questions to ask.'

The boy gestured to the shujan board between us. 'I have found that a good game of shujan always produces many fascinating questions. Shall we play?'

50

The Game

I hadn't realised how much I'd missed those games of shujan with Keliesh on the road to the Berabesq capital until I found myself playing against a god.

'I find there is a rhythm to shujan that liberates the mind,' he said, moving one of the pieces. 'Though the number of potential moves is mathematically finite, there are still so many as to give one the sense that anything is possible.'

The variation of the game we played involved each controlling one of the six sides of the board. Either of us could play the pieces of the other four sides, but because we could only move one piece on each turn, and such moves could simply be reversed by the other player on their next turn, it made more sense to focus on our respective armies. We'd agreed that with each turn we had the right to pose the other a question.

'What is your name?' I asked, moving one of my camels forward. While not the most pressing issue, this felt like a reasonable place to begin.

'The warrior,' he replied, then added, 'the gardener. The clockmaker, the penitent, the hea—'

'Your real name.'

'I don't know. Everyone in the temple calls me God.'

'You mentioned another voice you hear in your head. Who is he? What does he call you?'

'It's not your turn.' The boy moved an archer. 'What name would you like to call me?'

Though it sounded like an idle question, I had the strange sense that it was a kind of test.

I don't want to call you anything, I thought. *I don't want you to exist. I don't want for there to be gods who sit there choosing the destinies of others. What right does any god have to decide my fate?*

'And yet,' the boy said aloud in response to my unspoken words, 'now it is a god asking *you* to choose *his* fate.' He sat back in his chair. 'You still haven't answered my question.'

I stared down at the board, pondering my next move. He'd been wrong about the game allowing for nearly infinite moves. That was true at first, but the instant you made your opening gambit, you started down a path that would progressively allow fewer and fewer choices until at last there would be only one.

'Shujan,' I said at last. 'I would like to call you Shujan.'

A smile lit up his face. 'Shujan! Yes! I love it!' He reached across the game board and took my hand in his. 'Thank you, Kellen!'

He seemed so delighted I felt awkward, as if there was something I was supposed to do now to seal his happiness. I changed our grip so that we were now shaking hands and said, 'Nice to meet you, Shujan.'

He shook my hand vigorously in reply. 'Nice to meet you, Kellen!'

Then he took his hand away, and all the mirth was gone. 'It is your turn to ask a question.'

'You made it rain yesterday,' I said, moving my camel again. In shujan, the usual strategy is to get as many of your pieces in play as possible to encircle your opponent, but I wasn't ready for that yet. 'What else can you do?'

'When I was merely a babe in swaddling clothes and the viziers presented me to my people from the balcony of this spire, I brought down rain that made a hundred thousand flowers rise up from arid grounds around the city. On the next, I revealed to all who watched the movements of the sun and stars. I once made all sound in these lands, from the roaring of the wind to the flutter of butterfly wings, fade away so that all present knew a moment of pure, silent reflection. I have healed the sick and caused bitter enemies to beg each other's forgiveness.'

Five miracles, each one corresponding to one of the six faces of the Berabesq god: the gardener, the clockmaker, the hermit, the healer, the penitent. That left only one remaining: the warrior.

He said the malediction wasn't one of his miracles, so what is the sixth?

The answer, I realised then, was obvious. *It's the one the Arcanists are still inscribing onto his flesh. The miracle that will unite all the Berabesq sects into a single army that would march across the continent.*

I quieted that thought in hopes of keeping it from the young man sitting across from me.

'How did you discover you could work these miracles of yours?' I asked.

Shujan shook his head. Not my turn. After he moved one of his chariots two spaces, he asked, 'Regardless of my true nature, you believe me to be a threat to all that you love. Why have you not killed me?'

'Because I . . .' I trailed off. I really wasn't sure what was holding me back. I'd killed before and for less noble reasons than preventing a war. And while Shujan might *look* like an innocent, I'd been the victim of enough illusions in my life to distrust such naive notions. For all I knew, he could be a demon masquerading as a boy. Why wasn't I just coiling the Baojara Scourge around his neck and doing the job I was sent to do?

'I don't like being controlled,' I said finally. 'And killing you without knowing the truth feels too much like . . .'

'An act of submission?' he suggested.

I nodded.

'Interesting. Perhaps we are getting close to something.'

'I don't see how.'

'Move your next piece.'

I looked down at the board. It was still early in the game, but he'd made a mistake with his chariot. In shujan, a chariot can't be removed from the board, but it can be 'mounted'. I placed my eagle upon it. Now, though the eagle couldn't attack, it could move with the chariot and was immune to being removed by one of his pieces.

Yeah, it's a pretty weird game when you think about it.

'How did you know the things you could do?' I asked. 'The rain, the healings?'

'It's in the markings,' Nephenia said, confirming my earlier suspicion as she brought one of the leather-bound books over. 'The Arcanists are literally inscribing miracles into his flesh.'

'Like spells?'

She shook her head. 'There's no Jan'Tep spell that can do the kinds of things he's done. The scale is too big. The laws of physics just don't work that way, which is why I can't figure out how any of this is possible.'

367

'The shadowblack,' I said suddenly, my fingers instinctively reaching up to the winding lines on my own face. 'When I was at the Ebony Abbey, they said the shadowblack creates a kind of opening into other ethereal planes, where the laws that govern matter, energy and life work differently, allowing those alternate rules to momentarily seep through into our universe.'

'But that still requires a will to guide it,' Nephenia said. She pointed at Shujan. 'He was just a baby when he performed his first miracle. He couldn't have caused it himself.'

'How do you decide when to bring forth your "miracles"?' I asked him.

Shujan stared down at the game from which I'd given him his name. 'There is . . . another voice, one who speaks inside my mind. When the viziers bring me out to stand before my people, he helps me bring forth my gifts that I might bestow them upon others.'

His answer, while plain enough, frustrated the hells out of me. 'That doesn't explain anything. How can you even know it's you who's—'

He abruptly moved another piece, a wooden vizier this time, cutting off both my own pieces and my question. 'You claim to dislike being controlled, but can you tell me what it means to be free?'

I removed my eagle from the chariot and took his vizier. 'To make one's own choices, free from the influence of others.'

His archer mounted the chariot. I'd made an amateur mistake. No piece can attack from a chariot except an archer, but they can only mount a chariot abandoned by another player, which I'd just done. 'You are not free,' Shujan said. 'The shadowblack around your eye, the limitations of your own mortality, the need to stay alive – these inform every choice you make.'

'Not so much that last one,' Reichis grumbled. He appeared to be rooting around in a drawer of underclothes.

Why does he have to embarrass me in front of a god?

'Since you haven't asked a question,' I said, bringing my second eagle forward into play, 'why don't you explain to me why a god needs someone to tell him his abilities? Shouldn't you know who you are?'

Instead of answering, the boy rose and walked over to the partitioned study area. When he returned, he placed six heavy books in the middle of the board between us, scattering the carved wooden pieces and putting an abrupt end to our game. 'These are the codices of my people, the entirety of our holy texts. Find for me, if you please, where it says God must be all-knowing.'

I sat there staring at the leather-bound tomes, one for each of the Berabesq god's supposed 'faces'. Warrior. Gardener. Clockmaker. Hermit. Healer. Penitent. Ferius had implied the Argosi had something to do with these different variations, thus ensuring six distinct sects of religious traditions that would keep the Berabesq from uniting behind one theological banner. But that story didn't sound quite right – the Argosi weren't the sort to manipulate cultures in that way. More likely, most of the individual interpretations were oral traditions, and they'd simply made sure all six appeared in written form to prevent one single one from erasing all the others.

Click.

Not a sound, not really, but the tell-tale pinching of the skin around my left eye as my shadowblack markings began to turn.

369

To unlock.

'You haven't been honest with me, Shujan,' I said to the boy.

'No?'

His hesitation increased my certainty. I felt the second ring of my shadowblack markings turn.

'You said you weren't sure if you were God.'

'I'm not.'

'I think you do believe you're God . . . You just aren't sure which one.'

I felt the third twisting ring of my shadowblack markings turn. The enigmatism that my grandmother had banded me with as a child, the curse that made me a hunted outcast everywhere and never answered my questions until I found just the right one, unlocked.

The board between us grew, spreading out beyond the walls of the spire, past the temple grounds and the city itself. Shujan and I ceased to exist, becoming watchers without substance. There, upon the hexagonal fields below us, armies marched away from the board rather than towards its centre, each one led by Shujan himself. Only . . . he wasn't the same boy.

On one side he strode with a flaming sword in hand, his warriors cheering him on as he led them to conquer. They left the slaughtered corpses of other nations in their wake.

On another he carried a bag of seeds, his followers planting them across the land as they raised new crops, their success causing other nations to join them in exchange for the resources they needed to survive.

A different Shujan, this one the penitent, led his people in quiet prayer. They lived simple lives, sought out no great conquests, simply hoped to justify their existence through piety.

I watched one god after another lead the people of Berabesq, each in a different direction towards different lives – lives that affected those of everyone else on the continent.

'Show me,' the boy who was still inside that room in the spire begged. 'Show me which path must my people take so I may know which god I should be to them.'

But there was no answer – no good one. The warrior conquered territory at the cost of the lives of his own people. The clockmaker devised great plans for prosperity and dominance of the continent, yet his people grew indolent, relying on the labour of others. The gardener, the penitent . . . They each provided an answer, yet none was complete.

Then I felt the vision shatter, the shadowblack markings around my eye unwinding until they settled once again, revealing the same room I'd been in moments before, except now Nephenia, Reichis and Ishak were all on the floor, tiny darts dangling from their necks.

'I can tell you exactly what kind of god the world needs,' Torian Libri said, holding a blowpipe in one hand and the scourge she'd taken from me without my even noticing in the other. 'A dead one.'

51

The Dupe

Torian was saying something – something about me stepping aside so she could finish the job she'd known all along I couldn't be trusted with. I didn't hear much of it though. My eyes were on Nephenia and Ishak, who were unconscious on the floor, and Reichis, who lay so still I watched desperately for signs of him breathing, even as another part of me considered what I would do if he were dead. Poison's a tricky thing to work with. The dose to knock out a full-grown woman or even a hyena was more than enough to kill a squirrel cat.

'Are you *growling* at me, card player?' Torian asked. She held up the blowpipe for me to see. 'Never thought much of these as killing weapons, but I'm starting to appreciate them for getting rid of unwanted witnesses. I've got a dart just for you, if you'd rather not watch.'

'A moment, if you please,' I replied, still watching Reichis.

There, I thought, suddenly able to breathe again as I saw his side rise just a little, then fall again. *He's alive!*

'I was careful with the dosage,' Torian said. Evidently she knew me well enough to guess at what had me so worried. That only made the betrayal hurt more.

372

'You were the one who killed the vizier,' I said. 'You led the guards to the travellers' saloon so they'd arrest the first foreigner they saw leaving, which you knew would be me.'

'Now don't get all sore, card player. I knew you'd shake them soon enough.' She held up the scourge. 'I needed you to bring this to me, remember?'

Shujan, sitting across from me, held my gaze.

Perhaps this is the answer we both sought, he told me silently. *Perhaps we have both been free all along because neither of our choices really mattered.*

I rose to my feet and turned to face Torian. She shook her head and showed me the blowpipe again. 'I wouldn't suggest coming any closer. I think I might've dipped this last dart in the venom too long, and I know how much you hate it when I poison you.'

I waited there for a few seconds, trying to learn what I could from the way she stared back at me, from her posture, from the set of her jaw. Torian was hard to read though. She so proudly wore the mantle of heartless, cavalier enforcer – the ruthless agent of the empire – but there was always something else hiding beneath. Now it played under the surface of her features. Was it fear? Uncertainty?

'Don't,' she said, a sudden flush of anger coming to her cheeks.

'Don't what?'

'Don't look at me that way, with that Argosi gaze of yours, as if I'm some puzzle for you to solve with your arta precis or arta tuco or whatever it is.'

There were a range of responses to that one, some witty and disarming, some outraged. I let them all drift by me. First lesson Ferius ever taught me about arta loquit –

373

eloquence – was that a conversation is music, and sometimes it's best to let your partner be the notes, and you the silences.

'The queen's with the army, amassing at the southern border, did you know that?' she asked, a bitter timbre in her voice. 'A twelve-year-old girl in pretty armour that won't do her a lick of good when she's overrun by the Berabesq. She insisted she had to be there though. Told me some nonsense about monarchs having no right to send armies to die if they wouldn't ride alongside them into the abyss.'

I felt a stab of guilt and something harder, colder, in my gut. None of it surprised me; Ginevra showed herself to be that kind of ruler at every turn – the type who wants to *earn* the love of their people. The type who most often die trying.

'But here you are, sipping tea with the enemy, no doubt delving into all sorts of deep, philosophical discussions about the intricacies of religion. Debating, contemplating, searching for some great path to appear before you that will free you from having to do what needs to be done.'

I gave no reply, just waited for her to make her own way round to whatever it was she really wanted to say. Finally the words came out, not in a flurry of tears, but with the sorrow and confusion of a girl half her age all the same. 'You killed my father, Kellen.'

I didn't ask who'd told her. Emelda. One of the other Murmurers. Maybe someone else. It hardly mattered now. 'I'm sorry,' I said, not because it would do any good, but because it was how I felt. Jed Colfax had terrorised me when he'd set that white binder on me, brought my already miserable existence to the brink of utter and irreversible despair, yet every action he'd ever taken had been to protect the queen. I should've realised his daughter would be cut from the same cloth.

'You shot Ferius to keep her from coming with me,' I said.

'I could've killed her. That would've been a fair trade, don't you think? Goodness knows the world could use one less Argosi, but I kept my temper, just wounded her to keep her from interfering with the mission. I wanted to believe that if it was just you, if I gave you the chance, you'd do the right thing.'

The right thing.

Ancestors, I was almost as sick of people telling me the right thing to do as I was of trying to figure it out myself. Mostly, though, I was tired of listening to people lie to themselves.

'The reason you didn't kill Ferius is that if you had you'd've been forced to admit to yourself that all your talk of duty and loyalty is just more of the same garbage people like your mother feed the world to justify their actions.'

The outrage in her expression became so hardened that it was as if Arcanists had inscribed it onto her features. 'You pompous bastard. What gives you the right to judge me? You're an outlaw! A card sharp! Your whole life is tricking people!'

'You missed one,' I said. 'Did you forget I'm also a murderer?'

For a second I thought I'd pushed her too far and she'd just hit me with the dart and that would be the end of it. Problem was, I needed to make her so angry that knocking me out wouldn't be enough for her.

'You think you're so very clever, don't you?' she asked. 'The

375

spellslinging shadowblack Argosi who sees through everyone else's deceptions? You're the blindest one of all, Kellen! So convinced about who you trust, who you doubt, that you couldn't spot a trick so simple the lie was right there in plain black ink.'

I spun to Shujan, but he looked as confused as I was. My arta loquit picked up on two phrases from Torian's little tirade, repeating them over and over in my mind: *'who you trust . . . the lie was right there in plain black ink.'*

The word 'trust' had been filled with bitterness. Why?

She resents who you trust, I thought.

The lie in plain black ink. That could've referred to Shujan's markings, but I doubted it. There was no reason for her to believe that was some kind of ruse. My shadowblack? No, she knew that was real too. Besides, who would ever want to fake the . . .

No, please, not her!

Torian smiled as if she'd just beaten me in a duel.

'The queen,' I whispered, hoping my suspicion wasn't true, suddenly completely sure that it was.

A year ago, after the attempted coup that nearly brought down her reign, Ginevra had brought me into the palace throne room. I'd been preparing to depart Darome for good, wanting to get away from court intrigues and an endless parade of powerful nobles who wanted me dead. She'd forced me to watch as she pulled aside part of her dress, revealing the winding black markings that would be the end of her when she turned thirteen and by tradition had to present herself naked before the people she ruled. That's when I'd sworn to stay and protect her.

Ancestors, I am such a sucker sometimes.

'She was an eleven-year-old girl who'd just been tortured for days and had barely hung on to her crown,' Torian said. 'She needed a protector and she'd chosen you, the only person she could trust. But you were going to walk away and leave her to those wolves in fine silks who prowl about the palace waiting for their chance to destroy her. So she drew those markings on herself, knowing the shadowblack would be the one thing that would make you stay.'

'I thought . . . I knew there was a secret her tutors had over her. The shadowblack explained everything.'

'That's the problem with wanting the world to make sense, Kellen. It makes you gullible. Worse, it makes you demand other people live up to your expectations. Ginevra's a good girl. She's going to be a great queen. But she needs people around her who understand that you can't run away every time there's a difficult choice to be made. Doesn't matter how clever you are, card player – nobody gets to pull a fast one on destiny.'

I didn't know what to say to that. The part of my brain that's usually dedicated to clever retorts was trying desperately to come up with a reason why I shouldn't just walk away and let Torian do whatever she wanted, or stall her until some temple guard or Arcanist came along to kill her. Would a Berabesq empire be any worse than a Daroman one? This whole lousy continent seemed determined to destroy itself one way or another.

Why did you save me that day when my sister accidentally stopped my heart, Ferius? Why bother teaching me to see the world differently from other people if the end result is always the same?

'Just step aside, Kellen,' Torian said. 'I'll do what has to be done and then I'll help you get your friends away from here. Your Argosi mentor will recover and you can all ride off into the sunset together.'

It was strange, but the sarcasm in her tone as she mentioned Ferius became a kind of music to my ears, not just in the usual way that arta loquit makes you hear things, but because her disdain was so pure, made my mentor sound so ridiculous, that it created a kind of contradiction in the universe that couldn't be allowed to stand. Either Ferius Parfax was a joke, or everything she'd taught me was so real that it didn't matter where it led, only the path upon which it guided me.

I don't think I've ever had to make an easier choice.

I put up my hands for a moment to show Torian I wasn't going to try anything, then removed my hat and set it down on the floor. My coat came next, then, very slowly, the belt that held my powder holsters.

'What are you doing, Kellen?'

I unstrapped the leather case holding my deck of throwing cards and set that on the floor too. 'Getting ready,' I replied, and pulled my shirt with the castradazi coins in the hem over my head.

A confused rumbling came from the other side of the room. Reichis looked up at me, head trembling, eyes unfocused. 'Wha' happen? What are we . . . ?' His beady eyes stared at me quizzically, then at Torian, then he grumbled, 'Oh, you're going to mate,' before laying his head back down to go to sleep.

'I don't know how that messed-up brain of yours works, card player,' Torian said, a dubious smile crossing her mouth, 'but this really ain't going to go down the way I think you're hoping.'

'Put down the weapons,' I said. 'Take off that coat and your bandoleer of throwing knives.'

'Why would I do that?'

'Because otherwise you'll be too tempted to use them when I'm beating you senseless.'

She looked surprised. 'Now why would you think after everything that's happened that I'd risk my mission just to give you a few bruises?'

'Because the queen's wrong about us, Torian. She wanted us to be a couple. Maybe she figured that would somehow make up for the way your father died or the lie she told to keep me by her side. I don't know. But she misread what it is that you find attractive about me.'

Torian snorted. 'Your pretty face?'

I shook my head. 'You're not sure if you can take me in a fight.'

'Oh, I've no doubt on that score, card player.'

I ignored her attempt at arta valar. It wasn't very good. 'I used to wonder why you took it so personally when I got into some duel with a mage or bounty hunter and came back alive. Like the queen, I figured maybe deep down, underneath all the insults and threats, the times you dumped me in a jail cell, that you actually cared about me. And who knows? Maybe you do. But underneath that? What *really* bugs you about me is that you can't stand seeing a trickster defeat all those dangerous men – the ones you beat with strength, skill and courage.' I gestured to my gear on the floor. 'Well, now we see what happens when all the tricks are taken away.'

She stared at me a long while, the part of her that resented being pegged warring with the part that so desperately needed

379

to wipe the smug look off my face. 'No weapons?' she checked.

'I give you my word not to use any of mine. How about you?'

She set the blowpipe and scourge aside and began removing her coat. 'If that's how you want it. I'm kind of surprised you'd want to throw down with fists. Always took you for someone who imagines himself playing the chivalrous hero from the old romantic tales. Don't recall any of them going around beating up women.' She took another knife from the back of one boot and set it on the ground. 'I imagine you'll feel even less chivalrous when you're flat on your back looking up at me after I've broken both your arms and legs. You sure you want to make this play?'

I stood there, naked to the waist, acutely aware of how stupid I must look and how dangerously comfortable Torian appeared as she removed one weapon after another, always keeping an eye on me in case I might try to jump her and end the fight early.

'This is the last thing I wanted,' I said. 'Truth be told, I like you, Torian. A lot. You're fearless and daring, smart as anyone I've ever met and surprisingly fun to be around, even when you're arresting me. Even the squirrel cat has a crush on you.'

'I'm over it,' Reichis said in a little grumble before resuming his snoring.

I tilted my head left then right to loosen it up. I tend to get punched in the face a lot at times like these and a tight neck makes that worse. 'But then you went and nearly killed my mentor. You took out my friends and my business partner with poisoned darts. And now you want to kill this kid for no better reason than because you're so stubbornly determined to follow your mission that you can't see we're all being played for fools.'

She was expecting me to get into a guard position, but instead I stood with my feet together and extended my open hand towards her. Ferius had taught me to fight through the ways of dance, not violence. I hummed a few bars of a merry tune before I asked, 'Shall we begin?'

52

The Rules of War

Torian Libri was faster than me. She was better trained, less afraid of being hit (try *not* blinking when a fist is coming at your face) and, perhaps most important of all, more comfortable with violence.

'We done yet?' she asked.

I was, at that moment, stumbling backwards, the steady flow of blood from my nose dripping down my lips and chin. I had a cut over my right eye that was threatening to blind me and a particularly nasty elbow to the temple had left me reeling like a drunk.

I imagined I made a dashing sight.

Torian? She looked fine. Great in fact. Pummelling me really seemed to really bring out the blue of her eyes.

I can heal you, Shujan said silently.

No, I answered back.

I threw myself at Torian – almost literally, hurtling towards her as though a giant had tossed me in the air. There's really no way you can do much damage to an opponent that way. Trauma comes from either delivering maximum impact in the smallest area possible, using something hard against something weak, or taking control of a joint and twisting it past its natural range of motion. What I was doing had no chance of accomplishing either of those things.

I remembered the first time Ferius had taught me this technique. I'd asked her what possible good it could do. *'Ain't no way to defend if there ain't an attack,'* she'd replied, as if those words made any sense at all. There was a certain truth to it though: trained fighters learn to deal with blows or attempted grapples. They're never entirely sure what to do when you just appear to be falling into them. I mean, sure, Torian could have grabbed an arm and twisted it behind my back or punched me in the throat, but the lack of any visible threat on my part – the sense that I was merely stumbling around – made her hesitate.

In country dances, women get tossed around a lot – spun, twirled and generally flung around while the men do a lot of posing. Ferius had taught me that there was a certain magic to coming out of a toss or spin gracefully. So I let Torian slip to the right, her hands ready to add to my momentum and shove me into the room's back wall. But as she pushed, I turned with her. Now it really did look like we were dancing.

'What are you—'

'Weird, isn't it?' I said, during that brief moment when we were, in effect, waltzing.

Torian wasn't used to going with the flow of the dance however, so when I unexpectedly pulled hard on her waist while pushing against her shoulder, she found herself facing the other way. I gave her a good strong shove, at which it was her turn to take a stumble into the wall.

'That was stupid,' she said as she turned to face me. 'You could have gotten your arm around my neck from behind and choked me out. I won't give you that chance a second time.'

While I have little knowledge of fighting arts, Shujan spoke into my mind, *she appears to have a point.*

I'll be sure to let you know if I need any more critique of my technique.

Torian brought her fists up and began stalking me across the room again. I'd made a reasonable mental map of the available space before the fight began, so I could back my way around with reasonable confidence of not retreating into the edge of a partition or tripping over the furniture.

'If you're trying to tire me out, you're wasting your time,' Torian informed me. 'I once fought a Zhuban Elite for nearly two days without rest, and he was popping lightning weed into his mouth every hour.'

'Impressive,' I said.

A smile crossed her face as she closed the distance between us. 'He certainly thought so.'

'No, I meant it was impressive that he could swallow that much lightning weed without giving himself a heart attack. Also, doesn't excessive use of lightning weed cause painful erections in men? Maybe you won the fight by default.'

An unexpected laugh, like a sudden cough, threw off her rhythm. I raced forward, ducked under her reflexive round-house and delivered what I felt was a respectable uppercut to her jaw. She stepped back before I could press my advantage and delivered a front kick that would've taken my head off if I'd stayed in range of her foot.

'That's the problem with you, Kellen,' she said as she recovered her balance. 'You treat fighting as a game.'

A funny thing to say, because I could've sworn I'd once

384

flung those same words at Ferius when she was teaching me arta eres. She'd replied, with a smirk, 'And you keep wanting to treat it as a contest, kid.'

'What else is it if *not* a contest?' I'd protested. 'Fighting is about skill, power and reflexes, isn't it?'

'Fighting? Sure, kid. Fightin's all of those things,' she'd replied, backing away from me. 'But like I keep telling you over and over and over again, the Argosi don't have no fighting ways.'

'Then what is arta eres supposed to be?' I had asked, advancing on her.

It was right about then that I fell into a sinkhole and found myself tumbling down until I finally rolled to a stop arse over teakettle.

'Arta eres is about winning, kid. And if you need skill, power and reflexes to win, then you ain't doin' it right.'

Fascinating, Shujan's voice echoed in my head.

You can see into my memories?

When you're focusing on them.

Torian snuck under my guard and backhanded me so hard I thought my jaw would come off.

Which seems an odd thing to do in the middle of battle, Shujan added.

I fell back, rolling into a rather messy backwards somersault on the floor, nearly impaling myself on the assortment of weapons strewn there. My vision went blurry for a moment as I got back up a little too fast.

Torian was getting used to my fighting style – if you can call prancing around drunkenly a style. Didn't matter though. Everything was going according to plan.

'Your reflexes aren't bad,' Torian said, after I'd dodged a

flurry of kicks. 'You could've been a tough opponent with better training.'

She pressed her advantage, forcing me back and not giving me the room to manoeuvre. Soon I'd end up in a corner and then it would all be over. 'All that Argosi dancing of yours though? You've barely landed any punches.'

'The only punch that matters is the last one,' I said, backing up again. I figured I had another three feet between me and the corner next to the bed.

'Too bad for you that you're out of room and out of tricks.'

I smiled at that. 'Didn't I tell you once, Torian? I've always got one more trick left.'

My hands came up, fingers forming the somatic shape of my spell, and I said, with deadly finality, '*Carath!*'

'Son of a—'

Torian's arms came up to protect her face. Before she realised nothing had happened, I'd already barrelled into her, sending us both falling onto the bed. Our momentum kept us rolling, and I grabbed the edge of the blanket, causing the two of us to get wrapped up inside it. By the time we landed on the floor on the other side of the bed, we were cocooned together inside the blanket, neither of us able to get the distance needed to land a decent strike.

Ground fighting is its own sort of art, and one in which, as with all forms of violence, I was confident Torian was my superior. She'd already spun us around so she was on top of me, her elbow pressed into my neck.

I guess she felt something, because she gave a chuckle. 'Why, Kellen – is that a knife I feel pressing up against my thigh, or are you just glad to see me?'

Her breath was like a warm breeze on my face, and when

a drop of the sweat from her forehead fell into my mouth, I found it unexpectedly sweet.

'That would be a knife,' I replied. 'Yours in fact.'

At first her expression was one of disbelief, then confusion, and finally outrage. 'You cheated, you lousy—'

'I promised not to use any of my weapons. Never said anything about using yours. Oh, and in case you're wondering, the edge of the blade is pressed against the artery on your thigh. Make me so much as twitch and you're going to be bleeding a long time.'

She stared at me awhile, eyes locked on mine. They really were remarkable, especially when they were searching so deeply, the totality of her being focused entirely on me, trying to discern if I'd really do it. She tried subtly pressing her elbow down, just a bit, on my throat. I responded with commensurate pressure with the knife. I imagine the two of us, lying there on top of each other, wrapped in a blanket, must've looked pretty ridiculous.

'What now?' Torian asked finally.

'How about this? I remove the blade, you take your elbow away from my throat, and then the two of us get out of this ridiculous blanket without resorting to any more violence.'

'And then?'

'Then we do things my way.'

It wasn't an answer, or at least not one she liked, but she seemed to give it due consideration regardless. 'Well,' she said at last, withdrawing her elbow, 'whatever else you are, you're not a coward.'

'Thanks,' I said, and carefully removed the blade.

Getting ourselves out of the blanket and back to our feet was awkward and mutually embarrassing. It was only when we were both standing there, staring at each other, that I realised somewhere in all of that I'd lost the knife.

'You're not a coward, but you are kind of an idiot,' Torian said, showing me the blade. 'You ought to have figured out by now that no matter how badly I might want to beat you fair and square, I never let my feelings get in the way of protecting my queen.'

'And you should've learned how Kellen fights,' Nephenia said.

With seamless fluidity and grace, Torian spun on her heel and threw the blade with perfect accuracy. It met the iron-cloth fabric Nephenia was holding out in front of herself and clattered to the floor. An angry bundle of fur descended from the ceiling, landing on Torian's head and wrapping himself around her, his glider flaps blinding her. 'He may be dumb, and hideous to look at, but my partner's always got one more trick,' Reichis chittered.

There are times when I really do love that thieving, homicidal squirrel cat.

'Such purdy eyes,' he purred, claws pressed at the ridges of Torian's eye sockets.

53

The Peace

For someone who hates the Argosi so much, Torian Libri had a remarkable command of arta valar.

'What now?' she asked, showing not a shred of fear despite the very real possibility that she was about to lose her eyeballs down a squirrel cat's gullet. 'You planning to kill me? If you're squeamish you could just get your girlfriend to knock me out with one of those Jan'Tep sleep toys of hers and leave me for the Arcanists. I'm sure they'll get the job done. After a while.'

Nephenia bridled at that. 'I don't use sleep spells and I don't leave people to be tortured.'

I walked over to Torian and motioned for Reichis to get off her head. He made a few grumbling noises about squirrel cats' traditional rights of revenge for skinbags who'd knocked them out with poisoned darts, but finally complied, jumping onto my shoulder.

'The way I see it,' I began, measuring my words carefully to prevent the situation getting out of hand again, 'you pretend to give in, leave this temple with us, wait for your shot to try to kill Shujan again. Chances are it won't work, but in the process we'll probably get captured or killed and the queen will lose her two best protectors. Alternatively . . .'

She watched me closely, peering through the windows of those deep indigo eyes of hers. 'Let me guess. You want me to join your little troupe of travelling snake-oil salesmen peddling hope and kindness to the assembled armies of a continent on the brink of war?'

'Something like that.'

She shook her head in disbelief. 'Kellen, in the time we've known each other, I've jailed you, lied to you, poisoned you and beaten you half to death. Why would you trust me now?'

It was my turn to hold her gaze. 'Because not once has the outcome been what you expected, and I don't think you became one of the most legendary marshals in the service by repeating the same mistakes over again.'

'Even if I agree, how will you know I'm not just lying and biding my time?'

'Because even an outlaw knows that every once in a while you've just got to trust people.' I grinned. 'Besides, I'm pretty sure I've got this mesmerising thing figured out now, so it's not like you have a choice.'

Torian tried to keep a stoic expression, but it's hard to keep your emotions in check after a fight. Me? I usually start bawling like a three-year-old who's just dropped his dessert.

Torian broke out laughing. 'Okay, card player, we'll try it your way.'

Reichis sniffed the air suddenly.

'What is it?' I asked.

'Stinks of jealousy, and for once it ain't comin' from you.' His head swivelled towards Nephenia. 'Heh.'

'What did he say?' she asked.

'Nothing. He's just hungry again.'

Ishak yipped up at her. I was coming to learn that the hyena had a poor sense of discretion.

'I am *not* jealous,' Nephenia said, eyes narrowing as she stared daggers at Reichis.

'Hey, I calls 'em like I smells 'em,' he replied.

Torian found it all tremendously amusing. 'Yeah, this is definitely the group I'd send to negotiate an impossible peace treaty between warring nations.'

'The marshal has a point,' Nephenia said. 'What's your plan, Kellen?'

I looked over at Shujan, who was watching us intently. I suppose he'd never seen the chaos of normal human beings up close before. 'You still want to figure out what kind of god you should be?'

He nodded.

I glanced around the room, filled with trinkets and books and games, where viziers instructed him in what to believe and Arcanists sought to inscribe his destiny on his skin, where his only exposure to the outside world was being paraded on a balcony to look down upon the faces of adoring worshippers waiting for him to perform his miracles. How could anyone know themselves when their lives were so utterly circumscribed by the beliefs of others? In a way, he reminded me of myself before I'd met Ferius Parfax. Before I'd ever left the confining oasis of my own nation, my own people.

'Fancy going for a walk?' I asked.

54

The Patsy

Sneaking back down the spire, floor by floor, knowing our next step could see us surrounded by enemies, reminded me a lot of the nights I'd stayed up shuffling little wooden pieces around a hexagonal board with Keliesh, the commander of the penitent army. Shujan is often played with a set of sandglasses, some of which give you several minutes to choose your next move, others only seconds. In shujan, as in life, delay can cost you the game. So can haste.

Torian stopped at the end of the passage, pumping her fist twice in the air. I nearly tripped over her. She made a gesture with her hand, spreading her fingers out wide then holding up just three. I assumed this was a signal of some sort, but never having trained with the marshals, I had no idea what it meant.

'Eight coming,' she mouthed silently when it became obvious I hadn't understood.

It will be one of my viziers and his attendants, Shujan informed me. *It is time for my lessons.*

In the middle of the night? I asked silently.

My lessons take place six times a day, each with one of six different viziers.

392

One for each of the six codices? I asked.

Yes. They always come individually, their lessons spread throughout the day. I believe each of my viziers fears the teachings of the others risk polluting my education.

Six different viziers proselytising from six different holy books, hoping theirs would be the interpretation that shaped the god Shujan would one day become.

We waited in the shadows as a procession of robed figures passed by. The first was a man shorter than me and skinny, despite a protruding little belly that strained the silk of his vizier's vestments. On either side servants with shaved heads and smooth skin attended him. One suffered under the prodigious weight of a massive book, its thick wood-bound cover holding hundreds of pages, each of which must have been two feet tall. Yet the attendant bore the awkward burden as he walked without any word of complaint.

On the other side, a second shaved figure periodically reached over and turned the pages for the vizier to read aloud. Neither attendant seemed to see the world around them, which made sense once I caught sight of their milky-white eyes. They were blind.

A quartet of female guards in Berabesq armour followed behind. Like those of Keliesh and his troops, the bronze of their breastplates had been carved with intricate designs, though theirs depicted flowers and vines rising up from desert sands, the leaves guided towards the heavens by gentle hands.

'Gardeners,' I whispered to Torian after they had passed us by.

She gave me a look that said, *I don't care. This is stupid. You're stupid, and we're all going to die.* I happen to be intimately familiar with that particular look as Reichis gives it to me all the time.

After interminable shuffling and trudging, the vizier and his attendants finally reached the end of the corridor and made a right turn.

'You smell anyone else nearby?' I asked Reichis.

He chittered something at Ishak, who snuffled at the floor before yipping something back.

'This whole place is practically deserted except for the prayer rooms. The other skinbags are still packed in there.'

When I translated this for Torian she rubbed at her jaw. 'Why in all the hells aren't more of the guards circulating the corridors? Berabesq has as many spies as Darome does. They must've known we would send someone to—'

'That's precisely what they've been counting on,' Nephenia interrupted. Her arms were laden with the Arcanists' books she'd stolen from Shujan's room. There was a desperate urgency in her voice even though she spoke in that eerily quiet Argosi whisper of hers. 'You were right, Kellen. This whole thing has been a set-up.'

It was nice to know I got things right once in a while, even if I had no idea why or how.

Torian led us down to the next flight of stairs before we stopped to give Shujan the chance to catch his breath. He leaned a hand against the golden wall.

'Are you all right?' I asked.

He couldn't seem to get the words out. *I am so weak, Kellen. It's as if I have never grown from being a babe at all, but have merely been . . . stretched.*

His hand slipped and I had to catch him in my arms to keep him from falling down the stairs.

'What's wrong with him?' Torian asked.

'He's sick,' Nephenia said. She'd opened up one of the books she'd taken from his room to a page depicting exquisitely-drawn outlines of the human form. Surrounding each one were layers of concentric scrawls of Berabesq writing, and buried among those a half-dozen sigils Nephenia and I both recognised. 'I think the Arcanists have been using a mixture of sand and blood magic to make Shujan appear to mature,' she said, tracing a finger along the rows of symbols. 'It's not natural, though. His body can't sustain it.'

I leaned closer to try to make sense of the intricate markings. 'So all these miracles he's displaying, the way he's grown so quickly . . . it's all been weakening his physical body and making him sick.'

Ishak sniffed at the boy's feet before barking something at Reichis.

'The kid ain't sick,' the squirrel cat informed me. 'He's dying.'

I translated, first silently for Shujan, then, after he nodded, for the others. Torian shook her head. 'This makes no sense. What good is a dying god to the Berabesq leadership? For hundreds of years the six religious sects running this country have been waiting for their six-faced deity to finally arrive and reveal his true aspect once and for all.'

'And then what?' Nephenia asked. 'One sect turns out to be right, the others misguided? Generations of family traditions go up in smoke the moment the six faiths collapse into only one. People would unite, sure, but with a lingering reluctance.' She turned to me. 'What if the Arcanists never wanted a real god in the first place?'

My gaze went to Shujan, who stared back at me in

confusion. For all the philosophy and wisdom his teachers had imparted to him, for all the miracles the Arcanists had inscribed upon his flesh, this was something his innocence couldn't fathom. 'A god murdered by his people's enemies before he can reveal the answer his followers have been waiting centuries to hear would unite them in a new holy cause. Vengeance.'

I do not understand, he said silently to me. *Am I a fraud then?*

Right sentiment, wrong word. I quieted my thoughts to keep the true one from him.

Shujan pushed away from me and spread his arms. In the dim light of the stairwell he began to glow like a star, as the ceiling above us started to dance with images of the inner workings of plants, of animals, of the raw elements of life itself. *Is this not a miracle, Kellen?* he asked. *Is it merely a trick?*

'What the hells is he doing?' Torian whispered furiously. '*Trying* to bring the temple guards down on us?'

'Give me a second,' I said. I turned to Reichis. 'Can you do some reconnaissance and make sure nobody's on our tail without being seen?'

He snorted, then gave a shake of his fur, changing its colour to once again match the gold of the walls all around us. Without a word he scampered up the stairs and back into the corridor.

Shujan reached out a hand and touched my right shoulder. I felt a warmth that steadily took away the ache of one of the bruises Torian had given me.

I can heal the sick and wounded. Is this not a miracle?

He took his hand away. The pain was still gone, but I've

396

been injured enough times to know the difference between a wound that's healed versus one that's just been numbed.

'I don't know,' I said to him, the longing in his voice making me want to find some way to reassure him of something I myself was now sure wasn't true. 'Maybe divinity isn't just about power or knowledge.'

'Rumours of a god wouldn't be enough for the thousands of viziers who lead the six sects of believers,' Nephenia said.

Shujan spoke aloud, though he struggled from the effort. 'When I first appeared in the spire, the viziers questioned the meaning of my arrival. Over the months that followed, however, I grew so unnaturally quickly that they deemed this the first miracle prophesied in all six of the codices: a child would arrive who had not been born, who would grow to a man in his first year.'

Shujan stared down at his emaciated, gangly arms. 'Am I merely a doll made from too little cloth?'

I was still trying to come up with something reassuring to say when my attention was drawn elsewhere – to the book Nephenia still held in her hands. It was newer than the other books I'd seen, the pages still crisp, the paper not yellowed by time. But it was the unusual mix of Berabesq script and Jan'Tep sigils, drawn in a flowing, elegant hand, that had caught my eyes. I doubt I'd ever have recognised them were I not still holding a small stack of thirteen painted cards in my pocket. I'd kept them with me all this time, not with any purpose in mind, but simply as a memento of my mother.

Ancestors, I swore silently. *She'd been their prisoner for weeks after Ke'heops had sent her to spy on the Berabesq. She would have known not only the secrets of Jan'Tep magic, but of the shadowblack banding he'd brought back with him from the ruins of the Ebony Abbey.*

'Kellen?' Nephenia asked, looking up at me. 'What's wrong?'

The discordant clanging of a distant bell coming from one of the floors above us took me by surprise, making my heart skip a beat. Soon the chimes were picked up by other bells, spreading throughout the spire like wildfire. Shouts began to echo down from the corridors.

A skittering along the floor above us was followed by Reichis racing down the stairs. 'The guards are being released from the prayer rooms and those crazy guys in the black and gold robes are makin' weird signs in the air.'

'The Arcanists must've discovered Shujan's gone,' Nephenia said, after Ishak had translated for her. 'We need to get moving before—'

A gleam caught my eye, drawing my gaze to Shujan who was staring down in horror as the blackened inscriptions carved into his flesh began to writhe and pulse beneath the thin fabric of his robes. Though he made no sound himself, I could hear chanting coming from inside the cavern of his chest. He clawed at the front of his robes, revealing shadow-black words that were rewriting themselves before our eyes. 'The Arcanists are near! I can feel them altering my destiny, reshaping me into . . . Kellen, run!'

Before any of us could make a move, his hands rose up of their own accord. The air between us shimmered and shook as though the very laws of physics were beginning to crumble around him. A hurricane appeared out of nowhere, buffeting us around the confines of the stairwell. Reichis and Ishak went flying. Nephenia reached for them

398

only to be picked up by one of the winds herself and slammed into the wall so hard I could've sworn I heard something crack.

Torian grabbed hold of one of the bannisters with her right hand and used the other to keep me steady. 'Kellen,' she shouted. 'The Arcanists are forcing Shujan to kill us! You've got to use the scourge!'

I stared down at the desiccated length of rope wrapped around my arm, then at Shujan standing there before me, unmoved by the raging winds, his very nature being altered by the Arcanists even as he cried out, 'The marshal is right. I can feel all the possibilities of my future collapsing in on themselves. Kellen, you must strangle me with the scourge before I become the god of their design!'

Torian was saying something else, but I couldn't hear her above the roar of the chanting carried aloft by the impossible winds surrounding us. I began to unwrap the scourge from my arm, then stopped.

Destiny, I thought. *The predestined path set for us by others. The elimination of both free will and . . . chance.*

I reached into my pocket for the baojara dice. If I tried to throw the tiny wooden cubes into the storm they'd just be picked up by the wind and my intuition told me that would negate any power they might have over Shujan. As luck would have it though, the paltry Jan'Tep spells I'm capable of casting – unimpressive as they are by the standards of my people – just happen to involve breath magic.

I bent my fingers into a set of somatic shapes so simple even first-year initiates scoff when asked to demonstrate them by their teachers. The esoteric geometries I conjured in my mind were equally straightforward. As to the syllables I needed

399

to invoke? The only problem there was that hurricanes make it a little tricky to perfectly project specific sounds. I had to shout the words at the top of my lungs three times before I even began to feel the band around my forearm sparking. '*Elas'shep'shi!*' I screamed a fourth and final time. I tossed the dice in the air and willed them to resist the winds and roll of their own volition.

They flew so fast from my hands that I feared the spell had failed, but then I watched them begin to spin effortlessly in the air, their motion governed not by the Arcanists' storm but by the simple chaos of random probability. For just an instant we all watched them tumble over each other. A moment later the winds buffeting us disappeared and the baojara dice fell to the floor.

'You rolled a six,' Reichis said, fur sticking straight out as he shuffled unsteadily towards them. 'Is that lucky?'

'I don't know that it matters,' I replied. 'But the dice seem to have released Shujan from the Arcanists' hold.'

'For now,' Nephenia said. Ishak was licking and nuzzling her hand. 'We need to get him away from here before they can try again.'

Torian was staring at the boy, whose youthful features were now twisted into a mask of such misery that his suffering commanded sympathy even from the usually cold-hearted marshal. 'It's all been a ruse,' she said quietly. 'A trick to get us to destroy the evidence of the Arcanists' deception once they were done using him as their puppet. He's not God. He's not even an enemy. He's just . . .'

Shujan was so weak he could barely stand now. I had to pick him up in my arms to keep him from collapsing to the floor. His eyes, brimming with a boy's tears, stared up at mine.

400

There is a word there, in your mind, but you're trying to hide it from me. It's all right, Kellen. You can say it.

I knelt down to retrieve the dice. *I'm sorry, my friend.*

'He's a patsy,' I said aloud as I began to carry him down the stairs. 'And this whole thing is a con game.'

We managed to get out of the spire before either the guards caught up to us or the Arcanists could try their hand at taking control of Shujan again. Torian took the lead, guiding us back to the tunnel that ran beneath Makhan's walls to the ruins beneath the streets of Mebab. Even in the near perfect darkness, her steps were quick and sure. Maybe there really was something to this 'marshal's magic' of hers.

'What now?' she asked when we reached the sloping passage that would lead up to the little shop door and out to the street. The journey through the tunnels had given her time to armour herself in her usual cynicism. 'If your big plan was to ride to the Seven Sands in hopes that your little friend and my twelve-year-old queen could somehow hold back the tide of war, I can't see how we'll ever make it. This whole city is swarming with soldiers and viziers and who knows how many Faithful. We'll never reach the border.'

Would Shujan even survive that long? The only way out of this mess was to engineer some kind of peace treaty between him and Queen Ginevra. Berabesq is a theocracy, and under their laws the rule of the viziers exists only as interpretation of the will of their six-faced god. The Arcanists had gone to all the trouble of convincing their people that God now walked among them, which meant Shujan's word was law.

So long as we could stop anyone from murdering him first.

'We can't get to the Seven Sands without help,' I agreed.

401

'We need horses, supplies and probably a few distractions along the way.'

'And just who's going to supply them for us?' Torian asked.

Nephenia and I couldn't help but share a smile as I picked Shujan up in my arms once again and began to carry him up the slope while she pulled various charms and traps from her coat to help us escape whatever awaited us outside. 'Some folks who probably aren't going to take a shining to you, marshal.'

55

The Stand-Off

Ferius's voice bellowed loud enough to make the cavernous chamber of the travellers' saloon shake. 'I'm the one took an arrow in the back, and that means nobody kills this girl less'n it's me doin' the killin'.'

Her display of arta valar would've been more impressive had she been able to stand on her own two feet without both her mother and father holding her up. Torian's own swagger was remarkable to behold, given she was surrounded by nearly a hundred Argosi wielding just about every weapon imaginable and a few I'd never seen before and had no idea how they worked. I mean, sure, you can strangle someone with a silk scarf, I guess, but the way the Path of Emerald Steps brandished it managed to look a lot more frightening than I'd've thought possible.

'How about the lot of you get in a nice line and I'll kick your arses one at a time?' Torian asked.

Reichis, who adores a good show of bloodlust almost as much as the taste of butter biscuits, leaped from my shoulder to hers. 'Yeah, you Argosi scumbags. Come and get it!'

'Have you forgotten that a couple of hours ago you were the one who wanted to kill her?' I asked.

'Yeah, but . . .' The squirrel cat got that faintly sheepish look on his fuzzy face that he gets when he realises he's embarrassed himself. He jumped back onto my shoulder and muttered, 'Just thought it sounded cool is all.'

The stocky woman who called herself the Path of Floating Lilies came forward, each hand holding a trio of what looked like flattened steel flowers, balanced for throwing and with a sharpened point at the tip of each petal. 'The Daroman has made a most generous offer, one I am eager to accept.'

'Back off,' I warned.

Her eyes never left Torian's. 'She attacked the Path of the Wild Daisy. I will not let that go unanswered.'

'Aw,' Ferius said. 'Never knew how much you cared, Lily. Especially seein' as how you've wanted to kill me so many times.'

How did these people ever get a reputation as pacifist philosophers?

'You demanded that we give your teysan leave to end the threat of the god,' the Path of Emerald Steps noted. The small, black-haired woman gestured to where said god lay slumped in a chair at one of the tables, barely able to keep his eyes open. The further we'd got from the temple, the weaker his condition had become. 'Instead the Path of Endless Stars has brought the abomination here, adding yet another discordance to our decks.'

'You seem awful quick to want to condemn an innocent,' I said, hands at my powder holsters. 'Whatever happened to "The Way of the Argosi is the Way of Water"?'

Lily snorted. 'The Path of the Wild Daisy still spouts such nonsense to her teysani?' She turned to Ferius. 'Who knew you were such a traditionalist?'

'Must be old age,' she replied.

404

'Then perhaps you should heed time's warnings and let the rest of us correct your failures.'

She tried to take another step closer to Torian, but Nephenia got in her way, hands in the pockets of her coat, not yet revealing what charms she would draw should the situation get any further out of hand. Ishak loped to her side, snarling a warning to anyone who was considering making a move against his partner.

'You'd risk your life for this marshal?' Lily asked her. 'What is she to you?'

'Not much,' Neph replied. 'I can't stand her, as a matter of fact, but Kellen thinks she can help and that's good enough for me. Besides –' she took a step closer to the Path of Floating Lilies, ignoring the blades in the other woman's hands – 'I don't think I'd be taking much of a risk at all.'

A man could fall in love with Nephenia seven times a day if he wasn't careful.

'All this arta valar is startin' to stink up the place,' Ferius muttered. 'Kid, do me a favour and put a stop to this nonsense?'

'Yeah, sure,' I replied. I took in a deep breath. 'The marshal's with me,' I bellowed.

No one seemed to be listening – or lowering their weapons.

I flipped open my powder holsters and took out two pinches larger than I could afford, tossed them into the air and cast a variation of my spell. '*Cara'juru*,' I intoned.

The fire-fan isn't an especially dangerous form of breath magic, but the way it splits apart the licks of flame, shedding them like drops of water into the air above me, puts on quite a show.

Excellent, I thought, seeing the reaction of the other Argosi. *Now all the weapons are pointed at me.*

405

'The marshal's with me,' I repeated.

'She shot Ferius in the back!' the Path of Mountain Storms pointed out. He, even more than Lily or Emerald or any of the others, seemed determined to deliver some righteous vengeance upon Torian. I guess he felt the same loyalty to Ferius I did, on account of her being his maetri.

'Don't reckon it would've hurt any less in the front, Stormy,' Ferius said.

That, at least, got a chuckle here and there.

'Look,' I said, 'it's simple. Our only play is to get him out of the city and to the border where the queen's been amassing the Daroman army.'

'What good will that do?' Durral, Ferius's father, asked.

'In theory, Shujan is the Berabesq head of state.'

Durral's brow furrowed. '*Shujan*? Like the game?'

'He asked me to give him a – Look, can we just focus on the plan here? If I can put Shujan and the queen in a room together, explain what's been going on, they could hammer out some sort of deal.'

'Only if he stays alive that long,' Ferius said, pointing to the boy. 'He don't look so good to me.'

She can talk, Shujan said in my mind.

If you have something, you know, useful to offer, now would be the time, I replied.

He surprised me by pushing himself up from the chair. He managed two steps before he stumbled and fell. Oddly, it was Torian – her reflexes outstripping even those of the Argosi nearby – who caught him and pulled his arm over her shoulder to help him stand. He smiled at her before turning to the others.

'I have recently come to learn that I am not a god,' he said.

406

'Five miracles have I performed, yet none of them were mine to choose.' The hand that wasn't holding on to Torian shook as it reached up to pull at the neck of his robes, revealing the unfinished markings inscribed into the flesh of his shallow chest. 'I will never know what sixth marvel the Arcanists had in store for me.'

'You should sit back down,' Torian said quietly. 'Save your strength for—'

'No. Kellen is right. I wish to travel to the border, where in my name the machinations of destiny or distrust seem intent on bringing our war and bloodshed to other nations. I cannot do this alone, and so must one who had believed himself a god beg for the kindness of strangers.'

Rosie, who'd been silent up until now – which made me incredibly nervous, since I recalled she rarely bothered to announce her intentions before following the Way of Thunder – came closer and asked, 'You are weak, godling, and death stalks your footsteps. Whatever power you once had flees at his approach. Even if you survived the journey, what could you possibly hope to accomplish?'

His hand came away from the neck of his robes, falling limp at his side. One ragged breath after another accompanied the stuttering rise and fall of his chest. But when he spoke, he did so with a conviction that silenced us all. 'I would seek with what little is left of my life to finally perform a miracle of my own choosing.'

56

City of Fire

Makhan Mebab went to hells with a speed and ferocity only possible when the right words are spread like wildfire – whispered, shouted, wept, prayed: *They have killed our god.*

Chaos began as a manic, malignant thing. Smouldering anger and outrage, having nowhere else to go, burned inward. Men and women fought in the streets, accused each other of blasphemy, of bringing the end of Berabesq down upon the heads of the pious and the venal alike. Those who worshipped God the warrior blamed those who saw him as a penitent for so weakening their society that a foreign agent of Darome – for that part of the story everyone had clearly understood – had been able to enter the temple and murder him. Worshippers of the clockmaker blamed the militant, however, for their rank stupidity in failing to understand the intricacies of Berabesq's enemies. On and on it went, and the streets of Makhan Mebab flooded with blood.

'Ain't your fault, kid,' Ferius said as she and three other Argosi – the Path of Mountain Storms, the Path of Floating Lilies, and Rosie – guided Nephenia, Ishak, Torian, Shujan, Reichis and myself along connected rooftops, down hidden alleyways and sometimes beneath the streets themselves. 'This was gonna happen no matter what went down inside that temple.'

Shujan, for his part, wept endlessly as he witnessed the rabid bloodshed. 'Could I not . . . If I revealed myself, pretended to be who they wanted me to—'

'*Khata Batab*,' Rosie said, cutting him off.

Shujan looked horrified.

'What does that mean?' I asked, not recognising the term.

'It means "liar's face",' she said. 'The clockmaker's codex speaks of a false god who, should the true god be killed, will come to Berabesq to lead the unwitting and the unbelievers down to hell.'

The Path of Floating Lilies – though I was coming to think of her just as 'Lily' – grunted angrily. 'Bad enough we have to deal with a conspiracy; now we're up against religion itself.'

'Well, guess that's what happens when you have so many to choose from,' Torian said.

Lily turned on her. '*You* don't get to talk about this particular disaster, marshal, given it is a crisis of your making.'

'Leave it be,' Rosie warned. 'We must be like water now, and flow around the obstacles in our way.'

Lily snorted. 'Says the woman for whom the Way of Thunder has traditionally been the answer to all problems.'

'Just keep moving,' Ferius said, sounding as exhausted from the in-fighting as she was from her malediction.

It was strange how often the Argosi seemed to rub each other the wrong way. Alone they always seemed so calm, so wise and certain, but anytime two of them got together, it was like tinder on dry leaves, just waiting to ignite.

Maybe that's why they travel alone, I thought, remembering back to something Enna – Ferius's mother – had told me about her and her husband. *'Durral and I happen to be on the same path. One day, our paths will diverge and I'll have to say goodbye to him.'*

I looked over at Ferius as she trudged doggedly through the tunnel, ignoring the screams and shouts coming from the streets above, ignoring her own pain. Some part of me had hoped that if we could survive all this, she – along with Nephenia, Ishak, Reichis and myself – would resume our travels together. There had been a brief time when the five of us had been a kind of family. Those memories seemed almost childish now.

Ferius must've known I was staring at her, because she glanced over and flashed me a smile. 'Get a move on, kid. Can't carry you all the way to the border, you know.'

It took us three full days just to reach the outskirts of Makhan Mebab. We had to stop often, waiting for one mob or another to finish bringing whatever wave of destruction best suited their outrage to whichever group they blamed the most. Sometimes we had to turn back because fires had taken over entire city blocks. Our progress was slow, exhausting and heartbreaking.

'I've never seen anything like this,' Nephenia said one night when we were sitting away from the others.

'Me neither.'

She didn't seem to have heard me. Her eyes stared unfocused at the fires outside the broken window of the burned-out shop in which we'd taken temporary refuge. 'I thought I'd witnessed all kinds of horrors. The onyx worms. The massacre at the Ebony Abbey as the monks and the war coven tore at each other with spells and shadowblack and just pure hatred.' Her hand trembled as she brought it up to cover her mouth, as though her body were instinctively trying to keep the misery from spewing out of her. 'The things my father did to me . . . I used to think he was a monster. An aberration. Now I wonder if maybe he was just like everybody else, a fragile shell of a human being, just barely holding himself together until one day something cracked the veneer of civilisation to reveal all the cruelty and desire underneath.'

The longer she spoke, the quieter she became, as if the air was being drawn away from her lungs, leaving nothing but emptiness behind. My attempts at consoling people I care about have a habit of failing spectacularly. A wiser soul than mine would have long ago learned to keep silent.

'Eat?' I asked, handing her one of the sticks of gristly beef Rosie had provided.

She took it from me and, after a grudging inspection, bit down on it.

'Do you remember how much it bothered you when I covered up my shadowblack?' I asked, tapping the markings around my left eye.

Nephenia gave a mute nod. Jerky is remarkably tough to chew, which made it difficult for her to talk. That was pretty much my plan for getting through this uninterrupted.

'I used to think the shadowblack meant I was irredeemably broken – that some day a demon would take possession of my soul and turn me into a monster. Then a year ago, when I was first in Darome, a monk they called a "white binder" managed to control me through the markings. I discovered then that there are worse things to fear in this life than having a demon take your soul.'

411

I shuddered at the memory. Still to this day the visions it brought back made me sick to my stomach. Colfax had sworn to me, as his last breath was leaving him, that it had all been a set-up. A performance. The girl herself had written to me months later. She'd discovered the truth of why he'd hired her and hated having been a part of what the marshal and the white binder had done to me. I'd written back, thanking her for that kindness, but my self-hatred had remained. I hadn't been intimate with anyone since.

'Kellen?' Nephenia said, a hand on my arm. 'Are you okay?'

I almost laughed then. I'd been trying to devise a way to make her feel better, knowing it probably wouldn't work. But you don't fight despondency with inspiring words. With someone like Nephenia, you need to give her the opportunity to rescue you.

'Are you laughing at me?' she asked.

'Not you precisely,' I said.

'Then who? Because it certainly looks like you're laughing at—'

I leaned over and kissed her on the lips. She seemed surprised but didn't pull away, so neither did I.

Every kiss we'd ever shared had stayed with me throughout my travels. The first was just as she was about to face her final mage's trial, after my entire clan had seen that I was shadowblack. The next was when Ferius and I had found her in the desert, hunted down by the Faithful because she'd disguised herself as me to draw away their pursuit. Then there was that time outside the Ebony Abbey after my father's war coven had destroyed it. I'd wanted to follow Neph to wherever she was going next, but she said that while she thought she loved me, she'd never know for sure until she

412

met the man I would become once I finally stopped being the boy I'd once been.

So had I at last become that man? I couldn't say for sure. But, ancestors, I'd been trying.

I pulled away from her at last. She smiled at me, but the impenetrable sorrow of what we were witnessing all around us was still there. 'The world's full of darkness, Neph,' I said. 'Depredations and degradations and devils of every kind walking about in human form.' I took her hands in mine. 'But it's also got you, so really the scales are just about balanced, as far as I'm concerned.'

Not my best poetry, but it wasn't meant to be. I hadn't reached the punchline.

Neph raised an eyebrow. 'Because I'm still the pretty little flower upon whom you pin all your lovelorn hopes?'

'Because you're my hero.'

Her lips parted, but she didn't speak.

Every once in a while I get the words right.

After a pause, she leaned towards me, resting her forehead against mine. 'Kellen?'

'Yeah?'

'I've missed you a lot.'

'Yeah,' I said. 'Me too.'

57

City of Sorrow

I could have lived the rest of my life in that moment. In fact, I'm pretty sure we'd both started to drift off when a long, wailing scream pierced the darkness, coming from somewhere down the street outside our burned-out hideaway. It wasn't the first we'd heard that night. It wouldn't be the last.

'How long do we have to stay in this damned place?' Torian called out angrily. She'd been stewing by herself in a corner on the other side of the shop, between a pair of fallen shelves, their wares looted before the building had been set afire.

'Awhile yet,' Ferius said, her own attention still focused on the game of cards she was playing with Rosie and the Path of Mountain Storms, trying to discern a new pattern in the evidence we'd uncovered from the stolen Arcanists' books. I'd told her about seeing my mother's handwriting in the drawings describing their spells. She hadn't seemed surprised, which troubled me all the more.

'Why do we wait?' Torian demanded. 'Are we just sitting here so you can keep staring at those idiot Argosi cards.'

'Gotta learn to feel the rhythms, girl. We walk outta here now, we'll be swept up in the chaos. We wait a little longer, the thirst for blood will ease and we can make our way through the mobs without bein' noticed.'

That seemed to settle the matter, but a short while later Nephenia took hold of my chin and turned my head to where Torian was sitting. 'You'd better go talk to her,' Neph said.

'I think she wants to be alone.'

'Then your arta precis needs work.'

Reluctantly, I rose and walked to the shadows on the other side of the shop. Only then did I see that Torian had been weeping silently this whole time.

'Is this my fault?' she asked when I sat down next to her.

'How could it be?'

'I shot your friend, slowed you down. Maybe if you'd gotten here sooner, or if she'd gone to the temple with you, or if—'

'We were set up,' I said, cutting her off. 'All of us. It's as simple as that. Even if you hadn't come along, we'd still be in the same boat right now.'

'You don't know that.' She shook her head. 'My whole life I've refused to follow any order I didn't believe in. Told my mother a hundred times to go to hell – that I'd never join the Murmurers like her and become some spy or assassin, killing off the empire's enemies without ever letting them see my face. But this time I was so sure she was right. One death to stop a hundred thousand others? I knew you wouldn't make that trade. You're not built for it. I used to think I wasn't either.' She looked over at Shujan, who was slumped against one of the walls, one hand wearily petting Ishak, who sat next to him, keeping him warm. 'I never believed he was God,' Torian said. The words seemed to wrench at her.

'Why should you? The Daroman are no more religious than the Jan'Tep. None of us—'

415

'I never believed he was God, which meant he was just a boy. And I was going to kill him anyway. I was willing to take that scourge from you and wrap it around his throat and watch him choke to death.'

'None of us knew what—'

'You did,' she said. 'Right from the beginning, you refused to believe that assassination could be the path to peace.'

'Guess I've never seen it work out that way before, so why would it now?'

She wiped the back of her hand across her eyes, staunching the tears. 'I have. Every time I've hunted down a fugitive, whether it ended with me dragging him back in irons or leaving him drowning in his own blood, the end result has been a safer world for everyone else. A better world. It's not like I enjoy killing people. I mean, I love the fight. I love that look in a man's eyes when he's sure – right down to his bones sure – that he's going to break my pretty little face apart, only to find himself flat on the ground looking up at me and wondering if today's his last day on earth. But I've never killed unless I had to, unless there was no other choice.'

Over her shoulder I saw Ferius signalling quietly that it was time to leave.

'That's the problem with death,' I said, rising to my feet and extending a hand to Torian. 'You never really know if you have a choice until it's too late.'

By the time we finally reached Makhan Mebab's massive outer defensive walls, a change had come over the city. What had begun as chaotic, frenzied violence had gradually transformed into something far more dangerous. The council of viziers, with the help of the clerical guards and military commanders,

416

had, step by step, block by block, taken control. Now the people of Makhan Mebab, whether followers of the warrior, the gardener, or any of the other faces of God, were united in one purpose: to bring the enemies of Berabesq to justice.

'Well,' Ferius said as we made our way through one of the less-travelled gates out of the city, 'we sure stepped in that one.'

Her old student, the Path of Mountain Storms, looked back at the walls of Makhan Mebab with a despair I'd never seen on the face of an Argosi. 'Every foreigner will be suspect. They'll be rounded up and interrogated.'

'They'll be killed,' Rosie said. 'The Way of Thunder rules this place now, and the lightning will strike a great many before the storm passes.'

The young man winced at her choice of metaphors, and I wondered whether perhaps this had something to do with her opinion of the particular path he'd named himself after. 'I saw every deck of every Argosi at the saloon,' he said. 'Played every one of my cards to every one of theirs. None of us saw this pattern emerge. Not until it was too late.'

'We don't always get it right, kid,' Ferius said. 'Sometimes no matter how you count the cards, they all add up to war, and there ain't no play to make 'cept to save what few you can.'

I felt an odd jealousy at hearing her refer to him as 'kid'. I tried to shunt that away. 'It's not over yet. That commander we met, Keliesh, he wasn't a warmonger. If he—'

'The viziers seek control,' the Path of Floating Lilies said. 'They always have, but they've lacked the means to attain it. This little Daroman queen and her father before her were too prone to wisdom and restraint. My people live surrounded

417

by desert. It breeds in us the kind of thirst others cannot comprehend, and now our thirst will only be quenched with the blood of enemies.'

What they were saying was true. I knew it in my bones. Every experience I'd had travelling the long roads with Ferius, from the Jan'Tep territories to the Seven Sands, from Darome to Gitabria, and even to a land across the water, this war was like a machine being built before our eyes, gears attaching to other gears, with every culture helping to turn them until it became a behemoth that would trample across the continent.

Our thirst will only be slaked with the blood of enemies, Lily had said.

We were going to have to provide them an enemy soon.

Teleidos

City of Peace

City of Peace

The whole world longs for a land of peace, a shining city upon a hill, without walls, without guards.
They're so much easier to sack that way.

58

The Intruder

I lost track of the days for a while. The desert does that to you: by horse or camel you trudge along slippery paths, hour after hour, the sun rising and falling, the air becoming so hot you have to keep your mouth closed to avoid drying out your throat, then so cold you shiver in your tent all night. But I'd journeyed through deserts before, and as much as I hated them, their rhythms were familiar to me. What was different this time were the thoughts that haunted me along the way.

Shujan was dying. Whatever had been done to him to turn him into a believable imposter for a living god hadn't been designed to keep him alive beyond his first birthday. He slept, mostly, wrapped inside a nest of blankets we'd strapped in front of Torian's saddle whenever we rode. For some reason she'd designated herself in charge of his care.

Ferius was dying too. Despite Nephenia's charms and the healing tricks the other Argosi with us had discovered on their travels. Rosie, Lily and the man who kept trying and failing to get Ferius to go back to calling him the Path of Mountain Storms instead of 'Stormy' all shared in my despair as we watched her put on that brave face of hers day after day.

The malediction was relentless. Small things mostly. Accidents that caused her to trip when she shouldn't have, the resulting wound never quite easing in the way it gnawed at her. The curse was slowly eating her alive.

'Quit starin', kid,' she'd say every time she caught me checking on her. 'Gonna make me blush.'

At night she spent a lot of time with Rosie, the two of them sitting up in their tent, playing cards, arguing. Sometimes they were careful to make no sounds at all, and the rest of us knew well enough not to probe further.

Well, except Reichis, of course.

'They're doin' it again,' he'd chitter at me in our own little tent at night.

'Shut up, Reichis.'

'I'm just sayin', maybe you should watch.'

'What? Why would I—'

'Well,' he reasoned, 'you never seem to seal the deal with human females, and now Nephenia's back and I'm tired of watching you pine over her. So I figure maybe the problem is you're worried you won't know how to please her when the two of you start—'

I wrapped the folded blanket I was using as a pillow around my ears. 'Shut up, shut up, shut up!'

'I mean, I could give you pointers, but squirrel cat anatomy isn't exactly the same. I mean, our females really like it when you bite—' He suddenly perked up, his nose twitching as he sniffed at the air.

'What is it?'

'I thought I smelled . . .'

'Reichis, what is it?'

He got off his rump and sauntered right past me, out the

front flap of our little tent and off into the desert beyond our camp. I followed behind him, trying to get his attention without waking the others, but to no avail. It was as if he were being drawn by some phantasm conjured up by a mage's silk spell.

Just over two hundred yards from camp, past the crest of a tall dune, I found what had lured Reichis away. Was she beautiful? I couldn't say. Female squirrel cats aren't exactly my area of expertise.

'I gotta go,' Reichis said.

'What do you mean you've got to go?' I demanded. 'We're less than a day from where the queen's army is massing in preparation for war! We've got bigger problems than . . . Reichis?'

'I gotta go, Kellen.'

Without looking back, without even so much as a proper goodbye, he wandered off into the desert with the other squirrel cat, leaving me standing there like an idiot. I felt like shouting at him, calling him a coward and a traitor for abandoning me now of all times. The only thing was, I remembered something Ferius had started to say when we were travelling through here on our way to Berabesq. She'd been trying to warn me that Reichis had been away from his own kind too long, that it wasn't right for him to give that up just to go on watching my back all the time instead of creating a life – a family – for himself. If there was a tribe of squirrel cats out here, shouldn't he have the right to find them?

A cough alerted me to someone behind me. I spun around to find the Path of Mountain Storms standing there.

'What are you doing up?' I asked. 'I thought Lily was on watch tonight.'

'She is. Ferius had me scout ahead, to make sure we weren't heading into an ambush.'

That made sense. While our enemies wouldn't have known our precise location, if they assumed we were heading for the queen's encampment at the Berabesq border, then all they had to do was draw a straight line between that and Makhan Mebab and somewhere along the way they'd find us.

'How many of them?' I asked.

'Just one,' he replied. 'Ferius said you'd know who it was. She also told me to tell you and no one else. She said the play was up to you, and the rest of us shouldn't interfere.'

A weight descended on my shoulders, almost heavier than I could bear. 'She's right,' I said at last. 'This is my responsibility.'

He locked eyes with me, no doubt using some of the same Argosi skills Ferius had taught me to see if he could understand whether this was the right move or whether I was about to condemn us all. 'You sure you don't want back-up?'

'Don't reckon it would help,' I said.

The Path of Mountain Storms pointed northward. 'About a quarter-mile ahead, I think. Couldn't actually see anyone at first. No tracks, no fire, nothing.'

'Then how did you figure out someone was—'

He gave a passable impression of Ferius's drawl. '*When there ain't a single sign of an ambush, that's when ya know for sure trouble's comin'.*'

I smiled at that. I was going to miss all those sayings of hers.

I took off alone, my feet suddenly having trouble finding purchase on the loose sand. My hands started to shake before I'd gone a hundred paces.

I guess I'd always known I was going to die in the desert one day.

59

Reunion

Berabesq's northern region digs into the borders of three nations, like the three prongs of a trident: Darome to the north-east, the Seven Sands in the middle, and the Jan'Tep territories to the north-west. That paints a false picture though, because it makes it sound as if all these countries are geographically comparable to one another. They're not. The Berabesq lands are huge, spanning more of the continent than almost all the other countries combined. The mighty Daroman empire, by comparison, isn't half so big. The Seven Sands are even smaller. And my homeland? Well, let's just say you could fit the Jan'Tep territories into Berabesq fifty times and there'd still be room for more.

The same calculation works if you think in terms of population. They could swallow us up, every Jan'Tep mage from lords magi down to lowly initiate, every Sha'Tep cook, clerk and servant, the young, the old, the living and the dead, a dozen times over and still be hungry.

When you grow up with the marvel of magic all around you, it seems inconceivable that the rest of the world could see your nation as small. Weak. Trivial. Sometimes we were feared as potential spies or assassins, it's true, but most often we were seen as quirks of nature. Unusual, but ultimately insignificant novelties on a continent dominated by great armies and ever more sophisticated machines of war.

How does such a nation survive, slowly crushed between growing empires and powerful mercantile interests? And what if – instead of mere survival – what you really wanted was to rule? To overwhelm the disbelievers and prove yourself once and for all their superiors?

Now wouldn't that be a clever trick?

'Hello, Father,' I said quietly.

I still couldn't see him. Obscurement spells are funny things – easy to cast (if you've sparked your silk band), but hard to perfect. Few had the patience to work out all the kinks, to practise the esoteric geometries and calculate the exact somatic shapes required to make oneself invisible. Shalla was about the best at it I'd ever seen, but even with her, if you knew to look you'd find certain flaws in the air, a subtle, nagging feeling of someone watching you.

Ke'heops, by comparison, was a bit of an amateur. I could see now how the Path of Mountain Storms had sensed something wrong nearby.

'Ke'helios,' my father's voice replied.

'Kellen,' I corrected.

A sigh. 'And isn't that the crux of it all?'

A shimmer in the air preceded the release of his spell. He was standing closer to me than I'd anticipated – one of the many reasons I hate obscurement magic.

'You'd think a name was far too small a thing to bother a lord magus, never mind a clan prince and the mage sovereign of the entire Jan'Tep people,' I said.

My father smiled, a small, unexpected thing that seemed

428

to surprise even him. 'Flattery? That's a new trick for you, isn't it?'

He had a point – my usual assortment of tactics revolved around infuriating him through various insults both subtle and overt. So why not now? I suppose for two reasons. First, because it was far too late for such childish acts of rebellion, and second, because there was something I very much needed to tell him. 'I'm sorry about Bene'maat . . . Mother, I mean.'

It was a long time before he spoke. 'Do you miss her?'

The question took me aback. I suppose neither of us was in the mood for our usual ploys. 'I miss . . . I miss the way she smelled in the morning, after she'd spent the night making those astronomical charts of hers, that scent that came from those longs rolls of parchment she used.'

'It was the inks actually. She made them herself. Bene'maat never trusted the ones traders brought to our city – claimed they blotted on the parchment and her work was too precise.'

'*Precise*,' I repeated. Such a good word to describe her. Every word she uttered, every action she took, was so finely tuned somehow, as if she'd spent endless hours deciding what must be done before approaching the task at hand.

'She loved you,' Ke'heops said. 'I know that must be hard to accept, given how things ended when you left us. She never forgave me for forcing her hand, making her choose between her faith in me and her desire to protect you. The counter-banding we performed on you . . . She wore the shame of it like scars across every part of her body.'

'That's why she went to Berabesq, wasn't it? To discover the secrets of how the Arcanists devised the inscriptions that give the Faithful their powers.' I held up my right forearm. 'That's what this ember sigil is, isn't it? A different kind of inscription designed by Mother to create new pathways that can bypass the counter-glyphs.'

He nodded.

'You let me believe she went there to spy for you.'

'No son should ever carry the weight of his mother's death upon his shoulders.'

I had to clench my teeth to keep from saying something I'd regret. There was more to the story, most of which I'd surmised by now, but some small part of me hesitated to confront Ke'heops. I didn't want to give up that last tiny thread that still bound us together as father and son.

'Did she ask for me? I mean, at the end?'

Ke'heops nodded. 'The malediction broke her mind in those final days. She wanted so badly to speak to you, to hear your voice, to beg your forgiveness.'

He said it without ire, without any attempt to induce guilt in me, yet I felt the stab all the same. I didn't want to let him see, so instead I turned my thoughts to what must have happened next, and that brought a little comfort to me.

'Shalla told her she'd spoken to me, didn't she?'

One of my father's perfectly formed eyebrows rose a fraction. 'How did you know?'

'Because she's Shalla. She likes to fix things. People, mostly. I imagine she went to Mother's bedside, squeezing her hand excitedly. "I cast a spell, Mother. I found Kellen and told him. He's very far away, otherwise he'd ride here to see you. He wept for you, Mother, and begged me – yes, silly, arrogant Kellen *begged* me – to tell you that he forgave you long ago. He misses you, Mother, and he loves you very much."'

Ke'heops laughed at my outrageous impression. 'My daughter can be rather . . . predictable, at times.'

I laughed too, disarmed by my father's momentary descent from his usual lofty perch as head of the House of Ke, into simple parental sentiment. 'Did Mother believe her?'

A sombreness returned to him. 'I hope so. She wanted to.' A pause. 'So did I, but I know better.'

'It's strange,' I said. 'A year ago, a month ago . . . maybe even yesterday, I'd've said you were right. Some things are unforgivable, or at least I thought they were.' I shook my head. 'I can never get that image out of my mind, even now. The straps binding me to that table, the two of you standing over me. The needle in your hand, the metallic ink dripping from the end, biting into my skin.'

'I see it too,' he said softly. 'I see my own hand moving, pressing the needle into your forearm, drawing the counter-sigils. I scream at myself to stop, tell myself there's another way. There has to be another way.'

I rolled up the right sleeve of my shirt. The counter-banded tattoos used to look so ugly to me, a hideous reminder not only of what was taken from me, but of who had taken it. Now though? 'I never would have left home had you and Mother not done that to me.'

'I know.'

'No, I mean . . .'

How was I supposed to explain this to him? Travelling the long roads with Ferius, learning to survive with nothing more than a few Argosi tricks . . . arta eres, arta loquit, arta tuco; leaving behind dreams of having power over others in return for the knowledge that sometimes even the smallest, simplest, most human things, like learning to stand up straight and listen to a girl with your eyes, can be as magical as any spell; meeting Seneira in the Seven Sands, falling for her, discovering

431

love isn't the same as infatuation, and neither one is a cure for loneliness; running scared from the shadowblack, only to learn it's just as awful as I'd been told and yet, somehow, didn't have to be nearly so scary. Nephenia showing up every once in a while to turn my life upside down and remind me that I couldn't love anyone else until I learned to love myself. And Reichis. Always Reichis. The damned squirrel cat, who'd just walked out on me because he happened to catch the scent of a female of his species. The worst business partner in the entire world. The best friend I could ever have hoped for.

My life had been one mad, terrifying hell, and yet so full of outlandish wonders I laughed out loud just thinking of them all. I would've had none of that if I'd been allowed the life I'd always dreamed of – if my parents hadn't taken magic away from me.

'I do forgive Mother,' I said finally. 'I forgive you too, Father.'

'Truly?'

I don't think I've ever seen my father cry before. Even now, there was a kind of stern nobility to that lone tear at the corner of his eye.

'Truly.'

I took in a long, slow breath, and very carefully flipped open the clips on my powder holsters. 'But I won't let you pass.'

Neither my words nor my actions surprised him, but they seemed to hurt him nonetheless. I expected him to threaten or scold me, to remind me of just how much power he possessed, and how well he knew all my tricks. I thought perhaps he'd accuse me of lying just now when I'd claimed to forgive him.

So I was surprised when he asked, 'Will you allow me to explain myself, first, before either of us takes that final step from which we can never turn back?'

I hesitated. What paltry advantages I have in a duel come from fast hands and keeping people off-guard by saying things that make them falter in their own attacks. That my father was not simply offering to explain himself, but actually asking for my permission, told me several things. The first was that there was a lot more to the story than I knew.

The second was that we weren't alone.

60

Dreams of Sand

'Where is she?' I asked.

I suppose I should've felt gratified that my father didn't try to lie to me. 'Your sister is nearby. Listening.'

'She asked you to give me one more chance, didn't she?'

He nodded. 'Sha'maat has always believed that if I were to be honest with you, truly and completely honest, that you'd begin to see why the actions you deem so despicable have been necessary for the survival of our people, that given this understanding, you and I could . . .' He glanced back in the darkened desert to a spot I couldn't see. 'Sha'maat believes the truth will bring you back to us.'

I swallowed a dozen shrewd observations, a hundred mean-spirited retorts. None of them were clever enough to warrant the hurt they'd cause. Maybe I was finally becoming the man Ferius had been trying to teach me to become, the one Nephenia saw sometimes when she looked at me with that faraway stare right before disappearing from my life again. In the end, though, I think it was just that I'd already witnessed more suffering and heartache than I could stand lately, and I knew there was more to come.

'Speak then,' I said. 'I'm listening.'

'I showed you the bleak future that awaits our people as our ability to wield the primal forces of magic wanes. We have interbred for the talent for too many generations, and our own numbers are too small to adjust our course. We must . . .' Lines appeared at the corners of his eyes as though presaging the pain of his next words. 'We must bring outsiders into our midst.'

'The Daroman would've been good candidates in that endeavour, or the Berabesq for that matter. Too bad you decided to screw all of them.'

Parental fury played across his features, but he soon regained mastery of himself. 'I told you, the number of Jan'Tep blood-lines would be insufficient if we were forced to—'

'If the Jan'Tep lost too many mages helping the Daroman empire fight a war against Berabesq. Yeah, I remember. Only you forgot to mention the part where you decided that our people just surviving wasn't enough.'

'We are a nation of mages, Ke'helios, not servants to barbarians who measure themselves by the number of swords and horses they own, or by which asinine image of God haunts their fevered visions. These are the pursuits of superstitious children, not great civilisations. Would you have us become jesters begging for scraps at their tables for the next three hundred years?'

'We could have been teachers, Father. Bringing the gifts of our ancestors to those who never knew that they too could wield the magic of this continent.'

'Teachers?' Rage ran scarlet in the skin of his cheeks. 'To what end? So the barbarians can learn our secrets, take what is ours, only to return to their own people to whom they will always be loyal? To prove that there is nothing special

435

about the Jan'Tep except the exotic metals in the veins of ore beneath our oases?'

I shook my head, not sure whether to laugh or cry at the tragedy that was my people's enduring hubris.

'Do not chortle at me, boy! I am your father. I am your king. I am—'

'A trickster,' I said. 'A huckster who preys on the very same superstitions you keep mocking.' I held up my right arm, and the ember band where he'd managed to instil a new sigil over the counter-banding he and my mother had done. 'How did you do it, Father? How did you discover this new way to bind magic to a human being? That's how the Berabesq god came to be, isn't it? The Arcanists have always known the techniques to inscribe spells on flesh, but that wasn't enough. Miracles are far too complex. They require an entirely different set of physical laws, ones that can only be produced by . . .'

My fingers went to the black markings around my left eye. 'The shadowblack. At the Ebony Abbey, the abbot studied the patterns Grandmother had used to band me in shadow and found the means to repeat the process on others.'

My father nodded. 'Seren'tia uncovered the technique. We simply never understood what she'd done – why she had banded you in shadow. Iron, ember, blood, breath, silk, sand – these are single etheric planes from which only a narrow set of possibilities emerge. But shadow? There are dozens, perhaps hundreds, of different sets of physical laws from which to derive new spells, ones so complex as to be akin to—'

'Miracles,' I said. 'When Mother snuck into the Berabesq territories to learn the ways of the Arcanists, she figured out how the two techniques could be combined to concoct miracles.'

436

'That is a zealot's word. This is merely a new branch of magic, one whose wonders will take decades to fully decode.'

'Maybe, but until that day, they look like miracles to everyone else. So you fed Mother to the Arcanists, had her trick them into thinking *they* came up with the idea of creating a god for their people to worship. Just like you were the voice in Shujan's head telling him when and how to activate the spells carved onto his skin.'

He nodded. 'The Berabesq have their own problems. A people united only in the belief that God will one day return to them grows tired of waiting. We gave the Arcanists the means to at last rally their nation and destroy the Daroman empire they so despise.'

'Meanwhile you made a deal with the Murmurers in Darome to help them destroy the Berabesq.' I looked around us, at this poor, sad place whose beauty is so often missed by those other nations who happily tread upon it whenever they wish. 'You set them both up to wage war here, in the Seven Sands.'

'It was the only way. The two great nations of the continent will do battle and seek to annihilate the other, but they will both fail. Their armies will hurl themselves against each other, and when they are spent, the Jan'Tep will use our magic to defeat those who remain. They will be forced to make peace on *our* terms, and support us against Gitabria and Zhuban, should there be a need.'

'And all at once, a doomed culture will take dominion over the entire continent.' I practically spat the words. 'What made you think any of this would make me like you better, Father?'

He locked eyes with me a moment, then spread his hands. 'This.'

The tattooed bands on his arms glowed now, more powerful

than ever as he invoked the sand-shaping spell he'd first shown me in Darome. This time, though, his creation was bigger, more refined, as if a thousand master sculptors were giving form to his vision at the speed of thought.

Where once he had shown me glimpses of a single city, now the desert all around us became a map of the entire continent, with cities flourishing, new roads spreading out from the centre – from the Jan'Tep territories. It was breathtaking.

'We will not be tyrants,' Ke'heops said. 'Once we have the power to ensure our own survival, we will welcome those with the talent for magic from every other nation to join us. Then, over time – when we deem them ready – they will return to their countries, combining their spells with the skills of their people to build better cities and better lives for all.'

I had to turn to watch in awe as his words were brought to life in the sand, the desert for as far as I could see becoming a miniature version of the world he described.

'What do you see, Ke'helios?' my father asked.

'I see a golden age.'

'Yes. Yes!' He reached out to me, beckoning me as a father does his long-lost son. 'Tell me that Sha'maat was right. Tell me that you finally understand, that we can be a family once again!'

With two pinches of powder, a barely sparked breath band, and a single word, I blasted my father's golden age back to a hundred billion grains of sand.

61

Two Sides

My father was unharmed, of course. Only his pretty display of sand magic and self-delusion had been destroyed. A shimmer in the air behind him came and went, and in its place left Shalla. She was trying very hard to appear stern. Disappointed. Disinterested. Hard to do that when you've been crying.

'I'm sorry, Shalla,' I said.

'Sha'maat.' She walked towards us, feet unsteady on the loose sand, not helped by the ostentatious silver gown and uncomfortable-looking sandals. 'Shalla was a child's name, and we can't afford to be children any more, brother. The stakes are too high.'

'You've got that right. That's why I won't—'

She shook her head. 'No. No more bold declarations. No more frontier philosophy and Argosi tricks. No more wilful disregard of your duty to your country, to your family. I have tried so hard to help you, to guide you back to our family, but at every turn you defy your own people, to prove that we are the villains in this story you tell yourself, and you some kind of cunning hero. But heroes don't betray their families, brother.'

There was a cold cruelty to her words that felt more

characteristic of our father, as though she were trying to show him that she'd chosen once and for all to be his daughter rather than my sister.

'You keep using that word,' I said, my mind already setting itself to the myriad tricks I already knew wouldn't be enough to get me out of this situation. 'I'm not sure it means what you think it does.'

An eyebrow arched. 'What word?'

'Family.'

It was a low blow, so I suppose I shouldn't have been surprised at the hurt in her expression, nor the sudden, violent sparking of the iron band around our father's forearm. An invisible hand grabbed my jaw, preventing me from speaking.

'Above all else,' Ke'heops said, 'no more of your clever tongue.'

I felt myself being pulled up until my feet lost hold of the ground.

'The future of the Jan'Tep is not a matter for debate,' he said.

Something about that bothered me – bothered me even more than all his pompous elocution about family and duty and all the rest of it. 'What future did we leave the Mahdek?' I asked, forcing the words out against the pressure of his spell on my jaw. 'We massacred an entire people to take the oases from them rather than share the magic of these lands.'

He laughed at that. 'Share? You think the Mahdek wanted to *share* the oases with us? They expected us to be as servants to them. Children, allowed only brief periods of time inside the oases, given access to a mere fraction of our magical potential until *they* decided we were ready. No.' He slammed

440

his fist against his chest – an unusually uncontrolled gesture for him. 'No. We had the greater talent for wielding the primal forces of magic. Nature itself demanded we have control of the oases. What we did wasn't simply necessary – it was right.'

'Then why lie about it?'

'Kellen, stop goading him,' Shalla warned.

I ignored her, ignored the pain in my jaw and the threat in my father's gaze. 'Why the lie, Father? Why have fifteen generations of Jan'Tep lied to themselves and their children, claiming we were the ones who created the oases? Concocting tales of how the Mahdek tried to murder us with demon magic.' I pressed a finger to the twisting black marks around my eye. 'Telling those of us cursed with the shadowblack that it was evidence of some fault in us, when the truth was that we are the inheritors of the poison our ancestors brought upon our own people. You spoke of our future, Father. I wonder, what lie will you tell the rest of the Jan'Tep this time?'

'I will not lie to our people. I learned from you the price we pay for keeping secrets from each other. No. It is a harsh truth, but one we must face together.'

'Easy to say. Harder once you see how quickly they'll despise you.'

He smiled then, the small smile of a petty man who, for a long time now, has wanted to prove his moral superiority to his failed, exiled, worthless son.

He made a gesture with his right hand. I wondered what spell he was casting now, but it turned out to be no spell at all. It was a signal.

The air shimmered in waves behind us. One by one, mages

became visible, standing silent vigil at all that had unfolded. A Jan'Tep war coven. Seventy-seven mages. Not only had my father not lost his posse after the attack on the Ebony Abbey, but new mages had joined to replace those who'd died.

You could do a lot of damage to the world with seventy-seven mages. Once the Daroman and Berabesq armies had smashed themselves against each other, a full war coven would be able to subdue the rest with ease.

Suddenly all six of my father's bands sparked, and the glow from them cleaved the darkness. 'I am Ke'heops, head of the House of Ke, Lord Magus and Mage Sovereign of the Jan'Tep people, and the man who will secure the future of his nation, no matter the cost. I did not ask for this burden, but it is mine, and I will fulfil that destiny.'

I couldn't speak any more. My jaw ached too badly from the iron grip of his spell. As much as it hurt, some smaller, dispassionate part of myself wondered how long it would take for the bone to break.

'It's enough, Father,' Shalla said. 'Let Ke'helios down. I will put a sleep spell on him and we can—'

'No. No! Always you coddle him, despite my commands. For once he will see the truth unfold. For once he will understand that he has never had the power to stop us.' My father gestured with his fingers, as though beckoning me, and I found myself floating towards him. 'I am going to bring you with me now, as I go and kill that Berabesq boy as you were meant to do. I will kill the Argosi protecting him too, and that filthy nekhek rodent you call your "business partner" – was that too a way to mock us? Playing the fool who can't tell the difference between a familiar and a beastly little vermin whose entire species should have been eliminated long ago?' His other hand slapped the air,

442

and I felt a blow so hard I saw stars. 'But most of all, I am going to kill that Mahdek *bitch* Ferius Parfax, who came to our city three years ago and stole you from us. From me.'

'Father, please, that's enough.'

Ke'heops wasn't listening any more though. 'She's a Mahdek. Did you know that? Our ancient enemy, and yet you, boy, you listened to all her vile lies, lapped them up like a dog. Because you wanted to believe her. Because you *wanted* to hate us.'

With another wave of his hand, the iron spell faded, and I found myself flung to the sand.

'I am going to kill them all, Kellen, and you will witness every moment of it.' He came closer, leaning down so I could see the raw, unbreakable determination in his eyes. 'And then I am going to put a mind chain on you. For the rest of your life you will know exactly what happened, will see it over and over again, without ever being able to speak of it. I will bring you to the Daroman queen, and when I tell her of how we saved her from their god and that now she must go to war with Berabesq, she will turn to you, trusting in your loyalty, and ask if what I've said is true. And then, Kellen, though it tears your soul in two, you will find yourself nodding, and telling her that, yes, everything is as I've described it, and with love in your eyes and hate in your heart, you will urge her to trust me as she does you.'

Never before was I so terrified of Ke'heops, of my father, than in that moment. Mer'esan, dowager magus of our clan, had been one of the most powerful mages our people had ever produced, and yet I'd witnessed her suffering under the effects of the mind chain her husband had bound her with to keep her from revealing our people's past.

'Well, boy?' Ke'heops asked. 'No clever remarks now? Have

443

your Argosi masters not taught you some secret art to resist a mind chain?'

Already I saw the bands for iron, silk and blood glow brighter on his forearms. His finger twitched through a series of somatic forms too quick for me to follow. He was practising the motions of the spell.

Actually, Father,' I said, pushing myself up from the sand, 'I do have a trick that can stop a mind chain.'

It wasn't a lie, because while there was no Argosi training that could save me from the spell, and no way I would ever be able to break it, as I reached for the powders in my holsters, I knew one thing my father didn't: I would die before I let him cast it on me.

Always figured I'd end up blowing myself up with this spell one day, I thought. *Just never thought it would be on purpose.*

'No!' Shalla ran to our father, grabbing at his arm. On some level she's always known me better than he did. 'Father, no. Let me talk to Ke'helios, let me—'

He shoved her away. 'Enough, Sha'maat. I've acceded to your pleas for mercy one too many times. Tolerated your brother's disobedience more than any father should ever have to. Been diminished in my own eyes, in your mother's . . .' Anger and sorrow drifted away like grains of sand on the desert breeze until both the wounded father and the grieving husband were gone. Only Ke'heops, saviour of a doomed people's once glorious way of life, remained. 'Now *you* will heed *me*, Sha'maat. Go and make sure the Argosi and the others have not fled.'

'Oh, I wouldn't worry about that,' I said, only then realising something that should've been obvious to me a while ago. 'They're already here.'

444

Pretty much all card tricks involve misdirection – focusing the mark's attention on one thing so you can set up the reveal – so I wasn't surprised that Ferius and the others had used the cover of my father's magical demonstration of his mad dream to sneak up on us. I wasn't even particularly shocked at the fact that they'd actually buried themselves just under the sand and were now rising up as if from the ground itself. No, what I hadn't expected was that it wasn't just Ferius, Lily, Rosie, Storm, Nephenia and Ishak who'd showed up to save my neck, it was *all* the Argosi.

One after another they rose like ghosts from a hundred graves.

I caught sight of a tall, broad-chested man brushing the sand off his shaved head. Ebony markings twisted along his cheeks, coming to three points beneath each eye like black teardrops. The grin on his face hit me like one of those unpredictable, inexplicable rains that sometimes appear even during the worst desert droughts.

'Butelios?' I asked, halfway convinced he was some kind of mirage. 'What are you doing here?'

He gestured to the biggest woman I'd ever seen, who was, at that moment, sliding spiked knuckledusters onto her hands. 'When my meitri, the Path of Skyward Oaks, informed me that the end of the world was near, I naturally assumed I'd find my good friend Kellen nearby.'

A wave of snarls and growls swept over the dunes to the north. Everyone, Jan'Tep and Argosi alike, turned to witness dozens upon dozens of leaping and gliding bundles of fur-covered rage and fury descending upon us. At their lead was a particularly devilish-looking squirrel cat, his coat a blazing scarlet with jagged golden stripes like bolts of lightning.

445

Turned out my business partner hadn't forgotten about me after all.

'What?' he said, peering up at me with those devious eyes of his. 'I figured if there was one squirrel cat around, there had to be others, right?'

My father's posse looked suitably distressed by the sudden appearance of so many Argosi and even more so by the arrival of an entire tribe of nekhek. I caught many of their bands fading as their concentration failed them. But these were proper mages, many of them lords magi, and it didn't take long before the desert glistened with the reflected light of their magic.

'Well now,' Ferius said, dusting herself off and adjusting her frontier hat, 'looks like we've got ourselves a fight.'

62

The Game of Shujan

A tense stand-off held the desert in its grip, the only sound that of anxious breaths as each and every one of us waited for the spark that would set off a wildfire of violence and bloodshed. The sun was just beginning to peek out over the desert horizon, as if rising to see what would happen next.

I found myself taking one of my castradazi coins from the hem of my shirt in my left hand, feeling its weight, the coolness of it, but mostly the way it felt like a prophecy of this moment. Argosi and Jan'Tep. Tricksters and mages. Opposite sides of the same coin. Flip that coin and how would it land?

For once I wasn't scared. In fact, the moment was . . . beautiful, in a way. There's this thing that so many warriors I've met in my travels, from soldiers to marshals to Torian herself, talk about with an almost mystical awe. How had she put it?

'That look in a man's eyes when he's sure – right down to his bones sure – that he's going to break my pretty little face apart, only to find himself flat on the ground looking up at me and wondering if today's his last day on earth.'

No. That wasn't it, not exactly. I remember one night playing dice with a group of Daroman soldiers, asking them if they got scared going into battle. They told me fear was part of it, but if you dug underneath you found this strange sense of wonder. You wouldn't understand what it was at first, but then your eyes would go to the man or woman on your left, to the one on your right, and without a word being said you'd know that person was going to put their life on the line for you, and you for them. 'There's no other way to put it,' one of the soldiers had said to me. 'It's beyond fellowship, beyond friendship or family. It's like . . .'

The woman next to him, her face a patchwork of scars, with one eye covered by a worn black patch, said, 'It's like walking through the gates of the greatest city in the world. The one that can't exist because no architect could ever conceive of it. The one you'd never think twice of giving your life to protect, because though you know that once you've died defending its walls, your spirit will always be part of it.'

Standing there with Ferius and Nephenia and the other Argosi, with Reichis and his hastily recruited army of squirrel cats, I felt myself standing before the gates of that magnificent city. To fight alongside them would be glorious. A wonder for the ages as a battalion of rag-tag brothers-in-arms battled an implacable enemy to defend a peace that seemed impossible. That would be some kind of miracle.

But then my thoughts turned to a different game – the one I'd played with Keliesh all those nights on the road to Berabesq.

'Vizier Quozhu advises –' the quadan began all his lessons as if it were vitally important to ensure I knew any wisdom

448

he offered belonged to someone else – 'that for all the thousands of strategies written about shujan, there are only two ways to approach the game.' He held up one of his blue-painted wooden archers. 'Consider every piece as a living person whose fate is in your hands, or treat every life as if it were merely a piece on the board, to be used and discarded as needed.'

Despite my limited experience with both the game and Berabesq philosophy, I had recently become something of an expert in the ease with which people treated human lives as nothing more than little wooden pieces on a hexagonal board. As I pondered what would happen next, I felt the markings of my shadowblack being to pinch, eager to twist and turn and show me the potential outcomes of this new game. I forced the sensation away though. I didn't need my enigmatism to know what would happen next.

The Jan'Tep would wield their spells with deadly efficiency, countered by the myriad tricks of the Argosi and the fierce courage of the squirrel cats. Many on both sides would die, their screams eaten up by the vastness of the desert, their bones left to rot in the sand.

Somehow I knew I'd survive.

I'm not sure why I was so convinced of that outcome. I guess it's just that I'd faced so many terrible odds in the past few years I wasn't capable of imagining any scenario that didn't result in me standing there while someone else lay on the ground at my feet in a pool of their own blood.

All except one.

Sometimes life is a roll of the dice, but I've always been more of a card player myself.

My father waited, daring me to speak, to defy him. Slowly,

taking care to make sure I hadn't broken any ribs when he'd thrown me to the sand, I adjusted my powder holsters on my belt, made sure the strap holding my deck of throwing cards was secure around my thigh, checked for each of my other four castradazi coins, and only then turned back to my father and uttered the one-word incantation: 'No.'

63

The Countdown

There had been no magic behind the word I'd uttered, barely even any real defiance, yet it hit Ke'heops as hard as a slap across the face. 'No?' he asked, disbelieving.

'No, Father. No betrayal of your allies. No slaughter of their armies. No great Jan'Tep ascendancy to dominate the continent. No more.'

He gestured to the Argosi all around me. 'You can't believe that these wandering desert gamblers and a few nekhek can defeat a war coven?'

'I honestly don't know,' I replied. 'But I don't plan to find out.'

'You seem to think you have some say in the matter.'

He made his bands flare, which struck me as unnecessary showing-off.

'Yes, yes,' I said, waving his display of power away, 'you've got all sorts of fancy spells. But I've got a few tricks up my sleeve and I think you'll find, when push comes to shove, they're a lot more effective.' I stepped back and knelt down to draw a circle in the sand around myself.

An expression of confusion came to Ke'heops's noble features. 'You can't seriously propose to duel me?'

'Why not?' I asked. 'I've duelled bounty mages and hextrackers, initiates and lords magi. They all had more power than me, and not one of them ever beat me.'

Well, technically, Freckles, that kid back in the Seven Sands, had beaten me to a pulp. But he was thirteen years old and had no magic at all, so if the mathematics of it all applied, I should be able to defeat Ke'heops easy.

I turned to look at Ferius and all the Argosi around her. I wondered when was the last time so many of them had come to one place, ready to do the one thing the Argosi reviled more than anything else, the very opposite of what they stood for: to wage war. Worse, they were ready to do battle, to die here in this lousy desert, for me.

That thought was the one thing pushing me down this path, the one thing keeping me from falling to my knees and begging my father's forgiveness. The one thing holding me to the Way of Stone.

The Argosi and the squirrel cats had to live so there would be one final chance to stop chaos and destruction from washing over the continent. That meant this next part – weakening my father's rule in however small a way was possible – had to be my fight alone.

'Once it starts,' I told them, 'nobody interferes.'

My father shook his head, doing a very good job, I thought, of not looking back at his allies. 'I do not duel Sha'Tep.'

I held up my right fist, sending my will through the breath band until it sparked with shimmering blue light. 'I'm not Sha'Tep though, Father; you know that. Despite your best efforts, I still have my breath band. You know why? Because that "filthy nekhek" came and set me free from the table you had me strapped to.'

452

Ke'heops snorted as if he'd just won an argument. 'You said you forgave us, and yet still you—'

I felt the urge to sigh then, even despite the pounding drumbeat in my chest that threatened to make my entire body quiver. I was not ready for what was to come. Would never be ready. 'I do forgive you, Father,' I said. 'I swear I do. But I won't allow you to ruin the world, to desecrate all the beauty I've witnessed in the lands and people beyond our borders.'

Uncertainty played across his face. Was it simply the natural aversion to beating your own child in plain view of your followers? The embarrassment of even pretending this was a real fight? Or was there some small part of him that wondered whether his feeble, outcast son, who by rights should never have survived a day outside the protection of his clan and yet had taken down almost every man and woman who'd come to kill him, might actually be a threat?

My father, I had noticed, was vulnerable to arta valar.

'Come on now,' I said, goading him. 'The sun's coming up and I have a busy day ahead of me, unwinding this mess you've made.'

He didn't smile, didn't credit me with a response to my outlandish words. Somehow it always disappointed me that my father never took any pleasure in the fact that his son defied the odds even when those odds said he would surely lose.

'Very well,' he said, kneeling to draw a spell circle around himself in the sand. 'I suppose it was always going to come down to this.'

As with everything in life, my father proceeded methodically, painstakingly. His circle was a marvel of geometric

453

precision, as though there were some prize for such things. My eyes sought out Shalla, who stared back at me with such anger I almost wondered if she'd kill me before Ke'heops had the chance.

'Why?' she asked.

One word, so filled with pain and longing that it felt entirely too big to answer. And yet, answer it I must. She knew she was about to witness the final destruction of our family. We had no other brothers or sisters, no cousins, no uncles or aunts left. Our mother, whom Shalla had adored, admired and, regrettably, emulated in her loyalty to our father, was dead. There was just Shalla, my father and me. Now she was going to be forced to watch as one of us killed the other.

I think Ke'heops understood that something deeper than either he or I understood was about to be broken forever, because he tried one last time to reason with me. 'It doesn't have to be this way,' he said, though the words sounded very far away to me at that moment. 'I was hasty in my anger, Ke'helios. Let us talk more. Let me show you the calculations I've made, explain why my plans are necessary, and why they will, I promise you, lead to a better world not just for the Jan'Tep but for others on this continent. I know you care about these Daroman and Berabesq and Gitabrians. I know you have friends in the Seven Sands. Let me prove to you that their futures can be one with our own.'

'Just so long as you're in charge.'

He went silent again. There was nothing left for either of us to say.

'Would you like to set the countdown?' I asked my sister. She shook her head.

454

'No countdown,' Ke'heops said. 'None is needed. When you are ready, boy, come at me, and learn once and for all what happens when you toss paper cards into the flames of true magic.'

'Fair enough.'

I closed my eyes for a moment, using this time he'd given me to slow my breathing and steady my hands. A familiar smell came to my nostrils, of road dust and smoking reeds. Ferius. Something else too. A musky scent that went with fur and fury. Reichis.

'Hey, kid,' Ferius said. 'I ever tell you about the seventh form of arta tuco?'

'Little busy right now, Ferius.'

She chuckled. 'Fair enough. Let me see your eyes a second then.'

I opened my eyes and looked into hers. They were green, but not the colour of emeralds. More like a field of long grasses, waving in the breeze, telling you the world was a big place and the roads were calling to you.

I wondered what she saw in mine.

'Yeah,' she said, a smile crinkling at the corners of her mouth. 'You've got this.'

Reichis, sitting atop her shoulder, tilted his head. He was unusually quiet and I wondered if Shalla – who claimed her presence naturally silenced him – was the cause. But the squirrel cat just gave a sniff and said, 'Rip his throat out, Kellen.' Then, as an afterthought, added, 'But leave his eyeballs for me.'

Ferius turned and walked away to join the other Argosi.

Nephenia came and took her place. 'Hey,' she said.

'Hey. Listen, I appreciate the words of encouragement, but

455

I really don't think all these Jan'Tep mages are going to wait for—'

'You know that thing you like to tell people when they're warning you about taking reckless chances? The one about how you've always got one more trick up your sleeve?'

'Yeah.'

'You know nobody believes you, right? I mean, your arta valar is usually pretty good, but whenever you pull out that line, everyone around you can tell it's just bluster.'

'Really?'

She nodded, then leaned over into my sand circle and kissed my cheek. 'Except me. I fall for it every time.' When she pulled back, I saw the tears in her eyes. 'So would you mind saying it now?'

'Nephenia?'

'Yes?'

'You're going to want to find yourself a spot with a good view, because this last trick, the one I've been saving up . . . ? Let's just say it's going to be quite a show.'

She smiled, and chuckled, and I really don't think she believed me. But once she'd moved a safe distance away, I turned to my father, who, despite everything, I found I still loved, still admired, still so desperately wanted to be like, and said, 'Time's up.'

With that I flipped the coin in the air between us.

64

The Duel

The coin spun in the air, and though time itself didn't slow down, it felt as though all of us – my father, myself, Shalla, the Jan'Tep mages at their back and the Argosi at mine – were trapped in that moment; as if how the coin landed, which side came up, mattered in the slightest.

It didn't.

When it comes to gambling, Ferius likes to say that an amateur plays his cards, an expert plays his opponent's and a master plays the spaces in between.

I'd been trying to figure out what that meant almost since the day I met her.

Now, finally, I knew. The only problem was, getting to that point – reaching the moment when such things made the difference between victory and defeat, between who lived and who died – that came down to the cards in your hand.

My father had sparked all six of his Jan'Tep bands – a remarkable feat for any mage. He could wield the spells of our people from the most subtle to the most deadly, from the most complex, to the most ruthlessly simple. He could roast me alive before the coin I'd flipped landed on the sand at our feet.

He wouldn't though, because here, in front of his followers, he needed the illusion of a fair fight. He needed the image of the stolid mage sovereign doing only what he had to, of the reluctant father forced by a cruel world – despite all his own efforts to redeem his son – to save his son's twisted soul by taking his life.

That meant he had to wait for me to attack first.

The obvious one would be my powder spell. It was the only thing I had that passed for proper Jan'Tep magic, and so the one my father and his posse would expect.

So why disappoint them?

I tossed the powders in the air, formed the somatic shapes with my hands: index and middle fingers pointed straight out, the sign of direction; ring and little fingers pressed into my palm, the sign of restraint; and thumbs to the sky, reminding my ancestors that after all the crap they'd put me through, they owed me a little luck.

Twin red and black flames exploded, channelled by my spell, burning hot enough to melt steel. My father already had a shield up that could've taken a thousand such blasts. Of course, he wasn't the target.

I closed my eyes as the blast struck the coin lying on the ground, the tremendous heat turning the sand to glass. The luminary coin reflected the light of the flames back a hundred-fold, making the sun on the horizon look pale and sickly by comparison, blinding everyone but me.

Reflexively, my father struck out with a simple ember spell – a bolt of lightning that would've pierced me through the chest had I not dived to the ground.

All around us, you could hear the mumblings of mages casting variations of blood or sand spells to clear their vision.

458

Shalla had been first, of course, and had seen how our father had nearly killed me in that instant.

'Both of you, stop, please,' she said.

Someone grabbed her arm. 'Do not interfere in a mage's duel.'

Whoever that was found themselves flying through the air a moment later from Shalla's iron spell.

My father looked down at me, more irritated than anything else. 'A clever trick, but you failed to press your advantage. A war mage would've evaded the lightning while casting a counter-measure to disable his opponent.'

I rose back to my feet. 'Little late for lessons in duelling, don't you think?'

Grim determination set in his mouth. 'As you say.' His hands twitched as the next spell came to his lips.

My one advantage was that, despite not being able to cast much in the way of high magic, I'd been an exceptional student at school. I knew almost every somatic form – especially the ones used in duels. And I was a born coward, so I'd developed an instinctive eye for spells that could cause me pain. If none of that sounds particularly impressive, let me put it this way: I knew what spells my father intended even before he could finish casting them.

Also? I may be weak, I may only have a couple of spells, but I'm a damn sight faster on the draw than any lousy Jan'Tep lord magus.

Ke'heops's index finger wound a weaving circle in the air, his silk band glimmering. A fear snake, meant to induce panic in one's opponent. I could've evaded it, used another powder blast to force him to abandon it in favour of a shield. Instead I let it hit me full on.

459

My throat clenched, my hands shook. The muscles in my legs twitched in preparation to run as fast and as far as they could before my heart finally gave out.

I laughed out loud.

My father glanced down at his hand, as if perhaps some flaw in the movements of his fingers had warped the spell. That's not how the fear snake works, so I was as gratified by his confusion as I was by the fact that what he'd tried to do was throw me off my game – fill me with terror so I'd be too frightened to use any tricks or deceptions.

He's afraid of my tricks, I realised then. *They violate his sense of how the world works, how it* should *work.*

'Your spell didn't fail, Father,' I said. 'I can feel the fear snake inside me, writhing around, twisting everything into dread and panic.'

'You hide it well,' he said, though it was obvious he didn't believe me.

'Don't you get it?' I asked, circling him – it's not like my circle in the sand would do me any good – as I slowly reached into the deck of steel cards strapped to my thigh. 'I've been afraid every day since I left our home. People try to kill me, Father. All the time. I get terrified, I fight, I survive, and most nights I lie awake because I can't bear the thought that soon, whether the next day or the next week, it's all going to start over again.'

'Was that your vaunted final trick then?' he asked. The grey pulse of iron magic wound itself though his hands. 'Perhaps it's best this way then. Perhaps you've been waiting all this time for someone to release you from your fears.'

'Or maybe I've been waiting for the day you stopped taking the coward's way out and faced me like a man for once.'

He tried to laugh it aside, but I saw something smoulder in his eyes. 'You think you can goad me into . . . what? Exchanging fisticuffs with you?'

'Oh, never that, Father.' I continued circling him, forcing him to shift his feet to face me. Mages are used to keeping their bodies still – makes it easier to do likewise with the mind, which is rather crucial for spellcasting. 'Do you remember when you and Mother were counter-banding me?'

'This again?'

'I was thinking of the day Uncle Abydos – the brother you treated as a Sha'Tep servant – burst into your workroom. Do you remember that?'

'Abydos was a traitor.'

'Maybe, but what struck me most at the time was the way he came at you, asking if you'd face him without your magic for once.'

'A lord magus does not soil his hands with—'

'You looked so scared, Father, as if you knew – you *knew* – that without your spells, you had no chance against him.'

The iron magic wrapped around Ke'heops's hands didn't fade; instead it hardened, almost like actual metal. 'Then you were mistaken.'

I pretended not to hear. 'But then Mother saved you. Do you remember that part? You stood there, frozen in fear of your brother's wrath, and she stepped in front of you, telling him he'd have to go through her to get to you.' It was my turn to laugh. 'The look of relief on your face, Father. I swear, every time I look at you, I can't help but see it all over aga—'

Ke'heops gave a growl I'd never heard before and came at

461

me, the magic surrounding his fists like a metal club that would smash the bones of my jaw and silence me once and for all. That is, until his foot hit the patch of glass made when my blast had fused the sand between us. His sandalled foot slid on the unexpectedly slippery surface, and he went down on his arse in front of everyone – his enemies, his allies and his family.

Nobody laughed. Nobody was that stupid.

Nobody but me.

I heard Ferius, in barely more than a whisper, say, 'Kid . . .'

She's never liked tactics that involve shaming another person, and though when we travelled together she seemed to incessantly talk about me needing to 'become a man', the word never carried the sort of backwards, ugly connotations you sometimes found in other cultures on the continent. She'd never have countenanced me trying to make my father feel small by questioning his manhood – not least because it was likely to get me killed.

'Tricks,' he said, rising to his feet.

My father was a big man. Strong. Always in control. Now though, those big shoulders of his shook with rage beneath his robes. 'Always with you it is tricks.'

'Here's one you'll like,' I said. I held up a card – a regular paper one Ferius had given me not long after we'd first met. It depicted a young man, the beginnings of shadowblack markings around his eye and fire in his hands. The title of the card was 'The Spellslinger'. I turned the card around so he could see it from both sides. 'Now watch as the Incomparable Kellen makes it disappear!'

I flicked the card in the air, sending it spinning towards him, only it wasn't the same card any more. I'd substituted it with one of my razor-sharp steel cards. A cut three inches long appeared on Ke'heop's right hand, leaving behind a line of blood and a whole lot of anger.

Again I could hear Ferius say my name. She knew this wouldn't work. Usually if you can make a mage lose control of themselves, their spells fail them. But Ke'heops wasn't like other mages, nor even lords magi. He was the head of our house, always in control, and as deadly a war mage as the Jan'Tep ever produced.

His iron and blood bands flared. He closed his bleeding fist, uttered a single word – '*Bimei'ayda*' – and then spread his fingers apart, as wide as they would go.

Suddenly all four of my limbs were outstretched as if four horses had taken hold of them and were determined to tear me apart.

'Father, no!' Shalla cried out.

Damn, I thought, as I found myself lifted up in the air, spreadeagled like a sacrifice waiting for the blade. *He's even better at this than I thought.* My father had not only remained in control of himself, hadn't simply kept hold of his magic – he'd actually used the bleeding caused by my steel card to create a blood sympathy between us. So the more he spread his fingers out, the more I felt the pull on my own arms and legs.

'How do you like *my* trick?' he asked as he came closer.

Arta valar, I told myself. *It all comes down to arta valar now.*

'Always wondered where I got my propensity for deception,' I said, my voice calm as still water on a windless day. 'Mother never had need of such things, so I guess it had to come from somewhere.'

He pulled me to him with his spell. I was floating off the ground, eye to eye with him for the first time in our lives. 'I am nothing like you,' he said. With his free hand he slapped me so hard across the face it took me a second to be sure my jaw hadn't come right off. 'And *you* are nothing like me.'

Still using his magic to hold me up, he began squeezing his hand closed. My arms slammed into my sides, my legs pressing together, my ribs creaking as my own body began to crush itself. I tasted blood, considered spitting it in his face, then thought better of it. 'That's where you're wrong, Father,' I wheezed, forcing out what air I could to be heard. 'We're exactly the same, you and I. Don't you see it?'

'Are you mad? I am the Mage Sovereign of the Jan'Tep! The first in three hundred years! You are an outcast. An exile with nothing but a few card tricks and an endless desire to betray his father!'

I shook my head, which was hard to do as my skull, too, felt as if it was being squeezed by the hand of a giant. 'I never wanted to betray anyone. I wanted to be the hero. The one from the stories who saved his people from demons and devils, who brought them from the darkness into a brighter future.'

A grim laugh escaped his lips. 'You have an odd way of showing it.'

'Because I'm not a hero, Father, and neither are you. That's the one thing we've got in common. The two of us have spent our entire lives desperately wanting to be the chosen one of the stories, yet deep down we both knew the real chosen one was always meant to be someone else.'

The fury of his reaction couldn't have existed without him

knowing what I'd just said was true. I whispered the next part, forcing him to lean forward.

'What did you just say?' he demanded.

'Shalla was meant to be our people's saviour, Father,' I repeated, loud enough now for everyone to hear. 'It's always been Shalla. Never me. Never you. Always her.'

65

The Final Spell

My father would have killed me then, were he not even in his rage a man always in control of himself. He knew how it would look: I tell him his daughter is the real future of our people and then he kills me? Even in the middle of a mage's duel, with death the only outcome, it would look . . . weak.

So instead he took in a breath, composed himself and laughed.

'And there it is,' he said at last, shaking his head. 'The final trick. Only it's the same one you've always used, isn't it? Hiding behind your mother's skirts as a child when you were due to be punished. Letting the Argosi woman fight your battles for you. And now, finally, trying to set your own sister against her father.'

He flung his hand, and I went tumbling onto the sand. I heard something that felt important crack in my side. Shalla ran to Ke'heops. 'Please, Father, it's enough. Look at him! He can't harm us any more!'

Ke'heops pushed her away. She'd unwittingly made things worse – both for him and for me. 'How dare you interfere in a mage's duel! Or have you perhaps been swayed by his words, daughter. Would you seek to challenge me for our people's crown?'

'No, Father, no!' she said, horrified.

'Then obey your sovereign. Obey the head of your house. Obey your father.'

Shalla stepped back, still watching me, trying and failing to keep herself from crying in front of our father and his war coven.

'Rise,' he commanded me. 'Rise and face the judgement you've evaded for so long.'

Without his spell holding me together, I came to realise just how badly damaged I was now. I had to cough out the blood in my mouth to keep from choking on it. Several of my ribs were broken. I could barely move my arms, and only by a supreme act of will was I able to stagger to my feet.

'Ke'helios of the House of Ke,' he intoned, like a magistrate preparing to deliver a verdict, 'for the betrayal of your family, your house and your people, I now—'

'One second,' I said, spitting out more blood.

Ancestors, I think he's really killed me this time.

'No,' he said. 'No more tricks now.'

With considerably more effort than I would've thought possible, I held up my right arm. 'A spell then. A proper spell. Ember magic.'

He seemed almost amused by that. 'Ember magic? That would indeed be a fine trick without having ever sparked your ember band, and with all but one of the counter-sigils still in place.'

'I'm not saying it's going to be easy.'

'Even before we were forced to counter-band you, you were never able to spark your ember band. As a boy you sat there

467

staring at it, giving yourself nosebleeds from the sheer effort of trying to bring it to life. So determined, even though anyone could see it wasn't possible.' He paused for a moment, then said, 'You made me proud trying though.'

'Then let me make you proud one last time,' I said. I coughed up a little more blood. Something inside me was bleeding. I didn't have long.

He stepped back, shaking his head all the while. 'Very well then, Kellen,' he said. I wondered if he was even aware he'd called me by my childhood name. 'This is as good a way to end it as any.'

I spread my feet apart, shoulder width. Squared my shoulders. Faced my father one last time. 'I wish you were the man you pretend to be,' I said, my voice cracked, broken like the rest of me. 'I wish you could've seen the truth that I've seen, recognised that magic can be wondrous but it can also be foul, learned that there's more to our people than just spells and incantations. That you didn't have to betray half the world just to protect our little corner of it.'

'And again you lie to me!' he shouted. 'I offered you this last chance to prove yourself, to die at least *trying* to be a Jan'Tep, and yet you—'

'Oh, I've got a spell, Father.'

He started to speak again, but I cut him off.

'A real spell. An ember spell.' My arm was shaking from the effort of holding it up, but I forced it to steady. 'A bolt of lightning, Father. Not a metaphor, not an illusion. With true magic will I shake these sands, with thunder and lightning I will strike you down.'

'Then do it, boy!' He almost sounded like he wanted me to succeed, as if my breaking the chains fate had set upon

468

me would at last unshackle his own grand destiny. As if the two of us were linked by a bond greater than the one we'd both betrayed so many times, that of father and son.

I stared at the copper sigils of my ember band. All but one were dead, broken by counter-sigils. I focused my will into them anyway, commanding them to draw upon the primal force of ember magic. Ignoring their blunt refusal. Pushing more and more of myself inside them until I could've sworn I felt the band constrict tighter and tighter around my forearm.

I felt something drip onto my upper lip. Blood from my nose.

'Kellen, stop this,' Shalla said. 'Father, please—'

'Silence,' he replied. 'Let him have his moment.'

Oh, Father, I thought. *Why couldn't I have been the son you wanted? Why couldn't you have been the father I so badly needed?*

Even as I pushed more, felt the pressure in my mind building, found it harder and harder to draw breath into my lungs, I found my gaze going to Ferius Parfax. She stood there, leaning on Rosie for support, dying herself from the malediction whose source I was now sure was not some foreign god, but my own father. She must've realised it too, and yet I saw no rancour in her. No desire for revenge.

The Path of the Wild Daisy.

I love you, Ferius Parfax, I thought, feeling more and more blood dripping down my face. It was coming down my cheeks now too. I was bleeding from my eyes. *You taught me to laugh at the world. To search for light even in the shadowblack itself. To find something inside myself more precious than magic.*

She looked back at me, an uncertainty in her gaze. She didn't understand what I was doing. I almost laughed at that.

469

Maybe now, at the end, I'd finally pulled a trick even she couldn't see coming.

Reichis was on her shoulder, waiting for the moment, convinced that any second now I'd give him the signal and he'd leap into the air, spread his limbs so his furry glider flaps would catch the breeze and launch him onto our enemies, tearing at them with tooth and claw.

Best business partner an outlaw could ever hope for.

Someone was calling my name, but the sound was muffled. I think there was blood in my ear canals now.

And still the band wouldn't spark.

'Kellen, stop!' Shalla screamed. 'You're killing yourself!'

My sister has never been one for hyperbole, which was apt, because I was, in fact, killing myself.

'Enough, boy,' my father said, so gently I was surprised I'd heard him. 'Let it go now. The Grey Passage awaits. Tell our ancestors that you gave all you had. Without shame. Without dishonour.'

A better son would've taken that with some grace. Me though? 'Tell them yourself, you arsehole.'

The copper sigils of the ember band around my forearm were still flat, lifeless, all but the one my father had repaired. But of course there's no spell that can be cast with only one sigil. Still I pushed harder.

'Stop it, Kellen,' Shalla pleaded. Even through the blood seeping from my eyes I could see her steeling herself, her own magic swirling around her forearms. 'I won't allow this.'

'Then stop me,' I said. 'You've got the power. It's always been your choice to make.'

She looked uncertain at first, but then a creeping realisation came to her and finally she understood.

470

My last trick. The one that had taken me years to pull off. The one I hadn't even known I was preparing.

Ever since I'd left our people, all the thousands of miles I'd travelled, the things I'd learned, the secrets I'd unearthed, they had never been for me. Not really. Like I'd told our father, I wasn't the hero of the story and neither was he.

Turns out everything I'd gone through had been so I could offer my sister a choice, to show her a path that could only be seen from outside the world we'd grown up in. All those conversations we'd had when she'd use her scrying spells to appear to me in a pool of water or a patch of sand, listening to my pronouncements about the secrets I'd learned about our people, about the lands and cultures outside our home. Always Shalla had been pulled between the simple truths that had guided us since childhood and the far more troublesome ones that had cost me my innocence to discover, between the father she so badly wanted to emulate and the brother who, despite all his manifold flaws, she loved just the same.

Always she'd avoided a choice she must have known was waiting for her, delaying the inevitable moment when she'd either defy our father irrevocably, or watch me die.

Two paths, for a nation, for a family. For the most powerful young woman in the world, who just wanted her father and brother to love each other, as she loved them both. Two destinies, utterly irreconcilable.

Now that time was up.

I felt my legs beginning to give way beneath me, my consciousness crumbling apart. I tried to take in a breath, failed, and realised I'd pushed so hard I'd actually stopped my heart. With the last of my flagging strength, I extended my arm towards my father, and with the last bit of air inside me .said the magic word as an explosion shook the air all around us.

'*Ta-da.*'

City of Shadows

Why should we believe the dead languish in shallow graves beneath the ground? Does not every building cast its own shadow? Perhaps it is to such places that those for whom the city of the living no longer has a purpose are, in the end, granted admission.

66

The Grey Passage

I'd always suspected that the Grey Passage – that misty nether-world between life and afterlife where the Jan'Tep dead were met by their ancestors to be judged – was nonsense. A fable. The final remnants of a time when we still believed in comforting superstitions.

So I was rather surprised to find myself standing there, in near-perfect darkness – though I could see just fine – facing an old woman whose features were unfamiliar to me, though I was fairly sure I should have remembered her, given what she'd done to me all those years ago.

'Hello, Grandmother,' I said.

She smiled – not a nice smile, mind you. More of an unimpressed sneer.

'So you figured out who I am. Big deal. You think any of your other ancestors would waste time coming to greet you?' She took a step closer to me. 'Come on, boy. Show me you can do better.'

Arta precis, I thought. *Lately all anyone seems to want to do is test my arta precis.*

'Well,' I began, looking first at the black ocean in the

distance and then at the shards of onyx beneath my feet. 'I'm pretty sure I recognise this lousy sewer anyway.'

Seren'tia – the grandmother who'd banded me in shadow as a child – shrugged. 'Hardly a grand deduction.'

'And you're no ghost, nor are you some spirit ushering me to the afterlife.'

'Obviously,' she sneered, despite the hint of a more genuine smile appearing at the corners of her mouth.

I tapped the shadowblack markings around my left eye, though I felt nothing when I did. 'When you banded me in shadow, you embedded a piece of yourself inside me.'

She snorted. 'Now you're just pulling guesses out of your arse. Prove it.'

'The enigmatism. The ability to see into the secrets of others. It's supposed to unlock when I ask the right questions, only, in my experience it's been a little . . . temperamental.'

'Watch yourself, boy. Best not to make me angry.'

I see where Ke'heops got his temper.

'Like I care,' I said. 'You're not even real. My grandmother – may she rot in whatever hell her deeds consigned her to – imprinted a sliver of her psyche somewhere in the recesses of my mind. A kind of . . . mechanism.'

The apparition of Seren'tia made an unconvincing show of looking disinterested. 'Oh? Why would she do that?'

I walked towards her, got so close I could see the fine lines around her eyes, the patchiness of skin worn by time. She looked as real as anyone I'd ever seen, but when you've pulled as many con jobs as me, you learn that the more convincing something appears, the less you should believe it.

'My grandmother found out about our people's past,' I replied. 'About the massacre of the Mahdek, the taking of

478

the oases. Other things too, I'll bet. She was a smart woman, I'm told.'

'And beautiful,' the spectral figure added, stroking her long grey matted hair.

'I'm guessing she figured out that our people were in trouble, that the way we bred bloodlines for magic, our entire obsession with it, was going to slowly destroy the Jan'Tep way of life, along with the rest of the continent.'

The apparition shook her head. 'The rest of the continent? You think I care about a bunch of Daroman barbarians or Berabesq zealots? And the Gitabrians! Don't get me started on them. Ancestors, we should've blasted them from existence long ago. No, boy, I'm a loyal Jan'Tep through and through. It was our culture I wanted to save. Not the rotten, petty parts of it, mind you, but . . .'

She hesitated, then turned and waved a hand across the onyx landscape. The shards rose up, forming buildings, mages' sanctums, sigils floating in the air, arranging themselves in complex esoteric geometries that were beautiful to behold. 'Magic *can* be wondrous. But it twists much more easily into dark deeds than brighter pursuits.'

'Then why didn't you do something about it?' I asked, my voice rising in pitch in a desperate and rather unflattering way. 'You were a powerful mage. Respected. Admired. Why didn't you—'

'The Dowager Magus was admired too, boy. Look how she turned out – her own husband mind-chained her for three hundred years. Made sure it wouldn't go away even after he died.' My grandmother shook her head. 'No. This wasn't a problem my generation could solve. Nor your father's. Too stuck in the past, in the myths of our own glory.'

479

'Then why not Shalla? She's the one with the power.'

'Exactly.'

I waited for her to explain. When she didn't, I said, 'You know you didn't actually answer my question, right?'

'Even as a babe, you could see the raw potential for magic in her. She was so . . . perfect. The perfect Jan'Tep baby, waiting to become the most powerful mage in generations. But power – and here's the lesson you get for free, boy – power without humility is an arrow that destroys everything in its path, piercing one life after another until only at the very end does it return to slay the archer who fired it.'

The apparition of my grandmother reached out a hand then, and touched my cheek in a gesture so gentle it took me aback. 'I loved watching you as a boy. So determined to be a mage like your father, like your mother, and yet, I think even then some part of you must have sensed that it was never to be. Oh, you might have managed to pass your Jan'Tep trials and become a lesser mage of some sort. A lightshaper, had you sparked iron and ember; more likely a mere far-talker, with that breath band of yours. You would never have found joy in such things, Kellen, no more than had you attained your deepest desire to be a lord magus. Instead you became someone much more . . . interesting.'

'An outcast spellslinger?'

'A spellslinger. An outlaw. An Argosi. A trickster. But more than all those things, something I began to despair would disappear from our people forever.'

'What's that?'

She patted my cheek. 'A decent human being.'

I thought about that. It wasn't exactly the loftiest title I'd ever heard, but I could live with it.

Or not.

'What happens now?' I asked.

The image of Seren'tia shrugged. 'The future of our people is up to Sha'maat. That little gambit you pulled worked. She blasted your father to oblivion – with a lightning bolt no less.' She shot me a raised eyebrow. 'You really have a fascination with the theatrical, don't you? All that "watch me cast my mighty spell" nonsense, waiting for your sister to finally make her choice.'

'Always thought maybe I'd become a wandering actor when this was done.'

She made a face. 'Filthy profession. Anyway, Sha'maat will name herself Mage Sovereign now. She can't afford to do otherwise. She's seen what her father became, and he was the man she admired most in all the world. She won't let one of those other arseholes take charge.' She smiled. 'So be happy. You stopped a war, saved your people, and while no one's going to be singing songs about you, still you acquitted yourself well for a one-banded spellslinger.'

She turned as if to go, and I finally summoned up the courage to ask the question I'd been avoiding until now. 'And what about me? Am I dead?'

She stopped and turned back to me. 'Mostly.'

'*Mostly?*'

'Well, let's just say, your father's iron magic almost killed you, and that stunt of trying to force ember magic from your band to prove to Shalla that you were willing to kill yourself in the attempt took you the rest of the way. Anyway, do you really want to live? Seems to me it's a pretty lousy life out there for an outlaw, and not likely to get any better, what with all the enemies you've made. Besides, you know the world has

481

no use for a trickster after the final trick is played, right? Once things are settled, people like us just get in the way.'

'Good point,' I said, and made to go off into the distance, to let myself drift away into that endless sleep.

'You're not fooling anyone,' she said.

'Neither are you. "Do you really want to live?" I'm a coward, Grandmother. Of course I want to live.' I came back to her. 'So what do I have to do?'

The grin she gave me was just about the most terrifying thing I'd ever seen. 'Give granny a kiss.'

'A kiss?'

She nodded. 'A kiss.' She tapped her mouth. 'Right here on the lips, otherwise it won't work.'

'You're making this up.'

'Nope. You have to accept the kiss. That's the only way.'

Ancestors, I thought. *You really enjoy screwing with me, don't you?*

So I did it. I leaned in to kiss the apparition of my dead grandmother. I tried to do it lightly though. Just a quick peck on the lips – enough to satisfy whatever idiotic magic was behind this but not enough to make me gag. But Seren'tia grabbed the back of my head, holding me there, lips pressed against mine, her breath pumping into my mouth even as I tried to push her away.

'Now there's gratitude for you,' an entirely different voice said. This one was winded, exhausted.

'Ferius?' I gasped aloud.

My eyes opened, blinded by the light above me, the blurriness slowly resolving into the face I'd first seen in precisely these same conditions.

'We gotta stop meetin' like this, kid,' she said, that smirk of hers firmly in place, almost, but not quite, hiding the concern in her eyes. 'Folks are gonna think you're sweet on me.'

Instinct had me searching for a clever response to that, but somehow I found my hand reaching for hers, ignoring a stab of pain in my shoulder – guess my father had broken something there too – and squeezing as hard as I could manage. 'Folks would be right.'

'Well now,' she said, then repeated herself. 'Well now.'

Ancestors, I thought. *Ferius Parfax at a loss for words. We really must be in a new world now.*

Something heavy thumped onto my chest, and a fuzzy face with beady eyes stared down at me. 'You done lyin' there yet? I'm hungry.'

'Need a second,' I said, struggling to take in a breath.

'Get off him, ya danged squirrel cat,' Ferius said, shooing him away. 'You think I sat here pumping air into his lungs just so you could smother him?'

He gave her a growl that was surprisingly fierce, even for him.

'What's the matter?' I asked.

'Argosi bitch won't let me kill any of these skinbag mages. Won't even let me eat your daddy's eyeballs.'

Ugh. Squirrel cats have no sense of propriety whatsoever.

I reached for some sense of regret, of guilt over my father's death. It was there, I was sure of it, but an outlaw learns to survive by staying in the present, not looking to the past. And that meant there was someone else I was a lot more worried about right now. 'Shalla?' I asked, trying to push myself up to my elbows.

'Best leave her awhile,' Ferius said. 'She ain't ready to talk none yet.'

She meant Shalla wasn't ready to talk to *me*. I'd forced her to choose between her brother and her father, to decide which one of us would live and which would die. Nobody should have to make that choice.

'Did I do the right thing?' I asked Ferius.

'Ain't no way to tell for sure, kid.' She removed her frontier hat and wiped her brow with the sleeve of her shirt. 'Probably stopped a war. Saved a lot of folks from dyin' for a lie. But then, maybe your daddy was right. Maybe we'd all get along better with one country, one ruler, deciding for everybody how they're gonna live their lives.'

She reached into her black leather waistcoat and for once didn't take out a smoking reed. Instead she made a deck of cards appear. 'The Argosi don't believe in divination, kid. These cards don't tell the future – only what exists in the here and now that might shape it. All we can do is read 'em best we can, and then follow our path wherever it leads.'

I thought about her words. 'Ferius?' I asked eventually.

'Yeah, kid?'

'Would it kill you to just tell me I did the right thing?'

She smiled, made the deck of cards disappear into her waistcoat and, sure enough, pulled out a smoking reed. 'Reckon it might, kid. Reckon it just might.'

67

The Future

Those next weeks moved slow as frozen molasses. I've never tasted molasses, nor do I have any idea at what speed it moves when frozen, but Ferius assured me that was the right way to describe the pathetic crawl at which my health begrudgingly improved. Turns out getting your insides crushed isn't good for you.

Some of the mages in my father's war coven were assigned to keep me floating using breath magic as the lot of us – Jan'Tep and Argosi alike – made our way north-west to my homeland. None of my escorts gave me any trouble, though a few looked like they wanted to. I guess Shalla had made it clear there would be repercussions for anyone who caused me further damage.

There were negotiations apparently. A deal was struck between the recently crowned fifteen-year-old Mage Sovereign of the Jan'Tep, the twelve-year-old Queen of Darome, and the not yet one-year-old Living God of Berabesq. In two simultaneous acts of unusually poetic justice, the treaty was bound using the unwound strands of what was previously a rather nasty whip, and witnessed by my friend Seneira, formal emissary of the newly declared sovereign nation of the Seven Sands. It seems they were getting a little tired of people treating their land as the plaything of great powers who, it turned out, weren't nearly so great as they'd pretended.

I'm told that when his armies arrived, Shujan stood before them, proved himself their god through the performance of miracles and handed down two edicts. The first was a divine command to abide by the peace treaty. The second was a revelation: that a deity, like the people who worship him, is far too complex an idea to be described by any one book, or even six. Then Shujan, the six-faced god of the Berabesq, their ruler, my friend, fell to the ground and died.

He never saw his first birthday. I never said goodbye to him.

After her formal coronation, Shalla assembled all seven of the clan princes and their councils of lords magi. She presented them with the irrefutable facts of the slow decline they'd all noted in their own clans but had hidden from each other, not realising our entire nation was suffering the same failings. Then she'd allowed several of them to challenge her claim to the crown of the mage sovereign. She was gentle with them. I'm told all but one will recover, eventually.

'Our way of life is over,' she bluntly informed the great houses of the Jan'Tep. 'No longer can we afford to see the rest of the world as lesser than ourselves. No longer can we define our people solely by our magic. Instead, we must trust that there is something deeper within us, within our culture, something that survives beyond the limits of our spells.'

There was a lot of consternation at those words, and a burning question: what next?

'A school,' she announced. 'Founded on the same principles as the Academy of the Seven Sands. A place of inquiry that welcomes those with a talent for magic regardless of where they came from. We will bring students here, to my own clan's oasis, where they will learn from us, and we from them. And perhaps together we will discover if there is indeed something to be proud of in the name Jan'Tep.'

No one cheered. No one applauded. But they listened and, in the end, they agreed.

And, just like that, my people took the first step towards a different future than any of them had imagined.

The Path of the Humble Mage.

She never spoke to me during that time though, not even at our father's funeral which by her own directive I was forced to attend. Afterwards I was handed a letter by one of her attendants. It said nothing of Ke'heops's death, nor of the terrible choice I had forced upon her. Instead it listed the duties I was to perform as the first Chancellor of the Academy of the Oasis.

The gift of a good life. Perhaps even a noble one.

I left her a carefully worded note politely declining the position.

Other offers followed, most of these delivered in person, which was the part I liked. Refusing them was a little harder.

Seneira asked if I would consider coming back to Teleidos to help her and her father as they fought those within and without the Seven Sands who would try to undermine that newly declared nation, to prevent it from instituting a new form of government. Beren Thrane had come up with a perverse and preposterous system that involved – get this – every citizen *voting* for representatives who would then form the country's leadership for a limited time before being forced by law to step down so others could be voted in.

You can bet I declined that nightmare pretty quick. Even I'm not that big a sucker.

I convinced Seneira to hire Butelios for the job, since he's the only person I've ever met so preposterously idealistic that he might actually be able to make it work. He, in turn, extorted from Seneira the promise of a home and citizenship in her bizarre new country for the tribe of shadowblack families he'd rescued from the ashes of the Ebony Abbey.

I suspect I may have inadvertantly added to the list of countries where I'll be hanged if I ever show my face again.

I got to see Keliesh again, which was nice. We played several games of shujan. Unfortunately, being half dead doesn't do much for your game. I could have lived with losing every match, but having to listen to the collected thoughts of Viziers Quozhu, Calipho and – believe it or not – Sipha (Ferius had kindly gotten him a set of her writings), soon threatened to disrupt my recovery. He politely, almost sheepishly, asked if I might like to convert to the penitent religion and join his army. Apparently it's hard to find willing shujan players – even among your own troops – when you spend half the game lecturing them.

The hardest of the offers I had to decline was that of Queen Ginevra. She thought my refusal was due to the discovery of her duplicity. It took me a while to convince her that knowing she would never have to suffer from the shadowblack – and that I wouldn't have to throw myself in front of a bunch of her enemies when it was revealed – more than made up for any irritation I felt at the deception.

Besides, it was kind of reassuring to discover that there are even more shameless con artists than me out there.

The thing that really hurt came later as I was convalescing in my family's home and learned that all my friends were leaving me behind.

68

The Pack

It's funny how much you want to sleep after nearly dying. You'd figure it would work the other way – that you'd be terrified to close your eyes for fear of waking up in the Grey Passage with your hideous grandmother cackling at you about another kiss. Yet for weeks I couldn't seem to stop drifting in and out of unconsciousness. After the offers of employment stopped coming, bad news arrived in their place.

'The squirrel cat made a deal,' Ferius informed me when I asked her why Reichis wasn't there slapping at my face with his little paws, demanding I get my lazy arse out of bed.

'What do you mean, he made a deal?'

She was sitting on a little rocking chair at the foot of my bed. I had no idea where she'd gotten it – there had never been one in my family's home before. 'Little bastard had to convince all them other squirrel cats to come fight to save your life against a horde of war mages. That don't come free.' She snorted. 'Nothing does with those crazy varmints.'

'But they didn't fight! I duelled my father myself!'

'Yeah, reckon he should've been more specific when he was negotiatin' that deal.'

I sat there in my own misery. 'So what happens now?' I asked finally. 'He joins their tribe and I never see him again?'

She took a puff from her smoking reed. The healers my sister had assigned to me had tried to explain on a number of occasions that smoke wasn't conducive to my recovery, but Ferius refused to give them up. She was still recovering too, I guess, now that Shujan was dead and the malediction was fading from her. 'There ain't a lot of squirrel cats left in the world, kid,' she explained. 'Most of the smart ones are female, so there aren't that many males to go around.'

'So Reichis has to . . .'

She nodded. 'His part of the deal was to breed with any of the females who wanted him for as long as they needed him around. Little fella's goin' to be pretty exhausted for a while.' She shook her head. 'Poor little critter.'

'Somehow I think he'll survive,' I said.

Goodbye, Reichis, I thought. *I hope you find even half the happiness you deserve. I'm pretty sure you'll steal the rest.*

'What about Nephenia?' I asked.

'She tried to see you. Waited around as long as she could, but there's a riverboat leavin' these shores in a few days and if she waits for the next one she won't make the coast in time to catch her ship. Told me to tell you the story between you ain't done yet, that it had been a long time comin' and could wait awhile longer.'

'That doesn't sound like Nephenia at all.'

Ferius shrugged. 'Reckon I tell it better.'

I guess a part of me had known all along she wouldn't stay. Nephenia had more of the Argosi instincts about her than I did, and everyone knows each Argosi follows their own path, no two staying together forever.

491

My eyes had drifted shut and sleep overtook me before I'd fully considered what that meant.

Ferius was still there when I woke though, which surprised me. The night sky peeked in through the window of my room, stars twinkling as if calling to her.

'How many hours was I out?' I asked.

She chuckled. 'Hours? You've been out two whole days, kid.'

'Two days?'

'Yeah. Them healin' spells your people are so fond of do a real number on the body and mind.' She took a puff of her smoking reed. 'Me, I prefer the traditional ways.'

She moved from her rocking chair to a sofa a little ways away from my bed. I tried to get up to follow her, but despite all the healing magic I was still wrapped in so many bandages I could hardly move. She set to strumming that little guitar she carries around with her, humming a tune I didn't recognise. 'It's a Tristian song,' she said, though I hadn't asked. 'From across the water.'

'Is that where you're going?'

She nodded. 'Reckon a little vacation might do me good. See if I can learn a little about where the Argosi came from.'

'The Argosi didn't start on this continent?'

She shook her head. 'Nope.'

'You never told me that.'

'Never told you lots of things.' She strummed a chord on her guitar that drew my attention. It wasn't discordant, really, but haunting. Unfinished. Questioning.

'You're asking what I plan to do next,' I said.

492

She smiled. 'See? Knew you'd get the hang of arta loquit eventually.' She added a note to the chord, strumming it again, giving it a whimsical, almost laughing air. 'Heard you got plenty of offers. Lots of nice places to settle down.'

I didn't bother responding. Times like these it's best to just be the silence between the notes.

'Now, that Daroman palace the queen's got – that's a fine place. A body could learn to like it there, especially now that them Murmurers know you're the one as saved them all.' She set the guitar aside. 'Seven Sands ain't lacking for attractions either. That Seneira, I heard she ain't married yet, and what with you bein' sorta famous these days . . .'

'Ferius?'

'Yeah, kid?'

'You remember that talk we had a couple of years ago about you not giving me romantic advice?'

She put up her hands. 'Okay, kid. Okay.' She glanced around my room. 'This house ain't so bad, you know. You could live here, help your sister turn things around.'

'Shalla hasn't spoken to me once since I . . .' Part of me wanted to let the words hang there, but another part figured if you're going to cause a man's death, the least you can do is say his name. 'I made her kill Ke'heops. Our father.'

Ferius took out a deck from her waistcoat and tossed me a card. The markings on it were a deep crimson, showing the six of chains. 'A debt card?' I asked.

'Argosi don't waste no road on guilt, kid. You reckon you did something wrong, then follow the Way of Water and balance it out. No matter what else, your sister loves you; that ain't gonna change. Now that she knows a way to fix them counter-sigils or whatever they're called, you might even be able to become a proper mage one day. If that's what you want. Just don't stay in one place too long, kid. An Argosi never lets the past catch up to them.'

A pain in my ribs made me lean back into the bed. 'Don't let the past catch up to me? Ferius, I'm a wreck. I'm not even nineteen years old and I've got more scars than a corpse that's been picked over by buzzards. I feel . . . old inside.'

'Me too,' she said, carefully putting her guitar inside its leather case and rising – a little unsteadily, I noticed. 'Dang malediction really did a number on me. Mostly gone now, but I reckon it'll be a while before I'm doin' any dancing.'

She walked over to the bed and put a hand on my head. 'Still warm,' she said. 'Guess you got a few years in you yet.'

She turned and headed for the door, and I knew then that by morning she'd be gone.

'That's it?' I asked. 'Not even a goodbye?'

'You mean like the goodbye you gave me and Nephenia back in Gitabria when you took off in the middle of night cos you had to be so noble you figured you'd leave your friends behind and go off to face your enemies all on your lonesome?'

She had a point there.

'Will I ever see you again?'

Even before the words escaped my lips I regretted the question. The Argosi were all about the path, walking the present moment, not worrying about the future, never being held back by the past. Ferius had allowed her path to twist and turn so that she could save my life more times than either of us could count, and teach me to survive on my own. Now that time was done.

She turned back though, and gave me that grin of hers.

494

'Reckon there's no way to avoid our paths crossing again, kid. You know why?'

Hopefulness snuck through all the pain and the bandages and cracked ribs. 'Why?'

She tipped her hat at me. 'Because I'm a damned good tracker, kid.'

69

The Trickster

Later that night, I was arrested.

'You can't be serious,' I said, throwing the writ back at Torian Libri.

'Don't look at me. I'm a marshal, not a magistrate. I just go where they tell me.' She sat down on the edge of my bed, pushing aside the tails of that long, crimson leather coat of hers.

'First of all, we're in the Jan'Tep territories. You have no jurisdiction here.'

She smiled. 'Haven't you read that nice new treaty your sister signed? Great, long thing. Lots of clauses. One of them covers extradition of fugitives.' She made a show of brushing her nails against the leather of her coat. 'I've got a reputation to maintain, you know.'

I grabbed at the writ again. '"Assaulting a marshal"? "Inhibiting the course of justice"?'

She shrugged. 'You did punch me pretty good a couple of times back in that temple in Berabesq.' She took the writ from me. 'Don't worry your pretty little head about it though, card player. The queen's busy these days, what with the new treaty between Darome, Berabesq and the Jan'Tep territories. I'm sure she'll say some very flattering words at your trial.'

'My trial?'

'You'll like the magistrate. Nice fellow. Well, I suppose he's more one of those "hanging judges" you hear about, but he owes me a favour or two. I might be able to persuade him to sentence you to a year or two of house arrest.'

'You really like your job, don't you?'

She patted my chest. 'Arresting no-good card sharps and hunting down fugitives? Who wouldn't?'

'You know this "house arrest" nonsense won't hold, right?'

'Oh? Why not?'

'First of all, because even if you do get some crooked magistrate to pass the verdict, until the queen delivers my resignation letter to her court, I'm still a royal tutor, so any such sentence would automatically be commuted. Even if it wasn't, the queen will issue a pardon. Also,' I added, holding up the two-inch knife I'd pilfered from her coat, 'I'm an outlaw. We're pretty good at breaking out of places.'

She sighed. 'I suppose that's true. On the other hand, I have a plan for that.'

'Care to share it?'

She leaned an elbow on my chest, ignoring my grunt of pain. Oddly, I found I quite liked the sensation of her weight on me. She leaned down close to me, and I was soon staring into those twin sapphires of her eyes, tasting her breath. I felt her fingers intertwine with mine. 'See, when I said you'd be held under house arrest, I never specified whose house.'

'Marshal?' I asked. 'Are you trying to mesmerise me?'

'Can't say for sure. Is it working?'

'A little.'

The hand that wasn't holding mine came up and covered my eyes. 'There now, that's better. Can't mesmerise you now, can I?'

'Torian—'

Her lips found mine, and a thousand aches and pains found

497

themselves losing the fight for my attention. There was something wild in that kiss, something that made my hands want to pull Torian closer, made the feeling of her fingers sliding through my hair awaken something in me that I'd honestly thought might be lost in all the wounds and injuries and heartache.

'Stop.'

The word took us both by surprise, so much so that it took me a second to realise I was the one who'd said it.

Torian pulled away. 'I'm sorry, Kellen. I didn't realise . . .' She arched an eyebrow. 'Actually, I'm not sure *what* I was supposed to realise.'

'It's . . . I'm sorry. It's nothing to do with—'

'Card player, I swear if you finish that sentence you're going to need a whole lot more bandages.'

I heeded the warning. Torian sat there on the edge of the bed, staring at me awhile before she finally said, 'Well, damn.'

'What?'

'It's that charmcaster, isn't it? Nephenia? Didn't she leave your arse here while she's gone off who knows where?'

'It's complicated,' I said.

'Life is complicated. *We're* complicated. Why not take the complication that gives you a chance at happiness instead of waiting around for the one that may never come to pass?' She leaned closer to me on the bed. 'Look, Kellen, maybe you and me will never fall in love. Maybe it'll just be a few months of wild, animal passion and the occasional duel.'

'I try to avoid those when I can.'

She smirked. 'You're not good at it. Anyway, so what if it's not the great romance of your life? Darome's a fine place and the queen adores you. Why not help me look out for her? She could be the greatest ruler since the empire began if we just—'

498

'Because I don't belong there!'

I hadn't meant to put it so bluntly, or to shout. These past couple of weeks I'd tried hard to come up with flowery, poetic ways of letting people down, but now melancholy was giving way to bitterness.

'I don't belong in Darome, Torian. I don't belong in the Seven Sands or here or anywhere else.'

She frowned. 'That doesn't make sense. Everybody and their uncle has been trying to hire you. Practically the whole continent's offering you a job right now.'

I shook my head. 'I'm . . .'

How could I even begin to explain my grandmother's dire appraisal of my place in the world? Torian wouldn't understand. She'd just laugh, drown me in those sapphire eyes of hers and pretty soon I'd forget all about my troubles. A marshal's magic; not a bad place to lose oneself for a few months or years. But I'd paid a high price to become my own man – the kind of man who didn't flinch when Nephenia ran a fingertip along the shadowblack marks circling my left eye. The kind who could answer the unspoken but always present question in Ferius Parfax's smirk with a grin that said, Yeah, you were right to bet on me. I wasn't ready to give that up.

'People like me . . . we're meant to break things,' I said at last. 'To pull back the curtain when a society has gotten wrapped up in too many of its own deceptions.' I reached up and touched the shadowblack markings around my left eye. 'But when the dawn comes, when something new and good is being built, I just don't belong, Torian.'

I expected that to earn me a snide remark, but she just nodded as though my rambling explanation had made some kind of sense. 'So where will you go?'

499

'I don't know,' I replied. 'Pretty much every waking minute I've been asking myself that question.'

She leaned over and kissed me again, this time on the cheek. 'I hope you find out, Kellen.' She stood up and grinned. 'Because you know what? Even though you're a no-good, spellslinging shadowblack Argosi card sharp, there's one thing about you I'm really going to miss.'

She walked over to the door and I thought she was going to leave without another word.

'Mind telling me what that is?' I asked.

She turned back and gave me maybe the most salacious grin I've ever seen. 'Just close your eyes. You'll figure it out.'

She left me there, utterly confused. Having nothing better to do, I did as she suggested and closed my eyes. I'd nearly fallen back asleep when I heard a strange sound, like someone grinding their teeth. I opened my eyes again but the glow-glass lantern was barely flickering under the weak effect of my meagre magic. I gave up and decided to figure out Torian's mysterious message in the morning, only to hear the noise again.

'Who's there?' I said, grabbing for my powder holsters. 'If you're one of my father's friends or my sister's enemies or just about anybody else, you should know I haven't blasted a mage in weeks and my fingers are getting twitchy.'

Nothing.

I pushed my will into the lantern and got a little more light into the room. It still took me a moment to follow the slow, methodical sounds of mastication to the windowsill. There, in the shadows, a tubby, two-foot-tall squirrel cat sat on his haunches, staring back at me while chewing on what looked to be a butter biscuit.

'Reichis?'

'Yeah?'

'What the hells are you doing, skulking in the shadows?'

He took another nibble of butter biscuit. 'It looked as if you and that marshal were about to mate, and, well, you know, I figured I'd better not distract you in case me being here made you go all—'

'So you decided to just sit there and watch while chewing on butter biscuits?'

'I was hungry.'

'That doesn't explain what you're doing here. Ferius said you made a deal with that tribe of squirrel cats to—'

'Yeah . . . Could we maybe never talk about that? Leastways not until we're a good thousand miles from these territories?'

'What do you mean?'

'I mean, get out of that stinkin' bed – you people have to come up with some spells for cleanin' yourselves by the way – and let's get the hells out of this lousy country.'

Despite the bandages, it took me less time than I'd've expected to get myself up and dressed. Packing was even quicker. There's something to be said for being a mostly broke outlaw spellslinger with only two decent shirts to his name. Just before we walked out the door, I turned back and left the thirteen cards my mother had made on the bed where I knew Shalla would find them.

It wasn't long before the two of us had saddled up my old horse – Reichis claimed he'd found him wandering the hills outside the city and convinced him to come back with him – and soon we were back on the road that led due east out of the Jan'Tep territories.

501

'Where are we going?' I asked.

Lying on his back on his usual spot above the saddle, he gave a lazy shrug. 'Don't know. Don't care.'

I considered our options, but a different question kept getting in the way. 'Reichis?'

'Yeah?'

'How exactly did you get out of your deal with that tribe of squirrel cats? Your species seem pretty . . . stringent about contracts.'

A long, long pause. 'It's complicated.'

I let his evasion hang there awhile as our horse made its slow, plodding way along the road. Eventually I couldn't stop myself from asking, 'Is it possible that maybe – just maybe – those female squirrel cats weren't entirely taken with your charms?'

He gave a low growl.

I put up my hands. 'I'm just asking.'

'Well, don't!'

'It's just . . . I would've figured, what with you being the supreme master of mating techniques and all, I mean, how could they resist you?'

'My kind are barbarians, that's how! Couldn't convince even one of them to come with me to find a nice warm bath. They just laughed at me, Kellen! Made out like I was some dumb house pet. Can you believe that?'

'Inconceivable.'

'I even went and stole some butter biscuits from a store in the town nearby, and you know what those lousy females did? They took one bite and spat the rest out. They spat out butter biscuits, Kellen!'

'Shockingly uncivilised, if you ask me.'

'It's like they're not even the same species.'

'So the mating . . .'

'I did my duty,' he declared in a grumbling tone. 'Not that anybody thanked me. No gifts when I woke up the next morning, no flowers. Not even a decent compliment.'

'Is it possible you were doing it wrong?' I suggested amiably.

His upper lip curled as a snarl came from somewhere low in his throat. 'What?'

'I mean, did you try that thing where you drop down on all fours and wiggle your butt in their faces?'

'Shut up, Kellen.'

'And did you remember to make this sound? Female squirrel cats love it, you know.'

I proceeded to concoct the most horrific, unpleasant noises my body could produce, braying like a constipated sheep while Reichis roared a thousand and one threats at me.

I kept making those sounds all the way to the riverboat dock, where we bought passage for the coast. I'm pretty sure the captain overcharged me on account of him thinking I might be deranged, but it was worth it.

Once we set off from the shore, a glimmer of light drew my eyes back to a figure standing at the edge of the road. The six tattooed bands around her forearms glowed just brightly enough to illuminate the familiar cascade of perfectly arranged yellow hair, now circled by an elegant seven-pointed crown. She was too far away for me to make out whether she also wore her customary disapproving glare and downturned mouth to remind me that I was, yet again, running off in the wrong direction, ignoring my familial obligations. Maybe that's why she'd kept her distance; maybe she figured it was past time the two of us stopped trying to convince each other of the person we ought to be.

503

So I waved, and she waved back. From such clumsy, insignificant somatic gestures, hopeful spells are sometimes cast. Perhaps one day that arrogant, insufferable face I adored would appear in a patch of desert or a bowl of water. I would tell her of my travels and she would shake her head at me, causing grains of sand or droplets of water to scatter, and ask what in the world had caused me to believe I'd had any chance of catching up to Nephenia or Ferius, whose ships had surely left the shore long before I'd reached them.

I'd have to think up some clever, witty tale to tell, because Shalla would never understand the truth of it. I could only keep moving forward because there was no longer any way back for me; I had no home. I'd probably never have one again. 'The world has no use for a trickster once the final trick is played,' my grandmother had said to me. Reckon the crazy old bird knew what she was talking about.

So that left me curled up under the stars on a cramped little section on the top of a rickety old riverboat, an outlaw spellslinger, broke and covered in bandages over wounds that were going to take months to fully heal, with no future and a good portion of the world still looking for an excuse to kill me. All the while, my thieving, murderous, and now, it turned out, romantic failure of a squirrel cat business partner was droning on about the innumerable ways he'd remove, cook and devour my eyeballs if I ever again dared to question his virility.

I couldn't stop smiling.

See, I wasn't born to be an outlaw. Probably wasn't built for any of this. But whatever life lay ahead of me was mine, paid for in full, and every point of light in the sky above was another path for me to follow.

And there sure are a lot of stars up there.

Acknowledgements

A Thousand and One Magic Tricks

The word 'magic' has two commonly understood meanings in the English language: the use of supernatural means to control the natural world, and the art of performing seemingly impossible tricks. Fantasy has always taken a clear stand on which of those two is the most powerful and important, but with the Spellslinger series I found myself arguing that this second type of magic – obviously weaker and yet sometimes nobler and always more human – is the one we should turn to when the game is rigged and the odds against us seemingly insurmountable.

And this got me thinking about books . . .

We often talk about authors as if they're great and powerful mages whose strange magical abilities conjure up wondrous tales otherwise out of reach to mere mortals. Maybe that's true for some writers, but to me it's always felt like writing a book isn't supernatural at all; it's a really a long series of magic tricks performed not just by one lone author, but by many magicians working in concert. So I thought I'd tell you about a few of them here.

The book you're holding in your hand or listening to feels real, doesn't it? When you close your eyes, you picture it not simply as a collection of words, but as a kind of artefact with shape and form. That's because Nick Stearn envisioned something beautiful and tangible, Sam Hadley drew a vision of Kellen facing his father in the deadliest of duels, and Sally Taylor imagined a set of wondrous places where this battle could take place. Jamie Taylor and Alex May then took all those pictures and poured them like molten metal alongside my words into a finished book.

Of course a book is like a card in an infinitely large deck, and the odds of this one instead of countless others appearing in your hand is due to a long and complex series of tricks. My agents Heather Adams and Mike Bryan had to mesmerise people into believing that a fantasy series about the guy who *isn't* the chosen one, that features loads of magic spells that he can't cast, was a good idea. Mark Smith, then CEO of Bonnier Zaffre, and Jane Harris, MD of Hot Key Books, pulled not simply a rabbit but an entire team of amazing individuals out of a hat – and it's a big team that includes publicists, designers, sales reps and so many others. I owe you all better than a brief mention like this at the back of the book. I'll figure out how to do better next time, I promise.

There are a few magic tricks that astound me the most, and I want to tell you about some of those now, along with the one trick I've never been able to figure out.

First, if you're reading this book in a language other than English, then you and I have Ruth Logan and Ilaria Tarasconi – along with all those other wonderful publishers around the world – to thank. Want to see a real magic trick? Behold as a translator takes a book full of not just English idioms (evenly mixed between British and North American no less) but also bizarre ones made up by a merciless author and

508

somehow makes the whole story flow beautifully in an entirely different language. Just ask all the talented translators who've had to figure out how to make 'squirrel cat' sound like a real thing in your language.

Another of my favourite feats of illusion is the part of the process where the copy-edit comes back from Talya Baker and all of a sudden the hundred-thousand-word mess of sentence fragments and missing punctuation I laughingly call a final draft has been magically replaced with a smooth, flowing manuscript. Not only that, but every one of my countless splelling and grammaticalistical errors are made to disappear into thin air by Melissa Hyder. *Poof!* See?

Before that, though, my editor Felicity Alexander has to read multiple drafts and find the magic words that will get me to write the best version of the story for fans of the series instead of just the one that comes most easily to me. She took over the series from Matilda Johnson, who forced me to actually define how the Jan'Tep system of magic works and kept me from turning Kellen into a whiner. Well, she mostly kept me from turning Kellen into a whiner.

With his mystical third eye, Eric Torin perceives all the threads that could be fascinating but which I'd otherwise leave unexplored; Kim Tough identifies the pieces that *are* working early on and keeps me from losing them in the process of searching for new ones. At various stages of the process, Brad Denhert, Wil Arndt, Jim Hull and Nazia Khatun let me know if I've gotten the story right or managed to saw my own legs off.

Like a mad alchemist, Joe Jameson takes my words and brings them to life in over a hundred different voices he created for the audio editions of the Spellslinger series. Joe is without question the greatest audiobook narrator in the world (Wait, I didn't write that! How dare you take over my acknowledgments!?! Shut up, Sebastien, I'm in charge now.) Anyway, moving right along . . .

Without all those astonishing people and their bewildering tricks, Spellslinger simply wouldn't be the series it is now – one that I am so incredibly privileged to get to put my name on. Receiving your wonderfully kind and inspired letters and emails when you enjoy them is what magically makes my day better.

Oh, and you know that thing Kellen likes to say about there always being one trick left? Well, here's the one that continues to mystify me to this day:

Until the age of twenty-seven, I'd never written anything longer than a page that wasn't a university essay or a weird extended joke with friends. I'd heard so many authors talk about their 'unstoppable drive to write' – you know, the one that defined them from childhood and provided the evidence that they were meant to be artists. Me? I wrote nothing. Nada. Zip. Then I started dating Christina and all of a sudden someone who'd never demonstrated a single shred of discernible talent as a writer – who really hardly ever finished anything he started – was staring dumbly at the finished draft of a book.

Crownbreaker is my tenth novel in an utterly improbable and truly magical career, yet I still haven't figured out how she made that trick work.

Sebastien de Castell
August 2019
Vancouver, Canada

Postscript

Every story has a final page, the one we hesitate to turn for fear doing so closes the door on places, people and squirrel cats we've only begun to truly know. Yet turn the page we must, because there are thousands of stories awaiting each and every one of us, and it is unwise to linger too long inside just one.

'But what about . . . ?'

'Did they ever . . . ?'

'Will he one day . . . ?'

Questions. There are always questions. Even after the book is closed and given its place on the shelf – or, better yet, given to a friend – there remains that desire to tug on every remaining thread. Our own world is always, by necessity, unfinished, but must that also be true of the worlds of our stories?

Yes.

There has to come a time when the reader's own imagination becomes sovereign – when Kellen's path and Reichis's latest heist take place in your mind instead of in mine. A moment when it no longer matters what the writer thinks or intends. Otherwise the author becomes a kind of tyrant, and the book a cage inside which the reader is trapped.

None of this means there won't be more books in the

future featuring a certain tricky (and occasionally whiny) outlaw and his thieving, murderous, blackmailing (and more recently, loan sharking) business partner. Only that, for a while at least, we have to set them free.

'But what about . . . ?'

I don't know. Let your thoughts wander and see for yourself.

'Did she ever . . . ?'

Ask them. The two of them are as much in your mind as mine.

'Will he one day . . . ?'

I promise, the answer is waiting for you inside your own imagination.

It's easy. Let me show you . . .

. . . Picture a ship. A true Gitabrian long-voyage merchant vessel with long, sturdy oak planks curving to its hull and gleaming bronze caps atop each mast. The mainsail masters the wind so perfectly that the ship fairly glides across the ocean. The crew, hardy and experienced, can't remember a smoother voyage.

'I'm gonna die,' groans a figure leaning over the rail.

Normally such plaintive grousing could be attributed to a young Jan'Tep outlaw known for self-pity, but today, in a singular act of almost implausible supernatural justice, the victim of this terrible seasickness turns out to be a slightly tubby squirrel cat whose fur has turned the exact same green as the vomit he spews over the side and into the waters below.

'Maybe if you stopped eating those butter biscuits from the hold,' suggests his business partner, who is at this moment unaware that he is destined to wake up the next morning with bite marks on his legs and his black frontier hat filled to the brim with squirrel cat puke.

'It ain't the butter biscuits,' Reichis insists, before sending the regurgitations of a few more into the calm ocean below. 'It's this raging sea. Storm of the century, that's what it must be. This water's probably swirling with crocodiles.'

Kellen doesn't comment, for fear some of the crew members nearby will laugh at the squirrel cat's plight and then . . . Well, sailors do their job better with both eyeballs.

'It's unnatural,' Reichis moans. 'Creatures of the land aren't meant to travel by water.'

'Unnatural? You recall you leap from the tops of trees to glide in the air above canyons all the time, right?'

'That's completely different, *idjit.*' The squirrel cat turns his head, muzzle upturned. 'How come you ain't sick?'

Kellen shrugs. 'Don't know. I'm already claustrophobic and have a dozen other problems. I guess there's only so much bad luck you can fit into one person.'

'Then how come you look just as miserable as I feel?'

He doesn't respond. The answer will only make him sound as stupid as he feels.

Why did he think he'd get lucky enough to pick the ship Nephenia was on? He doubted she could've made it to the coast in time to catch the previous week's sailing, but perhaps she took a slower route and was still on their own continent, sitting in a travellers' saloon somewhere with Ishak at her side, maybe even hoping Kellen will walk through the door.

Stupid, stupid, stupid, he thinks. *Now I'm stuck on this ship for the next three weeks, headed for a place where I don't speak the language and have no idea how to behave. I'll probably end up stranded on the Island of Those Who Despise Spellslingers.*

Not that the sailors on this ship particularly like them

either. Recent events have left most sensible people distrustful of anyone with Jan'Tep blood. Kellen has had to keep vigil at night so Reichis could get some sleep in between bouts of seasickness. He keeps his castradazi coins in his pocket and a half-dozen steel throwing cards in his right hand at all times. Turns out it's hard to keep powder dry when you're at sea.

'How's your friend?' asks one of the sailors. He's about Kellen's height, but burlier and with a thick red beard that can't have been trimmed anytime in the last decade. He's also the only person who's been remotely polite to them.

'He's fine,' Kellen replies. 'He just likes throwing up a lot, that's all.'

The sailor chuckles. 'He seems a noble beast. No doubt a formidable adversary in a fight.'

'Got that right, ya big ugly bear,' Reichis chitters, then goes back to groaning.

'And you?' the sailor asks Kellen. 'Forgive me for saying, but you seem . . . lost.'

'I'm fine too. Happy as can be.'

The sailor claps him on the back. 'I've seen that look, friend. You stare out at the sea like a man wondering if perhaps falling in would be the best thing that could happen to him – that perhaps what he seeks will only ever be found at the bottom of the ocean.'

'Again, I'm fine, thanks for asking. Wouldn't want to keep you from your duties.'

He knows that's unlikely to be an issue. It's already late, and the stars have come out overhead. They're pretty enough, he thinks, but to his surprise he's discovered he prefers the stars over the desert. He's about to pick up the squirrel cat and make their way back to their cabin when the sailor clamps a hand on his shoulder. Kellen realises then that it's just the two of them out on this part of the deck.

'You should remove your hand, friend,' he says. 'I imagine you need it for pulling ropes and such things.'

The sailor ignores the warning as he points out to the gentle waves. 'There's an old Gitabrian sailing tradition – if ever we're lost at sea, we call out over the bow, shouting at the top of our lungs for the sea gods to send us that which we most desire.'

'You mean like an extra ration of liquor?'

The sailor just smiles. 'Usually it involves a woman.' He catches Kellen's look and says, 'Ah, is that what troubles you, lad? Some sweetheart you left behind?'

'One who left *me* behind is more like it.'

The sailor gives him a disapproving look. 'Self-pity is an unattractive quality, my friend. Best hope when you next find her you've rid yourself of it.'

Before Kellen can reply, the sailor claps him on the back again. 'Now, tell us this woman's name. Shout it to the sky with as much force as the oceans themselves during a storm, and see what the sea gods reply.'

'I'm not going to—'

'Just do it, you whiny little prat, or maybe I *will* push you over the side.'

When Kellen booked passage on the ship, an old man at the docks warned him every landlubber had to pay twice: the first time for the ticket, and the second for not knowing the ways of a ship. The ticket you paid for in coin, the ignorance with humiliation.

'Best not resist it,' the old man had said. 'Sailors are kind enough once they've had their fun with you, but if you avoid their jests, the games can turn ugly.'

'Fine,' Kellen says at last. No doubt a half-dozen other sailors were waiting to run out and perform some kind of unpleasantly witty prank on him once he fulfilled this bizarre little ritual.

'Go on then,' the sailor urges. 'Call out that which you most desire.'

With a deep breath, making sure to be so loud he'd interrupt the sleep of the off-duty sailors, Kellen shouted, 'Nephenia!'

'There!' the sailor says. 'Feels better, don't it?'

'It's embarrassing,' Kellen replies, but the truth is, there is a subtle sensation of catharsis in giving voice to his thoughts of her.

'Again,' the sailor says.

This time he doesn't hesitate. 'Nephenia!'

'One more time, for the sea gods love all things in threes.'

Kellen grabs hold of the railing, throws his head back and shouts, 'NEPHENIA!'

Nothing happens, of course. There's no such thing as sea gods, and if there were, they wouldn't be in the business of granting wishes to landlubbers on their first ocean voyage.

He turns and leans his back against the railing for stability, reaching into his pocket for the steel throwing cards he's keeping there. To the sailor he says, 'Let's get on with the rest of it, shall we?'

The burly man shrugs, long beard bobbing against his chest. 'As you wish.'

Kellen had been keeping watch on the man's hands, which

he reasoned were likely to grab hold of him, and on the shadowy vista of the deck over the sailor's shoulder in case others came running. That's why he was utterly unprepared for the real attack when it came.

The sailor kissed him.

'Ugh. This again,' Reichis groaned.

The man's big, hairy face mashed up against Kellen's, hands reaching around to hold him.

Okay, nobody warned me about this particular sailing tradition.

But something is off. Instead of the sensation of bristles against his mouth and chin, Kellen's lips feel only the smoothness of soft fabric. Silk.

Suddenly the sailor pulls back, a mildly disappointed expression on his face. 'That wasn't very good. No wonder she left without you.'

But Kellen, though occasionally a little slow, remains an Argosi, the student of Ferius Parfax herself, and even if he weren't, he'd still remember a time not so long ago when another stranger had kissed him in the desert.

'What surprises me,' he says at last, 'is that someone would be so cruel as to make her hyena hide out below deck for three days and nights just so she could play a lousy trick on a poor, heartbroken spellslinger.'

'Wait – what?' says Reichis.

The sound of paws scrabbling along the deck precede the arrival of a scruffy hyena who leaps up to put his paws against the railings, muzzle inches from Reichis's own, and says, in a perfect replica of the squirrel cat's own words from long ago, 'A demon!'

517

With a laugh, the sailor reaches up and tugs at the left side of his own face. At first it looks as if the skin is peeling off, but the instant it comes away, it changes to wide strips of red silk. Over and over the sailor unwinds the silk until it lies in a small pile at his feet and *he* is now *her*.

'Nephenia?' Kellen asks, still too nervous to really believe it is true.

She grins at him, that fierce, wild charmcaster grin of hers. 'Told you the sea gods answer all prayers.'

She kisses him again, and this time his lips feel hers, and as they stand there together on the gently swaying deck, arms wrapped around each other even as they sink together in a kiss that is going to last a very long time, all the while ignoring the running commentary of a particularly unhelpful squirrel cat and the yips of a highly entertained hyena, Kellen finds himself an unexpected believer in the benevolence of the sea.

. . . Maybe.

Maybe it doesn't happen that way. Maybe he sails clear across the ocean in search of her, only for her to have to rescue him from pirates, or – more likely, if past is prologue – they have to save each other. But I don't know for sure, because right now that story, that kiss, belongs to you as much as me. So let's allow, in this moment as the last page turns, for our individual imaginations to take over, and not look for a single, definitive answer to all our questions.

Because the only thing I know for sure is that when Kellen next sees Nephenia, he'll stare at her in wonder, as he so often has of late, amazed at how different she is from the shy, demure girl she seemed to be when they were younger. Then he'll remind himself that his own story is unfinished, and for all his flaws, for all his failures, both real and imagined, he, too, is so much more than the sum of his upbringing.

So am I.

So are you.

Sebastien de Castell
August 2019
Vancouver, Canada

Thank you for choosing a Hot Key book.

If you want to know more about our authors and what we publish, you can find us online.

You can start at our website

www.hotkeybooks.com

And you can also find us on:

We hope to see you soon!